CHARADES AND CHIVALRY

Highfield Hall
Book Two

Charlotte Wren

ARE YOU SIGNED UP FOR DRAGONBLADE'S BLOG?

You'll get the latest news and information on exclusive giveaways, exclusive excerpts, coming releases, sales, free books, cover reveals and more.

Check out our complete list of authors, too!

No spam, no junk. That's a promise!

Sign Up Here

www.dragonbladepublishing.com

Dearest Reader;

Thank you for your support of a small press. At Dragonblade Publishing, we strive to bring you the highest quality Historical Romance from some of the best authors in the business. Without your support, there is no 'us', so we sincerely hope you adore these stories and find some new favorite authors along the way.

Happy Reading!

CEO, Dragonblade Publishing

Additional Dragonblade books by Author Charlotte Wren

Highfield Hall Series
Doubts and Desires (Book 1)
Charades and Chivalry (Book 2)
Passion and Principles (Book 3)
Pride and Propriety (Book 4)
Obsession and Obligation (Book 5)
Vices and Virtues (Book 6)

The Highfield Chronicles
Of Christmas Past (Novella)
If the Fates Allow (Novella)
Loving Lysander (Novella)

The Lyon's Den Series
The Devilish Lyon

'To love is to find one's richness outside oneself.'
~ *Alain* ~

For Claire.

CHAPTER ONE

London
1846

T HIS WAS NOT the first time Julian had laid eyes on the Duchess of Rothbury. Her Grace had been present at several gatherings this past season, though not always accompanied by the duke, whose health was less than robust. She was his second duchess and not even half his age. Their marriage, two autumns before, had taken place as soon as the duke's required mourning period for his first wife had concluded, suggesting the new pairing of pedigree and title had been agreed upon well beforehand. Speculation naturally followed, but Julian, who abhorred shallow conversation, kept his thoughts to himself despite being aware of the broadly held opinion. It seemed obvious, after all.

Her Grace, being the Earl of Sedbergh's eldest daughter and a renowned beauty, had secured a coveted title and the benefits along with it. Meanwhile, the duke, who had already sired two healthy sons during his previous marriage, had obtained a much-coveted feather for his cap, as well as the envy of many of his peers, bachelors and otherwise.

So what? No harm done. Quite the contrary. Her Grace, whose enchanting beauty was complemented by an exuberant and magnetic personality, had been popular before the marriage. Since acquiring her title, her popularity had increased. Within minutes of her arrival at a society event, she would be surround-ed by a fawning retinue of male and female admirers, all jostling for attention. His Grace, whenever present, never showed any sign of jealousy. If anything, he took pleasure in his wife's popularity, strutting about as much as his one gouty foot would allow, while puffing out his chest like a cock pigeon.

Julian didn't fawn. His admiration for the lady was sincere, but elemental. They had never even been formally introduced. And, until this utterly unanticipated moment, he'd only ever seen her fully clothed. Now he stood in awed silence as he gazed upon her near-naked form, which lounged brazenly upon an ornate, red velvet chaise-longue. His hands rested quietly at his side while his bold gaze touched every visible part of her, lingering here and there to absorb detail. Her Grace, in turn, appeared to study him with equal audacity.

Her head, partially framed by the crook of her slender right arm, rested upon a gold silk pillow. A delicate blush of rose graced each defined cheek, contrasting sweetly with the flawless alabaster hue of her lovely complexion. Her lips, strawberry-red and deliciously plump, displayed the merest suggestion of a pout. A gold, laurel leaf circlet adorned her hair, which tumbled over her left shoulder in a cascade of glossy chocolate curls, veiling her right breast. The left breast, in erotic contrast, was fully exposed, firm and pale, the alluring dusky tip at its center drawing Julian's eye.

The lady's left arm, meanwhile, rested nonchalantly along the curved edge of her body, the bejeweled hand gracefully anchoring the swathe of ivory fabric draped over her hips. An evocative accessory rather than an attempt at modesty, Julian decided, since a seductive, heart-shaped shadow, at the apex of the lady's thighs, was easily visible through the diaphanous cloth. His gaze rested there a moment before continuing its journey, wandering over legs long and shapely, ankles finely turned, and feet, delightfully dainty.

His attention then moved back to the lady's face, where her flagrant, dark-eyed gaze remained fixed upon him. Come-hither eyes, not quite fully open, their intriguing depths lit by a sultry gleam. Tempting. Challenging.

And incredibly life-like.

"So, brother mine, what do you think? I have a few finishing touches to take care of and, of course, it has to be varnished and framed, but it is otherwise done."

Julian raked his gaze over the life-size portrait once more and shook his head in admiration. "It's exquisite, Joe. *She* is exquisite. You have a remarkable talent. Not sure I should be seeing Her Grace like this, however. Aren't you obliged to protect her privacy?"

Josiah snorted. "Absolutely, but your discretion is beyond question. Besides, I doubt very much Her Grace would object. The portrait is, apparently, to be hung in full view over the fireplace in her private parlor."

"Then I must assume His Grace is aware."

Josiah gave an acknowledging nod. "Fully."

"In that case, I shall set all gentlemanly considerations aside and continue to admire your artistic talent." Julian folded his arms and took another long look at the lady's splendid attributes. "She truly is beautiful. Of course, you must know my seeing her at any future society events from now on will never be the same. Her clothing, henceforth, will be invisible to me." Frowning, he took a moment to study the other elements of the portrait. "And I'm curious to know why she is reclining among the ruins of a Roman temple."

"Greek temple, actually, and purely imaginary. It was what she wanted. And yes, Rosalind is very beautiful, with or without clothing." Josiah heaved an exaggerated sigh as he regarded the portrait. "Definitely one of my more pleasurable commissions, all done here and very covertly, for obvious reasons."

"*Rosalind?*" Julian cocked a brow and regarded his brother. "Yes, well, I suppose propriety is superfluous under such circumstances."

"To the contrary, propriety is essential under such circumstances. Usually, anyway." The hint of a smile appeared. "The formalities just naturally disappeared over time."

Julian ignored the inference. "How long did it take to finish?"

"Almost a year." Josiah shrugged. "I'd have had it finished sooner, but the sittings with Her Grace often took longer than might be deemed normal."

"Did they, indeed." Julian gave in to humor and asked the unnecessary question. "And why, pray tell, was that?"

"Attention to detail." Josiah assumed a serious expression. "Rosalind had very specific demands that had to be met to her complete satisfaction. Not that she was difficult, mind you. As I said, she was a pleasure. A most willing subject, in fact. I shall miss her. I *do* miss her."

Julian grimaced. "You know, one of these days you're going to find yourself looking down the barrel of some husband's gun."

Josiah huffed. "Well, it won't be Rothbury's. Most of the time, he's got his gouty foot propped up on a footstool. Besides, it seems he can only manage verbal intercourse, so he makes allowances for his wife's occasional flirtations and turns a blind eye to them." A grin appeared. "Which isn't difficult, since he can't see a bloody thing without his spectacles."

Julian frowned. "Damn it, Joe, I'm being serious. You tend to play a little too close to the hearth at times. Just be careful you don't get burned."

Josiah's grin dissolved. "I'm always careful," he replied. "And where women are concerned, I also happen to be very selective. Compared to some of my academy associates, I live like a monk. Truth is, I never set out to seduce Rosalind. If anything, she seduced me."

"Ah, I see." Julian nodded. "And I suppose you put up a fight."

Josiah parted with a laugh. "Not much of one, I'll grant you. Can you blame me?"

Julian eyed the portrait once more, heaving a sigh as he shook his head. "No, I cannot. So, what else are you working on?"

"Not at liberty to say, I'm afraid. Secret project, and all that." Josiah threw him a challenging look. "Nothing risky, though, before you start lecturing."

"Glad to hear it." Julian gave his brother's shoulder an affectionate squeeze and cast an eye around the studio, which occupied the entire top floor of his brother's London apartments.

Sunlight, pouring through two large windows and a skylight, filled the entire, white-washed space, with the exception of a mysterious corner hidden behind a screen of faded, red silk curtains. Canvases of assorted sizes were stacked along one wall, while a diverse selection of jars containing an equally diverse collection of brushes and other implements occupied several wooden wall shelves. A large wooden table stood in the middle of the room, its surface a chaotic mosaic of paint spatters that had accumulated over time. Beside it, two empty easels awaited their next project. A large mirror, set in an ornate gilt frame, leant against the far wall, adding extra depth and light to the room.

It was more than a workspace, Julian thought. It was, in fact, a representation of his brother's character; colorful, abstract, not quite orderly but unquestionably brilliant, and not without a furtive edge of darkness and mystery. Then his gaze came to rest on the chaise-longue featured in the duchess's portrait.

"Borrowed," Josiah said, apparently following along. "The owner is coming to collect it this afternoon."

Julian smiled an acknowledgment. "So, you'll definitely be joining the family for dinner tonight?"

"Definitely." Josiah drew a cross over his heart. "I'll be there at five o'clock sharp."

"Then my mission is accomplished, and I shall leave you in peace." He gave the duchess a final admiring glance and then headed for the door. "Superb work, brother, truly. I'm proud of you."

"You are?" A hint of surprise edged Josiah's response.

"Unquestionably." Julian paused on the threshold and looked back. "We *all* are, Joe. See you tonight."

Minutes later, he stepped onto the street, intent on hailing a cab, but paused, his gaze drawn to a remarkably clear sky. A pleasant change, since the past several days had been damp and miserable. And for him, at least, this bright day marked the end of another London season. As usual, his time in the city had been enjoyable and entertaining, but not extraordinary.

As far as marriage prospects went, Julian had yet to meet the woman with whom he'd wish to spend a lifetime. He was in no particular hurry, however, so it mattered little. Tomorrow, utilizing both train and horse-drawn carriage, he would begin the journey back to Yorkshire, specifically Highfield Hall and all the responsibilities the estate entailed. Today, he decided to forgo transport and take advantage of this rather splendid day. It was not a long walk to the family's London home. Half an hour, perhaps. Tapping his hat firmly onto his head, he set out.

CHAPTER TWO

CLUTCHING HER SMALL, paper-wrapped purchase, Annie Fairfax stepped out of the Burlington Arcade and merged into the turbulent tide of man, beast, and carriage that walked, trotted, and rumbled along Piccadilly. After a week of wet and windy weather, the dawning of this calm, sunny day seemed to have brought forth half of the city's population, Annie included. Unfortunately, London's more disagreeable odors hung stubbornly in the motionless air, adding weight to the discomforting swell of humanity.

Nose wrinkling, Annie opened the silver vinaigrette that dangled on a fine chain about her neck and lifted it to her nostrils to savor the more agreeable scent of lavender. It calmed her somewhat, but she clutched her package a little tighter as she dodged and wound her way through the throng of people. Despite being born and raised in the city, or maybe because of it, she had never been comfortable in crowds.

"Are you still with me, Hattie?" she asked, glancing over her shoulder at the woman who had long served as matron, teacher, and maid to Annie.

"Right behind you," Hattie replied, wafting a hand like a fan beneath her nose. Annie nodded and turned back, a move that caused her to side-step directly into the path of someone coming toward her. She had no time to correct herself or even cry out as she ploughed into whoever it was.

It might as well have been a stone wall.

A decidedly male *"oof"* coincided with her choked cry as she toppled backwards, arms flailing, hands snatching at air. The package flew from her grasp, her heels caught in the hem of her skirt, and she sat down hard on the pavement. The vicious jolt caused her to bite her tongue, which brought instant, scalding tears to her eyes. From somewhere above, a man's voice uttered a mild curse, while another tittered. Winded and tasting blood, Annie flinched as the crowds continued to move past, their shapes creating dizzying waves of shadow and light. She tried and failed to take air. "Pl... please," she managed, struggling to fill her lungs. "Cannot br—"

"It's all right miss, I have you," a man said, and she felt herself being hoisted gently to her feet by a pair of strong, and undeniably masculine, arms. "My sincere apologies. That was quite the bump. Are you injured at all?"

Annie, at last, managed to draw a desperate lungful of air. She opened her eyes but squeezed them shut again when the world around her tilted nauseatingly. "Oh my."

The man's hands, cradling Annie's elbows, tightened slightly as she grabbed, blindly, onto his sleeves. "Take your time, miss," he said. "Catch your breath."

Hattie's concerned voice meandered into Annie's ear. "Gracious, my pet, you took quite the tumble. Are you hurt? You're as white as a sheet. Here, let go of the gentleman and lean on me."

"Just give me a moment, Hattie," Annie replied, and clutched the fabric of the man's sleeves tighter. Yes, she was hurt. Her tongue stung, her bottom ached, and her pride was not without injury either. It took an effort to keep the tears at bay.

"Do you feel faint, miss?" the man asked. "Perhaps you should sit for a while. Come, there's a bench over here."

Annie cringed inwardly at the thought of sitting on a hard bench. "No, I'd rather not," she replied, somewhat abruptly. Softening her tone, she continued, "That is, thank you, but I just need..." She squinted through her lashes. "I just need a moment or two."

"Of course," came the gentle response. "Take all the time you need. I'm in no hurry."

Annie knew she should probably let go of whoever *he* was, but didn't quite dare, mostly because her legs felt somewhat like jelly. Besides, nothing about this man's nearness gave her cause for concern or embarrassment. If anything, she found solace in his apparent strength. Who was he?

She breathed in a subtle hint of Eau De Cologne and dared to open her eyes fully, exhaling with relief to find her dizziness had almost abated. She blinked and stared at the blue silk cravat before her, the neat folds secured with a pearl-tipped, gold pin. As her composure returned, her gaze moved upward over a cleanly-shaven, masculine jaw, an unsmiling but pleasant mouth, and a finely sculpted nose. A second later, she found herself looking into a pair of arresting hazel eyes, gazing down at her from beneath a pair of dark brows, which were currently knitted together in a frown. Annie's breath caught and her stomach gave a queer little lurch. She opened her mouth to speak, but words failed her. All she could do was stare into the man's eyes. He stared back, his frown usurped by the hint of a smile.

"There now," he said, quietly. "Feeling better?"

His voice broke through the strange spell that had Annie in its grasp. She blinked again and loosened her grip on the man's sleeves, though her gaze remained locked with his.

"Yes," she replied. "Yes, I think so."

"Are you sure?" The man spoke as softly as before, his concerned gaze moving over her face.

Annie swallowed and found a smile from somewhere. "Yes, sir, quite sure," she replied. "Thank you."

He acknowledged with a nod and released his hold on her. Annie, to her bewilderment, experienced a brief sense of regret.

"Here, pet, let me brush some of this dust off your skirts," Hattie said, tutting as she stooped to the task. "There, that's better. Oh, but you're still rather pale. Lean on me, now, if you have need."

"I'm all right, Hattie, really." Annie's hand drifted to the base of her throat as if to settle the continuous wild beating of her heart. "Just a little shaken, that's all."

"Hardly surprising," Hattie said, her accusing tone obviously aimed at the stranger.

"And it was entirely my fault," Annie replied, giving Hattie a quick, reproachful glance before facing the man once more. "I was *not* watching where I was going. An apology, therefore, is entirely mine to make."

"Well, since it is unseemly to argue with a lady, I shall keep any further admissions of negligence to myself. However, I will not rescind them." The man stooped to pick up the package, which lay at his feet. "What is most important to me, miss, is your honest assurance that you are not injured in any way."

Hattie harumphed and Annie threw her another admonishing glare. "My dignity is a little bruised, perhaps," she replied, easily deciding not to mention her sore tongue or bruised backside. "But that is all, sir, truly. No harm done."

"Glad to hear it." The man's frown reappeared as he handed her the package. "Hopefully, no harm done to this either."

"None, to be sure," Annie gave the wrapping a cursory inspection, "since it is not a breakable item."

Hattie harumphed again. The man gave the maid a somewhat amused glance and then returned his attention to Annie, his gaze once again critical. "With respect, miss, may I ask about your plans for the rest of your day? Given how crowded the city is today, and despite your assurances, I'm loath to leave you and your companion unassisted."

"We have no further plans, sir," she replied. "We're going straight home."

The man nodded. "Then permit me to hail a cab for you."

Annie gave her head a brief shake. "A kind offer, but I do not live far. A short walk, only."

"Then at least allow me to escort you to your door," he countered. "Given what has occurred, I would be happier knowing you have arrived home without further mishap."

An odd little flutter arose beneath Annie's ribs at the thought of spending more time with him, even as she provided an argument against it. "But my direction is opposite to the one you were taking, therefore an inconvenience to you, surely."

His expression softened. "Not in the least."

Annie ignored the flutter and pondered for a moment. The man was a stranger, after all, though every bit of instinct she possessed insisted she had no cause to fear him. Besides, she reasoned, a faint headache now occupied a spot behind her eyes, her tongue and her bottom continued with their persistent throb, and her legs were still a *little* wobbly. It was probably prudent, then, to accept this handsome stranger's offer. And, she silently admitted, it had an undeniable appeal.

"With respect, my dear," Hattie's voice cut into her thoughts, "I believe you should accept the gentleman's offer. It'll do no harm."

Annie barely suppressed a surprised gasp as she regarded her maid, since not a minute earlier the wretched woman had been scowling at the fellow. "Perhaps you are right," she replied, and returned her gaze to the gentleman. "Therefore, sir, I accept your offer with gratitude."

"Excellent. And in that case, miss, allow me to introduce myself." He smiled, tipped his hat, and presented an elbow. "Julian Northcott, at your service."

Julian Northcott.

Annie absorbed the information as she tucked her hand into the fold of his arm. "A pleasure to make your acquaintance, Mr. Northcott. My name is Annabelle Fairfax."

"The pleasure is also mine, Miss Fairfax," he replied, "though I regret what precipitated it. Shall I carry the package for you?"

"No, it weighs nothing," she said, "but thank you."

Lifting a brow, he regarded Hattie, who had several packages tucked under her arms. "And what of you, ma'am? May I unburden you a little?"

"No, sir, you may not," Hattie replied, looking mildly affronted. "I am not injured and can manage quite well."

Annie noticed the same amused expression flicker across the man's face as he returned his attention to her. "Then let us be on our way," he said, "but you, Miss Fairfax, must be the one to set our pace. There is no hurry on my part. I ask only that you'll tell me if you feel in the least unwell or in need of a pause."

Annie nodded her assent. "I will, sir, thank you."

"Good. Now, where do you live?"

"Chester Street. Do you know of it?"

"I do. It's not far at all."

No, it wasn't, yet Annie felt genuinely glad of his support as they moved off. True, she still felt a little shaken, but deep down inside another sensation had sparked to life. One she had never felt before. It was, however, instinctually recognizable and, in truth, not entirely welcome. She took a steadying breath.

"Do you live in London permanently, Miss Fairfax?" he asked.

He had a pleasant voice, Annie thought. A decidedly masculine resonance, refined and confident, but not in the least haughty. It fell so easily into her ears, stimulating yet calming at the same time. Knowing this man's name, she realized, wasn't enough. A quick calculation in her head told her she had perhaps fifteen, maybe twenty, minutes till she arrived at her front door, where she would bid Julian Northcott farewell forever. And, for reasons she could not begin to fathom, she endeavored to learn as much as she could about him before the moment arrived. Not that doing so made any sense. This impromptu meeting with a chivalrous stranger would serve no life-changing purpose, after all. The direction of her future had been mapped out long since.

"Yes, I do. My father is a physician." The image of her father's face appeared in her mind, and she clutched her package tighter to her chest. "Now retired."

"A fine profession, indeed."

Annie smiled her response, aware that Julian Northcott, as decorum dictated, was making polite conversation. Propriety demanded she do likewise, which meant ignoring the growing list of less decorous questions arising in her brain. The crook of his arm clenched around her hand as he steered her through a cluster of pedestrians. Nothing more than a small gesture of protection, yet it sent a tingle of pleasure spiraling down Annie's spine.

"Actually, I have lived here all my life," she said. "What of you, sir? Do you live in the city?"

"Only temporarily," he replied. "In fact, I'm returning home tomorrow."

"Oh, I see." Annie masked a brief sense of disappointment with another smile, wishing she were bold enough to ask what had brought him to London in the first place. Business, perhaps, though she suspected it might have been for the Season. Although he hadn't introduced himself with a title, everything about him, from his comportment to his fine clothing, indicated he was a man of note. If not actual nobility, then connected somehow. Decorum must prevail, she decided, and settled on a less intrusive question. "And where might your permanent home be?"

"Yorkshire," he replied. "Specifically, not too far from Harrogate, if you happen to be familiar with the area."

"Not terribly, I'm afraid," she replied, the mention of northern lands provoking a vague and long-abandoned memory. "I've only been to the northern parts of England once, though I couldn't tell you whereabouts, exactly. I was but four years old, you see, and sent away from London when my mother became ill." A hazy image slid into Annie's mind, that of a thin, pale woman, recumbent upon the chaise-longue in the front parlor, perpetually accompanied by the smell of roses and something else undefined, medicinal, and not particularly pleasant. "I stayed at my aunt's house for several weeks, but have few recollections of it." More memories, long discarded and blurred with time, manifested themselves. "It was definitely somewhere in the countryside, though. I remember all the fields with stone walls. There were sheep in those fields and my aunt had a black-and-white dog that stood almost as tall as myself. Mind you, being but four years of age, I was probably not very tall. My aunt used to sing to me at bedtime, as well. She had a lovely voice. Oh, and I was awoken each morning by a rather loud cockerel and always had a speckled boiled egg for breakfast, served in a pretty blue-and-white eggcup with some kind of picture on it. And buttered toast!"

From somewhere behind came an exaggerated cough from Hattie. It served as a resonate nudge that made Annie groan inwardly even as an unwanted flush of heat washed over her face. *Oh, Annabelle! Blathering away like an idiot. Bedtime? Sheep, cockerels, and boiled eggs? What must he think of me?*

"What did she sing?" he asked.

Annie, her thoughts now flooded with self-castigation, regarded him blankly. "Pardon?"

"Your aunt," he replied. "You said she sang to you, and I just wondered what she sang."

"Oh." Annie, silently endeavoring to steer the conversation elsewhere, gave the question but a brief ponderance and responded honestly. "I'm afraid I do not recall, sir."

JULIAN BIT BACK a smile at Miss Fairfax's obvious embarrassment. As far as he was concerned, her chagrin was unnecessary. The young lady was refreshingly charming. Mannerly, yet lacking the stiff airs and graces so often found within the aristocracy. And, while she might not be deemed beautiful in the classical sense, she was far from plain. Undoubtedly younger than him by a few years, petite in stature, yet not without womanly curves. A pretty face, gentle of expression, previously pale, but currently lit by a flush of color. Otherwise, she possessed a flawless complexion except for a small mole that sat above the arch of her right eyebrow. The dark ringlets framing her face were closer to brown than black, and glinted with thin threads of dark coppery red when caught by the sun.

The duchess's portrait aside, Julian had never paid particular attention to a woman's eyes before. At least, not that he could recall. Yet his attention had been drawn to Miss Fairfax's, mostly because they had, at first, been closed, and fringed with an abundance of thick, dark lashes sparkling with captive tears. They bothered him, those sparkles, for they indicated distress and pain, which contradicted the young lady's denial of injury. And, although Julian could have done nothing to avoid the collision, he couldn't help but feel responsible. As he'd held her, feeling the soft tremble of her body so close to his, he had silently willed her eyes to open, that those wretched tears might dissipate and ease his conscience. At that point, he hadn't given any thought to the actual color of those eyes. They turned out to be quite exquisite, however. A dark bluish grey, dramatically edged in black, they had regarded him with unabashed curiosity. And perhaps trust, if he was not mistaken.

She interrupted his contemplation. "Please forgive my silly rambling, Mr. Northcott," she said, her cheeks still sweetly pink. "I'm afraid, at times, my mind has a propensity to wander."

Julian smiled. "Your childhood memories of this place are not in the least silly, Miss Fairfax. To the contrary, I find them charming. I trust your mother recovered from her illness?"

"I'm afraid she did not, sir," she replied, glancing away. "I only returned to London after her death."

"Ah." Julian winced inwardly. "Then please forgive my intrusiveness. We need not speak of it further."

"Oh no, it's quite all right. It all happened long ago." She gave a slight shrug. "In truth, I have few memories of Mama and even less of my aunt."

"Yet it seems this aunt of yours provided you with shelter and comfort during a difficult time."

Her brow furrowed slightly as she regarded him. "Yes, it seems she did."

He couldn't help but ask. "Which, with respect, leads me to

wonder why you cannot recall the whereabouts of her house."

"That is because my aunt also passed, and not long after Mama, so I was still a child. My father does not like to revisit the events of that time, so we have never spoken of it at any length. Actually, till today, I have not thought about it for many years." She slowed her step and glanced over her shoulder. "Do you happen to remember where it was, Hattie?"

"I remember you being sent away, of course," the woman replied, "but I was otherwise preoccupied with caring for your poor mama. True, 'twas a dreadful time. Hardly surprising your father does not care to visit the memories of it."

Julian frowned at what he perceived to be a hint of evasiveness in the maid's response. Perhaps he imagined it. Miss Fairfax, meanwhile, dropped her gaze to the pavement, effectively hiding her face beneath the brim of her bonnet. "Even so," she said, quietly, "I believe I shall ask him about it upon my return home today."

She fell silent and Julian sensed her continued chagrin, as if she'd somehow misspoken by voicing her innermost thoughts and memories. In an effort to ease her discomfort, he decided to do the very thing that had led to hers, and take a slight step beyond the formal boundaries to share some insight into his life.

He regarded her. Or rather, the top of her bonneted head.

"How are you feeling now, Miss Fairfax?" he asked, hoping she would look at him again. She did, her fingers tightening in the crook of his arm as he gazed into those pretty eyes once more.

"Much better, Mr. Northcott, thank you," she replied.

"Good." Julian focused on committing the vision of her face to memory. "You're certainly not as pale as you were, I must say."

"Which is likely due to a persistent sense of embarrassment," she replied, with a wry smile. "But I feel quite well, otherwise."

"Your embarrassment is not warranted. Not at all." He dared to probe again. "If you don't mind me asking, do you have any siblings?"

"Regrettably, I do not," she replied. "Do you?"

Julian nodded. "Five of them. Three sisters and two brothers, all younger than I, and not one of them beyond embarrassing me." He chuckled. "Or each other, come to that, though it is perhaps unfair to include my youngest brother in my accusation. Arthur is the quiet one. Then again, there are those who say, 'beware the quiet ones'."

"Five! How splendid." Miss Fairfax's curls danced as she shook her head. "I should imagine you have many tales to tell."

Julian grimaced. "One or two, perhaps."

She gave a soft laugh, followed by a wistful expression, there and gone. Then, "Your parents are still living?"

He nodded again. "They are, and both in good health, thank God."

"You are fortunate, sir." A sigh escaped her. "My father is quite ill, I'm afraid. Has been for some time."

The response raised more questions, though Julian resisted the temptation to ask what ailed the fellow. If the tone of Miss Fairfax's voice was any indication, however, the ailment sounded serious. He couldn't help but wonder what would become of her if and when her father died. "I'm sorry to hear that," he replied. "It must be difficult for you."

"More so for him." She gave a brief, cheerless smile. "He insisted I go out today to lift my spirits. *My* spirits, if you please! Yet he is the one suffering."

"I'm sure seeing him suffer cannot be easy for you, Miss Fairfax, and I'm equally sure he understands."

"No doubt. I'm fully aware of his motives and I'll be sure to tell him the outing was very pleasant." They turned onto her street, and her fingers, tucked into the crook of Julian's elbow, tightened a little. "Which it has been."

Julian gave the street sign a quick glance, which indicated more than Annabelle Fairfax's address. It also indicated that his time with her was almost at an end.

Three more minutes. Maybe four.

"Which number?" he asked, eyeing the row of elegant town-houses.

"Twenty-nine," she replied, gesturing. "The second house in from the far end, on this side."

Maybe five.

"Right," he muttered, falling silent as several different scenarios played out in his mind.

I suppose I have no choice but to leave her at the door and bid her farewell. Not sure why that bothers me. I know nothing of her, after all. Pity. I should like to know more. Not likely, though, since I'm leaving tomorrow. Besides, she might already be—

"I am very grateful to you, sir." Her voice broke into his thoughts once more. "I trust the detour has not been too much of an inconvenience."

"Not an inconvenience at all, Miss Fairfax," he replied, and finished his contemplation. *She might already be spoken for.* The possibility of it darkened his thoughts. Once again, he regarded the lady's bonneted head, but drew on the vision of her face he'd committed to memory.

Not even an hour earlier, he'd gazed upon the naked form, albeit a portrayal, of the Duchess of Rothbury. Unquestionably, the most beautiful woman he'd ever seen. And he'd seen almost every inch of her. It had been a pleasurable experience, but he desired nothing more from it. Beyond admiring her physical assets, he had no real interest in the lady, no compulsion to learn about any hidden beauty she might possess.

Yet he longed to know more about the young woman still attached to his arm. Her beauty might not be as remarkable as that of the duchess, but, for Julian, it held far more appeal. He yearned to solve the allure and mystery of her. And he had no time left in which to do so.

"Well, here we are," she said, with a touch of finality. "I must thank you again, sir."

Halting, Julian regarded the polished brass number on the door. *Of course! I could always—*

"Sir?"

Julian blinked. "Forgive me, Miss Fairfax. It seems my mind also has a propensity to wander." He cleared his throat. "I confess, I find myself unwilling to bid you a final farewell. That being so, and at the risk of being presumptuous, I wonder if you might be agreeable to an exchange of correspondence between us."

Even as the words were spoken, he groaned inwardly. *Bloody hell, Julian. Could you be any more pragmatic?*

Those lovely eyes widened as they had earlier. "Oh, Mr. Northcott, I…" She released his arm, looked past him to where her maid stood in silence, and then regarded him once more. "I'm afraid it would not be appropriate, sir." A smile, regretful rather than joyful, came and went. "You see, I am promised to another and due to be married in a fortnight."

The response landed rather like a punch to his gut. "Ah." Julian barely managed to summon up a smile of his own as he absorbed the news, unsure of what pained him more, disappointment or embarrassment. His cravat felt tight all of a sudden, and he suppressed an impulse to loosen it and to disappear, with all haste, back into the city streets. Holding onto his smile, he inclined his head. "In that case, Miss Fairfax, I apologize for my temerity and offer you my very best wishes for your future. I must also excuse myself from your company and allow you to continue with your day."

"Mr. Northcott, please." Gloved fingers touched his arm once more. "I feel compelled to tell you that, if circumstances were different, I would consider it an honor and a privilege to correspond with you. As it is, please allow me to thank you, again, for your chivalry. I shall never forget it."

Julian gazed into Annabelle Fairfax's eyes and wondered if Josiah would be able to capture their beauty on canvas. A random thought. Utterly pointless.

"I'm happy to have been of service to you," he replied, regarding both women as he tipped his hat. "I bid you both a good day."

Then, feeling overly warm and rather deflated, he walked away, taking several good strides before allowing himself the luxury of a hefty, and heartfelt, sigh.

He needed a drink.

CHAPTER THREE

ANNIE STEPPED INTO the soothing coolness of the hallway, released a slow breath, and set her package down on an occasional chair. "You will say nothing to Papa of what happened today, Hattie," she said, barely able to keep a quiver from her voice. "It would serve no purpose other than to agitate him, and I will not have that." She pulled off her gloves and began to remove her bonnet, still seeing the image of Julian Northcott walking away from her. Why did she feel as though she'd made a terrible mistake by denying him? She could not have done otherwise, after all. She was engaged to Leo, had been since childhood, and they were soon to be married. Yet she had the strangest feeling she'd just been offered something of extraordinary value and had refused it. The impression still lingered, though it made little sense.

"My lips are sealed." Hattie closed the front door using her derriere, and set her armful of packages on the console table. "Besides, there is really nothing of import to tell, now, is there?"

"Nothing at all." Annie ignored the penetrative undertones of the maid's voice and picked up her package from the chair. "I shall be with Papa in the parlor. Would you ask Bridget to send some tea, please? I'm quite parched."

There followed a telling silence that dragged on for several seconds. Annie bit back a sigh and regarded the woman who had been a part of her life for sixteen years. A maid officially, but the relationship had long since evolved into something more. The woman was the closest thing to a mother Annie had ever known. "Is there something you want to say to me, Hattie?"

"Oh, hum, no, not really." Hattie sniffed and tugged down on her sleeve cuffs. "I was only thinking that Mr. Northcott seemed like a very nice young man."

Annie gasped. "Then it appears you've had a change of opinion, since I had the distinct impression you didn't approve of him at all. In fact, I thought you were unnecessarily curt to him."

Hattie shrugged. "Perhaps a little at first, but I was simply being cautious. Can't trust anyone these days. Men especially. Soon became apparent to me that he was a gentleman, though. A decent man. Treated you very kindly, he did."

Annie looked down and fiddled with a corner of the package. "Yes, he did."

Hattie sniffed. "It's a pity, really."

"What is?" Annie, already at odds with herself, felt her patience unraveling and glared at the woman. "Please get to the point, Hattie. I'm not in the mood for guessing games."

"That you had to refuse the gentleman's offer of correspondence."

Annie scoffed. "Well, it would hardly have been appropriate to accept, now, would it? I'm to be married in a fortnight."

"Yes, indeed you are." The woman clucked her tongue. "And you well know my opinion on—"

"That is *quite* enough, I think." Annie gave an exasperated sigh and turned away. "I'll be in the parlor with Papa. Just do as I ask, please. Bridget, tea, and then I suggest you put your feet up for a while. You must be worn out from carrying all those opinions of yours."

There followed a brief pause, then, "Speaking of carrying, shall I put all these packages in your room?"

Annie capitulated to a smile and answered without turning. "Yes, Hattie. Thank you."

Not a minute later, she entered the parlor, settled onto the tufted stool beside a large, well-worn leather chair and gave the chair's fragile occupant a critical inspection.

"How are you feeling this afternoon, Papa?" Annie set the package she'd been holding on the floor and reached for her father's hand, the flesh disturbingly cool and paper-thin to the touch. "Are you warm enough? Can I fetch you anything? I've ordered some tea, if you'd like a cup."

Clarence Fairfax, her father, was a man who had aided and cured many souls in his fifty-four years upon the earth. But his own health had been gradually failing for some time, and notably for the past several weeks. His self-made diagnosis, as well as that of a colleague who'd been attending him, was concluded to be a disorder of the liver. Whatever, it had thus far acted without mercy, stealing his strength and fortitude with steadfast rapidity.

Initially, Annie had chosen to ignore her father's impending demise, as if constructing a wall of denial might serve to keep the inevitable at bay. But lately, reality had leached through her defenses, creating a sickening mix of fear and despondency that gnawed incessantly at her stomach. Her prayers for her father's recovery had not been answered. Now she prayed he would at least be well enough to walk her down the aisle two weeks hence.

Smiling, he gazed down at her, the whites of his slate-grey eyes sullied by a faint, yellowish hue. "I'm feeling quite well, my dear. Very comfortable, in fact. I even took a brief stroll around the garden earlier and enjoyed a bit of sunshine." His fingers squeezed hers. "Did you enjoy your outing?"

She answered him honestly. "I did, Papa, but felt guilty about leaving you alone."

"Ah, but I'm not alone, am I? Bridget is here." He gave her fingers another feeble squeeze. "You can't stay cooped up in the house all the time, Annie. It's not healthy. Now, tell me about your excursion. Where did you go? Did you purchase some nice things for yourself?"

"I went to the Burlington Arcade, and yes, I purchased a few items, though mostly frivolous. Some ribbons, lace, and notepaper." She gave a slight shrug. "And I also bought you a gift."

"Oh, my dear child." He closed his eyes briefly. "I have no need of anything."

"Well, I couldn't resist, and it is *not* a frivolous item." Annie released his hand and picked up the package, noticing, for the first time, a faint smudge on the wrapper. From the pavement, no doubt, after she'd collided with Julian Northcott. The image of his face still lingered in her mind, as did the unsettling impression of having made a mistake by bidding him a permanent farewell. With some effort, she shoved both image and impression aside, and turned her attention back to the parcel. "Shall I unwrap it for you, Papa?"

He nodded. "Yes please, my dear."

She did so, and then set the open wrapping on his lap so he could see what lay within. "I noticed the one you were wearing last night looked a little worn," she said. "This one is made from the finest Spanish wool, though it feels like silk. It's a light weave, more suited for the summer months."

Her father lifted the sleeping-cap from the paper and studied it, eyes widening slightly. "Oh, it's perfect, Annie, thank you." He brought it to his face and nestled his cheek against the cream-colored fabric. "And yes, so soft! I shall wear it tonight and no doubt sleep better for it."

"I hope so." Frowning, Annie glanced down and brushed an imaginary speck from her skirts while wondering how to broach the subject of her mother's death, and the events which had taken place around that time. A door, long closed, had recently reopened in her mind, and she felt compelled to explore its hidden contents further, to discover what childhood memories had been set aside and forgotten.

"Good lord, look at that frown," her father said. "May I know the cause? Nothing is wrong, I hope."

Biting her lip, Annie met his gaze. "No, nothing is wrong, Papa. It's just that I remembered something about my childhood today, and wish to enquire about it."

His eyes widened. "Well, now I'm thoroughly intrigued," he replied, shifting in his seat. "All right. What is it you remembered?"

"The time I went to stay with Aunt Sybil."

He blinked, and his entire expression changed to one of obvious disapproval. "When your dear Mama was ill, yes. What about it?"

"Well, I should like to know the whereabouts of Aunt Sybil's house, and the name of the nearest village or town, too. Where, exactly, are they located? Somewhere in the countryside, I know, but which county?"

The expression remained. "Annie, I do not care to resurrect my memories of that time. I find them distressing, as I'm sure you're aware."

Guilt sent a slight flush to Annie's face. Her father was, after all, poorly, and she had no wish to upset him, but she was determined to press him a little further. "Yes, I do know, Papa, but I am not really asking much. I'm simply curious about where Aunt Sybil lived, that's all. I stayed with her for quite a few weeks, did I not?"

A tic came to his left eye. "May I know what brought this about?"

A fair question. Annie took a moment to find a response that lacked specifics, but was not entirely dishonest. "I overheard part of a conversation today and, well, it might have been due to their accents, but I was reminded of that time. I have a few vague memories of Aunt Sybil's house and just wondered where it was. That's all."

"I see," he said, without enthusiasm. "Well, unfortunately, my dear, I'm not sure I can recall the exact location. Somewhere in Yorkshire, perhaps. Or maybe Lancashire."

"Yorkshire?" It came out almost as a squeak, and her next question escaped before she could prevent it. "Might it have been anywhere near Harrogate?"

"Harrogate?" Her father gave her an odd look. "I couldn't say,

Annie. Doesn't ring any bells, though, I'm afraid."

"Oh." Annie bit her lip again, trying, and failing, to visualize the precise position of the county on a map of England. "But you must remember the name of the place, surely."

"No, I do not. I do not believe I was ever aware of it, in fact. I was never there, you see. Sybil came to collect you and escorted you there herself, since I could not leave your mother." His expression hardened, as did his voice. "Nor does it matter, since both of them are long gone. I only recall that it was a sad time, one I prefer not to dwell upon."

Annie stifled a sigh of frustration. "I understand, Papa. I just hoped you might be able to shed a litt—"

A knock on the door interrupted whatever remained of the conversation, and Bridget entered with a tea tray. "Shall I pour, Miss Annabelle?"

"No, I'll pour," Annie replied, rising. "Thank you, Bridget."

Bridget set the tray on the nearby sideboard, gave Annie a sympathetic smile, and left. Silence then descended, disturbed only by the clink of a teaspoon as Annie stirred a sprinkle of sugar into her father's tea. She turned and halted, overwhelmed by a sudden rush of compassion as she regarded him. He appeared to be examining the sleeping-cap she'd purchased for him, turning it over and over in his hands. Yet she had the distinct impression his thoughts were elsewhere. Nowhere pleasant, either, judging by the lost expression on his face.

Annie smothered another sigh and silently cursed her thoughtlessness. What did it matter, really, where her long-deceased aunt used to live? The question had only arisen because of a brief encounter with a charming stranger who, in mere minutes, had somehow managed to instill a foolish ache of attraction in her heart. Foolish, yes, and worthless besides. Under different circumstances, their meeting might have led to something more substantial. *But my destiny lies elsewhere and I'm quite happy about it.* She straightened her shoulders. *Yes, quite happy.*

"Forgive me, Papa." She approached, set his teacup on the small table at his side, and bent to kiss his cheek. "I should not have upset you. It was thoughtless of me."

"Oh, that's all right, my dear." He tutted and shook his head. "I must also beg your forgiveness. Some memories are simply too painful to recall."

"I understand, of course." She lifted an errant strand of silver hair from his brow and patted it into place. "Now, drink your tea, and then perhaps you should take a nap. In case you've forgotten, Leo will be joining us for dinner this evening."

"No, I hadn't forgotten." A frown appeared, followed by the clearing of his throat. "Actually, I've been meaning to speak to you about Leo. More specifically, the marriage."

Annie blinked. "What of it?"

"I need to be assured you are happy with the arrangement."

An obscure little tingle shot across her scalp. "I don't understand, Papa."

Her father leaned forward, his gaze now intense and searching. "Do you have any misgivings about marrying the fellow, Annie? If so, you must tell me now, before it's too late."

Misgivings? Annie knew Hattie disapproved of the match, but now her father was questioning it as well? "I'm not sure how to respond, Papa. I haven't really thought about it. Leo has always been a part of my future."

"Yes, because the union was arranged years ago, when you were children. It was never, however, an agreement set in stone. Frederick, may God rest his soul, was a dear friend and colleague, and it seemed fitting at the time to foresee his son and my daughter wed to one another. But Fred has been gone twelve years now, and your mother fifteen." Frowning, he looked away for a moment. "Muriel was always a touch ambivalent about the arrangement, as I recall. I'm not sure she ever took it seriously." His gaze snapped back to her. "I need to know what lies in your heart, child. Do you truly care for Leopold? Love him, even?"

The unexpected questions took Annie aback. "Why, yes, of

course, Papa. I…" Her brain stumbled over several responses. *Yes, I care for him. Indisputably. And I love him, too. I'm sure I do. I always have.*

Certainly, when Leo had gone to work for his uncle in Prussia four years ago, Annie's young heart had entertained a fairytale impression of love-lost. She had even wept for several nights afterward. But, in hindsight, her sorrow had not been overly taxing and had soon ebbed. Leo, as promised, had written to her fairly regularly. Well, at first anyway. Annie had looked forward to his epistles, which, for the most part, detailed his daily life in the city of Berlin, aiding his uncle and cousin in their tobacco import business. His descriptions of the city, along with the Prussian traditions and culture, fascinated her. While his penned voice was friendly rather than poetic, he always signed off with "affectionately yours."

As time passed, the weekly letters from Leo dwindled to maybe two a month, and then one every few weeks. By that time, each letter included an apology for the lengthy gaps in his correspondence, attributed to his workload due to the ongoing success of his uncle's business. Despite Leo's lapses, however, Annie had continued to write to him faithfully once a week. The past eighteen months had seen but a dozen responses from him, the last three months ago, which had arrived soon after Annie had written to tell him of her father's illness. It appeared Leo had responded with haste, writing to say he was, at last, returning to England.

He'd arrived not quite a fortnight after his letter.

Annie silently admitted she'd entertained a *few* reservations since his return. Nothing more than some little whispers of uncertainty here and there, all without any real foundation. The youthful, carefree boy she remembered had been replaced by a man with a more serious and assertive disposition that could be a little intimidating at times. He was still as handsome as ever though, and unquestionably charming.

An image of him slid into her mind, standing before the fireplace where she now sat. Tall and slender of form, clad in his usual dark garb, sandy-blond hair impeccably groomed, thumb tucked nonchalantly into his vest pocket. Then Leo's image faded, and was replaced by the one of Julian Northcott walking away from her not even twenty minutes before. She blinked the image away and supplied her father with an emphatic response. "Yes, of course I love Leo," she announced, aware of a sudden warm flush upon her cheeks, "and I'm sure he loves me too."

Yet her words sounded hollow, somehow. Lacking substance.

"It bothers me you had to think about it," her father replied, looking unconvinced.

"With respect, Papa, it bothers me you thought it necessary to ask the question," she countered. "It took me by surprise."

He groaned softly. "Forgive me, my dear. I perhaps should not be asking such things. Maybe it's because the fellow has been away these past four years, yet not once did he take the time to visit us. Germany is not the end of the world, after all. Even now, his return appears to have been prompted solely upon hearing of my illness. If not for that, he might still be abroad. And he has yet to fully explain how he means to support you."

"I think he has explained it well enough, Papa," Annie replied. "Even as we speak, he is visiting a couple of potential properties which might serve as the new London location for his uncle's business, of which he will be the manager."

"Yes, yes, but it all seems to be..." He grimaced and waved a hand, as if searching for what to say. "Convenient. Oh, I don't know, Annie. He is not the young man I remember, though I cannot quite say what has changed."

"Well, of course he is not the same, Papa. How could he be? Given the time that has passed and the experiences he has endured, it's hardly surprising. He is no longer a youth, and working long hours for his uncle is what kept him away. He regrets his unbroken absence, but is proud the business has become so successful, which is why an expansion to London is now possible."

"Yes, he did explain all that," her father replied, looking anything but convinced. "Perhaps my concerns are unfounded, then."

"I'm sure they are! Leo and I have spent a good amount of time together over these past few weeks, and we get along well enough. I see no reason why our marriage will not be a loving one." Annie then voiced the question that had thrust its way to the front of her brain. "I confess to being puzzled, Papa. Why would you wish to discuss all this now, with the wedding but a fortnight away?"

"Because weddings can be cancelled, my dear. Marriages, not so easily." His taut expression softened as he collapsed back into his chair. "I simply need to be sure this union is what you want. I need to know you'll be cared for and protected. I need to be assured of your future happiness."

Before I die.

Those final three words were not spoken, yet Annie heard her father's silent declaration quite clearly. It was deafening, in fact, the intensity of it sending a chill into the depths of her bones.

And so, driven by little more than a heartfelt need to placate her ailing father, to eliminate any and all of his fears, Annie could supply but one response. "Please do not fret, Papa," she said. "I have no doubt Leo will take good care of me. I want this union, truly I do. He and I will be happy together, I'm sure of it."

CHAPTER FOUR

B Y THE TIME Julian arrived at his family's London home, he'd managed to smooth out the dent in his ego. Well, almost. He cringed as he replayed Miss Fairfax's gentle rejection for the umpteenth time. Not that she was to blame. He'd been guilty of assumption and acted impulsively, which was not usually his way. But no harm done. Nothing lost.

Still, he paused before the columned portico of the elegant townhouse and took a moment to shrug off a lingering remnant of despondency. Then he entered the house, only to be greeted by a crescendo of chatter and laughter coming from the front parlor, the door to which stood wide open.

"What have I missed, Hewitt?" he asked, handing his hat to the butler who had hurried across the foyer to greet him.

"Mr. and Mrs. Harlow have recently returned from the continent, sir," the man replied, gesturing to the parlor. "They arrived not a half-hour since."

"Max and Louisa are here?" Julian's subdued spirit lifted instantly. "Oh, now, that *is* welcome news!"

A smile appeared. "Indeed, sir."

Julian tugged down on his vest and approached the open door, where he paused for a moment on the threshold to absorb the scene before him. With the exception of Josiah, his entire family was present. Aldous and Grace, his parents, were seated on one of the settees. His twin sisters, Evie and Clara, were perched on the edge of another. Arthur, his youngest sibling, was seated in an armchair, his face bright with a smile as he regarded Louisa and Maxwell, who were standing by the hearth. Julian's gaze came to rest on them as well, and his subsequent smile surely matched Arthur's.

"My favorite was definitely Florence," Louisa was saying, her voice ringing with enthusiasm. "There is something about it that touches my soul. But the entire journey was wonderful, truly wonderful. We're glad to be home, though." She then cast a glance at Maxwell, her rapt expression one Julian recognized, for didn't his mother often wear the same expression when she looked at his father? It spoke plainly of a deep and profound love. And, judging by the reciprocal look Maxwell had given Louisa, it was totally mutual.

Julian was happy to have been proved wrong about his sister's somewhat scandalous marriage to her Anglo-Scottish industrialist the previous year. In the beginning, he'd harbored reservations about the union, serious reservations. But no longer. Louisa was obviously content, and Maxwell didn't look too miserable either. It gladdened Julian's heart to see it. He could only hope to be similarly blessed in marriage someday. So far, though, his bachelorhood was not at any risk of ending. This past London season had been enjoyable enough, but he'd yet to meet a woman who intrigued and captivated him to the point of proposal. Well, until today, of course, if his heart had not misled him. No, he was certain it hadn't. His attraction to Miss Fairfax had been genuine enough, but sadly misplaced.

"Julian, there you are." Louisa's cry pulled him from his musing. "We're back!"

"So I see." Smiling, he went to her and dropped a kiss on her cheek before shaking Maxwell's hand. "Welcome home, both. Have I missed some good stories?"

"One or two," Louisa replied, "but I have plenty more to tell."

Maxwell chuckled and gave her another fond glance. "We've

barely scratched the surface, Julian," he said. "In fact, by day's end, you might all wish we'd bypassed London and continued straight on to Yorkshire."

"Not I," Evie retorted. "I love hearing about foreign lands. I hope I have the good fortune to see some of the places you describe, Lou."

"Same," Clara piped up.

"I hope you do too, both of you," Louisa replied and wrinkled her nose at Maxwell.

"Did you manage to find Josiah?" Grace asked.

"I did, Mama," Julian replied, "and he promised he'll be here for dinner."

Grace placed a hand on her chest and heaved a sigh. "Oh, that pleases me very much, and it'll be all the more special now Max and Louisa are here. Truly a nice surprise for him."

Louisa's face lit up with another smile. "Our timing couldn't be more perfect, arriving here the day before you all leave for Highfield! I feared we might have missed you, but now we can all travel back together. We've had a wonderful trip, but I am so looking forward to going home."

Julian glanced at the window and the city beyond. "So am I," he said, all at once eager for time and distance to erase a persistent sense of disappointment.

So am I.

"And, um, well, I suppose we should *really* wait till tonight, when everyone will be present, but I fear I simply cannot," Louisa continued.

"Wait for what?" her father asked.

Louisa cast another loving glance at her husband, who chuckled softly and appeared to give her a nod of approval. She slid her hand into his and regarded everyone once more. "Maxwell and I have an announcement to make."

"UNCLE JOSIAH."

Julian, who had been deep in thought, lifted his head and regarded his brother. "Do you like the sound of it?"

"Yes, I believe I do." Josiah frowned into his glass of cognac. "I've never been an uncle before. Maybe 'Uncle Joe' would be more appropriate. Easier, at least."

Julian smiled. "I'm very happy for them. I confess I had some doubts about Harlow at first, but no longer."

"I liked him immediately." Josiah took a sip and licked his lips. "He's not a man to be messed with, but he's a decent fellow at heart and obviously besotted with Louisa."

"Louisa was besotted from the start," Julian replied, his gaze drawn to the mantel clock as it struck the midnight hour. With the long journey to Highfield looming a few hours hence, everyone else had retired for the night. Julian, however, wasn't quite ready to surrender his busy mind to the stillness of the bedchamber, where sleep would undoubtedly be elusive.

Nursing a near-empty glass of fine French cognac, he presently sat beside Josiah in the lantern-lit billiard room. Well-sated, perhaps not quite sober, he returned to his ruminations. He'd already revisited his afternoon interlude with Miss Fairfax umpteen times. Of course, nothing about it ever changed. Nothing ever could. Now, in an effort to ease a persistent sense of despondency, his focus shifted to the north, specifically to Highfield Hall and his on-going responsibilities as heir apparent. He sank deep into his thoughts again and drifted amongst them for a while, until Josiah's voice intruded once more. "Does she have a name?"

Julian blinked. "Who?"

"Whoever is responsible for the witless expression on your face." Josiah cradled his glass and swirled the contents as he spoke. "You've been staring at the hearthrug for the last five minutes."

"Have I?" Julian gave his head a slight shake. "No, she doesn't have a name. As a matter of fact, it's not a woman, but something far less baffling. Try barley, malt, and livestock yields, not to mention tenants and rents. In other words, the various complexities of estate management."

"Then may the Lord have mercy." Josiah crossed himself and took a generous swig of cognac before continuing. "At times like this, I'm reminded how blessed I am to be a lowly Northcott spare. Please take good care of yourself, Jules, because there's no way in hell I could ever step into your shoes and assume responsibility for Highfield. I'd sooner hang myself."

"We do have a very competent steward, Joe, so it's actually quite—wait." Julian frowned. "Did you just call me witless?"

Josiah tutted. "Not precisely. I said you had a witless expression, which you did. Totally gormless, in fact."

Julian failed to suppress a chuckle. "Bugger off. But if I *had* been thinking about a woman just now, her name would be Annabelle." A sigh escaped. "Annabelle Fairfax."

Josiah had just taken another sip of his drink and all but choked on it. "Bloody hell, you've kept that quiet." He frowned. "Fairfax, you say? Not a name I immediately recognize. Whose offspring is she?"

"No one we know. She is a physician's daughter, and I only met her this afternoon." A slight, bitter-sweet ache tightened his gut. "After I left you."

"Met her where? I thought you were going straight home."

"I was." Julian downed the remainder of his drink and stared at the hearthrug again. "But since I knocked the dear lady on her derriere, I felt obliged to see her safely to her front door, and on foot besides, because she refused the offer of a cab. We ended up spending a half-hour or so together. Not alone, I might add. The young lady was chaperoned by a disobliging dragon named…um," he frowned and searched his mind, "Hattie, I believe."

"After you knocked the dear lady on her derriere?" Josiah scratched his chin. "Er, a bit bloody drastic, don't you think? Couldn't you have just tipped your hat and introduced yourself?"

"I did, once I'd set her back on her feet. It was an accident, Joe. And, actually, she bumped into me."

"Did she indeed. Tell me more. What is she like?"

"She's rather lovely."

"Detail, Julian, I'd like detail. Paint me a picture."

Julian snorted. "That's your forte, not mine."

"Just try. It's really not too difficult." Josiah got to his feet and waved his glass as he headed toward the sideboard. "Want another?"

"Thank you, no," Julian replied. "And not too difficult for the artists among us, perhaps, but all right, I'll try. First, she had the most beautiful grayish-blue eyes, edged in black. Truly remarkable. Oh, and a sweet little freckle." He prodded a spot above his brow. "Right here. Her hair… her hair is the color of… oh, I don't know. It's darker than mine and has little hints of copper in it."

"Mahogany?" Josiah offered.

"Not a word I'd have thought to use, but yes." Julian nodded his approval. "And the most kissable lips. She's about the same height as Louisa, I think, and slender, though not without some rather lovely curves. Ah, but it was more than just her appearance, Joe. There was something about her. Can't properly explain it. It's just a feeling."

"A wonderful description, which leaves me wondering why you never mentioned the lady till now, given the effect she's apparently had on you."

"I didn't mention her because there's little point." Julian eyed his empty glass, wondering if he should, in fact, have another drink. "Since I won't be seeing her again."

"Uh-oh. I take it she didn't much appreciate being knocked on her arse, then."

Julian grimaced. "Actually, it's because she's promised to another. Getting married in a fortnight."

"Damn." Josiah sat down again. "That's too bad. I haven't seen you this taken with a woman in ages. If ever, actually."

Julian huffed. "I'm still trying to make sense of it. Like I said, we only spent a half-hour together."

"'The heart has its reasons which reason knows not,'" Josiah replied, and took a sip of his drink.

"Good lord," Julian muttered, "he's a bloody poet as well."

Josiah shook his head. "Cannot take the credit, brother. 'Twas a French fellow by the name of Pascal who wrote that particular line."

"Still, the fact you can quote the stuff with such ease is impressive."

"The ladies like it," he replied. "Truly, though, it's too bad your Miss Fairfax is spoken for."

Yes, life was unfair at times, Julian thought, and decided he would have another drink after all. He rose and wandered over to the sideboard. "Like I said, there was something about her, but it is not to be, so that's that. What about you, Joe? Other than the fine lady whose portrait I saw today, is there anyone significant in your life?"

"I will never be with a woman indefinitely and to the exclusion of all others, Jules. I much prefer…" Josiah glanced over at the door as if to reassure himself no one was listening, "mutually satisfying temporary associations, for want of a better description. No obligations or commitments for me, thank you very much."

"Fair enough." Julian poured himself a half-measure. "But you don't intend to maintain that lifestyle indefinitely, do you?"

"I do indeed. I have absolutely no intention of marrying. The mere thought of shackling myself to one woman for life has me reaching for the laudanum. I'm quite happy to leave the misery of domestic imprisonment to you. And I thought you didn't want another drink."

"Changed my mind." Julian returned to his seat. "What about children?"

Josiah gave him a sideways glance. "There are ways to avoid that particular consequence."

"No, I mean, don't you actually want any?"

He sucked air through his teeth. "Lord, no! This city already has a surplus. I see them wandering the streets every day, poor little devils."

"Hmm." Julian sat back. "Still, you never know. The day may come when *you'll* bump into someone and be knocked on *your* arse."

"I suppose there is a slight possibility of that," Josiah replied, waggling a brow, "but only by a jealous husband and not by accident. Which is why I'm so careful."

Julian laughed. "Again, that is not what I meant. And a jealous husband might do more than knock you on your arse."

Josiah huffed. "Stop carping. Like I said, I'm very selective about the company I keep, male or female. I have to be. You'd likely be surprised at who wanders in and out of my social circle."

"No doubt," Julian replied, tamping down a twinge of something that resembled guilt. Truth was, he and Aldous, their father, had long since made it their business to *know* who wandered in and out of Josiah's social circle. Their observance was not intended to be intrusive so much as protective, and its purpose actually extended beyond Josiah's personal well-being to that of the entire Northcott family. Aldous was prepared, with quiet reservations, to make allowances for his second son's free-spirited ways, but harbored a guarded fear that he might be lured into London's dark underbelly, where the foundations of law and common decency had extremely loose footings. Those who prowled its shadows came from all levels of society, from the highest to the lowest and everywhere in between. It was a dangerous and unpredictable realm.

Josiah appeared to have no idea his actions and interactions were, to some degree, being monitored. And so far, his ventures had given little cause for worry, including his secret and lucrative pastime of painting erotic scenes on the walls and ceilings of some of London's more illustrious homes. He worked incognito, his real identity unknown, at least for the most part. Both Aldous and Julian, however, had recently been made aware of it.

"You needn't worry about me, brother," Josiah said, as if

following the direction of Julian's thoughts. "I know I'm considered to be the black sheep in the Northcott fold, but I'm not a fool. I can hold my own."

Frowning, Julian lowered his gaze and swirled the cognac in his glass, feeling uneasy in the midst of his, albeit well-intended, deception. Then he leaned forward, looked his brother in the eye, and spoke with utter truthfulness. "You have a propensity to underestimate your value to us, Joe, and you are mistaken in doing so. I have never once thought you a fool. Far from it. I truly admire your talent and your certitude. We all do, unquestionably. Never doubt it. Not even for a moment."

Josiah, wide-eyed, regarded Julian for a moment, then blinked. "Thank you. That means a lot," he replied, shifting in his seat. "So, are you looking forward to going back to Highfield and all those complexities?"

"Yes." Julian nodded as if to reassure himself. "Yes, actually, I am. You should consider coming for a visit as well, and sooner rather than later. You've yet to meet your long-lost uncle. He's in fairly good health, all things considered, but he's not getting any younger. Would be a pity if you missed the opportunity to see him."

"Mama mentioned the same thing to me earlier this evening." Josiah gave a slight shrug. "And I do want to meet him, believe me. But, as I said earlier, I'm finishing up a special commission right now. I'll head north as soon as it's done, which will likely be in a month or so."

"Anyone I know?" Julian asked.

"The commission? Quite possibly, yes. In fact, I'm sure it is, but my lips are sealed."

"A portrait?"

"No. Yes." Josiah grimaced and tugged on his earlobe. "Sort of."

Julian laughed, got to his feet again, and downed the rest of his drink. "Well, I'm calling it a day. See you at breakfast."

"No, actually, you won't." Setting his empty glass aside, Josiah rose also. "I'm not staying. The night is yet young."

"Another carefully selected liaison?" Julian shook his head in feigned disapproval. "I thought you said you lived like a monk."

"I do. And monks have long upheld a reputation for keeping odd hours." Josiah winked and gave Julian's shoulder a squeeze. "Goodnight, brother. See you in a month or so."

CHAPTER FIVE

"Three more." Hattie fastened the final few buttons on the back of Annie's bodice and patted them lightly. "There, all done." She moved around to the front, eyes visibly brimming as she regarded Annie. "Oh, my pet," she said, her voice barely more than a whisper, "you quite steal my breath away."

Annie turned to the mirror, her own breath catching at the sight of her reflection. "Goodness," she said, with a slight shake of her head. "I do look rather…"

"Beautiful," Hattie finished. "You look absolutely beautiful."

Annie looked down at herself as if to verify the reality of her reflection. Made from fine Scottish muslin, embellished with cream lace and embroidered with tiny pink flowers, her gown was indeed exquisite. "It is splendid. Truly."

Hattie huffed as if in agreement. "Indeed. But then, Estelle Gilbert is a wonderful modiste. One of the best in the city, in my opinion, if not the entire country."

"She is certainly talented."

"And a good-hearted soul besides." Hattie heaved a sigh. "I swear I can hardly fathom it. My little Annabelle, a bride. It seems only yesterday you were in pinafores. Where have all the years gone?"

A lump came to Annie's throat. "No matter where, they've been good years for the most part," she said. "Please don't become maudlin, Hattie. You'll have me in tears, and I'm not sure Leo would appreciate his bride sporting red eyes and a nose to match."

"Appreciate his bride?" Hattie harumphed. "I hope the wretched man knows just how fortunate he actually is. I confess to having some doubts."

Annie gasped. "That is *quite* enough," she said, ignoring an odd little flutter in her belly. "You force me to remind you of your place."

Hattie huffed again. "Oh, I never forget my place, pet, but there are times when I must speak as I see it. The father was a good man, but something about the son bothers me. He's not the lad I remember, and I suspect your father feels the same way."

Another flutter arose in Annie's belly as she recalled her father's words from a fortnight ago, which seemed to support Hattie's opinion. A whisper of doubt brushed across her mind, but she sloughed it off. Yes, Leo was assertive by nature, but he was a good man and sure to be a good husband.

Hattie sniffed and glanced briefly over her shoulder as if to verify their privacy. "I'm curious. Do you ever think of the other one?"

The question took Annie momentarily aback. She knew exactly who Hattie meant, but feigned ignorance. "The 'other one'?"

The maid clucked her tongue. "Apparently you do. I can see it in your eyes."

Was it that obvious? In truth, Annie had thought about Julian Northcott many times since that day. Indeed, she remembered every detail of their short time together. But the memory of him walking away was the one most often occupying her mind. Without fail, the image would be accompanied by a feeling she'd been presented with an opportunity but had chosen to ignore it. And, in doing so, she had made an irrevocable mistake. None of which made any sense, for it had been such a brief encounter. In truth, she knew practically nothing at all about Julian Northcott.

Even now, the same twinge of regret arose beneath Annie's ribs, immediately followed by a spontaneous thrust of resentment. "There are times, Hattie Henshaw," she said, through gritted teeth, "when you truly overstep your bounds. This is one of those times. You do me a serious discourtesy to speak of such things on any day, but especially on this, my wedding day. It is one of the most important days of my life, yet you continue to voice your unwarranted opinions on my husband-to-be and actually have the *audacity*..." Annie drew a shaky breath, "the audacity to remind me of another, who never had, nor will ever have, a place in my life. I want you to be happy for me on this day and all the days to come. Is that asking too much?"

Hattie's face had fallen during Annie's rebuttal, and her hands now flew to her reddening cheeks. "Oh, my dear child, you are quite correct. What was I thinking? Please forgive me! I swear my mouth is an entity unto itself at times. You are right to be angry. I should never have mentioned the gentleman at all. I never will again, not ever, I swear it." Her voice wavered with obvious emotion. "Your happiness is the most important thing to me, my lovely. The most important thing. Always has been. I want you to be happy in this marriage, truly I do. Believe me, I want it more than anything."

Annie closed her eyes for a moment, reaching for a semblance of calm before giving Hattie the benefit of a forgiving smile. "I know you do," she replied, taking in another slightly shaky breath as she turned back to regard her reflection. "And I will be happy. *We* will be happy."

"Yes, yes, of course you will. Take no notice of me," Hattie replied, her voice now edged with remorse. "Now, let's get your veil sorted." She set about arranging the floral garland and lace veil onto Annie's head. "There," she announced, stepping back. "The finishing-touch. Perfect. Just perfect."

Annie straightened her spine, lifted her chin, and gave her reflection a final, critical inspection. Though she did not consider herself vain, she silently admitted to being more than pleased with what she saw. "Thank you, Hattie." She glanced at the clock on her mantelpiece and pulled in a deep breath. "It's almost time to leave."

"Yes, indeed." Hattie cleared her throat. "Um, do you have any more questions for this foolish old woman? About tonight, I mean?"

Annie shook her head as a faint blush warmed her cheeks. "No, thank you. I believe you've already explained things quite clearly."

A couple of days earlier, Hattie had taken it upon herself to assume a maternal role, and had described, in simple detail, what occurred in the marriage bed and how the act was required in order to conceive a child. Annie had feigned her ignorance and astonishment. Only her blush had been genuine, prompted by a sense of guilt.

Being a physician, Annie's father possessed an extensive scientific and medical library. As a child, Annie had little interest in it, but the approach to womanhood raised questions. In the absence of a mother, Annie had turned, covertly, to her father's bookshelves in search of answers.

She had found them and more besides, including answers to questions she had never thought to ask. The detailed anatomical drawings of men and women performing the sexual act had shocked her. So much so, she had shoved the book back onto its shelf and left the room, silently swearing never to return.

The resolution lasted barely a day. Curiosity drove Annie back to the library and the book was pulled from the shelf once more. Her initial shock rapidly evolved into a guilty fascination, which also left her with frustratingly unanswered questions. The drawings were merely clinical descriptions and diagrams, emotionless and unfeeling. Yet her own body's reaction to them was unsettling; the soft pulse between her legs, the enhanced sensitivity of her breasts, and an underlying yearning for something she could not quite identify. She also had a desire to touch herself intimately, but resisted the urge. To capitulate to such a thing had to be wrong, somehow. Unnatural. Harmful, even. Consequently, the book was once again returned to its place, where it had remained, undisturbed, for some time now.

"And you are not a foolish old woman, Hattie," Annie continued, and then grinned. "Well, not old at least. Seriously, though, you have been as a mother to me, and I shall be forever grateful."

Hattie sniffed, pulled a handkerchief from her sleeve, and scrubbed it over her nose. "Your dear mother is watching over you always," she said, "so I have no doubt she'll be watching over you today. Now, you'd best be off because I'm about to shed a bucketful of tears and would prefer to do so without an audience. I'll see you at the church."

ANNIE STOOD BEFORE the church of St. James and gazed up at the steeple, which pointed at gray skies. So far, though, London's rooftops had remained dry, and a pleasantly mild breeze wandered the city streets. Not that Annie cared too much about the weather. The day ahead surely promised a variety of other blessings. Besides, the one she'd hoped and prayed for had already been granted.

She turned to him. "Ready, Papa?"

"I am, my dear," he replied.

"And you're sure you're feeling quite well?"

"Well enough to walk my daughter down the aisle, I assure you." He offered his elbow and then patted her hand as it settled on his forearm. "It will be one of the proudest moments of my life. Let's go."

Annie heaved a happy sigh, leaned in, and kissed his pale cheek. Yes, her prayers had been answered. Due to her father's continued frailty, however, she had insisted on a quiet celebration. They had no immediate family to speak of anyway, only distant relations, rarely seen.

The creak of the vestry door echoed through the silent interior of the church. Annie stepped inside and inhaled the cool, stale air that somehow suggested the passing of many years. The opening of the door prompted the few guests to rise to their feet, and Annie's veiled gaze went straight to the altar where Leo stood waiting. He turned as they entered and inclined his head, as if acknowledging their presence. The Reverend Talbot, standing before the altar with a prayer book clasped in his hands, shifted on his feet as they approached. It suggested the man's impatience, perhaps prompted by the slow pace of her father. Not that they were late arriving, but there would undoubtedly be another marriage ceremony after this, and probably one or two more after that. Saturday mornings, at this time of year, were busy for the clergy.

Too bad, Annie thought. The vicar had long known of her father's illness and, as a godly man, should surely make allowances. Besides, it would be but a simple service, a quiet exchange of vows before God and the blessing of the church. In less than an hour from now, she would have set aside her Fairfax name, and become Mrs. De Witte. It was the most important day of Annie's life, thus far at least, and she was determined to enjoy it.

In her peripheral vision, she became aware of Hattie and Bridget standing quietly in their pew on the right side of the church. Then another figure came into view; a dark silhouette, that of a woman, standing in shadows on the other side of the nave. A stranger. Annie gave her but a brief glance. A church volunteer probably, or maybe an onlooker who'd wandered in from the street to watch the proceedings. Such a thing was not unknown.

Leo had not once taken his eyes off Annie as she approached. As she drew near, his shoulders straightened slightly and a faint smile appeared. He looked as immaculate as ever. The dark tailcoat accentuated the broad lines of his shoulders, his gray trousers complimented his long legs, the silk cravat at his throat matched the pale blue of his eyes, and not a single blond hair on his head was out of place. At that precise moment, the fear—the doubt—Annie had encountered mere minutes ago dissipated like smoke in the wind. Her future—*their* future—surely held much promise. As they arrived at the foot of the altar steps, Annie's father released her to her husband-to-be. "You look beautiful, Annie," Leo whispered. "I'm a very lucky fellow."

Annie opened her mouth to respond, but didn't get the chance.

"Let us begin." Reverend Talbot's voice filled the cavernous church and cut off Annie's reply. At that same moment, she heard the now familiar groan of the church door being opened and wondered who it was. Leo gave but a half-glance over his shoulder and shifted on his feet as if irritated by the interruption. The reverend lifted his gaze, his expression unchanging as he regarded whoever had entered. Then, as the door groaned shut, he turned his attention back to his prayer book.

"Dearly beloved," he began. "We are gathered here in the sight of God…"

Annie listened as the introductory part of the ceremony continued. Then came the preamble to a moment of meaningful silence.

"Therefore, if any man can show any just cause why they may not lawfully be joined together," the reverend said, "let him now speak, or else hereafter forever hold his peace."

The moment of silence came and went without interruption and the reverend continued. "I require and charge you both, as you will answer at the dreadful day of judgment when the secrets of all hearts shall be disclosed, that if either of you know any impediment why you may not be lawfully joined together in matrimony, you do now confess it. For be you well assured, that so many as are coupled together otherwise than God's Word doth allow are not joined together by God; neither is their matrimony lawful."

There followed a brief, calculated pause, then the reverend's gaze came to rest on Leo.

"Leopold Harvey," he said, "wilt thou have this woman to thy wedded wife, to live together after God's ordinance in the holy estate of matrimony? Wilt thou love her, comfort her, honor, and keep her, in sickness and in health; and, forsaking all others, keep thyself only unto her, so long as you both shall live?"

Leo gave Annie a fond glance. "I will," he replied, the resonance of his voice rivaling that of Reverend Talbot's, who nodded his approval and turned his attention to Annie. But before the man could speak, the sound of a slow but emphatic handclap came from somewhere behind them. Annie gasped at the intrusion and turned to see a man—a stranger—standing half-way down the aisle. With the exception of a stark, white collar, he was clad entirely in black, from his top-hat to his polished boots. Leo turned also, sucked in a breath, and muttered something Annie didn't quite catch. She glanced up to see an expression of fury on his face.

"Very convincing delivery, De Witte," the man said, moving closer. "Though I'm not too happy about the 'forsaking all others' part. Would you care to elaborate on that?" He spoke with a pronounced foreign accent. German, Annie thought, as she regarded Leo once more.

"Leo, who is thi—?"

"I'm waiting." The man halted, widened his stance and put his fisted hands on his hips. "Come on, you blackguard. Explain it to me. Where will this sham of a marriage leave my sister, eh? Or, more accurately, the innocent young woman you first ruined and then abandoned, along with her unborn child. *Your* bastard."

Annie gasped and pressed a hand to her chest, her mind stumbling over what the man had just said. *Sham? A child?* "Leo," she began again. "Who is this man, and what is he talking about?"

"That's what I should like to know." Pale-faced and frowning, Annie's father looked from one man to the other. "Well, Leopold? Are these accusations valid? Have you done what this fellow is accusing you of?"

"I have done *nothing*." Leo's mouth lifted in a sneer as he regarded his accuser. "This *dummkopf* is lying. The girl is no innocent, and the child is not mine."

The man gave a soft, bitter laugh. "You know damn well it is, you worthless piece of shit. It is fortunate for you I am not armed, for I would be tempted to shoot you where you stand."

"I must remind you that this is a house of God, sir!" The reverend's voice thundered over Annie's head. "What is your purpose here? Are you declaring a legal impediment to this marriage? If so, state it now that I might proceed accordingly. If, however, no such impediment exists, you will cease this blasphemous interruption and leave this house immediately."

"My sincere apologies, Reverend, to you and the Almighty." The man removed his hat and came closer still. Annie, her mind reeling with confusion, lifted her veil to better see him. Of similar height, he also looked to be of a similar age to Leo, clean-shaven with an unruly head of brown curls, his dark clothes elegant and finely tailored. "And my answer to your question must be no," he continued, eyes narrowing as he regarded Leo. "What this scoundrel has done is reprehensible, but not illegal, so there is no impediment in the eyes of the law. However, I find I cannot, in good heart, allow him to continue with this charade of a marriage without exposing him for the snake he is." He moved his gaze to Annie, clicked his heels together, and bowed. "My name is Karl Hoffman, *Fraulein*. Please forgive the intrusion, but I feel it is my duty to warn you that the charming boy you once knew no longer exists and it would be a mistake to continue with this..." He gestured with his hand. "This *farce*. I notice there is no one here from his side of the family. Have you not asked yourselves why?"

Leo hissed through his teeth. "Shut your mouth, Hoffman."

"I'll tell you why. It is because they want nothing more to do with him. De Witte is a charlatan and a liar. A man without honor who will undoubtedly take all he can from you and then cast you aside while he moves on to—"

Leo parted with a throaty roar and launched himself at his accuser. Annie barely stifled a cry, unable to do anything but watch as the two men grappled with each other in the aisle. Other cries of alarm from Hattie and Bridget echoed around the church.

"Stop," her father shouted and moved toward them. "Stop this *at once*. Good Lord."

"Papa, no, leave them!" Annie reached out to grab his coat, but he pulled away. "Please, you might be—"

Leo's elbow, crooked to throw a punch, struck her father hard in the face. He staggered back a step, then another, yet remained upright, body swaying slightly, arms hanging loose at his side. The fight stopped, the subsequent silence disturbed by Annie's hesitant voice. "Papa?"

He didn't reply. Like a man seeking mercy, he fell to his knees, his upper body remaining rigid for a moment before he toppled, face-down, onto the cold, stone floor. The silence endured a moment longer, and then someone screamed; a high-pitched, blood-chilling sound, like that of an animal snared in a trap. Only when Annie felt the harsh burn of it on her throat did she realize the sound had been of her own making.

Dropping her bouquet, she stumbled to where her father lay and fell to her knees beside him. His head was half-turned toward her, the left side of his face visible, the left eye wide open and staring. Blood trickled lazily from both nostrils, forming a dark, viscous pool on the floor. There was no other sign of injury that Annie could see, yet a shiver of apprehension set her teeth chattering. With trembling fingers, she brushed several strands of hair from his face. "Papa, please," she said, tears blurring her vision. "Can you hear me? Say something."

A shadow fell across her, accompanied by Leo's voice. "This is entirely your fault, Hoffman," he said, his tone as cold and hard as the church floor. "Not mine."

There followed a scoff as someone knelt at Annie's side. Karl Hoffman, she realized. "Christ have mercy, De Witte, you are beyond despicable," he said. "*Fraulein*, allow me to examine your father. I do have some medical knowledge."

Shivering, Annie nodded her permission and sat back slightly as the man turned her father gently onto his back. There was no resistance, no sign of movement. No sign of life at all. Clarence Fairfax simply lay there, staring up at the ceiling. The trickle of blood from his nose seemed to have slowed. Was that not a good sign? Annie prayed in silence and reached for a semblance of hope.

At that precise moment, shafts of sunlight tumbled through the stained-glass windows, glinting off a ringed finger as Karl Hoffman probed beneath her father's jaw. Annie held her breath when Hoffman winced briefly and gave his head a slight shake.

"Papa, please," she whispered, willing him not only to breathe but to blink, for his eyes remained wide open, yet somehow horribly bereft of life. "Please stay with me."

"Someone fetch a doctor," came the wail from Hattie. "Quickly."

"I fear it is too late for that." Heaving a sigh, Karl Hoffman sat back on his heels. Annie felt his gaze upon her and dared to meet it. "I am very sorry, *Fraulein*, but he is gone."

"No, that is…" Unable to grasp the truth of the man's words, Annie shook her head. "That is not possible, sir. You must be mistaken. Please, check again."

"There is no mistake, dear lady," he replied. "I only wish there was."

Teeth chattering, Annie regarded her father. "Are you sure?"

"I am certain."

"Then may God rest his soul," the reverend said. "This is outrageous. Outrageous, I say!"

Someone, either Hattie or Bridget, began to sob. Leo muttered something under his breath and his shadow, looming over Annie, drew back. There followed a fading echo of hurried footsteps on stone and the familiar creak of the church door opening and closing.

In Annie's bewildered mind, it seemed as though every detail was somehow enhanced, like a terrible nightmare from which she could not awaken. She took hold of her father's hand, the fragile flesh still warm, and pressed it to her cheek as grief swelled like a stone in her throat. "No, Papa, not today. Not like this. It should not be like this." She then turned to Karl Hoffman. "His eyes, sir. Please. Can they be closed? I cannot bear it."

He nodded and brushed his hand lightly over her father's eyes, closing them. *"Es ist geschafft, Fraulein,"* he said, a moment later. "It is done."

CHAPTER SIX

HATTIE THREW BACK the curtains in the parlor with a spirited *swish*. "We're going out this morning," she said. "A walk will do you good."

Seated in her father's chair, Annie flinched at the sudden onslaught of daylight and gripped the chair arms. "No, Hattie, I really don't feel like—"

"It rained earlier, but I stuck my nose out of the kitchen door just now and the skies have cleared. We're going for a stroll, and I'll hear no argument."

"It has been but a fortnight since Papa's passing." Annie rubbed her temple, trying to erase an ever-persistent throb. "It is not seemly to go for a stroll."

"It is not healthy to sit in darkness day after day, starving yourself, either. No wonder you suffer with these constant headaches."

"I am not starv—"

"Your papa would agree with me, pet, you know he would." Hattie came to stand before her. "Lord help us, just look at you! Pale as a ghost. Come now. On your feet. You need some fresh air."

Annie flinched inwardly at the mention of her father, mostly because she knew Hattie's comment had merit. To embrace any sense of normalcy, however, seemed inappropriate these days. Grief was a demon that clawed mercilessly at her soul while torturing her mind with visions of those final, horrifying moments in the church. The image of her father lying lifeless on the cold, stone floor remained disturbingly clear, as did the sound of Leo's fading footsteps and the church door opening and closing as he left.

She squinted up at her maid. "We live in London, Hattie. Fresh air is not generally in great supply."

"A change of air then," Hattie countered. "And as for living in London, that is something else we need to discuss."

"What do you mean?" Annie frowned. "Where else would I live? I am not even going to *consider* selling the house, if that's what you're suggesting."

Hattie shook her head. "I'm not suggesting any such thing, but a change might be good for you. An extended holiday, if you will. Somewhere quiet, where the air *is* fresh. You need to recuperate. It's been such a terrible time of late. The only saving grace is that your father no longer suffers. And he did suffer, Annie, for a good while. You know he did."

"Yes, that thought has occurred to me as well, but for his life to end the way it did…" Annie dropped her gaze to her lap as she struggled against the familiar threat of tears. "I can neither accept it in my mind nor reconcile it in my heart."

"Perhaps it was not the only saving grace, after all," Hattie muttered, seemingly to herself. "At least you didn't end up married to that scoundrel, wherever he might be."

Weary to the bone, Annie closed her eyes and pinched the bridge of her nose wondering, for the umpteenth time, how she could have been so easily misled, be so blind to Leo's charade. His whereabouts remained a mystery, with neither sight nor sound of him since that fateful day. Karl Hoffman had also disappeared, but not before he'd further speculated on the motivation for Leo's sudden return to England. Learning about Clarence Fairfax's illness and imminent demise had presented the man with an opportunity. Greed, Karl suggested, was what lured Leopold De Witte to Clarence Fairfax's front door.

Marriage to Annie, as far as Leo was concerned, meant the acquisition of a fine house in London and taking control of whatever else had been left to her after her father's death. As for his setting up a business office in London, Karl highly doubted the claim. Then, vowing to track Leo down, he'd taken his leave of her, though he was apparently acting alone in his resolve.

Given that Leo had shown no intent to harm Annie's father, the death had been ruled as accidental. Consequently, Leo was not being sought by the authorities for any kind of offense. Annie could not argue that her father had put himself in harm's way, but she still placed the blame entirely at Leo's feet, even though Karl Hoffman had incited the situation. True enough, his intervention had resulted in a tragic twist of fate. It had also, however, saved Annie from a potentially disastrous marriage. The difficulty came in trying to reconcile the consequences. A nearly impossible task.

Adding to the heartbreak, and to Annie's absolute dismay, the awful events of that day had merited a couple of paragraphs in *The Morning Herald*. As a result, her father's funeral had drawn a small crowd of curious onlookers, adding to the number of those who had actually known him and who genuinely wanted to offer their condolences. Till then, Annie would never have considered being veiled in black as a blessing. As it was, the folds of black tulle had allowed her a modicum of privacy as she'd moved through the crowd at the end of her father's funeral service. Never had she been so relieved to climb into a coach, to close the door against prying eyes. All she wanted to do was go home, where she could retreat from the world until she felt able to face it again. Thankfully, the newspaper report and the response to it had quickly lapsed into the past. Even so, the mere thought of venturing beyond her front door still made her cower inwardly.

"Just a short walk," Hattie said, in a tone that implied she was not about to take no for an answer.

Annie set her willfulness aside, heaved a sigh, and gazed up at her maid. "Very well. But under protest."

Hattie's expression brightened. "Thank heavens. Come on, then. Let's tidy you up a little bit."

A short while later, feeling definitely tidied, Annie stepped out into the June sunshine. Pausing on the step, she breathed in the prominent scents of wet earth and stale smoke. A soft breeze rippled the taffeta of her gown and toyed with the curls peeking out from beneath her matching bonnet. Fiddling with the vinaigrette at the throat, she glanced about, fearful of being seen as an object of curiosity.

"Here, pet." Hattie snapped open the black lace parasol she carried and handed it to Annie. "There's no one about, so don't fret."

At that precise moment, an elderly couple, walking arm-in-arm, passed by and nodded a silent greeting. Their expressions merely reflected sympathy, prompted, no doubt, by Annie's black mourning garb. Annie returned the nod and then gave Hattie a scathing look. "Is there something wrong with your eyes, Hattie?"

"What I meant was, there is no one of *note* about." She sniffed and stepped down onto the pavement. "Things have long since calmed down. Come on. Let's go."

Instead, struck by a sudden sense of nostalgia, Annie remained where she was and took another unhurried look up and down the street. This was, after all, the backdrop to her life. She had been raised here, had always been happy here.

Across the street, a small brown dog had its gaze fixed on the leafy branches of a nearby plane tree, barking at only he knew what, his little tail wagging furiously. The rhythmic clip-clop of a horse's hooves next drew her attention, and she watched as a hansom cab passed by, pulled by a fine-looking gray. The cab itself appeared to have but one passenger: a man, his features obscured. The horse's approach scattered several pigeons that had been strutting about in the middle of the road. With a flutter of wings, they rose into the air only to settle back onto the road once the cab had gone on its way. Meanwhile, beyond the sanctity of this pleasant, though unremarkable, street, the city bustled as it always had.

"Annie?"

She blinked and shifted her attention to Hattie. "Yes, I'm coming," she said, gathering her skirts as she stepped onto the pavement. "Where are we going? Do you have somewhere in mind?"

"Not particularly," Hattie replied. "I'm just content to be out and about. Is there anywhere you'd like to go?"

Annie first looked left and then right, her gaze lingering on the latter as the memory of a recent encounter with a handsome gentleman arose in her mind. "This way," she said, struck by an unbidden moment of fancy. "I'd like to go this way."

"HE WAS AT the door not even ten minutes after you left, Miss Annie." Teary-eyed, Bridget sniffed, pulled a crumpled handkerchief from her pinny pocket, and scrubbed it over her nose. "I told him you weren't home and to come back later, but he insisted he wait here. All but pushed his way in, so he did. Been waiting in the parlor ever since."

"The nerve of him," Hattie muttered. "Want me to send for a bobby?"

Frowning, Annie set her parasol in the hallstand, removed her bonnet, and looked toward the parlor door. "No." She drew a deep breath and placed a hand on her stomach, as if to quell its churning. "At least, not yet. I'll see what he wants."

"Nothing good, I'm sure," Hattie said, folding her arms. "You'll not be going in there on your own, either. I'll be right behind you."

"I'm sorry if I've done wrong, Miss Annie, but he scared me." Bridget sniffed again. "Shall I bring tea?"

A ripple of fury subdued the flutter of nerves in Annie's stomach. *How dare he come here unannounced and frighten her?* "No, Bridget, no tea," she replied. "And don't upset yourself. You've done nothing wrong."

With Hattie in her wake, Annie went to the parlor door, opened it with a determined flourish, and stepped inside. Her fury increased when she saw him seated in her father's chair.

"You were not expected, Leo," she said, clenching her fists as he rose to his feet. "And given the timing of this impromptu visit, I can only conclude that you have been spying on me."

A brief expression of surprise, or perhaps guilt, crossed Leo's face. "What an odd accusation, my dear. Spying? What on earth would compel me to do such a thing?"

"Because you feared I would refuse to see you," Annie replied, "which is why you waited till I was not at home and then bullied my maid into allowing you access."

His subsequent laugh was more derisive than humorous. "Utterly ridiculous. My visit is entirely coincidental to your absence. Yes, I insisted upon waiting, but the girl had no reason to fear me. She is obviously prone to fancy."

Annie heaved a sigh. "Why are you here? What do you want?"

"We have things to discuss." He gave Hattie a pointed look. "Alone."

Annie scoffed. "I am certain you and I have nothing to discuss at all, alone or otherwise."

Leo moved toward her. "I beg to differ, my love. We need to discuss the circumstances of your father's death, for one thing. I trust you do not apply any blame for his demise on me, for I was not the one responsible. That distinction belongs entirely to Karl Hoffman."

Struck silent by the sheer audacity of Leo's statement, Annie recoiled a step, though more from revulsion than fear. "First of all, I am *not* your love, nor I suspect, have I ever been. A fortnight has passed since my father's death, and over a week since his funeral, all without a single word from you. Not a single word!

Where have you been? As to laying blame, Papa's death inarguably came about due to your violent reaction to Mr. Hoffman's accusations. Did he find you? He swore he was going to track you down after you ran off."

"Hoffman?" Leo's lip furled. "No, fortunately for me and for him, I have not seen him."

"Well, if you're here looking for absolution, you'll be disappointed. This discussion is now concluded, sir, nor will there be any more between us in the future." Annie stepped to the side and gestured to the door. "Please leave. You are no longer welcome in this house."

Leo sucked in a hard breath and Annie barely suppressed a shiver of apprehension. Had she pushed him too far? But then his shoulders dropped, and his expression softened. "Annie, please, I beg of you, at least give me a chance to explain. I insisted on waiting this morning because I needed to speak to you. I need to bare my soul and yes, I am here to beg your forgiveness. That is *exactly* why I am here, in fact. I admit I lost my temper in the church, but it was purely in response to Hoffman's lies and filthy accusations. My uncle could not be present at the wedding because he is simply too busy to travel. I believe I explained that to you. I never intended to hurt your father, you must surely know that. I always had the greatest respect for him. His death was an accident, a terrible, terrible accident, and the law agrees with me on this. But seeing him lying there, realizing he was gone, and knowing I was the one who..." He winced as if in pain. "May God forgive me, Annie, I could not bear the shame of my actions. And, until I learned where I stood with the law, I also feared the consequences of them. Prison, perhaps, or transportation to the other side of the world. So, I panicked and fled, taking refuge in a miserable rented room this past while. It was wrong of me, of course. I see that now. I should never have left you alone. I should have stayed by your side and faced the consequences. The blame, after all, was never mine to bear. Karl Hoffman was entirely the one responsible. If not for him, I would now be married to the woman I love. And I do love you, Annie. I have loved you since childhood." Leo's jaw clenched momentarily. "But that… that bloody bastard ruined everything."

"Language," Hattie muttered.

"Yes, I beg your pardon." Leo inclined his head. "I am simply speaking from my heart."

Weighed down by grief and fatigue, Annie's resolve wavered. The explanation and apology had sounded sincere, as had the declaration of love. But, with Karl Hoffman's words playing in her mind, she studied Leo in continued silence, seeking any signs of pretense or deceit. He rewarded her with a smile, but one that held no warmth, no emotion. It appeared to be nothing more than a physical manipulation. A counterfeit response. Hattie appeared to agree, judging by the whispered word that brushed softly across Annie's left ear. "Snake."

Annie propped up her sagging determination, drew breath, and fired a question at him. "What of Karl Hoffman's sister?"

The smile vanished. "What of her? As I said, Hoffman's accusations were false."

Annie shrugged. "There is no smoke without fire, Leo. Upon consideration, I find it difficult to believe Mr. Hoffman would go to the trouble of traveling all the way to England to confront you unless there was some truth in those accusations."

Leo scoffed. "You do me an injustice, my dear. Hoffman's sister is notoriously free with her favors. The child could be anybody's."

Annie arched a brow. "Are you saying, then, that the child *might* be yours?"

He groaned. "No, that is not what I am saying at all. Think, Annie! We have known each other all of our lives. Our fathers, yours, and mine, wanted us to be together, and I see no reason why that still cannot be. This world, this city, is unsafe and, as a young woman alone, you are particularly vulnerable, at the mercy of those who might exploit you. You need a husband, a protector, someone to look after your interests. That someone has always been me, and you need me now more than ever. You must see that."

"And you must see how your assurances ring hollow," Annie cried, throwing her arms wide. "You abandoned me at one of the most frightening times in my life, a fact that makes a mockery of everything you have just declared."

He grimaced and inclined his head. "Yes, to my shame, I did. But I swear I shall spend the rest of my life making amends for it, if you'll let me. Please consider it."

Annie fell silent as she pondered. Facing the future alone was certainly daunting, but the idea of submitting to Leo's pleas, to resume any kind of relationship with him, stirred nothing within her. His declarations of regret and shame had not quite reached her heart, nor had his expression of love. As she hesitated over her response, Karl Hoffman's words once again drifted into her mind.

A man without honor who will undoubtedly take all he can from you and then cast you aside...

Annie then turned her thoughts to that morning and the stroll she'd taken, retracing the path of a man she would likely never see again. A man who, in a mere fragment of time, had made her feel something she'd never felt before. Not love, of course, but maybe an introduction to it.

During her walk with Hattie that morning, she'd given full rein to fancy and dared to imagine Julian Northcott to be at her side once more, sharing stories of family and life beyond the city. A foolish daydream, but she'd found comfort in it.

"We can start again, Annie." Leo's voice intruded into her reverie. "You will not regret it. You have my word."

Annie frowned. There was no way of knowing what life might yet bring, what challenges awaited. But, in that moment, she knew which direction to take.

Forward.

Not back.

"My answer is no, Leo." She went to the door and opened it

wider. "What we shared in the past is over. There really is nothing else to discuss. I would like you to leave now and never return. As I said earlier, you are no longer welcome in this house."

Leo's expression darkened visibly. "You are allowing your grief to guide you," he said, nostrils flaring. "You are not of sound mind."

"At least my grief is sincere." Annie gripped the door handle to stop her hand from shaking. "And my mind, sound or otherwise, is made up. Please leave."

Hattie moved to stand beside her. "You heard my lady," she said, glaring at Leo.

"Hush," Annie muttered.

Leo parted with another humorless laugh. "As you wish, then," he said, "but I fear you'll live to regret your decision. The day will come, and no doubt soon, when you'll seek me out to beg for my help and protection. You know nothing of the world, Annie. Nothing. You cannot possibly survive on your own." Lip furling, he gestured toward Hattie. "You cannot even control your staff."

Jaw set like steel, he went to move past them, but paused beside Annie and gazed down at her, his expression softening. For a moment, she thought she saw a flicker of remorse in his eyes. Then he raised his hand and touched his knuckles to her cheek. Hattie, standing beside her, sucked in a quick breath. Annie merely turned her cheek away and remained silent.

Leo's hand dropped and another soulless smile appeared. "Take heed, my little Annabelle," he murmured, his sour breath warm against her face. "You will live to regret this."

Moments later, the slamming of the front door rattled through the house.

Annie leaned against the wall, heaved a lungful of air, and pressed a hand to her stomach again. "Dear Lord," she said, exhaling. "Now, I definitely need some tea."

Hattie moved into the hallway and stared at the front door.

"You also need to make an appointment with Archibald Mason. And sooner rather than later."

"Papa's solicitor?" Annie straightened and followed Hattie's gaze. "Why?"

"Because we have not seen the last of Leopold De Witte. He'll be back, mark my words."

"That may be so, but I am not obliged to let him in." Annie shrugged. "I shall make sure Bridget understands she is not to answer the door if, and whenever, I am absent."

"I fear it won't be enough." Hattie regarded her. "The man is not used to taking 'no' for an answer."

"Well, since I'm not about to change my mind, he has no choice." Annie frowned. "And none of this explains why you think I need to make an appointment with Archibald Mason."

"Because you'll need him to take care of the legal requirements and whatever else has to be done when you put this house up for rent."

Annie widened her eyes. "What?"

Hattie tutted and folded her arms. "I believe you heard me. If not, the mannerly response would be 'pardon'."

"Yes, but I…" Bewildered, Annie stared at her maid, trying to make sense of what had been said. "Are you mad? I have no intention of putting the house up for rent. This is my home."

"Ah, my pet." Hattie released a sigh and tucked an errant curl behind Annie's ear. "How I wish I'd been mistaken about Leo. I truly hoped my suspicions about him had no real foundation, that my instincts were wrong." She grimaced. "It appears, sadly, that is not the case. As I said before, he is not the boy I remember. Mind you, even back then I thought him a tad arrogant if not a touch sly, but I put it down to the impudence of youth. Not my place to voice opinions back then, though, so I kept them to myself."

Leo's remark barged into Annie's thoughts. *You cannot even control your staff.* She bit down against a temptation to correct her maid.

"I know what you're thinking." Hattie gave her a wry smile.

"Not my place to voice my opinions these days either, right? But I'll not apologize for speaking my mind, Annie. Not when it comes to your well-being. I promised your mother I'd take care of you for as long as I was able, and that promise still stands. Things have changed and not for the better. Leopold De Witte is a dangerous man, and he is also correct; you are alone and vulnerable. Which is why I think we need to leave London."

"And I think you're overreacting," Annie replied, obstinately.

"He threatened you not five minutes ago."

"Threatened me with what, exactly?"

"Nothing specific, but I fear it remains to be seen."

"And I fear you are sorely mistaken," Annie replied, even as a prickle of apprehension crawled over her scalp. "I do not believe him capable of doing me actual harm."

"Then you force me to remind you what he *is* capable of." Hattie heaved another sigh, her voice soft. "Leo is an arrogant brute whose… whose *flagrant* proposal has just been rejected, and by a woman no less. He's not upset, Annie. He's bloody furious. Just like he was in the church when Karl Hoffman challenged him. Need I say more?"

Images, still cruelly fresh, arose in Annie's mind and pushed tears to her eyes. "But I cannot believe he would actually think of—"

"I am convinced of it." Hattie took Annie's hand. "Please believe me. It is not safe for you to remain here."

Something akin to fear edged Hattie's voice, weakening Annie's obstinance, yet still she resisted. "You're asking me to give up my *home*, Hattie."

"You are not giving up your home, pet. You are merely vacating it for a while, for your own safety."

"But for how long?" Annie pulled her hand free from Hattie's grasp and tugged her shawl tighter about her shoulders. "And where would we go?"

"How long is difficult to say right now," Hattie replied. "As for where, I know of a place. A place where I'm sure you'll be safe."

Annie blinked. "And just where is this place?"

Hattie shook her head. "First things first. You need to speak with Archibald Mason, and the sooner the better. Today, in fact. I'll go with you."

THE OFFICE OF Archibald Mason Esquire, Solicitor, exuded a blended essence of camphor, mint, and well-weathered books, the latter of which filled a large bookcase adjacent to a city-smudged window. The man himself, mousy-brown hair combed back and plastered to his skull by a pomade of some sort, sat in attentive silence behind his large, leather-topped desk.

His customary staid demeanor faltered a little as Annie proceeded to explain her reasons for being there. A bead of sweat left a glistening trail as it made its way down his temple. A slight frown appeared, and his hands, at first clasped quietly together on the blotter in front of him, now fidgeted, fingers locking and unlocking in a slow rhythm. Annie suspected the man was likely biting his tongue whilst forming an opinion similar to Leo's; that she was obviously of an unsound mind. Overwrought. Overreacting. Barely managing to keep the tears at bay, she relayed all that had happened, all that had been said, as well as the plans for leasing the house and leaving the city.

"And that about sums it up, Mr. Mason," she said, finally. "Leaving my home, I'm sure you understand, is not an easy decision to make. I am seeking your advice and opinion on this matter, both professional and personal. And please, sir, do not moderate your response with sympathy. It is raw honesty I seek. Not platitudes."

Still silent, Archibald Mason sat back, frown locked in place, eyes flicking from her face to Hattie's. Annie waited, half expecting him to ignore her request for honesty, and instead offer a gracious response intended to soothe her feminine angst, making light of the whole affair.

Then, as if arriving at his opinion, his frown cleared, and a grim smile appeared. "Given what I've heard today, Miss Fairfax, and taking into account the tragic events at St. James, I can but support your decision to leave London," he said. "In fact, I'm of the opinion the sooner you leave, the better."

Hattie huffed her apparent approval and squeezed Annie's hand. Annie raised her brows in surprise. "The sooner the better?"

He nodded. "I think so, yes. It may well be this fellow is all bluster, but, given his recent behavior, I'd rather not put it to the test. Better safe than sorry, as they say. I assume you have somewhere to go?"

Annie shook her head. "Er, no, actually. At least, not—"

"Yes!" Hattie's snappy interruption made Annie jump. "That is, yes, Mr. Mason, we *do* have somewhere to go. I have a distant cousin in Derbyshire who will be quite happy to provide us lodging for as long as needed."

"Very good," the man replied, with another nod. "Will you require assistance readying the house for leasing, Miss Fairfax? I assume it will be leased furnished, but the personal effects belonging to you and your father will need to be packed away."

Annie, who had been gaping speechlessly at Hattie, blinked and shifted her attention back to Archibald Mason. "Yes. Yes, of course," she replied, a sense of dread seizing her at the thought of sorting through her father's effects. "What isn't to be donated can be packed away in the attic, I suppose. Will that be acceptable?"

The man nodded. "Certainly. And if you need someone to help with that, let me know. I have people I can recommend. If there isn't one already, you'll also need to put a lock on the attic door. With your approval, I'll take care of the arrangements regarding the lease, including the interviewing of potential tenants, *etcetera*. I doubt you'll have any trouble leasing the place. I shall keep you fully advised, of course. We can keep the leases short term if you wish, so you can return when you deem it safe to do so without too much of a delay. With that in mind, I should also like to make a report to the police regarding Mr. De Witte. Specifically, to my brother-in-law, who is an inspector with Scotland Yard."

Annie's eyes widened. "Scotland Yard? Is that really necessary, sir?"

"As a precautionary measure, yes, I believe it is," he replied. "You've been threatened, after all. Do I have your permission?"

"I suppose... I mean, yes, of course, if you think it best." Annie drew in a breath and endeavored to sort through the chaos in her weary mind. Despite everything, she was still not convinced all these proceedings were necessary. Beneath the weight of doubt and grief, however, flickered a guilty little spark of excitement. Annie had been raised quietly. Sheltered, even, some might say. Other than a mostly forgotten visit to somewhere to the rural north, and summer trips to Eastbourne, she'd seen little of the world outside of London. The idea of traveling beyond her familiar boundaries was not, therefore, entirely unattractive. The guilt came from acknowledging these proceedings were due entirely to her father's sad demise and Leo's questionable behavior.

"Do you have any questions for me, Miss Fairfax?" Archibald Mason's voice roused Annie from her thoughts. "Is there anything needing further clarification, perhaps?"

Perhaps there was, but Annie was beyond thinking straight and responded accordingly. "Nothing I can think of, sir."

His expression softened. "I'm sure you have more than enough to consider at the moment, my dear. For the time being, I shall draw up a summary of today's discussion and send a copy to you. Go over it carefully, and if there is anything further you wish to discuss, or if you have any questions at all, please do not hesitate to contact me."

Annie smiled. "Thank you, Mr. Mason. I appreciate your help."

He returned the smile. "Your father was a good man, Miss

Fairfax, a man to be admired and respected. I considered him to be more than a client. Indeed, he was a friend and colleague. If there is anything else I can do for you, please do not hesitate to ask."

Minutes later, after brief goodbyes and a promise to check in with her prior to their departure, they made their way out of the solicitor's office. Hattie closed the front door behind them. "Well, it all seems fairly straightforward," she said. "Very reassuring, don't you think? I certainly feel less worried than I did an hour ago."

"Derbyshire." Annie paused on the doorstep, squinted up at the rainy skies, and snapped her umbrella open. "I know that's where you grew up, Hattie, but I didn't know you had a relative there. How come you've never mentioned her? Or is it a him?"

"Like I said, she's a distant cousin. Her name is Janet, and I'm sure I must have mentioned her at some point. We've kept in contact over the years. You know, an occasional letter here and there." Hattie moved to Annie's side and also regarded the sky. "Oops, I left my umbrella behind. I swear I'd forget my head if it were loose. Wait here, pet. I'll be back in a minute."

Annie threw her a sideways glance. "You're actually going to leave me out here all alone? Aren't you afraid I'll be snatched away by the wicked Leopold and held to ransom?"

"It's nothing to joke about, Annie." Frowning, Hattie glanced up and down the street as if to reassure herself no such danger existed. "Just wait here, please. I'll only be a minute."

As soon as Hattie went back into Archibald Mason's office, Annie lost the sardonic smile she'd been wearing. No, none of this ugly business was anything to joke about. Since her father's death, her days had been cloaked in shadow, her spirit burdened with grief and uncertainty. Of the two, uncertainty was the most difficult to manage. Grief was a vicious entity, one that would accompany her for a long time to come. She knew to expect it, knew she had no choice but to live with it. Uncertainty, meanwhile, was devious and erratic, akin to a persistent fog that obscured her way ahead, leaving her feeling lost and afraid.

Today, however, the fog seemed to have lifted somewhat. *Janet. Derbyshire.* Annie pondered, shaking her head. She couldn't recall Hattie ever mentioning either one. Then again, maybe she had, the words falling on the deaf ears of a girl whose mind was frequently occupied with daydreams.

Even now, the world around her faded away as thoughts danced in her head. Derbyshire. What did she know of it? *The home of Chatsworth House, seat of the Duke of Devonshire. And... pottery?* She frowned. Nothing else came to mind, though she envisaged a rural landscape. *Does Janet live in a town or in the country? In a house? A country cottage, perhaps?* Annie supposed it didn't really matter as long as the place was clean, though she doubted Hattie would have suggested it otherwise. She resolved to open her father's atlas that evening and study the county's location. Deep inside, a little spark of excitement flared anew, followed by the familiar twinge of guilt.

The whinny of a horse roused Annie from her musing, and she turned to look at the door, wondering what was taking Hattie so long. Even as the thought crossed her mind, the door opened and the woman exited, umbrella in hand.

"I was about to come looking for you," Annie said, eyeing her red-faced maid with a frown. "Goodness. Is everything all right? You look a little flustered."

Hattie appeared to assert herself and conjured up a smile. "Everything is fine," she replied. "I suppose I'll not be settled till we're on our way out of the city, and we have much to do before then."

"I think we'll manage," Annie said, stepping onto the pavement. "I must say, I feel better after speaking with Mr. Mason. He'll steer us through it all."

"Yes, I'm sure he will." Hattie opened her umbrella. "Looks like this weather has set in for the day."

"What is her last name?" Annie asked.

"Who?"

"Your distant cousin."

There followed a moment of hesitation, then, "Caldridge."

"Is she married?"

Hattie shook her head. "A spinster."

"How old?"

"Does it matter?"

"No, not really. Just curious."

Hattie tutted. "Um, let's see. Janet will now be, I believe, in her thirty-eighth year. Two years younger than me."

Frowning, Annie chewed on her lip. "So, not terribly old then. How come she's never married?"

Hattie gave her a sardonic look. "No, not terribly old. And she almost married, but the poor fellow passed away. Don't think she's ever got over it."

"How sad." Annie tutted and shook her head. "Janet Caldridge. No, I'm sure you've never mentioned her before. I've always believed you had no family."

"Well, like I said, she's a *distant* cousin," Hattie replied. "And maybe you weren't paying attention when I mentioned her previously. You've always been a bit of a woolgatherer."

"I suppose," Annie replied, choosing capitulation over an argument. "Where does she live? In a town, or in the country?"

"In the country."

Annie absorbed the response. "In a house?"

"Yes. It's a nice area. Very quiet."

"Are you sure she has room for us?"

"Yes, don't worry about that. Her house is not grandiose, but it's very comfortable."

"And you're sure she'll be willing to accommodate us at such short notice?"

"I'm certain of it. I'll get a letter sent off today."

"But how can you be certain? When did you last see her?"

Hattie heaved a sigh. "So many questions, child."

Annie frowned. "Which are justified, are they not? It appears I know nothing of this woman, yet I'm soon to be moving into her home, apparently."

"Yes, of course. Forgive me." Hattie cleared her throat. "Well, let me see. The last time I met Janet was actually here in London, when she came to see a sick friend. Some time ago, now. I haven't been to Little Langby in many years, though. Since before you were born, in fact."

"Little Langby," Annie repeated. "It's a village?"

Hattie smiled. "Barely even that, though it does have a lovely old church. Janet does the flower arrangements for it. As I said, we've kept in touch through letters, and she's always made it quite clear I'd be welcome to stay with her if I ever had the need. And that need, though unfortunate, has now presented itself."

"Unfortunate, yes." Annie heaved a sigh of her own and then gasped as a sudden realization entered her mind. "Oh, gracious! What about Bridget? I hadn't thought about her till now. How shameful of me. I'm not sure she'll want to come with us, though. Her entire family lives in London."

"Better if she stays behind, I think." Hattie shrugged. "You can give her a good reference. I'm sure she'll have no trouble securing a new position. Besides, who knows? She might be kept on by the new tenant."

"Whoever that might be."

"Mr. Mason will ensure it's someone suitable, I have no doubt."

"Yes, but still, it seems so unfair. She's been with us forever." Fatigue, sudden and unexpected, washed over Annie like an invisible wave. "I'm so very tired, Hattie. It's all such a mess. Overwhelming, in fact. I cannot quite grasp everything that has happened. Everything that *is* happening."

Hattie slid her arm through Annie's and drew her close. "I know, pet, I know. Hush, now. Don't upset yourself. We've done enough for today. Come on, let's get you home."

CHAPTER SEVEN

Two weeks later
Ferndale Grange
Derbyshire

A NOISE UNLIKE any she had ever heard roused Annie from sleep. She opened her eyes, blinking as they adjusted to the room's dusky light. A brief frisson of panic followed, for nothing about the room was familiar. The panic subsided a moment later, when her foggy brain made sense of it all. Well, all except for the strange noise she'd *thought* she'd heard. It had sounded like a nasty coughing attack, or someone choking. Maybe she'd imagined it. Or maybe it had been part of a dream, the other details forgotten the moment she'd opened her eyes. Stifling a yawn, Annie rolled onto her back, wondering at the hour. Early morning, judging by the low light seeping through the faded yellow curtains and the muffled sound of birdsong beyond her window. The feathered chorus was richer than the dawn clatter of London's streets, and heralded her first full day in her new home.

Annie closed her eyes briefly and pinched the bridge of her nose. No, *this* wasn't her home. She'd left that behind two days before, her burden of contrasting emotions weighing more than her travelling-trunk. There had been no further contact with Leo, no sign of him at all, in fact, but Hattie refused to believe he was no longer a threat. Annie's renewed resistance to leaving London quickly faltered. She simply did not have the energy to argue any further. Still grieving, and uncertain of what the future held, she dared to hope this change, this *escape*, might lead to something worthy. Much of her train ride north had been spent with her nose pressed to the window, watching as the world beyond the city slid by, a world of which she knew so little. The journey, by train and horse-drawn carriage, had been uneventful, and they'd arrived at Ferndale the previous night.

Janet Caldridge had given them a warm welcome, with declarations of delight at their arrival and gentle hugs all round. An equally warm welcome had come from Janet's little terrier, who, given his wiry coat, was appropriately named Ruffy.

A petite, handsome woman, Janet matched Annie's height, and appeared older than her purported thirty-seven years. Faint frown lines were already etched permanently onto her brow, while others fanned out at the corners of her eyes. Her dark hair already played host to a few silver threads, which glinted at her temples. Annie had the impression the woman's life had not been without challenges. And perhaps she'd just been presented with two more, since her guests would be staying for an indefinite amount of time.

As for Ferndale Grange, it was, in a word, charming and a fine stone house of considerable age, judging by the low, beamed ceilings, mullioned windows, and lead-paned glass. Annie had yet to explore it fully, since their late arrival the previous night had not leant itself to such an endeavor. Weary from the journey, she'd picked at a light supper and then retired to bed. Despite her fatigue, however, or perhaps because of it, sleep had been elusive.

Lost in her reflections, Annie jumped as the same strange noise sounded again. Not part of a dream, then, but definitely someone—or something—outside. Intent on solving the mystery, she threw the bedcovers aside and went to the window, bare boards creaking beneath her feet. Rubbing the sleep from her eyes, she pulled back one of the faded yellow curtains and squinted through the thick, leaded panes of glass. The world beyond appeared blurred and disjointed, the details indistinct, yet enticing. Eager to see the view clearly, Annie lifted the latch, pushed the window open, and gasped.

Softened by the pale light of dawn, the patchwork of mead-ows and hills stretched off into the distance, all stitched together by rugged stone walls and checkered with dark swathes of woodland. Annie breathed in a lungful of fresh morning air, an invigorating blend of damp earth and floral sweetness. To add to her delight, opening the window had given her a front-row seat to the full glory of the dawn chorus. But then the strange choking sound came again. Frowning, Annie peered down into a small, walled courtyard. Surrounded by a variety of outbuildings, the area appeared to be empty, providing no clue as to the source of the noise. "What *is* that?" she muttered, and then turned as a soft tap came to her door. Grabbing her shawl from the bedroom chair, she went to the door and opened it. "Good morning, Hattie, I think someone might be—oh, Janet, forgive me!" Annie wrapped her shawl around her shoulders and gave the woman a sheepish smile. "I expected to see Hattie."

Janet, clad in a loose cotton dressing gown, with a lace night-cap atop her head, returned the smile. "Good morning, Annie. Hattie's downstairs nursing her second cup of tea. We heard the floorboards creak, so knew you were awake. Did you sleep well, dear?"

"Yes, I did, thank you." The lie came easily enough. Annie regarded the woman for a moment, noting the dark shadows beneath her eyes. "Did you? I mean, I hope our being here isn't too much of an inconvenience."

"Not an inconvenience at all," Janet replied, with a shake of her head. "I hope I made that clear last night. To the contrary. It's truly a pleasure having you here, and you're both welcome to stay as long as you need to, or even as long as you wish."

"You're very kind. Thank you. Oh, and…" Annie threw a quick glance over her shoulder, "I keep hearing the strangest noise from outside. It sounds like someone coughing or choking."

Janet frowned and peered past her. "That's odd. None of the staff are here yet, and the door to the courtyard is always locked at ni—"

"There it is again!" Eyes widening, Annie looked toward the window. "Can you hear it?"

Janet laughed. "Oh, gracious, yes. I probably should have warned you about that. It's only Lancelot. Nothing to worry about."

Annie raised her brows. "Lancelot?"

"The cockerel." Janet looked decidedly amused. "I agree, he sounds as though he's being strangled, but he's old, so I make allowances. I'm afraid you'll have to put up with his morning serenade. Now, seeing you're up and about, put your slippers on and come downstairs."

Annie looked down at herself. "But I am not yet dressed."

Janet shrugged. "Neither am I and neither is Hattie. It'll only be the three of us for breakfast. Unless, of course, you'd prefer to dress now?"

Annie shook her head. "No, not especially. I usually… um, well, I suppose things are a little less regimented in the country."

"Generally, yes," Janet replied, with a smile. "We do have our ways, though, but you'll get used to them soon enough. Come on then, get your slippers on, and we'll start your first day here with a good Derbyshire breakfast."

A WEEK LATER, Annie had learned much about the way of things at Ferndale Grange. It was, in fact, a working farm, though most of the land was rented out to other local farmers. The house had retained most of its original features, including outer walls two feet thick, a wooden staircase whose treads were blackened by countless footfalls, and the ancient oak beams in the ceilings. It also had a well-stocked vegetable patch, as well as an exquisite, walled flower garden. The latter occasionally provided flowers for the village church, and as Hattie had said Janet would do the arrangements as required.

The stable was home to Albert the carthorse, Tulip, the pony responsible for pulling the trap, and Melody, the Guernsey cow, who provided the creamiest milk Annie had ever tasted. Lancelot, meanwhile, continued with his questionable morning rhapsody and lorded over his hens and the grounds in general. Even the barn cats avoided the cantankerous cockerel. Ruffy tended to disappear most days, but always returned before dark. "Hunting rabbits, most likely," Janet said, when Annie asked about it. "It's in his nature. Though I believe he might also have a lady friend in the village."

Janet had two people in her immediate employ. Gwen, a shy, mousy-haired woman from the nearby village, worked as a domestic, helping out around the house three days a week. Like Hattie, she was an older woman, but unlike Hattie, Gwen spoke only when spoken to, answering quietly, and lowering her gaze each time. Amos, meanwhile, was a true jack-of-all-trades, handling everything from repairs to taking care of the gardens and livestock. Ever cheerful and good-natured, he was a man on the younger side of middle-age, never without a twill flat-cap on his head or a clay pipe in his mouth, the latter sometimes lit, sometimes not. He addressed her as "Miss Annie" and always greeted her with a touch to his cap and a friendly wink.

Hattie appeared to be quite at home. More than once, she'd announced her relief to be away from the city, or more specifically, the danger she applied to it. Though grateful for Janet's hospitality, Annie could not, as yet, bring herself to echo Hattie's sentiments.

Janet and Hattie were obviously close. Indeed, there was something of a conspiratorial air about them. Thick as thieves, as the saying went, or so it seemed to Annie. Earlier in the week, in the middle of the night, she'd been awakened by their voices coming from, she surmised, the kitchen. She couldn't make out what was being said, but the resonance had a solemnity about it, implying a serious discussion rather than a friendly chit-chat. There was no sharing of laughter either, only occasional moments of silence, as if discourse had given way to thought. Driven by curiosity, Annie had left her bed and tiptoed to her door to see if she might be able to make sense of what was being discussed. But the instant she'd stepped on a creaky floorboard, the conversation had ceased. They'd been talking about her, of that Annie felt certain. Not that it worried her too much. Hattie had likely been sharing details of the past few horrible weeks.

So far, the nights at Ferndale were no more restful for Annie than her nights in London had been. The unaccustomed silence only served to accentuate her anguish. Alone in the darkness, she found it impossible to manage her thoughts, which invariably dragged her down roads paved with sadness and edged with fear. Even the wind, whenever it brushed past her window at night, had a mournful sound. Grief and guilt unfailingly cast shadows over the joys of her day. As to her future, it remained uncertain. How long might they be there? Weeks? Months? Was Leo truly a threat? Was he even still looking for her? Annie doubted it, but knew better than to try and convince Hattie. At least for now.

Sleep, when it did come, was restless and plagued with strange dreams. Oddly, Lancelot's questionable dawn greeting had become something Annie welcomed, for it signaled the end of another night. Or, rather, the start of another day.

And, so far, Annie had quite enjoyed her days at Ferndale, since they offered many welcome distractions. A vague but pleasurable sense of familiarity would emerge now and then, as if her childhood impressions of pastoral life had been awakened. And, of course, there were no crowds.

Mornings were her favorite, when the house smelled of freshly baked bread and sizzling bacon or sausages. On rainy days there were books to read, needlework to do, or tunes to be badly played on the cottage piano in the parlor. On Saturday, she had accompanied Janet to the small village church and watched as she had placed fresh flowers at the foot of the altar. And yesterday, the Sabbath, she had attended the morning service with Janet and Hattie, their presence drawing unabashedly curious glances from those in the congregation. After the service, there had been a few quick, basic introductions before Janet whisked them back to Ferndale in the pony and trap. Annie was grateful for the abrupt departure, for she had no desire to answer or deflect questions about the reason for her presence there. Indeed, she quietly decided there would be no more visits to the church. At least, for a while.

For now, weather permitting, she would continue to explore the surrounding countryside at her leisure. No chaperone required, just a warning not to wander too far. Feeling like some intrepid explorer, she'd already taken herself off on three relatively short adventures, content to lose herself only in the beauty and fascination of the countryside.

London, at such times, felt as distant as the moon.

CHAPTER EIGHT

July 1846
Highfield Hall
Yorkshire

AFTERNOON SUN SPARKLED off the crystal chandeliers, throwing tiny rainbows across the walls of the music room at Highfield Hall. Most of the chairs in the music room were occupied, and a pleasant hum of chit-chat filled the air.

"Viola?" Lady Whickham addressed her daughter and then glanced at the piano.

Miss Viola Aitken, youngest daughter of Viscount Whickham, nodded her understanding and rose to her feet, prompting Julian, who had been seated beside her, to do the same. She gave him a smile, and then wandered over to the pianoforte, where she settled onto the piano bench, arranged her skirts, and straightened the music sheets on the rack. Julian took his seat again.

The audience, such as it was, fell into a respectful silence in anticipation of what was to follow. Something special, according to Julian's mother, who herself was accomplished at the keys. Julian shared in the anticipation, though in his case it encompassed a little more than the young lady's renowned musical proficiency. Having spent much of the afternoon in Miss Aitken's company, he dared to consider he might, at last, have found someone suitable.

Suitable.

The impassivity of the word gave him pause, for it simply indicated a measure of approval, as might be applied to a new item of clothing or a room at a roadside inn. It was a start, however. Suitability, at least in Julian's world, was generally gauged by the practicalities of wealth and social standing. Such things had their place, of course, but for Julian they were merely a precursor to what came next. What came next would be the rest of his life and possibly, in this case, the rest of Miss Aitken's. With that in mind, he did not think it unreasonable to strive for other things in a relationship. Mostly frivolous, impractical things, such as affection, contentment, passion.

And love.

Highfield Hall was currently playing host to Lord and Lady Whickham, their younger son, Mr. Frederick Aitken, and, of course, Miss Viola Aitken. Lord Whickham, recently returned from India, was a lifelong friend of Julian's father, and Julian was under no illusion his introduction to Miss Aitken had been a chance encounter. Without a doubt, it had been pre-arranged, and the one responsible was unquestionably his mother, Grace.

Even now, Julian felt his mother's eyes on him, though he steadfastly refused to meet her gaze, knowing she would raise a triumphant brow as one might raise a victory banner. Too soon for that, as far as Julian was concerned. He understood why she wanted to see him married and settled, but the tangible thought of a life-long commitment to Miss Aitken had not even begun to materialize in Julian's brain.

For now, such possibilities were mere suggestions. He and Miss Aitken had only got as far as sharing pleasantries. Certainly, Julian wanted to spend more time with the girl, to get to know her a little better. Instinct told him she felt the same. As if to bear that out, she regarded him and spoke. "I wonder, Mr. Northcott, if you would be kind enough to turn the pages for me?"

"With pleasure," he replied, rising and going over to the piano, where he stood at her side and regarded the piece of music she would be playing.

"*Für Elise*," he murmured. "A favorite of mine."

Miss Aitken answered him with a smile, one that caused

Julian to regard his mother at last. Grace smiled at him in a similar fashion… and arched a brow.

THE KNOCK—A SINGLE but confident rap—came to Julian's bedroom door later that night. Julian, who was already abed and about to lower the wick on his lantern, frowned at the interruption. After a day of continuous socializing, he'd been looking forward to his bed and the solitude that came with it. For a moment, he toyed with the idea of pretending to be asleep, but then the door creaked open, and Josiah stuck his head around it.

"Good, you're still awake," he said. "Hoped you would be."

Julian bit back a sigh and sat up. "And if I hadn't been? Oh, and yes, come in, by all means."

"Thanks. And I'd have woken you if you'd been asleep." Josiah bounced onto the bed and sat cross-legged, much as he might have done as a child. "Because we need to talk, brother."

"About what?" Julian stifled a yawn. "I'm tired, Joe, and possibly not quite sober. Can whatever this is not wait till morning?"

"No, it cannot. I haven't had a proper chance to talk to you all bloody day, in case you hadn't noticed. Since the moment I arrived here today, I've been appropriated by parents, offspring, and a couple of our illustrious guests, not to mention the couple of hours I spent playing dominoes with our uncle. I'm not complaining about that part, however."

Julian smiled. "I'm glad you've had the chance to meet him. He's remarkable, isn't he?"

"He's magnificently tragic," Josiah replied, glancing away for a moment. "A part of his shattered mind remains wholly intact and shines through that one blue eye as brightly as the sun. It was humbling being in his company. And yes, I'm also glad, *very* glad, I've had the chance to meet him. The journey here was worth it for that opportunity alone."

"Nicely put." Julian cocked his head, already toying with an inkling of what had brought his brother to his door. "All right, come on. Out with it. What cannot wait till morning?"

Josiah glanced about the room. "Is this new wallpaper? Looks good."

"No, it isn't." Julian sighed. "Get to the point."

"Right-oh." He waggled a brow. "Miss Viola Aitken."

Julian groaned and flopped back on his pillow. "God, I knew it. What about her?"

Josiah shrugged. "I'm just curious, that's all."

"I'm sure you are. Go on, then. Let's have it."

"Is she 'the one'?"

Julian hesitated. "She might be."

Josiah wagged a finger at him. "Ah! See, that 'might' bit bothers me."

Julian grimaced and rubbed his forehead. "I only met her yesterday, Joe. In fact, the girl has not even been officially debuted because Whickham has been in India for the past eighteen months. They've only been back in England for three weeks."

Josiah waved a nonchalant hand. "Yes, I'm fully aware of that. So, you're currently first in the marriage queue."

Julian chuckled. "I think that's the idea."

"She is quite the prize, I must admit."

"Yes, she is. Jealous?"

"You know I'm not." Josiah tipped his chin up. "Describe her to me."

Julian huffed. "What for? You already know what she looks like."

"Yes, but pretend I don't. Humor me. Describe her."

"Do you actually have a point to make?"

"I do," he replied, with a nod. "A very important point, I promise."

"Very well, let's get this foolishness over with." Scratching his jaw, Julian gazed up at the bed canopy. "Viola is pretty. No, she's *lovely*. Charming and intelligent. Well-mannered. Quite tall, I suppose. Fair hair. A nice body. A *very* nice body, actually. And she has a delightful smile."

Several moments of silence followed, interrupted by a snort from Josiah. "Is that it? You're all done?"

Julian linked his hands behind his head. "What more do you want?"

"Lord, help us," Josiah muttered, "Detail, Julian, I want detail. We did this once before, remember? Paint me a picture."

A memory stirred to life, as did the tightness in Julian's throat that always came with it. "What is this about, Joe? What's going on?"

"I'm waiting for you to describe Miss Aitken."

"Which I believe I have already done."

"In an inanimate fashion, I suppose. Is that the best you can do?"

"Yes, it bloody well is. You said there was a point, so get to it, will you?

"I'm about to, once you've told me the color of the lovely Miss Viola's eyes."

Julian groaned again. "I'm not sure what color they are, exactly. Brown, I think. Or maybe green. I don't know, to be honest. That's it, Joe. No more games."

"Well, then, it appears I was right." Josiah shrugged. "Usually am, of course."

"Right about what?"

"You, failing the test."

"What bloody test?"

"The one that *might* have proved your undying attraction to this girl."

Julian scoffed. "Like I said, I hardly know her, but so far, no complaints. I like what I see. Either make your point, if you actually have one, or leave and let me get some sleep."

"All right, all right, keep your voice down." Josiah cleared his throat. "Thing is, I have some interesting news. Wanted to share it with you as soon as I arrived, but never had the chance, and then I found out you were pursuing the lovely Viola, and I wondered if sharing this news was even…" He tapped a finger on his bottom lip and appeared to ponder. "Um, did Mama arrange it, by the way? You and Viola? I have a suspicion she might have."

Julian sighed. "The point, Josiah."

"Right. So, then I wondered if sharing this news with you was even necessary. I am now of the opinion it most certainly is, since we have just ascertained Miss Viola Aitken is not for you."

Julian sat up again, leaned forward, and touched the back of his hand to Josiah's forehead. "It's rather odd," he said, frowning. "No fever, and you don't appear to be drunk, yet something is clearly wrong with you."

Josiah clucked his tongue. "Maybe it has something to do with this." He pulled a slip of paper from his vest pocket and handed it to Julian. "Here. Read it."

Julian took the small piece of newsprint and squinted at it in the low light. "What's it about?"

"Just read it," Josiah replied. "I wondered, at first, if it was all just an incredible coincidence, but the dates and the names match, as does the poor fellow's profession. It has to be her, brother. Has to be."

"Her?" A tingle ran across Julian's scalp. He leaned into the lantern's halo of light and read the brief report about a wedding at St James' Church, Piccadilly. It told of a young bride whose father had died in the church following a violent altercation between the groom and another man who had challenged the union. The groom, a Leopold Harvey De Witte, had then fled the scene, leaving his bride, Annabelle Edwina Fairfax, alone, unwed, and weeping beside the body of her father, Dr. Clarence Geoffrey Fairfax, a retired physician.

"Good God," Julian muttered, and read the report a second time, his hand shaking so much he could barely make out the words. He lifted his gaze. "Is it her, do you think? Is it Annabelle?"

Josiah huffed. "How many Annabelle Fairfax's do you know?

Let's take that further. How many Annabelle Fairfax's do you know who was, if I recall correctly, due to be married around the same time, and whose father is also a physician? Of course, it's her."

"I suppose it must be." Julian, his mind reeling, read the article yet again. "What a bloody mess. I cannot begin to imagine the anguish she must have felt. Must *still* be feeling. The poor girl!"

"I agree," Josiah replied. "And you should know it was by pure chance that I happened upon the article. I never read the *Herald* as a rule, but it was sitting on a table in Lord Bethany's Mayfair foyer, so I picked it up and read it while I was waiting to see him. There are no such things as coincidences, Jules. Things like this happen for a reason." He jabbed a finger at the cutting. "I was *meant* to read that because you were *meant* to know about it."

Julian raised a brow. "Do you really believe that?"

"No, of course not, don't be daft." Josiah grinned. "But now you *do* know, so you can do something about it."

Julian blinked. "Like what?"

"Like getting your arse back to London and calling on the lady."

That utterly absurd notion had already barged its way into Julian's brain, but he'd hesitated to embrace it. "No, I cannot possibly do that."

"Why ever not?"

"Well, because…" Frowning, he ran his fingers through his hair. "Because it's irrational, Joe. It's folly. It's *madness*."

Josiah heaved a sigh. "What color are Annabelle's eyes, Julian?"

Julian turned his sight inward and looked upon the face he'd committed to memory several weeks earlier, every detail still intact. "Blue," he murmured, unable to prevent a smile from appearing. "An exquisite grayish-blue. Edged in black."

"Point made." Josiah clicked his tongue. "If I were you, I'd start packing right away."

"But you're not me, Joe." Julian regarded the scrap of paper in his hand. "This doesn't give me permission to go gallivanting off to London with no explanation. We have guests, in case you hadn't noticed. I have obligations to them and to Mama and Papa."

"Yes, of course. My apologies." Josiah gave him a contrite smile. "Perhaps I shouldn't have shown it to you—"

"No, it's all right. I'm glad you did, believe me."

Josiah tutted. "I was *going* to say, perhaps I shouldn't have shown it to you till the end of the week."

"Perhaps," Julian replied. "But at least now I know not to rush into things. Good God, listen to me. What am I saying?"

"You're simply confirming what I said earlier, brother." Josiah shrugged. "Miss Viola Aitken, whilst lovely indeed, is not for you."

"Well, I'm not going to rush into anything, either way." He heaved a sigh. "Half-an-hour, Joe. I was with Annabelle Fairfax for half an hour. Don't you think she'll find it strange if I show up at her door unannounced? She might not even remember me."

"Stop being so bloody pessimistic. This is an opportunity not to be missed. Nothing ventured, as they say. You can travel to London with me next week." Josiah slid off the bed and brushed the creases from his trousers. "Right, I'm off to bed. See you in the morning. Sleep well."

Julian scoffed. "At the risk of being bloody pessimistic, I doubt I'll sleep a wink now, but thanks. And I really mean that. Thank you."

"You're welcome," Josiah said, and opened the door.

A single, unrelated question drifted to the front of Julian's chaotic mind. "Er, Joe?"

He paused on the threshold and looked back. "Mmm?"

"Just curious. What were you doing at Lord Bethany's?"

He smiled and tapped the side of his nose. "Sorry, brother. Not at liberty to say."

A WEEK LATER, Lord and Lady Whickham's carriage, with Lord, Lady and offspring safely ensconced, rumbled over Highfield's cobbled courtyard, passed beneath the ancient gatehouse, and disappeared into the pale, morning mist. Julian, standing on the steps with his parents, waited to hear an anticipated comment from his mother. It was his father, however, who spoke first.

"Speaking generally," Aldous said, "I think the week went rather well."

"I agree," Grace replied, turning to go into the house. "They're lovely people, and Miss Aitken is charming. I'm very pleased."

"Is that it, Mama?" Julian frowned. "Aren't you going to say anything else?"

"About what, dear?" she replied, pausing mid-step.

"About Miss Aitken. Specifically, my intentions toward her."

Grace's brows lifted. "What do you want me to say? I can tell you're not quite decided, if that's what you mean."

"Best not to rush into these things." Aldous winked. "Now, if you'll both excuse me, I think I'll just trot over to the stables. I want a quick word with Willis."

"I confess I was expecting you to comment on my lack of decision, Mama," Julian said, as he followed his mother into the house.

"Then your expectation was misplaced." Grace headed into the Morning Room, where the aromas of breakfast still lingered. "I personally think it's an excellent match, but I also agree with your father—there's no great hurry. You've only just met. Now, I believe I'd like another coffee. Will you take some? It should still be fresh."

"Yes, I'll get it, Mama. Extra cream, as always, of course." Julian headed for the sideboard. "And your lack of critique makes what I'm about to say a little easier."

"Not sure I like the sound of that." Grace settled onto one of the settees. "I do hope it's not an outright dismissal of the girl's hand, Julian. You'll be seeing her at Myddleton in a few weeks. At least wait till then before making a final decision."

"Miss Aitken may have already made the decision for me." Julian handed his mother her black coffee and settled himself in an adjacent chair. "Or does she not have a say in it?"

"Yes, of course she does." Grace took a sip of coffee and then set her cup down on the small table beside the settee. "But I suspect the young lady is already smitten and simply waiting for a proposal. So, what is it you want to say?"

Smitten? Not something Julian wanted to hear. Frowning into his coffee cup, he also took a sip and then lifted his gaze. "I'll be leaving with Josiah in the morning, Mama."

"Leaving?" Her brows lifted again. "You're going to London?"

"Yes."

"What for?"

"I've received some worrying news about a friend and would like to assure myself that all is well."

"Oh dear. Is it anyone I know?"

"No, Mama, I'm certain it isn't."

"I see," she replied, her puzzled expression implying the opposite. "Well, I hope it's nothing too serious. How did you receive this news?"

Julian hesitated. "Josiah told me about it."

"And you absolutely have to go to London? I mean, can this assurance not be obtained by way of correspondence?"

"No, I'm afraid it cannot. And I'd rather go in person, actually." Unsettled by his intentional ambiguity, Julian set his cup down, got to his feet, and wandered over to the bay window. It overlooked the rose garden, which was currently at its peak, although it all looked rather gloomy draped in fog. "I'm not sure how long I'll be gone. A week at least, I should think."

A response came, but only after a notable stretch of silence. "Is this friend a woman?"

He couldn't lie. "Yes."

"Ah." There followed a brief rustle of skirts. "A woman you care about, obviously."

Parting with a soft sigh, he turned. "To tell the truth, Mama, I know very little of her."

Grace frowned. "Then why are you going all the way to London for her sake?"

"Because he can't get her out of his mind." Josiah, looking rather like he'd slept in the clothes he was wearing, sauntered into the room, and approached the sideboard. "Is the coffee still fresh? Oh, and good morning, Mama."

"Yes, it's fresh," Julian replied, "and your lack of tact is not appreciated."

"I thought it was a fair question." Josiah poured himself a cup. "Not keen on coffee that's been sitting a while."

"Not what I meant, and you know it," Julian said, frowning.

"Am I to understand you've met this young lady as well, Josiah?" Grace asked.

He shook his head. "No, Mama, I have not."

"Then, how do you know of her?"

"Because Julian told me about their meeting, and I learned about her dilemma from another source just recently." Clasping his coffee cup, Josiah sank into a nearby chair and stifled a yawn. "Wasn't sure I should tell Julian about it, to be honest, but then I saw him with Miss Aitken and was left with no choice."

Julian groaned. "Joe, don't."

Grace's eyes widened. "You don't like Miss Aitken?"

"I think she's absolutely delightful," Josiah replied. "She's just not right for Julian."

"Please ignore him, Mama," Julian said, taking his seat once more, "which is what I tend to do for the most part."

Grace toyed with the pearl pendant at her throat. "Well, Julian, I confess I find all this rather confusing, but if it's a matter of following your heart, then you have my blessing."

Julian gave her a dubious look. "Even though you know

nothing of her, Mama?"

"Nothing of *her*, no." Grace's gentle smile, so well-known to him, appeared. "But I believe I *do* know a thing or two about my eldest son and trust him to do what he feels he must. Especially when it comes to matters of the heart."

"I appreciate that. Thank you." He shrugged. "It might all be for nought, however."

"Why do you say that?" Grace asked. "She's not ill, is she?"

Julian shook his head. "No, not ill. She recently lost her father in a tragic way, and I simply want to make sure she's all right, that's all."

"I see. Yes, I'm sure that must have been upsetting. What of her mother?"

"Her mother died many years ago."

"Siblings?"

"None."

"So, she's alone."

"Not quite. She has a maid. That is, a companion of sorts, but that is all, as far as I know." Julian heaved a sigh. "We met briefly in London several weeks ago and she made an impression on me. Actually, it was the day Max and Louisa returned from their holiday. And yes, though my dear brother's remark was something of an overstatement, I have thought about the young lady many times since. There was something special about her."

Grace nodded and glanced away briefly. "Is she the reason you're undecided about Miss Aitken?"

Josiah snorted and Julian threw him a scowl. "No, she is not," he replied. "At least, she *was* not. The loss of her father is a recent event, but there is more to this tale. With respect, however, I would rather not discuss it further. Not till I return from London."

"Discuss what?" Aldous stepped into the room, a questioning expression on his face. "Why are you going to London? Has something happened?"

"Nothing of concern to the family, Papa," Julian replied, his nerves beginning to fray. "I simply want to check on the well-being of a friend and would prefer to do so in person."

"I see." Aldous exchanged a prolonged glance with Grace, one that Julian recognized as a silent form of communication perfected through years of marriage. "So, when do you leave?"

"Tomorrow morning."

"With Josiah, I assume."

"Yes."

"But where will you stay? The house is closed up."

"He can stay with me, Papa," Josiah said. "As long as he doesn't mind sleeping on the settee."

"Don't mind at all," Julian replied.

"Well, that's that then. I hope it all turns out for the best." Aldous gestured to the sideboard. "Is the coffee still fresh?"

"I think it has sat long enough, Papa." Josiah gave Julian a glance that denoted a triumph of sorts. It was not only their parents, apparently, who could communicate without uttering a word. "You might want to ring for more."

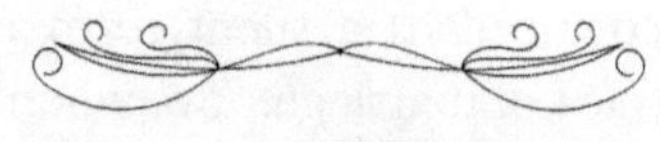

CHAPTER NINE

TWENTY-NINE CHESTER STREET was exactly as Julian remembered it. A handsome but unassuming house, its red-brick façade and black door were an exact replica of the house on either side. Unlike the others, however, Twenty-Nine exuded a vague air of abandonment. It manifested in the unpolished number on the door and the brass doorknocker, as well as the assortment of street debris nestling in the corners of the stone steps. Mostly, though, it was due to the fact that the curtains were drawn shut on every window, upstairs and down.

Still, he'd come this far, so he figured he might as well take futility that little bit further. Heaving a sigh, he climbed the unswept steps, lifted the dull brass knocker, and landed four solid raps on the door. An expected span of silence followed, adding credence to the conviction that Miss Annabelle Fairfax was not at home and hadn't been for a while.

Disappointment, as well as a touch of chagrin, accompanied Julian back to the pavement, where he turned and looked up at the house once more. Maybe he should have written to Annabelle first, explaining how he'd heard about the events at her wedding, and wished to offer his sympathy. Or maybe he should simply have stayed in Yorkshire, accepted the fact that he'd spent less than a half-hour of his life with a girl he'd never see again, and set all thoughts of a trip to London aside.

"There's no one at home, sir," came a male voice. "Hasn't

been for a couple of weeks."

Julian looked to his left, where a white-haired gentleman stood on the pavement in front of the neighboring house, a set of keys clutched in his hand.

"That's a pity." Julian grasped at a possible straw. "I was hoping to speak with Miss Fairfax. Do you happen to know where she went?"

The man shook his head as he mounted the steps to his door. "No idea, I'm afraid. The lady left rather suddenly and without a word. I assume you're aware of what happened at the wedding?"

"Yes, though I only learned of it recently," Julian replied. "Which is why I'm here, to offer my condolences. Is she expected back any time soon?"

Another shake of the head. "I shouldn't think so. The house is up for lease. The family solicitor will likely know how to contact her, though. Archibald Mason is his name. I believe his office is on Tothill Street. It was a dreadful business! Clarence Fairfax was a good man and a fine physician."

"Yes, dreadful indeed." Not wishing to be drawn into a conversation, Julian tipped his hat. "Thank you for the information, sir. Much appreciated. I bid you a good day."

Julian went back the way he'd come, toward Grosvenor Place, where he hailed a cab, intent on seeking out the solicitor the neighbor had mentioned. He hoped the fellow would at least have a forwarding address for Annabelle or be able to provide more detail about her intentions. As it happened, his hope was short-lived.

"Miss Fairfax is currently traveling abroad, Mr. Northcott." Archibald Mason cleared his throat and pushed his spectacles farther up his nose. "I'm afraid I cannot say when she might return to these shores."

The clip-clop of a horse-drawn carriage drifted in from the street, the sound synchronizing perfectly with the tick-tock of the clock on a nearby wall. Julian glanced at the clock briefly, though his mind did not register the hour. It was too busy trying to figure out why Annabelle Fairfax's solicitor was lying. "There is no forwarding address?"

"Since she is traveling, no." The man cleared his throat again. "May I ask how you know the lady, sir? I confess I do not recall her ever mentioning your name to me."

Julian saw no reason to lie. He met the man's gaze. "Miss Fairfax and I met briefly several weeks ago. I learned of her father's death through the newspaper report. Since I'm in London, I thought to call on the lady to pay my respects."

"I see." The fellow gave a thin smile. "Well, I regret that will not be possible."

Julian blinked as comprehension flared to life. "You're protecting her, aren't you?" His chair creaked as he leaned forward. "Why would that be necessary, Mr. Mason? Is Miss Fairfax in danger?"

A tic appeared beneath the man's left eye. "I cannot say more than I already have, sir. If you'd care to leave your contact information with me, I'll make sure Miss Fairfax gets it when next she is in touch. Unfortunately, I don't know when that will be." He got to his feet. "Now, I do have other appointments today, so with respect, I must call an end to this one. Do you wish to leave a card?"

"Yes, I do." Julian rose to his feet as well, reached into his waistcoat pocket, and handed a card over. "This is my brother's address. My father's London house is currently closed."

Archibald Mason regarded it, one eyebrow arching as he did so. "I appreciate your concern for my client, Mr. Northcott," he said, "and I bid you a good day."

"THAT'S IT?" JOSIAH shook his head. "That's all he had to say?"

"That's all." Julian heaved a sigh and flopped onto the settee. "I don't believe she's traveling abroad, though. I believe she's still in England, and Archibald Mason is fully aware of her location. He's protecting her, Joe, I'm guessing from the fellow she was meant to marry. I can't criticize him for that. He's doing his duty."

"Maybe if you pushed him," Josiah said. "Y'know, throw your societal status in his face. Nephew of an earl and suchlike. He might be a bit more forthcoming."

Julian frowned. "I could never do that. It's disrespectful to Uncle Isaac."

"I'm not saying you use the name. Just the title."

Julian shook his head. "No, can't do it. The fellow has my card and said he'd pass on the information when and if he can."

"Or he might just drop it in the waste-paper basket." Josiah cocked his head. "So, is that it? That's all you're prepared to do for now?"

"I don't see what else I *can* do."

"Hire someone. A private investigator."

Julian groaned. "Come on, Joe, that's taking things a bit far, don't you think? I mean, if you look at this entire venture from an impassive standpoint, it translates to me tracking down a young woman I hardly know, a young woman who clearly prefers not to be found. Yes, it bothers the hell out of me that the girl has deemed it necessary to go into hiding, but steps have obviously been taken to ensure her safety. I've done all I can do for now, or at least, all I'm reasonably able and willing to do. Besides, to take things further might do more harm than good."

Josiah grimaced. "You're giving up, in other words."

"I'm capitulating to circumstance," Julian replied, with a shake of his head. "Am I disappointed? Yes, very. But all at once, this endeavor feels like a bootless errand. I have obligations elsewhere and I cannot ignore them. At this time of year, I should be at Highfield. Not here, traipsing around London trying to locate a woman who doesn't want to be located. Maybe, if and when the solicitor tells her of my visit, she'll contact me."

"And if she doesn't?"

Julian shrugged. "Then I suppose I'll have to take a fatalistic approach and assume a liaison with Miss Fairfax was never meant to be."

"Hmm." Josiah nodded, his frown indicative of thought. "Well, in that case, feel like getting drunk?"

Julian opened his mouth to refuse but hesitated. "Yes, actually," he said, after a moment. "I do."

"Ever been to The Elysium?"

"I've heard of it," Julian shook his head, "but no, never frequented the place."

Josiah waggled a brow. "I highly recommend it. It's rather exclusive and the entertainment is of the highest quality. The ideal place for a gentleman to drown his sorrows, in fact. Fancy it?"

"Oh, what the hell. Why not?" he replied, capitulating to a rare desire to throw caution to the wind. "Lead on, Joe."

❧

LESS THAN A week later, Julian was back at Highfield.

"So unfortunately, no, I didn't actually see the young lady," he said, having just given his mother a trimmed version of events, "but I've been assured she's in good health."

Grace smiled and nodded. "Well, I'm glad it wasn't a wasted journey, dear. You do look rather tired, though. Perhaps you should take a day or two to rest. It wouldn't do to have you falling ill."

"I'm fine, Mama," he replied. "But the city was brutally hot and the air foul. Not a drop of rain fell the entire week I was there. It was exhausting. Believe me, I'm more than happy to be back in the cooler and fresher climes of Yorkshire."

He didn't tell her about the shadow of disappointment that had accompanied him back home. That, and a vague sense of failure. It might not have been a wasted journey, but neither did it yield the result he'd hoped for.

The responsible side of him told him he was being foolish. Maybe Archibald Mason had been telling the truth. Maybe Annabelle Fairfax was, indeed, traveling abroad. Julian could wait, of course, to see if she responded to the message he'd left with the solicitor. But for how long? How long was reasonable? How long was *un*reasonable?

In a little less than a month, he'd be in Miss Aitken's company once more, this time at Myddleton House, his uncle's Derbyshire seat. And it seemed likely a decision would have to be made at that time, if not for his sake, then for Miss Aitken's.

Grace's voice cut into his thoughts. "Oh, by the way, a letter arrived for you, dear. Two days ago. I put it in your room. Very pretty handwriting! I should imagine a response will be required."

The intonation in his mother's voice was clear. So too, it seemed, was the timing. To wait for any kind of response from Miss Fairfax was futility at its finest. There was no expectation, no inevitability. Common sense demanded he set foot on the path that had recently been laid out for him. A path clearly defined and certainly more suited to his status.

"Thank you, Mama." He stood, ignored the slight ache beneath his ribs, and straightened his shoulders. "I'll go and read it right away."

CHAPTER TEN

Ferndale Grange

ON THIS PARTICULAR morning, prompted by Lancelot's operatic solo, Annie had left her bed and opened her window to cloudless skies and the freshness of a mild breeze. She breathed deep through her nose, relishing the air, while giving silent thanks for the fine, sunny day she had wished for. For today, she intended to venture a little farther into the wilds of Derbyshire. Well, at least to the top of the distant ridge. She'd reached the foot of it a few days ago, but a sudden feeling of isolation had prompted her to glance back at Ferndale. Only the roof and chimneys had been visible, which added to her angst. She'd then wavered between attempting to climb the hill or turning back. In the end, she'd turned back, a decision she'd quickly regretted, for it left her with a sense of defeat. Still, it wasn't as though the hill was about to disappear.

Today, she would not be defeated, nor would she even turn to look back till she'd climbed the hill. Besides, her curiosity demanded to see what lay on the other side. She could quite easily get the answer from Janet or Amos, but she preferred to retain the enticing sense of mystery this morning's walk promised.

Breakfast first, though, and one that brought back a memory the moment she stepped into the kitchen.

"Oh, my goodness. This looks so much like the one I remember from when I stayed with my aunt." Annie seated herself at the kitchen table and bent to examine the little figures on her eggcup.

"I'd almost swear it's the same pattern."

Janet looked over from where she stood at the stove. "I have four of them. They belonged to my mother."

"They're lovely," Annie replied, a faint blush warming her cheeks as she recalled her conversation with Julian Northcott. Specifically, her embarrassing ramble about her childhood memory of egg cups and speckled brown eggs. She looked up to find Hattie's gaze on her and knew, instinctively, that they were both thinking the same thing. Annie gave her head a slight shake as her eyes flicked briefly toward Janet. *Please, do not mention him.* Hattie smiled a quick smile and acknowledged with a brief nod. "So, what do you have planned today, pet?" she asked, glancing at the window. "It's a fine one, by the looks of it."

"I'm going for a long walk," Annie said, following Hattie's glance. "And yes, it's a glorious day."

Soon after, having fed, washed, and dressed, Annie paused on the front doorstep to tie the ribbons of her bonnet. "Splendid," she muttered, gazing up at the cloudless sky. "Absolutely splendid."

"Keep your bonnet on and take this as well." Hattie handed her a parasol. "The sun does dreadful things to the complexion. What do you have on your feet?"

"My walking boots, of course." Annie lifted her skirts and pointed a foot. "I've worn them for every one of my walks. They're very comfortable."

"Stop fussing, Hattie," Janet said, folding her arms. "Let the girl be on her way. She'll be perfectly fine."

Ruffy, his tail wagging furiously, yapped his apparent agreement.

"Yes, Hattie, stop fussing." Annie bent to pet the terrier, who had accompanied her on all her walks so far. Or, at least, part of them. More often than not, the dog would abandon Annie to pursue his own path, returning home in time for his dinner, dirty, panting, and inarguably happy. "Besides, if the boots do begin to hurt, I shall simply remove them and my stockings and continue barefoot."

Hattie gasped. "You'll do no such thi—"

"Goodbye, both!" Waving a hand, Annie set off toward the gate. "I might be late for luncheon. No apologies. This weather is *glorious!*"

"The weather can change quickly, so don't go too far!" Hattie's appeal followed her out onto the road, but Annie ignored it.

A short while later, with Ruffy leading the way, Annie clambered over the stone stile and took the now-familiar path that skirted a patch of woodland. As usual, she was met by the raucous clatter of a resident flock of crows from their nearby tree-top roosts. And, as usual, she paused for a few moments beside the small brook that ran partway alongside the path, the clear water gurgling and splashing over rocks as it disappeared into the woods. It was a soothing sound, Annie thought, as was the rustle of leaves stirred by the soft, summer breeze. She gave silent thanks for the latter, since the black of her mourning dress captured the heat mercilessly and held onto it. For now, fortunately, the sun was not long above the horizon and the air was yet cool.

Annie looked ahead to her destination, though the crest of the ridge was only partially visible at this point. Once she turned away from the woods, she knew she'd be able to see all of it. Without thinking, she almost looked back at Ferndale, but stopped herself, resolved to keep looking forward till she reached her destination. How silly, she thought, with a rueful smile. What difference would it make whether she looked back now or later? No difference at all, really, but she found some satisfaction in creating and achieving these simple resolutions for herself. They were a test of will, stemming from a desire to control even a small part of her life, while facing a future that still seemed chaotic and unpredictable.

The path circled around, eventually taking Annie to where it split, with a narrow offshoot leading upward. "Well, here we go,

Ruffy. Are you ready?" She looked down, saw no sign of the dog, and huffed. "All right. Fine. I'll do it by myself."

Lifting her skirts with one hand and grasping the parasol in the other, she began the climb, which zigzagged ever upward. Fortunately, the slope was not too extreme, and the path felt dry and firm underfoot. Knee-high grass, their soft feathery tips rippling like waves, blanketed much of the hillside. Here and there, patches of heather hinted at their imminent display of color. Mostly, though, Annie kept her eyes on her path, placing her booted feet with care. She sucked in a breath when a bee buzzed close to her ear. At least, she hoped it was a bee, and not some other stinging insect she hadn't encountered before. The countryside, it seemed, was home to an endless variety of multi-legged insects, winged and otherwise, some of them alarmingly large.

By the time the path began to level out, the climb had taken its toll. Perspiration dripped into Annie's eyes, her legs ached, and her galloping heart felt like it was about to break out of her chest. She paused, dropped her handful of skirts, pulled a handkerchief from her sleeve, and mopped her brow. Then, sucking in a determined breath, she took the few final steps onto the broad crest of the hill. The distant horizon seemed to rise up and greet her. Her subsequent gasp expressed what words, at that moment, could not.

Never could she have imagined such a view. Enchanted, she moved to where a massive slab of flat rock jutted out from the hillside; a natural balcony with a dizzying drop, reserved solely for those brave enough to use it. Annie felt no fear, only fascination. She stepped onto the ancient ledge, filled her lungs with fresh, cool air, and swept her gaze over the breathtaking scenery. The world, it seemed, lay at her feet. Or perhaps, she fancied, she was gazing upon a fragment of Heaven that had fallen to Earth in times past.

Moorland and forest merged into emerald-green meadows dotted with white sheep. A sunlit river, like molten silver, snaked its way across the land. But of all the things visible, the one that drew and held Annie's attention was the house. Even without the sparkle of sunlight on its splendid array of windows, she would have noticed it immediately.

It occupied a spot at the center of the vista, as if its architect had once stood in Annie's place and purposely chosen the precise location. Only the upper part of the house was visible, the lower part hidden behind the undulations of the landscape and barricades of trees. Judging by the gables and chimneys, however, the house was obviously the centerpiece of a substantial estate. Annie wondered who lived there. A duke, perhaps. Or maybe a wealthy industrialist. Was it home to a solitary owner, or to a large family? The latter part of the question brought Julian Northcott to mind for the second time that day, for she recalled he'd spoken with fondness about his five siblings. Distracted by things new and unfamiliar, she thought of him less and less these days, though the memory of her encounter with him remained fully intact. She suspected it always would.

"Three sisters and two brothers," she murmured, and shifted her gaze to the far horizon, unsure of where, exactly, Yorkshire was. "You must be out there, somewhere. Do you ever think of me, I wonder?" She dared to believe he did, and then pondered the fickleness of life. The only predictable thing about it was its ruthless unpredictability.

A soft gust of wind brought Annie back to the moment, and her focus shifted once more to the great house. The question about what lay beyond the hill had been answered, but other questions now lifted their heads, demanding answers. And that's when Annie, at last, looked back to where those answers lay.

Ferndale Grange.

"IT'S CALLED MYDDLETON House." Janet, spectacles balanced on the end of her nose, frowned as she attempted to thread a sewing needle. "And it is home to the Earl of Hutton."

"The Earl of Hutton," Annie repeated, settling onto one of the chairs at the kitchen table. "I guessed it would be an aristocrat. Have you met him?"

Janet regarded Annie over the rim of her spectacles. "Not personally, no. Lady Hutton, yes. Many times, in fact."

"His wife? The countess?"

"Yes. Ouch!" Frowning, Janet stuck a fingertip in her mouth. "Time to get new spectacles, I think."

"Here, Janet, give it to me." Hattie held out a hand. "I'll thread it for you."

"Why?" Annie asked.

"Because my eyesight is still perfect," Hattie replied.

Annie shook her head. "No, I mean, how come you've met the countess, Janet?"

Janet handed the bobbin and needle to Hattie. "Because, on occasion, I'm asked to help with the flower arrangements at Myddleton, and Lady Hutton sometimes insists on being involved. She loves her garden and her flowers."

Annie pondered the response. She'd never met a member of the aristocracy before. "Is she nice?"

"She is utterly delightful. A fine lady with a kind heart. Thank you, Hattie." Janet took the threaded needle back. "The entire family is delightful, actually. Though, the dowager countess can be rather overbearing at times, I understand. Mind you, I've only met her once, but it left an impression. She must be in her nineties by now."

"So, you've actually been inside the house."

Janet picked up the apron that had been sitting on the table. "Many a time," she replied, frowning as she inspected the part in need of repair.

"What is it like?"

"Well, I'm not familiar with the *entire* house, of course, but what I have seen is as splendid as you might expect. Especially the long gallery."

"The long gallery."

"Yes. It's where most of the family's art collection is located. It's very impressive."

"Oh, I should love to see it. It sounds wonderful."

Janet didn't look up from her mending, but she smiled. "It is."

Annie heaved a sigh and shifted her gaze to the window as she reflected on her morning excursion. "It was beautiful up there," she said, as much to herself as the others. "The view from the ledge is incredible."

"Freya's Farewell? I haven't been up there for years," Janet said, head still bent, her needle darting in-and-out with practiced efficiency. "I never dared to step onto the ledge. Just thinking about the drop makes me shudder. I don't like heights."

"Freya's Farewell?" Annie pulled her gaze from the window. "Is that what it's called?"

Janet grimaced. "Named after a young lady who supposedly threw herself off there when her sweetheart married another. I suspect it's just a made-up tale, though. Lots of them in these parts."

"Poor Freya." Annie shook her head. "I do hope it's not true."

"I'm fairly sure it isn't." Janet shrugged. "In any case, don't let it stop you from going back up there."

"Is it wrong, do you think," Annie said, after a moment, "for me to be roaming all over the countryside? I mean, Papa has only been gone for six weeks."

Janet paused her mending and looked at Hattie, who answered with a firm shake of her head. "No, pet, of course it isn't wrong. What would be gained by staying cooped up in the house all day? Nothing at all, that's what. Your father wouldn't want you to do that, either, you know he wouldn't. He'd say it wasn't healthy, and he'd be right. Wearing that black garb doesn't mean you should stop living. Life goes on and we're obliged to get on with it."

"I suppose." Annie heaved a sigh, wishing she could lose the niggling burden of guilt that made her feel as though enjoyment of any description was inappropriate.

"Will you do something for me, Annie?" Janet asked, without looking up from her task. "There's a small, white envelope in the hall-table drawer. Will you fetch it for me, please?"

"Yes, of course." Annie scraped her chair back and went in search of the envelope, returning with it moments later. "Is this the one?"

Janet glanced at the envelope in Annie's outstretched hand. "Yes, that's it. There's a note inside. Take it out and read it, will you?"

Annie raised her brows. "Have you not read it?"

"Of course I have." Janet took a small pair of scissors from the table and snipped off the thread. "But I'd like *you* to read it."

"Out loud?"

"If you wish, though it's not necessary. I just thought you might be interested in what it says, that's all."

Intrigued, Annie took out the folded piece of paper, opened it, and silently read the short message, her eyes widening before she was even half-way through.

Monday, June 19th, 1846

Dear Miss Caldridge,

I trust this request finds you in good health.

Your valued services are required at Myddleton House on Thursday, August 6th of this year. Your early arrival would be greatly appreciated, and you should expect to be here for the better part of the day. Luncheon will, of course, be provided.

In anticipation of your prompt and positive response, I remain,

Your friend.

Mrs. Shelburne,
Housekeeper
Myddleton House.

"Oh, my goodness!" Annie lifted her gaze. "Are you to do the flower-arranging, Janet?"

"Yes. Well, some of it, at least." Janet stood, shook out the apron she'd been mending, and then folded it neatly. "There's obviously a gathering of some description scheduled. A house party, most likely."

"Um, would I be allowed to go with you?" Annie winced. "I mean, would it even be permitted? I'd really love to see the house."

The beginnings of another smile appeared. "I thought you might," Janet replied. "I responded to Mrs. Shelburne before you arrived, but I'll send her another note to say I'm bringing an assistant. I shouldn't think she'll mind. Not that you can go wandering about the place willy-nilly, young lady. Myddleton House is, first and foremost, a private home. You'll be obliged to stay with me. You can help me with the flowers."

"Yes, of course. I understand." Annie cupped her hands to her face, felt the glow of pleasure on her cheeks, and decided to ignore the anticipated twinge of guilt. "Oh, I can't wait to see the place. Maybe you could give me a few lessons on flower arranging before then?"

"Yes, of course," Janet replied, and then smiled as a scratching sound came to the back door followed by a recognizable bark. "There he is. Let him in, will you, Annie?"

CHAPTER ELEVEN

O F ALL THE women Julian might have expected to see at Myddleton House, she would not have been one of them. The sight of her instantly transported him back to that unforgettable day in London when he'd gazed into the depths of her eyes. And her eyes weren't the only things about her that came to mind.

Of course, Her Grace, the Duchess of Rothbury, looked as lovely as ever. Unlike her portrayal in oils, however, she was elegantly dressed, gloriously bejeweled, and perfectly coiffed, none of which was of any consequence to Julian. With little effort on his part, her clothing melted away before his eyes, replaced by a translucent piece of fabric that left little to the imagination. Her splendid hair, meanwhile, freed itself from its pins to tumble down over her breasts. Overall, a detailed recollection, and unquestionably inappropriate, given that the lady was currently deep in conversation with Julian's aunt. Still, he couldn't help himself, nor was it his fault. He blamed Josiah entirely.

"I should think she's praying he'll wait till he returns to Wiltshire before breathing his last."

Julian regarded his father, who had come to stand beside him. "His Grace, you mean?"

"Yes," Aldous replied. "They arrived not a half-hour ago, but he has yet to make it up the stairs. He's currently taking a noisy nap in the library."

"Noisy?"

"Snoring impressively." Aldous grimaced. "Poor old chap. I really mustn't be so ungracious. I'm surprised he made the effort to come to Myddleton, given his frailty. They're here a day early to give him time to recover from the journey."

"He likes to keep an eye on his wife," Julian said, shifting his attention back to the duchess. "He enjoys her popularity."

"Yes, so I've noticed," Aldous replied. "How are you feeling, Julian?"

Julian gave him a sideways glance. "I'm feeling fine, Papa. Why do you ask?"

"No reason." He cleared his throat. "I assume you're looking forward to seeing Miss Aitkin?"

"Yes," he replied, and not without honesty, "I am."

Aldous nodded. "Glad to hear it."

Julian didn't answer. He guessed there was more to come. Sure enough, after a few moments of silence, his father cleared his throat again. "What of this other young lady who has caught your eye?"

Julian, knowing full well his mother was behind this mild inquisition, and that his father was acting under protest, smothered a sympathetic smile. "What of her? I have no idea where she is, Papa. I've already made that clear." He swallowed against what felt like a mild but unwelcome sense of despair. "I only met her the one time, and it's highly unlikely I'll ever meet her again."

"So, you're still considering a possible engagement to Miss Aitken?"

"I believe I've made that clear as well," he replied. "Though, as you yourself said, these things should not be rushed."

"No, in my opinion, they should not." Aldous narrowed his gaze slightly. "On the other hand, over-delaying might lead to irrevocable disappointment."

Julian stifled a sigh. "What do you consider over-delaying, Papa? Thus far, Miss Aitken and I have barely spent a week together. A very enjoyable week, I might add. And I'm sure these next few days will allow us to get to know each other even better."

"No doubt," his father replied. "It's the existence of this mystery woman that has your mother in a bit of a dither, that's all."

"Yes, I've gathered that." Julian tamped down a touch of frustration. "But if I *am* delaying my decision about an engagement to Miss Aitken, it's for no other reason than I'd like a little more time to get to know her. If, in the meantime, she has a change of heart, then so be it. But I will not be rushed."

Aldous parted with a sigh. "Which is what I told your mother, but you know how she is. I'll just wander back to the parlor and tell her again, I suppose. Want to come with me?"

Julian laughed. "No, thank you, Papa, I'll leave you to it. Think I'll take a walk before luncheon, actually. Where are the twins, by the way? I haven't seen either of them or Arthur this morning."

"I believe they're in the conservatory. No idea where Arthur is. The games room, probably." Aldous gestured toward a rain-spattered window. "You'll need an umbrella."

"No, I'll just take a turn indoors." Julian gave his father's shoulder a squeeze. "I'll see you and Mama at luncheon."

Throwing another quick glance at the duchess, who was still conversing with his aunt, Julian wandered out into the hallway where he paused to gather himself. Despite what he'd told his father, he was actually contemplating a serious proposal to Miss Aitken at some point over the next couple of days. Why wait, after all? It would put an end to the speculation and pressure from eager parents. Besides, he could think of no profound or justifiable reason to refuse the union. They got along very nicely. Viola Aitken was a beautiful woman; intelligent, sweet natured, and handsomely placed in society. Quite the prize, to quote Josiah. Yet a small measure of doubt remained in Julian's heart. A stubborn impediment that refused to capitulate to the faultless reasoning of his brain. And, if he were to be totally honest with himself, he knew the reason for it, which meant he'd just been less than honest with his father.

"Damn it," he muttered.

"Am I interrupting, Mr. Northcott?"

At the sound of the soft, female voice, he spun round and found himself gazing in a pair of familiar eyes. Authentic, this time. Not replicated on virgin canvas by the touch of an artist's brush.

"Your Grace." Julian inclined his head. "Forgive me. I didn't realize you were there."

The duchess waved a dismissive hand. "My fault entirely for sneaking up on you. You wandered off just as I was about to suggest to your aunt we be introduced, so I excused myself and followed you. It's about time we met, I think, especially since I've heard so much about you."

Julian flinched. "All good, I hope."

"Mostly." A twinkle came to those eyes. "So, am I? Interrupting you, that is?"

"Not at all, Duchess," Julian replied. "Since the weather is disagreeable, I was about to take a turn indoors. Would you care to join me?"

"I would indeed, Mr. Northcott. Thank you."

Julian presented an elbow. "Mostly?"

She laughed—a musical, unforced sound—and tucked her hand into the crook of Julian's arm as they set off. "The way your wonderful aunt sings your praises, I can't understand why there isn't a halo permanently circling your head."

Julian chuckled. "Lady Hutton is my godmother, so she might be a little biased."

"Possibly," the duchess replied. "Your brother, however, while also complimentary in his descriptions of you, is perhaps a little more realistic."

"Er…" Julian almost gave himself away. "My brother?"

The duchess tutted. "It's very sweet of you to feign ignorance, Mr. Northcott, but not necessary. Actually, may I call you Julian? At least, when we're alone together. All this formality seems rather superfluous, don't you think? I mean, given that I know that *you* know. Or rather, I know how *much* of me you know."

Since it appeared Josiah and the duchess were still enjoying each other's company, Julian set all pretense aside. "Point taken, Duchess," he replied, breathing in subtle hints of flora and citrus that surrounded her. "You may call me Julian, of course, but I'd prefer to address you in the appropriate manner, if you have no objection."

"Josiah said you were a stickler for the rules." Head cocked, she regarded him, a blatantly mischievous expression on her face. "So, tell me, Julian, what did you think of it?"

"It?" Of course, Julian knew exactly to what she referred, but his brain stumbled over an appropriate response. It didn't help that the image of Her Grace, reclining near-naked on a red chaise-longue, arose in his mind.

"My portrait."

"Ah." Julian cleared his throat. "Well, first of all, I should assure you that I have not spoken a word ab—"

She tutted again. "I don't doubt your discretion, silly boy, I'm simply curious to know what you thought."

He allowed himself a very genuine smile. "I *think* it is beautiful. Remarkable, in fact."

"Thank you." Smiling also, she nodded. "That pleases me."

"Do you like it?" he asked.

"I love it." A fleeting expression crossed her face, there and gone in the blink of an eye, too quick for Julian to identify. She glanced away. "He's very talented, your brother."

"Yes, he is."

"Free-spirited."

"Indeed. Always has been."

"I envy him that." There followed a few moments of silence, then, "I'm extremely fond of him, Julian."

Julian didn't respond, simply because there was nothing of value to be said. He understood fully what the duchess meant. He also understood why her declaration had an air of sadness about it. No one would argue she had gained much by wedding the old duke; status, untold wealth, a life free from hardship. Yet she had also become the embodiment of a bird in a gilded cage, allowed out now and then to stretch her wings, but always obliged to return to the one who owned her. At least, till death parted them. Then again, he mused, she had made her choice, and willingly. Did Josiah know of what lay in her heart, he wondered?

"I haven't told him, nor do I intend to," the duchess said, as if reading Julian's thoughts. "And neither will you. Oh, is that lemon brandy?" This last referred to a passing footman carrying a tray of drinks, who nodded and paused. The duchess let go of Julian's arm, helped herself to a glass, and arched a brow at him. "I trust I'll not be drinking alone, sir."

"No, of course not." Julian took a glass for himself as his thoughts turned to his own future. Being a tad lower than her on the societal ladder, his familial obligations were not quite as rigid. Nevertheless, as heir to Highfield Hall and its estates, he was expected to marry responsibly. Marriage to the daughter of a viscount was a fine feather in his hat. And search as he might, he could find no fault with Miss Aitken. Quite the contrary, may his hesitant heart be damned.

"I trust your thoughts are worth a penny, at least." The duchess's voice drew him from his contemplation.

Julian winced. "Forgive me, Duchess, my mind wandered."

"Hmm." She narrowed her eyes at him. "Would it have anything to do with Miss Aitken, by chance?"

He cleared his throat. "It would seem my aunt has kept you well-informed."

"Not without a little prompting from me." She took a sip of her drink. "I was curious to know more about you. Your aunt indicated an engagement to the young lady might be in your future."

"It does seem likely, yes."

The duchess appeared to study him for a moment. "Miss

Aitken is very fortunate, I think."

"Thank you, Duchess. I consider myself fortunate also."

"Despite your uncertainty?"

Julian took a sip of his drink. "You're very perceptive."

"I pride myself on it." She gave him a playful nudge. "You're not difficult to read, sir. And please take that as a compliment."

He grimaced. "But stay away from the gaming tables?"

She laughed. "Yes, probably wise."

Seeking to change the subject, Julian looked to where the double doors of the long gallery stood wide open. Judging by the sunlight spilling through the gallery's impressive line of windows, the rain had stopped. "I probably should have asked earlier. Have you been to Myddleton House before?"

A vague look of amusement came to her face. "No, regrettably."

"Ah, then you are in for a treat, Your Grace." In a dramatic fashion, he swept his hand through the air toward the gallery doorway. "Please allow me to escort you."

"With pleasure, sir," she replied, and took him by the arm again as they entered the gallery. "Are any of Josiah's works on display here?"

"I don't believe so," Julian replied, pausing to gaze upon an impressive landscape scene. "He rarely comes north, and when he does, he never stays for very long. He prefers the city."

"Yes, that he does." The duchess studied the painting for a few moments before moving onto the next. "It appears to be a remarkable collection."

"One of the best, north of London." Both Julian and the duchess turned at the sound of Lady Hutton's voice. "I trust my godson is being hospitable, Duchess?"

"He is, indeed." Smiling, the duchess glanced up at Julian and released his arm. "Hospitable *and* charming."

"Glad to hear it," his aunt replied. "I would have expected nothing less from him. But then, all the Northcott men are mindful of…"

The rest of his aunt's remark sank into obscurity as Julian's attention drifted to the figure of a solitary woman, standing some distance away at the rear wall of the gallery. Dark-haired, petite, and clad entirely in black, she had her back to him and looked to be busy arranging some flowers in a vase on the nearby table. Judging by the few blooms sitting askew in the vase, it appeared she'd barely begun her task. The remaining flowers occupied two large buckets at her feet.

The woman had a grace of movement that seemed oddly familiar, yet her approach to her task lacked efficiency. Or perhaps confidence. Even as he watched, she took a single flower from the bucket and placed it in the vase, only to remove it a moment later and return it to the bucket. Then she stepped back, head cocked as she appeared to study the vase. An odd little tingle crept across Julian's scalp, causing him to frown.

His aunt's voice, close to his ear, drew him from his scrutiny. "I used to do a lot of Myddleton's flower arrangements myself, albeit with Catherine's help," she said. "Catherine is no longer at Myddleton, of course, but I still like to arrange the odd one now and then. It's a very relaxing pastime."

Julian glanced at his aunt and then pointed his chin at the woman, who was currently taking her time studying the buckets before choosing a different bloom. "Not in this young lady's case, Aunt. I get the impression she doesn't really know what she's doing."

"Maybe she's simply a perfectionist," the duchess said, as the previously chosen bloom went back into the bucket again. "Though I agree, she does make the task look rather laborious."

"I don't recall seeing her here before." Lady Hutton appeared to ponder. "I believe Janet is doing most of the arrangements today. She must have taken on an assistant."

"Who appears to be in mourning," the duchess said, "given her sad attire."

"She's young to be in mourning." His aunt flicked her fan open and wafted it at her throat. "I imagine you're looking forward to seeing Miss Aitken tomorrow, my dear."

Julian hid a twinge of irritation behind a smile. "Yes, I am, Aunt."

Perhaps he hadn't hidden his irritation well enough, given how his aunt's brows first lifted and then fell into a brief frown. Julian took another sip of his drink and steeled himself against what was sure to be a coercive attack. It appeared the duchess was correct about him being easy to read.

"Your parents' expectations of you do not include entering into a loveless marriage, dear." His aunt snapped the fan shut and used it to tap his shoulder. "Obligations have their limits."

Julian gaped at her for a moment and then laughed. "I confess, Aunt Eleanor, that was not at all the response I expected, but I thank you for it."

"And I'm in total agreement with your aunt," the duchess added. "You're young, handsome, and eligible, Mr. Northcott. You can have your choice, I should think."

His aunt nodded. "Of course, that's not to say you shouldn't marry well, Julian. You're the heir to that marvelous estate, after all, which is where most of those obligations come in."

"I'm fully aware of that, Aunt." Julian's gaze shifted, carelessly, back to the flower girl. "As it happens, Miss Aitken and I get along extremely well, and I'm seriously considering a propo—"

Julian's ability to speak further, to even take his next breath, deserted him. All he could do was stare at the young woman in the gallery who, not even a minute earlier, was bent over a bucket of flowers, her back toward him. She was still there, standing beside the buckets, a white flower clutched in her hand. Except she was now standing upright and looking straight at him.

Recognition washed over him in a heated wave, stealing his breath. His glass slid from his grasp and shattered at his feet, yet he remained stock-still, looking upon a face he never thought to see again.

Annabelle?

His aunt's voice, edged with urgency, pushed through the

strange rushing sound in his head. "Julian, dear, what on earth is the matter?"

Intending to respond, he opened his mouth, but immediately forgot what his aunt had said. Then he felt a touch on his arm, and the duchess spoke. "What is it, Julian? What's wrong?"

Then his aunt's voice again, anxious. Fearful. "Are you ill, dear? Answer me. Should we fetch someone?"

Julian blinked once, twice, and tore his gaze away from the one who held it.

"Er, no, I'm…" He swallowed and then drew breath. "I'm all right, Aunt Eleanor, quite all right. Forgive me. I was taken by surprise, that's all."

"Taken by surprise?" She shook her head. "How come?"

"I wasn't prepared to see, I mean, I never imagined…" Fearful he'd been mistaken, he looked again, and his stomach clenched. A single, white flower lay on the floor and the buckets now stood alone. "What? Where…?"

Did I imagine her? No, I didn't. It was definitely her. Miss Fairfax. Annabelle. She was definitely there.

As if to affirm her presence, or rather her sudden departure, the north door at the other end of the gallery banged shut, the sound echoing through the vast space. It further reassured him he had not been mistaken. Besides, the look of shock on Annabelle's face surely indicated she'd recognized him too. But why had she run? Perhaps she simply feared facing him. Feared answering the questions raised by her presence at Myddleton House. She couldn't know he was already cognizant of what had occurred on her wedding day, and how her father had died.

"Wasn't prepared to see *what*, Julian?" His aunt's demand intruded into his thoughts once more, followed by the audible click of her fan opening. "Gracious, I thought you were having an epilepsy."

Julian turned to see her fanning herself so hard that the delicate pink feather in her hair looked about to take flight. He parted with a remorseful groan. "Forgive me, Aunt Eleanor. I didn't mean to frighten you." He looked down at the mess on the floor. "And I'm sorry about the glass."

His aunt huffed and continued to fan herself. "I couldn't care less about the glass, my dear. I'm just worried about you."

"Has it something to do with that girl?" the duchess asked. "The one arranging the flowers? Do you know her?"

"I'm fine, Aunt, really. And yes, Duchess, I do know the young lady. Well, sort of." Again, Julian looked at the buckets of flowers, uncertainty and certainty swapping places in his head. "At least, I think…no, I'm sure it was her."

"Who is she?" his aunt demanded. "And where has she gone? She hasn't finished the arrangement yet. How come you know her, Julian?"

"Of all the places on earth," he continued, as much to himself as anyone. "I can hardly believe it."

"But who *is* she?" The duchess linked her hands, prayer-like, beneath her chin. "Tell us, please. I just know there's a story here."

"A rather long story, actually," Julian replied, and set off through the gallery, throwing an apology over his shoulder as he went. "Forgive me, Aunt Eleanor, Duchess. I'll explain later!"

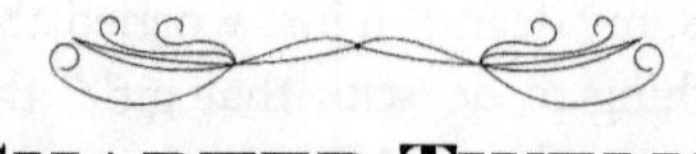

CHAPTER TWELVE

EARLIER THAT SAME morning, traveling by pony and trap, Annie and Janet had arrived at Myddleton House shortly after dawn beneath cloudy skies. Annie could only gape as they passed through the palatial wrought-iron gates. The gravel driveway cut a wide swathe through neat lawns of emerald grass and passed beneath the canopies of oak and elm. And then came the house itself, a majestic three-story edifice of gleaming windows, elegant gables, and handsome chimneys. The bottom portion of the house, which Annie hadn't been able to see from Freya's Farewell, was just as lovely as the top. She couldn't wait to view the inside.

Janet had steered the trap around to the rear of the house, where a stable lad had taken charge of Tulip the pony. They had then entered through a nondescript rear door, and into the underbelly of the great house. Annie, awed by the sheer grandeur of it all, had stayed in Janet's shadow as they'd been given the necessary instructions.

It was now close to midday and, with a half-dozen completed arrangements behind them, Annie found herself alone in Myddleton's long gallery with two buckets of flowers at her feet, and a large empty vase on a plinth. "Carry on," Janet had said, before disappearing in search of some "specific" greenery, whatever that meant. "See what you can do till I get back. I'll not be long. And do *not* wander off."

Annie loved flowers, but she'd come to realize the arranging of them in a fancy vessel of some sort was not really her forte. Still, as instructed, she'd continued with her efforts while listening to the rhythmic patter of rain on the many windows. She quietly admitted she'd be glad when Janet returned to finish the display, their fifth that day. After this, only one remained. *Thank goodness.*

On the bright side, her palatial surroundings were nothing short of spectacular. She could have spent the entire day in the gallery, wandering around, admiring the paintings and the sculptures, marveling at the sheer opulence of the place. Perhaps, when the flower display had been completed, and if the gallery remained empty, she might be allowed to indulge herself for a while.

That particular hope, however, had been short-lived. Not long after Janet left, the sound of footfalls and muted conversation had drifted in from the main gallery doorway. Annie wondered who it was but resisted an urge to look. Family or guests, undoubtedly. Perhaps both. Maybe even the earl and his countess. A touch of nervousness set Annie's heart racing, since she now had a potential audience who might bear witness to her ineptitude. She hoped Janet was right when she'd said that servants tended to be invisible to their wealthy employers. If so, they likely wouldn't pay her any attention. Nevertheless, a snippet of advice from Janet echoed in her head. *Speak only if spoken to.*

May Heaven forbid.

The hum of conversation continued on behind her, though Annie couldn't quite make out what was being said. Only when a man's laughter carried through the air did she dare to glance over her shoulder.

Three people. An older woman and a younger couple. The women in particular captured Annie's attention and her fascination. The older lady was startlingly elegant, her dress, of what appeared to be cream silk, nothing short of magnificent. As was the pearl collar at her throat and the immaculate coiffure of her silver hair, the latter adorned by a single, pale pink feather. Annie wondered if the lady might actually be the countess.

The younger woman, even from this distance, appeared to be worthy of portraiture. She reminded Annie of a porcelain doll, complete with a flawless complexion and perfect figure. Her hair, a rich, glossy brown, was also perfectly styled and curled, while the intense blue of her gown was reminiscent of bright, summer mornings. A jewel with a bluish hue glinted at her throat and surely matched the sparkling earrings that dangled from her ears. Annie gave the young man but a quick, cursory glance, wondered briefly if he was the younger lady's husband, and then returned to her sorry attempt at flower arranging.

It took a second or two for Annie's brain to catch up with what, or rather *who*, her eyes had beheld in that previous little fragment of time. With a gasp, she spun fully around, stomach clenching as her gaze fixed solely on the man. As if someone had drawn a curtain around her, all other sights and sounds faded into shadow. She saw him. Only him.

Julian Northcott.

Chatting with the older lady, he paid Annie no attention at first. But then, for whatever reason, he turned and looked straight at her. The subsequent expression of shock on his face indicated, beyond any doubt, that he recognized her also. The glass he'd been holding slid from his grasp and shattered at his feet, yet his gaze remained locked with hers. Annie's presence of mind spiraled into chaos as a horde of emotions besieged her, though only one of them took complete control.

Panic.

Run, her brain screamed, over the thunderous rattle of her heart. *Go, now. He cannot see you like this. He must not see you like this.* And yet she couldn't move, couldn't tear her gaze from his. Only when he looked away did whatever had tethered her to him snap. Willing her legs to work, Annie dropped the flower she was holding, hoisted her skirts, and fled. Moments later, she stumbled out of the gallery and raced along the hall to the servants' door.

Flinging that open, she flew down the wooden stairs and all but fell into the hallway at the bottom. There, she halted a moment to spare her poor heart, which was about to erupt from her chest, or so it seemed. As for her wits, they had scattered like loose beads on a tiled floor.

Julian Northcott. I cannot believe it. I cannot! He recognized me, too, I'm sure of it. What is he doing here? He said he lived in Yorkshire.

Not once had she imagined seeing him at Myddleton House. It seemed apparent he was a guest of the earl and the countess. *I knew he was a gentleman of note. I knew it! Oh, but why did I run from him? Why?*

The answer came swiftly. She ran because he would, likewise, demand the reason for her presence at Myddleton House, and she had no desire to explain it. To do so would be akin to poking at a wound not yet healed. And, if she was to be totally honest with herself, the telling of it would be embarrassing. Shameful, even. For now, caught unawares and unprepared, Annie could not bear the thought of facing him. She needed to find Janet, but had no idea where to begin looking.

Then, from somewhere above came the sound of the door opening and closing, followed by a cascade of footfalls on the stairs. They sounded masculine in nature. Urgent, as well. Annie's stomach clenched. Was it him? She wasn't about to wait and see. Seeking a potential hiding place, she looked left and right. Choosing to go left, she hoisted her skirts once more and sped off down the hallway.

Below-stairs at Myddleton House was no peaceful haven. Down here, beneath the grandeur and elegance of the upper floors, existed the inner workings of the great house. Men and women, young and old, skilled and novice, were the wheels and cogs of a machine that kept everything above stairs running efficiently. It did not run silently, however, nor did it move sedately, which for Annie was a blessing. The constant comings-and-goings meant her hurried presence went largely unnoticed. Or so she hoped.

When almost at the end of the corridor, she found a small room that appeared to offer sanctuary. It was unlit, unoccupied, and had a vague herbal smell, not too unpleasant. With a quick glance over her shoulder, Annie ducked inside, closed the door, and slipped into the shadows, giving silent thanks for the obscurity of her black mourning garb.

Disoriented and breathless, she pressed her back against the far wall, placed a hand over her heart, and tried to tame her wild emotions. The initial wave of shock receded a little, allowing rational thought to creep in, bringing a measure of regret with it. She had acted impulsively, she realized, without aforethought or reason.

She had, indeed, panicked.

"Oh, Lord, Annie," she muttered, cheeks burning as she buried her face in her hands. "What were you thinking? Stupid girl. You've just made things worse for yourself. Should've stayed where you were, waited till he approached, and explained your presence. The shame is not yours to bear, after all. You should have spoken to him, like… like a normal person. What must he think of you now? Deranged, most likely. A madwoman." She groaned. "God help me."

With her face still buried in her hands, Annie slid down the wall and sank to the floor, skirts ballooning out around her. The action seemed to mirror her composure, which, though carefully maintained and guarded over the past few weeks, now crumbled like dry clay.

Overwhelmed and entirely bewildered, Annie surrendered to the merciless unpredictability of her life and gave freedom to her pent-up tears. Hard sobs, one after another, erupted in near silence. Meanwhile, beyond the door of the sad little room, the clamor of Myddleton House continued as usual. Life went on, apparently unaware of Annie's presence or predicament.

But then, from outside the door, she heard a familiar masculine voice, the words unclear, the inflexion that of a question being asked. Annie's breath caught and the next sob stuck like a pebble in her throat. There followed a click as the door handle turned and a soft creak as the door swung open. Then a floorboard squeaked, followed by another, and Annie knew, without doubt or explanation, who had entered the room. She swallowed the trapped sob, dropped her hands, and lifted her gaze.

With the pale light of the corridor behind him, Julian Northcott appeared almost as a silhouette, detail visible, but subdued. Fists loosely clenched, he wore a slight frown, his expression one of concern; an expression she'd seen once before. His chest rose and fell visibly, though he had yet to utter a word. Annie, unsettled by his silence, scrubbed the tears from her eyes, sniffed, and gave him an utterly understated greeting, her voice slightly wobbly. "Good day to you, Mr. Northcott. It's nice to see you again."

His chest heaved once more, and his expression relaxed into a smile. "Good day to you, Miss Fairfax. It's nice to see you again, as well. I have been looking for you."

The nearness of him, the sound of his voice, and his smile, did indescribable things to Annie's stomach and heart. She waited, expecting him to ask what she was doing at Myddleton, but the question never came. Instead, he continued to gaze down at her, stretching the silence between them, compelling her to speak.

"Yes, sir, and for that I must apologize," she replied at last, with another sniff. "I should not have run off like that. I… I'm not really sure why I did."

The frown returned as he pulled a folded handkerchief from his vest pocket and crouched before her. "Not quite what I meant, but I'll explain later," he said, leaning over to dab the remaining tears from her cheeks. "And an apology is not necessary. There, that's better." He tucked the handkerchief back in its place, stood not quite upright, and held out his hands. "Come on, let me help you up. I doubt you're very comfortable down there."

Explain later? Explain what?

Annie wiped her damp hands on her skirts and then reached

for him. "It occurs to me, sir, that this is not the first time you've set me back on my feet," she said, as he hoisted her gently from the floor, his touch causing a little tingle that lifted the hairs on her nape. "I fear it is becoming quite a habit."

The smile reappeared. "Happy to be of assistance, Miss Fair-fax."

"I did not expect to see you here." Another understatement.

"Likewise, I can assure you." His expression softened as he gave her hands a slight squeeze. "And before anything else is said, please accept my condolences on the death of your father."

"Thank you." Annie glanced down at her black skirts, which had obviously announced her bereaved status. "Are you a guest here, Mr. Northcott?"

"You could say that." He released her. "Now, unless you're feeling less than able, I believe we have a task to complete."

Annie furled her fingers to preserve the warmth of his touch for a moment longer. "A task?"

"Yes." He gestured to the open door and the hallway beyond. "Arranging the flowers in the gallery."

"Oh." Annie swallowed against a twinge of confusion and disappointment. It seemed she had just been put in her place, wherever Julian Northcott considered that to be. Was this part of his delayed explanation? Had he only come looking for her to make sure she completed her floral task? Things must have changed since the time he'd suggested they correspond with each other. Or maybe, in her naivety, she'd misunderstood his intentions, though it sickened her to think so. *First Leo, and now him. Are all men prone to duplicity, then? No, not all. Papa, at least, was an honest and honorable man.*

A shadow of disappointment cast a chill over her. It also stirred up a touch of indignation. "I understand, sir, of course." She met his gaze and bobbed a slight curtsey. "I shall see to it right away." Biting down against another threat of tears, she brushed by him and went into the hallway.

His voice followed her. "Miss Fairfax, wait, please."

Shoring up the sorry remains of her defenses, Annie paused, lifted her chin, and turned. "Yes, Mr...?" Her voice faltered as he stepped out of the doorway and approached. She cleared her throat, linked her fingers together at her waist, and tried again. "Yes, Mr. Northcott?"

He halted barely a hand-span away and Annie found herself staring, as she had once before, at the pin in his cravat. Not tipped with a pearl this time, but a faceted, pale-blue stone. With little confidence in her fraying emotions, she purposely kept her gaze on that bright little jewel.

"I believe I said 'we'." With a hooked finger, he gently tipped her chin up. "I apologize if my intent was not made clear."

Annie's wretched heart skipped a beat as she gazed into his eyes. There was not a hint of duplicity in them, and she feared, suddenly, that all this was nothing more than a bizarre dream. That at any moment she'd hear Lancelot's lamentable crowing and awaken to see a pair of faded yellow curtains at her window. "Your intent?"

"Yes," he replied. "I actually thought to assist you with the flower arrangement, if you have no objection."

"Assist me?" Annie pondered. "You mean, as an observer?"

His mouth twitched. "While I'm certain that would be most pleasant, I fear it would not be particularly productive. I was rather hoping to be of some use to you, though I confess to having no knowledge of such things. However, if you tell me what flower goes next into that silly vase, I'm sure I'll be able to manage it. In any case, I am entirely at your disposal."

Annie's cheeks warmed anew. "Forgive me, Mr. Northcott, but are you saying you wish to *help* me with the flower arrangement?"

"That is exactly what I'm saying." He cocked his head. "But only if agreeable to you, of course."

"Oh, yes! I mean, yes, of course." An errant tear slid down the side of Annie's nose and she brushed it away. "That would be most agreeable."

"Excellent." He smiled and, as he had once before on that busy London street, offered her his arm. "Then let's go."

Still not fully convinced any of this was real, Annie hesitated for a moment before she dared to place her hand on it. Immediately, Julian Northcott crooked his elbow around her fingers, his hold firm yet gentle, and sweetly familiar. Just as well, since Annie now felt deliciously lightheaded, as though she'd consumed a tad too much wine. Or perhaps she was, after all, merely trapped in the unearthly realm between sleep and wakefulness. Holding her breath, she made a fist with her other hand and dug her fingernails into her palm till it hurt.

No Lancelot. No faded yellow curtains.

She just needed to be sure.

MISS ANNABELLE FAIRFAX was still in mourning, a fact that demanded the appropriate solemnity. That being so, Julian kept reminding himself to stop grinning like an idiot. But a moment later, he'd forget everything except the fact the young lady was actually walking beside him, her hand tucked into the crook of his arm. And the grin would return. He simply couldn't help it. It was as if he'd found a lost treasure.

Annabelle.

He gazed down at the top of her head as he had once before. No bonnet this time, hiding her curls. No time restrictions, either. At least, none he knew of.

"I must confess, Mr. Northcott," Annabelle began, as they started up the stairs, "I find it strange you have not yet asked me the anticipated question."

"You mean, what is Miss Fairfax doing in Derbyshire?" His grin became a smile. "Flower arranging at Myddleton House, apparently."

Annabelle regarded him, her expression serious. "There's actually a bit more to it than that, sir."

Chagrin dissolved the smile in an instant. "Forgive my levity, Miss Fairfax. I meant no disrespect."

"Oh, no, Mr. Northcott, there's nothing to forgive." Eyes wide and bright with what looked like more tears, she shook her head. "You cannot possibly know all that has occurred since last we met."

"Actually, I think I might be aware of most of it." Julian heaved a sigh, halted on the landing at the top of the stairs, and gently turned her to face him. "I'm aware of the circumstances surrounding your father's death, Miss Fairfax. Again, allow me to offer my deepest sympathy. It must have been terrible for you."

Expressions of confusion and dismay skittered across her face. "How did you learn of it?"

"From the newspaper report."

"Oh my!" Color came to her cheeks as her gaze dropped to the floor. "I didn't realize it had traveled beyond London."

"I'm not sure it did in the way you think," Julian replied, tipping her chin up again. "It's clear we each have things to say, and I thought we might do so while completing your flower arrangement. A pleasing distraction, so to speak."

"Then perhaps I should begin immediately and with a confession," she said, soberly. "The truth is, like you, I have little knowledge of flower-arranging. I came here today with Miss Caldridge, the lady with whom I am lodging. She lives nearby and is regularly summoned to Myddleton House when flower arrangements are required. I accompanied her because I wanted to see the house, that is all. She went off in search of some greenery and left me alone in the gallery. I was awaiting her return when you and the two ladies entered."

Julian heard every word she'd said. He even opened his mouth to respond, but his disarrayed mind was still reveling in the fact that Annabelle Fairfax was no longer lost to him. She was not hiding in London *or* traveling around Europe. She was here at Myddleton House, standing before him in an obscure hallway. The reality of her presence was more intoxicating than wine, and he consumed it without restraint. Breathing in her fresh, floral scent, he studied the face that had occupied his mind for several weeks. Those soft, dark curls, the little beauty spot above a perfectly arched brow, the unforgettable allure of her eyes and, of course, the exquisite lines of her mouth. His gaze lingered a little longer on her lips.

"Mr. Northcott?"

He blinked. "I beg your pardon, Miss Fairfax. I was just thinking about our previous encounter. Much has happened since, obviously." He resisted an urge to reach for her hand and instead gestured down the hallway. "Let's return to the gallery. Maybe Miss Caldridge has already finished the arrangement."

"I hope so," she replied, as she moved into step beside him. "And, if so, she'll be wondering where I am, since I was under strict instructions not to move from that spot. Will the two ladies still be there, do you think?"

"Possibly," he replied, glancing at her. "I expect they're curious to know why you ran off and why I ran after you."

"No doubt." She peered up at him. "May I—forgive me my forwardness—know who they are?"

"Of course. The younger lady is Her Grace, the Duchess of Rothbury, and the older lady is the Countess of Hutton."

"The countess herself?" Annabelle groaned. "Oh, my goodness, I had a feeling that's who she was. I can't believe I ran off like I did. How embarrassing."

"No need to be embarrassed," Julian said. "Like I said, I think we've stirred their curiosity more than anything else."

She heaved a sigh. "I panicked because I feared the inevitability of your questions, sir. I didn't know you'd read the newspaper report. Nor does it tell the whole story, unfortunately. There is yet more to it, most of it unpleasant."

Julian heard the tremor in her voice and silently cursed his disordered thoughts. Attempting to gather his wits yet again, he halted and turned to face her again. "There is more to my side of things as well, Miss Fairfax. Things you should know before we go any further, in fact. To begin, I'm fully aware you left London some weeks ago. What I *didn't* know, till today, was where you'd gone."

Her brows lifted. "But how did you know I'd left London? My departure was not mentioned in the newspaper report."

"Because after I read the report, I went to London intent on paying you a visit," he replied. "That's what I meant earlier, when I said I'd been looking for you."

Those beautiful eyes continued to stare at him for a moment. Then a frown appeared, followed by a brief averted gaze and a chewed bottom lip. "Mr. Northcott, are you saying you went all the way to London just to see *me?*"

Julian winced inwardly at the incredulity in her voice. Given how little time they'd previously spent together, he supposed his admission did sound a little outlandish. "Yes, but you'd already gone by the time I got there." He cleared his throat. "The truth is, Miss Fairfax, I've thought about you often since our brief encounter, though not once did I think I'd actually see you again. Then Josiah, my brother, arrived from London and brought a copy of the *Herald* with him. That's how I learned about what had occurred at the church and I just… I just felt compelled to see you to offer my assistance should it ever be required. Your neighbor kindly directed me to your solicitor, who told me you were traveling abroad and could not be contacted. I had a feeling there was more to it than that, but I also understood he was protecting your privacy. So, I left my card with him and returned to Highfield, none the wiser." He laughed softly and shook his head. "Seeing you here is the answer to a question I'd deemed unanswerable. I can still hardly grasp the reality of it." He gestured with his hand. "But, if all this is in any way discomforting, please say so. The last thing I want is to cause you any additional anguish. You're not obliged to remain here, and you certainly don't have to apologize for anything. You've done nothing wrong. Nothing at all. If you'd prefer to go home right away, I'll arrange for someone to escort you."

She appeared to ponder his words, then, "All that way, just to see me," she repeated, so quietly he barely heard it.

"Yes."

A soft sigh escaped her. "That was so incredibly kind of you, Mr. Northcott. I'm very grateful. And no, you have not caused me any additional anguish. Quite the contrary, in fact. I have often thought of you as well, and never believed I'd see you again, either. That's why seeing you in the gallery today was such a shock. The odds against it must be…"

Julian arched a brow. "Incalculable?"

She smiled. "Unfathomable."

"Dare I suggest, then, that it was somehow fated? And that being so, might we possibly spend some time together whilst I'm here?"

Her expression sobered. "That must surely depend on certain circumstances, sir."

"Such as?"

She parted with a soft sigh. "Well, since it appears you know more about me than I know about you, may I ask you some questions?"

"Of course. Anything."

"You mentioned Highfield earlier. Where, or what, is that?"

"It is my home," he replied. "Highfield Hall, in Yorkshire."

"Yorkshire, yes, that's what I'd understood when we last met." A pensive frown appeared. "Then, why are you here? What is your connection to Myddleton House?"

"I'm a nephew of the earl. My father is his youngest brother."

"The earl who lives here?" Eyes widening, Annabelle pressed a hand to the base of her throat. "Lord Hutton? *That* earl?"

Julian barely managed to hide his amusement. "Yes, *that* earl."

"So, Lady Hutton is your aunt."

"She is indeed. Northcott is our family name."

"I didn't know that, or I would probably have made the connection." She shook her head. "And I cannot help but wonder why the nephew of an earl would show any interest in someone like…"

"In someone like you?" Julian tutted. "Is that what you were about to say, Miss Fairfax? I do hope not."

"Actually, it was, though I was not about to belittle myself." Her chin lifted. "I am neither without education nor means, sir, but our social standing is, you must agree, clearly disparate. I am a physician's daughter, whereas you are—"

"An untitled gentleman who has been bewitched by a physician's daughter?"

That brought a touch of color to her cheeks. "Bewitched?"

"Totally."

"Impossible." She looked at him askance. "You hardly know me."

"Which clearly supports my claim of bewitchment." He shrugged. "What other explanation could there be, other than you have somehow cast a spell on me?"

Annabelle Fairfax's subsequent laughter and the accompanying sparkle in her eyes forged a moment, Julian knew, that would be forever indelible on his memory. In the next moment, however, a concern that had lingered in the back of his mind this entire time pushed itself forward. "I have some questions for *you*, Miss Fairfax, if I may."

"Yes, of course."

He moved closer, inhaling her fresh, floral scent while fighting a growing desire to touch her. "Why did you leave the city? Was it simply to grieve in a more peaceful environment? Or was it because you deemed it too dangerous to stay? I got the impression Archibald Mason was protecting more than your privacy. Has the man you were meant to marry now become a threat to you?"

The brightness in Annabelle's expression had faded as he'd spoken. "My former fiancé has, sadly, proven himself to be possessed of an exceedingly unpleasant temper." she said, "I doubt he would actually hurt me. Hattie disagrees, however, and so does Archibald Mason. They both urged me to leave the city, and I capitulated, mostly because I was too weary to argue against it. But I left with no small amount of reluctance. I was never traveling abroad, though. I never left England."

"I guessed that was the case. And Hattie left with you, I take it?"

"Yes. In fact, she arranged our accommodation. Miss Caldridge is a distant cousin of hers. She didn't come with us today, though. She stayed behind at the house."

"I see," Julian replied, quietly resolving to have a private chat with Hattie with regards to Leopold De Witte. "Well, speaking personally, I'm very glad you capitulated."

"So am I, Mr. Northcott, and not only because of our meeting today. As it happens, I've found some unexpected peace here and do not miss my London home as much as I thought I would."

"I'm pleased to hear it." His fingers furled against the unrelenting temptation to touch her. "And I'm also curious. Has your return to the country awakened additional memories of your childhood experience? Any more recollections?"

"Nothing specific." A slight frown appeared. "Well, other than a vague sense of familiarity now and then." Her expression cleared. "May I ask how long you'll be staying at Myddleton, sir?"

"Till Tuesday morning," he replied, and then shrugged. "Or perhaps, as of today, a little bit longer."

The sound of distant voices drifted down the hallway, followed by the closing of a door somewhere. The interruption reminded Julian that his continued absence had probably surpassed a reasonable limit. "In the meantime, Miss Fairfax, I wonder if I might introduce you to a few members of my family."

She gasped. "Today?"

He chuckled. "Within the next hour, preferably, but if you'd rather not, please say so."

"If circumstances were different, it would be an honor to meet them, but given how I ran off like that... well, what must they think?" She fiddled with one of her ringlets and looked down at herself. "Besides, I fear I'm not exactly at my best."

Julian stopped himself from voicing a direct contradiction and instead searched for a response that would not be conceived as trite. Such things, he knew, were more Josiah's forte; he would undoubtedly snap out an appropriate, poetic response without hesitation. Julian went for simple honesty. "In my eyes, Miss Fairfax, you are absolutely lovely. As to the eyes of others, I expect they will see a beautiful young woman whose attire indicates quite clearly she is in mourning, and I'm certain she'll be afforded the respect she deserves. And, as to your running off like that, I did exactly the same thing without any explanation. Don't worry. I'll do all the explaining when the introductions are made. I guarantee they're curious to find out what this is all about and who you are."

"I'm a physician's daughter, Mr. Northcott."

"I believe we've already established that, Miss Fairfax."

"Are they aware of the newspaper report?"

"No." Julian gentled his voice, wishing he could do more to comfort her. "They know only that your father passed away."

Annabelle inhaled a shaky breath. "Very well, but you should know I would rather you didn't share the details of Papa's death with them at this time. Suffice to say he'd been ill for a good while and then passed suddenly."

"I understand, of course, though I imagine decorum will not allow for too many questions anyway."

"You're probably right." She cringed. "And speaking of decorum, I must warn you, sir, I cannot recall the last time I conversed with an earl and his countess, so I hope I'm able to conduct myself appropriately."

Julian laughed. "I'll give you cues if I think it necessary, but don't worry if you make a mistake. They won't throw you in the dungeon. They're actually very nice people."

"That's what Janet—I mean, Miss Caldridge—said when I asked what the duchess was like..." Annabelle blushed and pressed a hand to her stomach. "I mean...well. That's a relief."

Julian was reminded of the first time they met. She was so affably charming, sweetly innocent, and refreshingly honest. Who wouldn't find her alluring?"

"I mean it, dear lady. There's no need to be nervous." Julian surrendered to his relentless urge, reached for her hand, and brought it gently to his lips. "I'll be beside you the entire time."

CHAPTER THIRTEEN

"THERE YOU ARE, at last," Janet announced, as Annie approached with Julian Northcott. The woman stood alone in the gallery, the buckets of flowers, emptier than before, still at her feet. The flower arrangement had taken visible shape but was obviously not quite finished. As for the countess and the duchess, both ladies had apparently gone elsewhere. Annie gave silent thanks for the reprieve.

Janet spoke again, her voice unexpectedly stern. "I trust you have apologized to Mr. Northcott for your untoward behavior, Annie, running off like that. I have already apologized to Lady Hutton on your behalf, and explained you are not quite yourself due to being so recently bereaved."

The unanticipated reprimand left Annie momentarily speechless and not a little embarrassed. Resentment tightened her throat, but before she could respond, Julian Northcott cut in.

"I do not require an apology, madam," he said, calmly. "Miss Fairfax had a bit of a shock, that is all. As did I, in truth." He smiled down at Annie, which set off the now-familiar flutter in her stomach. "A very pleasant shock, I might add."

"I see." Janet's subsequent smile held little warmth as she directed her gaze, once more, to Annie. "Till today, sir, I was not aware my young guest had met you before. I find it odd, frankly, that she's never mentioned it."

Once again, Annie opened her mouth, meaning to explain,

but Julian Northcott didn't give her the chance. "How long do you anticipate being at Myddleton House today, Miss…" he frowned. "Forgive me. Miss Caldridge, is that correct?"

"Yes sir," Janet replied, her expression still sour. "I expect we shall be finished here by mid-afternoon."

"Good, then we have some time. My reason for asking is because I'm stealing Miss Fairfax away for the next while and was wondering how long I might keep her." He took Annie's hand and tucked it into the crook of his arm once more. "I trust you can manage on your own, Miss Caldridge, for the time being?"

Annie's conscience gave her a nudge. "Um, actually, Mr. Northcott, perhaps I should stay and help Miss Caldridge with the flowers."

"Indeed, sir, I would much prefer the young lady remain with me," Janet said. "She came here to assist me, after all."

Julian's eyes narrowed slightly. "A compromise, then," he said, in a tone that brooked no argument. "Miss Fairfax will spend the better part of the next hour with me, after which time she will return and assist you with whatever work remains. I trust that is agreeable?"

It obviously wasn't, judging by the expression on Janet's face. "As you wish, sir," she replied, giving Annie another sour glance. "I'll see you later, then, Annabelle."

Annie, struggling to find any suitable rejoinder, merely nodded her response. She could not imagine what had got into the woman. She fully intended, however, to find out later. Now was not the time.

"Uh oh," Julian muttered as they headed for the door. "From 'Annie' to 'Annabelle' in less than a minute. I fear things do not bode well for you, Miss Fairfax. But do not lose heart! If you're evicted from your current lodging later today, I'm sure we can find room for you here."

Annie smothered an urge to laugh, which also helped to hide her dismay at Janet's uncharacteristic behavior. "I'm sure Miss Caldridge won't go that far, Mr. Northcott. And I must confess, I do feel somewhat guilty about leaving her."

"You shouldn't." He shrugged. "You told me you have little talent for flower arranging, so tell yourself you're doing the lady a favor by absconding, since you'd probably be more of a hindrance than a help if you stayed. You came here to see Myddleton House and see it you shall."

Annie's conscience refused to be quiet. "But she's been so very kind to me, sir."

"One hour, Miss Fairfax," Julian replied. "That is all I ask. One hour."

THROWING CAUTION TO the wind and acting without afore-thought wasn't like him at all. But then, Julian had never felt like this before, nor could he begin to describe the feeling. Not for the first time that day, he dared to imagine fate had intervened, albeit in a tragic fashion, to ensure his and Annabelle's paths would cross again. To be so fanciful, so fatalistic, was not like him either.

No matter how it came about, whether by the blessings of fate or the paths of misfortune, Annabelle Fairfax now stood beside him in Myddleton's imposing library. Having issued an apology along with a succinct explanation about what had precipitated the events in the gallery, Julian now finished off by introducing Annabelle to his uncle and aunt, propriety demand-ing the initial introduction be made to them.

As Annabelle rose from a perfect curtsey, Lord Hutton peered down at her from beneath his impressive pair of silver brows. "Well now, that's quite the coincidence," he said, in response to Julian's account. "Welcome to Myddleton House, Miss Fairfax. And please accept our condolences on the loss of your father."

"Thank you, Lord Hutton," she replied. "And thank you for allowing me into your magnificent home."

"You're most welcome." He cleared his throat. "Are you

related to the Middlesborough Fairfax's by chance?"

Annabelle blinked. "Er, no, my lord, I don't believe so."

"Hmm. Just as well, perhaps." Lord Hutton appeared to mull for a moment or two. "So, you're staying at Ferndale Grange, eh? Nice little farm. Used to be part of the old medieval estate. Somewhere along the way, it slid into independent ownership." His silver brows knitted together as he glanced away briefly. "Can't remember quite how it all came about. I'll have to read up on it. It's changed hands a few times since then, of course."

"That's very interesting, my lord," Annabelle replied. "I have wondered about its history. It's a charming house."

"Yes, quite." Lord Hutton nodded. "Well, if you'll excuse me, ladies, nephew, I have some correspondence awaiting my attention before luncheon. A pleasure to make your acquaintance, Miss Fairfax. Enjoy your visit." He bowed slightly.

Annabelle inclined her head. "Thank you, my lord."

Lady Hutton stayed where she was, a smile tugging at her lips as her husband wandered off. "There now, my dear," she said to Annabelle. "That wasn't so bad, was it?"

Annabelle smiled also and shook her head. "No, Lady Hutton, not at all. Thank you."

"You're welcome, my dear." The countess then turned her attention to Julian. "You'll find your parents in the conservatory, Julian, and I wouldn't dally if I were you. They'll be sounding the luncheon gong shortly."

"Understood, Aunt, thank you," Julian replied, and presented his elbow once more. "Miss Fairfax?"

"They were very gracious," Annabelle said, as they made their way into the hallway.

"Always are. I told you there was nothing to fear."

"And the library is incredible." She gazed up at the murals as they passed through Myddleton's main entrance-hall. "So is that ceiling. Goodness. Is Highfield Hall as grand as this?"

"No, not quite," Julian replied. "Though it's just as impressive in its own way. It's been in my mother's family for over six hundred years, though the house today bears little resemblance to the original castle."

"It was a *castle*?"

"Once upon a time," he replied. "Drawbridges and dungeons and all that. It was torn down a couple of hundred years ago, and the stones were reused to build the current house. There have been other changes made as well over the years, so it's become something of a glorious hodge-podge. The medieval gatehouse is still standing and there's a ruined watchtower on the moor road. The old chapel still exists in the house and a corner of the cellar is also original."

"It sounds wonderful."

"It is." He stopped himself from suggesting she might see it for herself one day, though he dared to believe she would. There was plenty of time for that, however.

Annabelle appeared to ponder for a moment. Then, "Is it haunted?"

Julian groaned. "My dear Miss Fairfax, I cannot believe you asked that question. Of *course* it's haunted. A ghost or two is mandatory for any historically-burdened house."

She gave him an amused glance. "Are you teasing me, Mr. Northcott?"

"Absolutely not." Biting back a smile, he kept his gaze to the front. "And this is Myddleton's conservatory."

"Heavens," she murmured as they paused at the entrance. "I could never have imagined anything like this. It's extraordinary."

"Yes, it is rather splendid," Julian replied, frowning as he cast his gaze over the jungle of giant palms, exotic ferns, and sweet-scented flowers, searching for his parents. "Ah, there they are, look. Over by the pond."

He felt Annabelle's resistance on his arm. "Who is sitting with them?" she asked. "My goodness, those two young ladies are twins, surely."

"Yes, my sisters, and they're sitting beside my youngest brother. Arthur. The quiet one I told you about."

"Should there not be two more?'

Impressed, Julian glanced at her. "You remembered."

She gave a slight shrug. "I remember everything about that day, sir."

Something stirred beneath Julian's ribs. "As do I," he replied, soberly, "and yes, you are correct. Louisa, my eldest sister, and Maxwell, her husband, are not here, and neither is Josiah. I believe I mentioned him to you already."

"Yes, you did. Do I curtsey?"

"You don't have to. My father should be addressed as 'Captain Northcott' initially and 'sir' after that, and my mother as 'Mrs. Northcott'."

"Right." Annabelle heaved a sigh and smoothed her skirts. "I do believe I was less nervous meeting Lord and Lady Hutton."

"You don't need to be nervous," Julian said. "Come on. I promise they won't bite."

Annabelle didn't quite look convinced as she fell into step beside him.

"Ah, there you are!" Aldous, Julian's father, got to his feet as they approached, prompting those seated with him to do the same. "We were about to send out a search party."

"We were with Uncle Isaac and Aunt Eleanor. Aunt Eleanor told us where to find you." Julian gave Annabelle a surreptitious wink. "Papa, Mama, everyone, may I present Miss Annabelle Fairfax, the young lady I met several weeks ago in London. I had assumed our meeting to be a singular event, but it seems fate has decided otherwise. It turns out Miss Fairfax is currently recuperating a few miles from here following the recent death of her father. Miss Fairfax, this is my father, Captain Aldous Northcott, and my mother, the Honorable Grace Northcott. These two young ladies are my sisters, Miss Evie and Miss Clara, and this young fellow is Master Arthur Northcott, my brother."

"A pleasure to meet you, Miss Fairfax," Aldous said, inclining his head. "And please accept our sincere condolences on the loss of your father."

"Thank you, Captain Northcott," Annabelle replied. "You're very kind. I'm honored to meet you all, and perhaps a little overwhelmed as well, in truth."

To Julian's surprise and delight, Grace stepped forward and took Annabelle's hand. "I'm not in the least surprised, my dear, under the circumstances. Come and sit beside me. Would you like a drink? There's some lemonade left."

"Thank you, Mrs. Northcott, but no," Annabelle replied, a sweet blush on her cheeks as she settled onto the cushioned seat of the large lattice settee. "What a remarkable space this is. I've never seen anything like it."

"It is rather splendid," Grace replied, glancing about. "It's also eternally summer, which is probably why I enjoy it most in the winter, when the weather is miserable and the days short. Sitting in here at such times lifts the spirits. How are you finding the countryside, dear? Have you spent time outside of the city before?"

"I have, yes, and somewhere up here in the north, though I don't remember the actual location," Annabelle replied. "It was many years ago, when I was a child."

Julian, sensing his father's scrutiny, exchanged glances with him. Aldous raised a brow that implied he was equally impressed, and perhaps surprised, by Grace's sweet response to Annabelle. Julian responded with a slight shrug and took his seat beside Evie. Then he watched and listened as his mother's propensity for easy chit-chat proceeded to put Annabelle at ease. Within minutes, the tension on her face disappeared, the stiffness in her shoulders softened, and she settled back, obviously relaxed, into the cushions. Incredulity lifted its head once more. Not in a million years—at least, a few hours ago—could Julian have imagined Annabelle Fairfax would be seated beneath a palm tree in Myddleton's conservatory, having a conversation with his mother. It truly beggared belief.

Evie leaned in. "Your lady friend is very pretty, Jules," she muttered, ventriloquist-fashion through a stiff smile.

"Yes, she is," he replied, quietly. "Why are you smiling like that? Is something wrong with your mouth?"

"You remind me of Jester, my old pony," Arthur said. "Remember him? When it was close to feeding time, he'd stick his nose over the gate and show his teeth."

Seated on the other side of Evie, Clara stifled a giggle. "Don't worry, Evie," she said. "The luncheon gong is going to sound any minute now."

"I doubt they'll have fresh hay on the menu, however," Julian added, which drew another giggle from Clara.

Evie's smile dissolved. "I was trying to be discreet," she said, scowling.

Julian tutted. "Don't know about discreet, but it was definitely amusing."

Evie cocked her head, leaned in again, and peered at him through narrowed eyes. "I'm curious, dear brother," she said, her voice barely above a whisper, "does this mean the musical Miss Aitken has been set aside?"

Julian gave her a stern look. "That's enough, Evie."

A smug smile appeared. "Which means *yes*," she replied, sitting back. "Not that it's a catastrophe, mind you. We're not overly keen, right, Clara?"

Clara gave a nod. "Right."

"What are you chittering about over there?" Grace asked. "Not 'overly keen' about what?"

Evie opened her mouth, but Julian interrupted. "Nothing of note, Mama. Evie is hungry, apparently, so we're speculating about what'll be on the luncheon menu."

Arthur chuckled, Clara snorted, Evie scowled again, and Grace sighed as she turned back to Annabelle. "I understand you are an only child, Miss Fairfax."

"I am, yes," Annabelle replied, giving Julian an amused glance.

"Hmm." Grace winced. "Then I should probably warn you about my children's frequently questionable behavior."

"Indeed," Aldous added. "Please accept our apologies in advance."

Annabelle laughed. "I'm sure they won't be required, Captain. That is—Mr. Northcott—your eldest son speaks very highly of his siblings."

"He does?" Evie leaned forward. "What does he say about me, Miss Fairfax?"

"Nothing at all," Julian said. "I never speak of you individually, Evie. You and your sister are, in my opinion, one entity. When and if I voice an observation, it generally applies to both of you."

"So, what did you tell Miss Fairfax about *us*, then, Julian?" Clara demanded.

"Hmm." He frowned. "I believe I told Miss Fairfax the next Season will undoubtedly be one of the most memorable in Northcott history and that London will never be the same."

Arthur sniggered, while the twins regarded each other for a moment and then looked at Julian. "You did not say that!" they exclaimed, in perfect unison.

There followed laughter all round. "No," Annabelle said, with a shake of her head, "your brother did not say that. The truth is, he hasn't told me anything specific about either of you, or any of his siblings for that matter. But I definitely get the impression he cares about you all very much."

"We quite like him as well." Clara wrinkled her nose. "Most of the time, anyway."

Evie snorted and was rewarded with a disapproving glance from Grace.

"You have no close family at all, Miss Fairfax?" Aldous asked.

"None, Captain," Annabelle replied. "Upon consideration, I suppose I've led a sheltered life, but not an unhappy one. My father made sure I had a broad education. As a child, I had an excellent governess, and my maid, Hattie, has been like a mother to me."

"Do you have a favorite pursuit?" Evie asked. "Do you ride, play the pianoforte, perhaps, or do needlework?"

"Actually, I do recall riding a pony when I was little, though I'm not sure where that was," she replied, frowning. "But my answer must be no, I do not ride. I play the pianoforte rather poorly, but I play anyway because I enjoy it. Needlework is not a favorite pastime, but I pick it up on occasion. I enjoy walking and I love to read. I read a lot, and all kinds of books. My father encouraged it, and he had quite an extensive library. Nothing compared to Myddleton's of course."

"You have that in common with our sister, Louisa," Clara said. "She always has a book in her hands."

"Your brother mentioned her to me." Annabelle glanced at Julian. "She and her husband are not here, though, I understand."

"Louisa is in an interesting condition," Grace explained, "so she and Maxwell thought it best to remain home."

"Ah, I see." Annabelle nodded. "And there is also another brother, I believe."

"Josiah." Aldous shifted in his seat. "He's an artist. Lives in London, prefers it to the country."

Annabelle's eyes widened. "An artist. How fascinating. What does he paint?"

Aldous smiled. "Portraits, mostly."

"Really?" She appeared to ponder a moment. "Are any of them on display here?"

"No. At least, not yet. He specializes in private commissions." Aldous's gaze flicked briefly to Julian. "He's in great demand, apparently."

Immediately, the image of the duchess arose in Julian's mind. He suppressed a smile and wondered, vaguely, where Her Grace was. In her room, most likely, given that His Grace had obviously awoken and vacated the library.

The sound of Annabelle's laughter shifted Julian's focus back to the present, where he watched and listened as the conversation continued around him.

It wasn't possible, he thought, a short while later, to love someone you hardly knew. Someone with whom you'd spent so little time. It simply wasn't possible. So, whatever had taken up residence in an empty corner of his heart couldn't be love. But perhaps it was the prospect of it, or even the precursor to it. Watching Annabelle Fairfax with his family for these past twenty minutes had convinced him that she was exactly where she was supposed to be. She was genuinely animated, her cheeks sweetly pink, eyes bright as she listened, hands moving as she chatted. Not a hint of nerves or shyness remained.

She belonged with them. She belonged with *him*.

Smiling to himself, his gaze drifted away from Annabelle and met that of his mother. She responded to his smile with one of her own and gave her head a slight shake. But it wasn't a contradictory message. Rather, it implied an understanding of what lay behind Julian's recent excursion to London, and perhaps an acknowledgment of what now lay in his heart. At that same moment, as if calling an end to their meeting, the luncheon gong sounded a cacophonous summons.

"Will you be joining us for luncheon, Miss Fairfax?" Grace asked, rising to her feet, with everyone else following suit.

Julian hoped she'd say yes, but expected a refusal, which came instantly.

"It's exceedingly tempting," Annabelle replied, "but I really must return to Miss Caldridge. I promised not to leave her alone with her task. It has, however, been an absolute pleasure to meet you all. Thank you so much for your kindness and hospitality."

Aldous gave a nod. "The pleasure is ours, Miss Fairfax. I'm sure we'll meet again."

"No doubt," Grace added, with a quick glance at Julian.

"Indeed." Julian moved to Annabelle's side. "If you'll excuse me, Mama, Papa, I'll escort Miss Fairfax back to the gallery, or wherever Miss Caldridge happens to be. I won't be long."

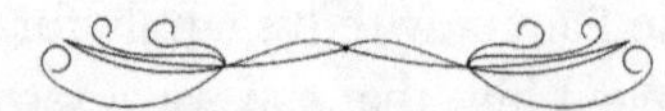

CHAPTER FOURTEEN

FROM EXCITEMENT TO despair to joyfulness, what a day it had been! Annie could hardly make sense of all that had happened thus far, and the day was not quite over yet. She was still with Julian Northcott, still beside him, as they headed down the hallway toward the gallery.

He spoke. "May I call on you, Miss Fairfax?"

At last. The question she had wished for, hoped for. He had asked it softly, almost whisper-like, exactly as Annie might have imagined if she'd been daydreaming about him in a moment of solitude. But this was no daydream. The actuality of it almost robbed her of the ability to reply. It also unsettled her a little, though she couldn't quite fathom why.

"Yes sir, you may," she replied, near breathless with anticipation. "I would like that very much."

"Then I'm already looking forward to it." Wearing a slight frown, Julian cleared his throat. "The thing is, I fear I cannot call on you till Monday. The reason I'm at Myddleton House is because I was invited to my uncle and aunt's party, which, of course, begins tomorrow and continues till Sunday. I could arrange an invitation for you, but given that you are in mourning, I'm not sure it would be appropriate."

"It would not, sir, but thank you," Annie replied, with a shake of her head. "Monday is perfectly fine. I'm already looking forward to it as well."

Minutes later, they paused at the doorway to the gallery and looked over to where Janet stood, beside the completed flower arrangement. Annie felt a slight twinge of anxiety, wondering if there was about to be another unpleasant exchange.

"What do you think?" Julian Northcott gave her a questioning look. "Is it safe for us to approach?"

Annie grabbed the opportunity his question presented. "I think that I shall not allow anything or anyone to spoil my happy mood, Mr. Northcott," she replied. "You may leave me here, sir. I'll be fine. Please rejoin your family and enjoy your luncheon."

He looked doubtful. "Are you sure you don't need a body-guard?"

"Absolutely certain."

"Till Monday then." He placed a gentle kiss to the back of her hand and then glanced over to where Janet stood. "In the meantime, I hope you're back to being 'Annie' again."

She stifled a laugh. "Till Monday," she replied, and watched him walk away from her as he had once before. This time, though, there was no regret, no sense of loss. Quite the opposite.

"I've decided to have luncheon back at Ferndale," Janet said, as Annie approached. "I'm all finished here, so no reason to linger. I assume you're finished hob-nobbing?"

Annie barely stopped herself from snapping out a defensive reply. Why was the woman being so obnoxious? "I thought you had another arrangement to do."

"It's done. You were gone a while." Janet looked past her to the doorway, where Julian had been standing. "Well? Are you staying here or coming back with me?"

"I *had* intended to return with you," Annie replied, keeping her voice purposely soft, "but I believe I shall walk back on my own."

Janet scoffed. "Don't be ridiculous. It's throwing it down."

Annie shrugged. "Not bothered by a bit of rain. Besides, I brought my umbrella."

"You'll catch your death. It's three miles through the fields and almost five by road."

"Fields it is, then." Annie smiled over her growing irritation. "As to my being silly, I'd rather face a three mile walk in the rain than suffer any more of your inexplicable rudeness, especially since I haven't a clue what I've done to merit it. You embarrassed me earlier, Janet. I have since, however, experienced one of the happiest hours of my life with someone I never thought to see again, and I will not allow you, or anyone else, to besmirch that happiness."

Janet heaved an audible sigh, closed her eyes briefly, and pinched the bridge of her nose. "You're out of your depth, young lady," she said. "Trust me. Whatever you believe exists between you and Julian Northcott is temporary at best. His sort do not entertain serious relationships with our kind."

"Our *kind?*" Annie gasped. "What does that mean? Are you saying I'm not good enough for him?"

Janet shook her head. "When it comes to marriage, no, you're not. At least, not in his eyes. Has he said he'd like to see you again?"

"As a matter of fact, yes, he has. He asked if he could call on me."

She frowned. "And you agreed?"

Annie nodded. "He'll be paying me a call on Monday. You misjudge him, Janet, you really do! Julian Northcott is courteous, kind, and attentive. The epitome of a gentleman, in fact. He introduced me to his family today, including Lord and Lady Hutton. Would he have done such a thing if he considered me unworthy?"

Janet's eyes had widened at Annie's words. "He introduced you to his family?"

Annie nodded. "His parents, two of his sisters, and his youngest brother. They were all very gracious. His mother, especially, is just the *sweetest* lady. Would that I had been blessed with such a mother."

Janet opened her mouth as if to reply, but hesitated as if rethinking her response. "Well, I'm… I'm glad they were kind to you, at least," she said at last. "And I suppose I might have misjudged the young man, but I still say his intentions remain to be seen. In any case, you don't have to walk. I apologize for the things I said. I just don't want to see you… that is, I don't want you to be misled or hurt."

"Julian Northcott is not capable of doing either, I guarantee it," Annie replied. "Even Hattie approved of him, and you know how opinionated she can be."

Janet gasped. "Hattie has met him as well?"

"Yes, she was with me that first time." Annie shrugged. "I'll tell you about it on the way home."

The drive home was quiet. At least, Annie did most of the talking, relating the tale, as promised, of how she first met Julian Northcott. Janet had acknowledged the account with an occasional nod or smile but showed little interest otherwise. She seemed preoccupied. Downcast, even. Not unlike the miserable weather. There was something about the sound of rain pelting an open umbrella that made Annie yearn for a cozy chair, a warm blanket, and a cup of hot, sweet tea. Perhaps some of Janet's mood could be attributed to the miserable conditions.

They arrived back at Ferndale to find Hattie a bit rattled.

"Thank God you're home," she said to Annie before any other greeting had been exchanged. "He's been waiting for you this past hour. Left London yesterday afternoon, apparently."

An icy prickle of dread skittered down Annie's spine. "Leopold?"

"Lord love us, no, pet, not him! I wouldn't let that wretch set foot in the place. But it does concern him, I think, though the fellow wouldn't give me any details. Says he wants to speak to you. Must be important, as well, since he's come all this way."

"Who is he?"

"I'd rather he told you himself. He's waiting in the parlor." Hattie looked Annie up and down. "Are your clothes wet? Do you need to change?"

"No, I had my umbrella." Annie pressed a hand to her stomach. What news had this man brought? She suppressed a shiver. "But I'd like a hot tea, please, Hattie."

"Of course." Frowning, she glanced at Janet and then back at Annie. "Is everything all right? How was your visit?"

"It surpassed all my expectations," Annie said, with a pointed look at Janet who, so far, had not uttered a word. "I have so much to tell you, Hattie, but it appears it'll have to wait."

"For now, yes," Hattie replied, still frowning. "Then again, maybe Janet can fill me in while I'm making the tea."

Annie chose not to reply to that. Instead, she headed for the parlor, pausing at the hallstand mirror to check her hair, smooth her skirts, and to take a slow, steadying breath. The parlor door creaked as she pushed it open, and a man, seated in an armchair by the fireplace, rose to his feet. Tall and trim, he was younger than Annie had expected. Smartly-dressed, handsome too, with finely-chiseled features and a wealth of dark blond curls. He held himself confidently, chin slightly raised, spine straight, and shoulders back.

"Good day to you, sir." Annie approached, gazed into a pair of intelligent brown eyes, and inhaled the pungent smell of tobacco smoke. "I'm Annabelle Fairfax, and I'm told you wish to speak with me."

The man's right eyebrow lifted slightly as he nodded his acknowledgment. "A pleasure to make your acquaintance, Miss Fairfax, and please forgive this intrusion. My name is Oliver Taggart. I'm an inspector with Scotland Yard and also Archibald Mason's brother-in-law. I believe he mentioned me to you."

"Yes, he did." Annie's hand went to the locket at her throat. "Has something happened? But of course, it must have, or you wouldn't be here."

"Well, first of all, Miss Fairfax, there's no reason to upset yourself. I'm not here in an official capacity, although what I'm about to tell you does concern a police matter. Please be assured, however, that I do not believe there's any need for alarm where you're concerned. It's simply a matter of caution. Having discussed it with Archibald, we decided I should take the time to visit you in person and relay the information verbally rather than by correspondence. He's taking your privacy and safety very seriously."

"Yes, I know he is, and I appreciate it." Annie gestured to the armchair. "Please be seated, Inspector. I see you've already had some tea. Would you care for more before we continue?"

"No, but thank you," he replied, as he retook his seat.

Annie took the chair opposite. "So, what information do you wish to relay, sir?"

Taggart cleared his throat and opened his mouth to answer, but hesitated as the sound of raised voices drifted in from the kitchen.

Annie heaved an exaggerated sigh. "Be good enough to ignore them, sir. It is simply two opinionated women having a friendly discussion. Please, go ahead with what you have to say."

The hint of a smile came and went. "First of all, Miss Fairfax, I must ask if you have seen or heard from Leopold De Witte since you left London."

"No, sir, I have not. He doesn't know where I am."

"That is my understanding, but I just wanted to be sure he hasn't, somehow, become aware of your location."

Annie tensed. "Is there a possibility he has?"

The man grimaced. "I suppose there is always a possibility of it, albeit highly unlikely. As previously stated, in my opinion there is no cause for alarm."

The sound of raised voices in the kitchen subsided, much to Annie's relief. "Then with respect, sir, why are you here?"

"Simply because you need to be made aware of that unlikely possibility, Miss Fairfax." He cleared his throat. "Archibald Mason's office was broken into several days ago. A few things were stolen, though nothing of great value. The filing cabinet, where Archibald keeps his customer files under lock and key, including yours, does not appear to have been compromised.

Nevertheless, I would ask you to remain vigilant."

Annie absorbed the information. "Thank you, Inspector, I appreciate being kept informed, but while I have no desire to see Leopold again, I still maintain he would do me no physical harm."

"Better safe than sorry, Miss Fairfax," Taggart replied, his eyes narrowing slightly as he regarded her. "That said, I should inform you we are currently investigating another incident that may or may not be connected to Leopold De Witte."

Annie frowned. "What kind of incident?"

"It concerns the whereabouts of Mr. Karl Hoffman, the fellow who interrupted your wedding ceremony. You remember him, of course."

"Of course."

"Well, it would appear Mr. Hoffman has gone missing."

Annie shifted in her seat. "Missing?"

Taggart nodded. "It seems he never returned to Germany. Have you seen him at all since the day of the wedding?"

"I have not, sir. He stayed with me till the police left and the undertaker came to collect my father." Annie's throat tightened. "But he left immediately afterward and I haven't seen or heard from him since."

Frowning, the inspector leaned forward. "I apologize, Miss Fairfax, if you find this upsetting."

"I'm all right, sir, but thank you. Actually, now I come to think of it, I believe Mr. Hoffman gave the police his London address."

"Yes, he did, but he apparently vacated the place three weeks ago without notice."

"I see. How did you learn of this? I mean, that Mr. Hoffman never went home?"

"We recently had a visit from his father. The family received a letter from Mr. Hoffman not long after he arrived in London, but they've heard nothing since. Naturally, they're worr—"

There came a couple of quick knocks on the door, which then

opened, and Hattie entered, balancing a tea tray on one hand, her expression a little pinched. "Here you are." She set the tray down on the small table next to Annie's chair. "Shall I pour?"

"No, it's all right, I can manage," Annie replied. "Thank you, Hattie. That'll be all."

Taggart shifted in his seat. "Actually, I'd like Mrs. Henshaw to stay here for now. What I have to say next concerns her."

Hattie's eyes widened. "Me?"

"Yes," he replied. "Specifically, your visit to Archibald Mason's office and what you told him that day."

"Ah." Hattie fiddled with her apron.

"What *you* told Mr. Mason, Hattie?" Annie shook her head. "I don't recall you telling him anything, specifically."

"That's because you were not present at the time, Miss Fairfax," Taggart said. "And I'm assuming, from your reaction, that Mrs. Henshaw has not yet spoken to you about it."

Annie threw a questioning look at Hattie. "You spoke to Mr. Mason alone? When?"

"That same day," Hattie replied. "If you recall, I left my umbrella behind. I spoke to Mr. Mason when I went to collect it."

Confused, Annie shook her head. "Spoke to him about what?"

Hattie gestured to the settee. "May I sit?"

Annie gave a nod. "Please do."

Hattie perched herself on the edge of the settee and looked expectedly at the inspector. "Do you want me to repeat what I told Mr. Mason that day, sir?"

"Actually, no, Mrs. Henshaw," Taggart replied, after a moment. "I'd prefer to relay what I've been told and for you to correct me if necessary. So, to begin, you told Mr. Mason you'd noticed a ring on Leopold De Witte's finger when he came to visit Miss Fairfax a fortnight after the funeral. Is that right?"

Hattie nodded. "Yes, that's right."

Taggart looked at Annie. "Is Mr. De Witte in the habit of wearing a ring, Miss Fairfax?"

Annie, who had been staring at Hattie, pushed through the fog of confusion in her mind and shifted her attention to Taggart. "Er, yes, he is, actually. A gold signet ring."

Taggart nodded. "Now, Mrs. Henshaw, can you describe the ring you saw when Mr. De Witte visited that day?"

"It was not a signet ring," Hattie said, with a firm shake of her head. "It was a simple gold band with a single jewel embedded in it. A diamond, I assume, since it had no color."

"And I believe you told Mr. Mason you were certain you'd seen that same ring on Karl Hoffman's finger."

Annie gasped. "Surely not."

"That's what I told him, yes." Hattie regarded Annie. "I remember it, because the day of the wedding was cloudy at first, but the sun came through the windows while Mr. Hoffman was, um, while he was checking your poor father for a pulse. The ring he was wearing, or rather, the jewel in it, glinted, and it caught my eye."

A memory flared and Annie gripped the chair arms. "Actually, yes, I noticed that as well."

Taggart nodded. "Good. Please go on, Mrs. Henshaw. Tell me why you suspect Leopold De Witte to be involved in Mr. Hoffman's disappearance."

Hattie cleared her throat. "Because the day Leo came to the house and, in my opinion, threatened Miss Fairfax, he was also wearing a ring. I might not have noticed it if he hadn't lifted his hand to touch your cheek, Annie. You turned your cheek away, remember? That's when I saw it, and I knew I'd seen it before, and I also knew where. It was the same ring I'd seen on Mr. Hoffman's finger." She shook her head. "My blood ran cold, let me tell you. I knew, right then, that I had to get you out of the city, and the sooner the better."

"Why didn't you tell me about this, Hattie?" Annie demanded, but the answer occurred to her as soon as the words left her mouth. "Never mind. I know what you're going to say. You didn't want to frighten me. It just makes me wonder what else you haven't mentioned."

"Just watching out for you, pet," Hattie replied. "That's all."

Taggart appeared to ponder. "What threat was made to you, Miss Fairfax?"

Annie blinked. "Er, if I recall correctly, he said I would live to regret my decision."

"A decision pertaining to…?"

"Renewing our engagement."

"You decided against it, of course."

"Yes."

"Leopold De Witte is a dangerous man, and no one will convince me otherwise," Hattie retorted. "I'd bet everything I own he's responsible for Mr. Hoffman's disappearance."

"But there's no proof, Hattie," Annie pointed out. "It could be he simply owns a similar ring."

Hattie huffed. "In all the times you spent with him, did you ever see him wearing a ring like that?"

"Not that I recall, no, but—"

"Well, there you are then," Hattie replied, with a resolute nod.

"It is speculative at the moment," Taggart said, "but worthy of investigation, I think. Thank you, Mrs. Henshaw. That will be all."

"Ah. Right." Hattie got to her feet. "Well, I'll be in the kitchen if you need me." She gave what Annie knew to be a false smile. "Janet tells me you had an exceptionally interesting day, Miss Annie. I look forward to hearing about it later."

Annie merely nodded. *I swear, Hattie Henshaw, there are times…* "I suppose I should have asked at the beginning, Inspector," she said, as Hattie left and closed the door, "but have you actually spoken to Leopold?"

"Not since he was cleared following the events in the church, Miss Fairfax, no. Unfortunately, like Karl Hoffman, he seems to have disappeared. It could be he's no longer in the country, but we're still on the lookout for him."

"The last time we spoke, he said he'd rented rooms some-where."

"Yes, we're aware of that, but he's no longer at that address."

"Karl Hoffman swore he'd track him down," Annie said. "It was the last thing he said to me at the end of that horrible day."

"And perhaps he did," Taggart replied. "There's a possibility a confrontation took place between these two men, and it did not end well for one of them."

Annie sighed and slumped back in her chair. "What a mess."

"Indeed." Taggart leaned forward. "You've been through a lot, Miss Fairfax. There is just one more issue to be cleared up, then I shall leave you in peace."

Annie frowned. "What issue?"

"Julian Northcott."

Her stomach did a flip. "What of him?"

"You know the gentleman?"

"Yes, I do."

"Are you aware he visited Archibald several weeks ago and enquired as to your whereabouts? Left his card, apparently."

"Yes, fully aware." Annie couldn't help but smile. "I actually spent some time with Mr. Northcott today, at Myddleton House. Our meeting was coincidental. A complete surprise. That's what Hattie was referring to just now."

"Ah, I see. Yes, he's Lord Hutton's nephew, I understand." Taggart rose to his feet and returned the smile. "I didn't think he was a risk. Now, I must take my leave of you."

"You're very thorough, Inspector Taggart," Annie said, rising also, "and I'm very grateful. I appreciate you coming all this way."

"You're very welcome, Miss Fairfax."

"Are you heading back to London today, sir?" Annie asked, as they stepped out into the hallway. "I didn't notice a horse or carriage outside."

"No, I'm staying at the Black Horse Inn tonight. A nice little place. A half-hour walk, maybe. It's nice to breathe some country air, to be honest. Heading back to the city first thing tomorrow." He took his hat and umbrella from the hallstand, and then turned to her, his expression serious. "If you need to contact me for any reason, Miss Fairfax, do not hesitate. You can do so through Archibald or directly through Scotland Yard. In the meantime, to reiterate, though I do not actually fear for your safety, please remain vigilant."

After the inspector left, Annie waited in the hall for a few minutes, seeking calm. The day, so far, had been an endless seesaw of emotions, from dismal to euphoric. She needed to think, to explore all that had happened that day, to put things in perspective or at least into some kind of order.

The creak of the kitchen door pulled her from her reflection.

"He's gone then," Hattie said.

"Yes, he has." Annie moved past her into the kitchen. "And I've no doubt he's wondering what all the shouting was about while we were trying to hold a conversation."

Janet looked up from kneading some dough on the kitchen table. "If I want to raise my voice in this house, young lady, I will do so."

Annie, weary of Janet's persistent mood, opened her mouth to counter the remark, but stopped herself. Her subsequent apology, however, was not without a touch of resentment. "You're quite right, Janet, this is your house," she said, barely managing a smile, "and I apologize for bringing the chaos of my life into it. I assume Hattie has told you why the inspector was here?"

Janet heaved a sigh and looked contrite. "Yes, she has. Are you worried?"

"Not in the least, and neither is he," Annie replied, and gestured to the kitchen door. "Hattie, may I speak with you in private please?"

"I know what this is about, Annie, love," Hattie said, following her along the hallway and into the parlor. "Janet's in a bit of a mood, but it's nothing to worry about."

"I'm more puzzled than worried," Annie replied. "May I know what you and Janet were arguing about earlier?"

"We weren't arguing. We were conversing loudly."

"And I assume it had to do with me and Mr. Northcott."

"Well, yes, actually, it did." Hattie winced. "Janet was a little put out that I hadn't mentioned your previous encounter with the fellow, but I explained I'd had no cause to mention it. I wasn't aware of the Northcott connection to Myddleton House, so not for a moment did I think you'd bump into him there, or anywhere else, come to that. Could have knocked me down with a feather when she told me you'd met him today, not to mention his family. I mean, really, what are the odds?"

"But why is she so against it, Hattie? That is what I cannot understand. I'd have thought she'd be pleased for me, but it seems the opposite is true. She embarrassed me today, speaking to me the way she did in front of Mr. Northcott. I was shocked, frankly."

"Oh, dear." Hattie frowned. "Perhaps she is afraid you're heading for heartbreak, that your Mr. Northcott is not being sincere in his dealings with you."

Scowling, Annie folded her arms. "Well, I hope you told her."

Hattie blinked. "Told her what?"

"That Julian Northcott is a respectable man. A true gentleman, by birth and by nature, and he is simply not capable of taking advantage of a woman."

"Yes, of course I did! That is, I told her he seemed to be an honorable man, and I had no cause to believe otherwise. But she's of the opinion that things are not always as they seem, especially since you're not, it has to be said, the kind of woman who moves in the same circles as he does."

There was some truth in that. Annie had even alluded to it herself in conversation with Julian Northcott, but he'd brushed her concerns aside, and more than once. Annie drew a deep breath and took a moment to search for any remaining doubts of her own, traces of trepidation she might have chosen to ignore.

But they no longer existed, if they ever really had.

"Janet is wrong about him, Hattie, totally wrong," she said, with solid conviction. "And frankly, even though we're currently residing beneath her roof, my relationship with him is none of her business. I think her opinions and fears are misplaced, and I cannot help but wonder why she refuses to believe otherwise. Might it have something to do with what happened to her all those years ago? I confess I find it odd that she never remarried."

Hattie's cheeks colored slightly. "It's possible. It's a bit of a long story, to be honest, and it's not my place to elaborate on it. Suffice to say, certain events took place which broke her heart."

"Which is sad, indeed," Annie replied. "But it makes no sense to assume that what happened to her will also happen to me."

"When it comes to heartbreak, it already has, pet." Hattie shrugged. "Well, in a way."

Annie shook her head. "Leo's behavior shocked and disappointed me, but he didn't break my heart. The collective circumstances of that awful day broke my heart. In any case, I refuse to believe that Julian Northcott is anything less than an honorable man, and while I'll be forever grateful to Janet for allowing us into her home, I think it's time to consider moving back to the city."

"Oh, no." Hattie pressed a hand to her chest. "No, please, Annie, it's not what you… I mean, I'm certain Janet doesn't want you to leave. I have no doubt the inspector would urge you to stay here as well, for the time being at least."

Frowning, Annie rubbed her temple. "Forgive me if I sound ungrateful, Hattie, but I'm getting a little tired of being herded. So far, I've followed everyone's well-meant advice and done exactly as I'm told. I'll grant you, it was probably all for the best, but things have been said today that lead me to believe we've outstayed our welcome here. Besides, all this nonsense really isn't fair on Janet. She's done more than enough, I think. That being so, I intend to write to Archibald Mason and ask him not to renew the lease at the end of September, so we can move back home. In the meantime, I'll ask him to find a suitable place for us to rent in the city."

"Annie, love, please reconsider." Hattie moved closer, her gaze intent. "It's been a strange day. An extraordinary day. Not a day to make rash decisions. I guarantee you're not thinking straight right now and neither is Janet. At least wait till there's news on the whereabouts of Leopold De Witte before you even consider returning to London."

"Wait for how long?" Annie threw her arms wide. "How much time should I allow before I consider it 'safe' to return to London? A month? Six months? A year? No, I'm sorry, but I refuse to be cowed by an irrational fear. And I totally resent the implication I'm not good enough to be taken seriously by a man like Julian Northcott."

"You misunderstand, pet," Hattie replied, softly.

"If I do, it's only because the reasoning makes no sense."

"Janet is worried about you. That's all."

"Well, she has an odd way of showing it." Stifling a sigh, Annie wandered over to the rain-spattered window, hugging herself as she gazed out at the lane and the fields beyond. Despite Janet's assumptions, Hattie's opinions, and Inspector Taggart's suspicions, Annie's optimism would not be subdued. Extraordinary didn't quite sum up the day. It had been unimaginable. Pivotal. A day she would never forget. The persistent shadows of uncertainty and apprehension had all but dissipated. In their place was a promise of happiness and a future she'd only ever dreamed of. Right now, as earlier, she wanted nothing more than solitude. A quiet place to revisit, over and over, all that had happened since that morning. Specifically, her time spent with Julian Northcott and his family.

"I need to think," she said. "I'm going upstairs for a while."

"But luncheon is almost ready."

"I'm not hungry."

"But you haven't eaten since breakfast."

"I'm not hungry, Hattie."

Hattie scowled. "Now you're being childish."

"No, I'm simply doing what I actually want to do." Annie went to the door and opened it. "You're right. It's been an extraordinary day. That being so, I'd like some quiet time to consider all it has held. I'll be down for dinner, I promise."

CHAPTER FIFTEEN

FRIDAY DAWNED IN a more agreeable mood than its Thursday predecessor, though gray skies lingered. The endless crunch of carriage wheels on gravel began mid-morning as a variety of guests arrived at Myddleton House, resulting in a fluctuating wall of wooden and leather luggage outside the confines of the portico.

Julian, who'd barely slept a wink, stood in the window of his aunt's private sitting room and observed the proceedings. Or at least, that was the impression he gave. In truth, his mind was otherwise occupied with thoughts of Annabelle. He wondered if she'd lain awake as well, and what she might be doing at that moment, and was she thinking of him as he was thinking of her.

Evie's voice, laced with a hint of impishness, meandered into his ear. "Are you waiting for someone special, brother dear? You've been standing there for ages."

"Not particularly," he replied, and then corrected himself. "Well, actually, since you took the time to ask, yes, I am. I'm looking forward to seeing Uncle Edmund and the cousins. We haven't all been together since Christmas. What about you, Evie? Is there a secret beau's name somewhere on Aunt Eleanor's guest list? There better hadn't be."

"Wouldn't admit it if there was." She wrinkled her nose at him, turned back to the window, and parted with an exaggerated gasp. "Oh, now, just *look* at this next arrival. What an impressive conveyance! The matched set of grays is absolutely splendid, don't you think? Mmm, that crest is awfully familiar, too. I'm sure I've seen it somewhere before. Whose is it, I wonder? Help me out here, Jules."

Julian watched as the Whitcombe carriage drew to a halt beneath the portico. "You're beyond help, Evie," he replied, somewhat surprised Miss Aitken's arrival had not stirred his conscience in some way. Then again, he'd done nothing to justify any kind of self-castigation. No promises made, no obligations pending. If anything, he felt a measure of relief knowing he had not committed himself, despite the subtleties of parental and peer pressure. He had little doubt there'd soon be a private discourse between the respective parents, during which time a certain situation would be made clear.

"Seriously, though," his sister continued, "aren't you looking forward to telling Miss Aitken she's no longer suited?"

"Evie Beatrice Northcott, for shame!"

Julian glanced over his shoulder to see his mother approaching, her face wearing a rarely-seen scowl. "Oh, you're in for it now, missy," he muttered, giving Evie a nudge. "And rightly so."

"I beg your pardon, Mama." Assuming a contrite expression, Evie gave Julian a retaliatory prod in the ribs. "I didn't mean it."

"I should hope not." Grace peered past them to where the Whitcombe's were exiting the carriage. "There'll be no more such comments, young lady, spoken, whispered, or even thought of. Understood?"

Evie nodded. "Understood, Mama."

Grace regarded Julian. "It's just as well no promises have been made," she said, echoing his thoughts. "Even so, your father and I feel obliged to inform Lord and Lady Whitcombe of your change in circumstance."

"Of course, Mama," Julian replied. "And I'm certain Miss Aitken will not be lacking future suitors."

THE SUN PUT in an appearance that afternoon, tempting a number of Myddleton's guests to venture outside, where they now mingled on the Grand Terrace. Julian, leaning against the balustrade, straightened as Miss Aitken approached. They had spoken briefly at luncheon, which had been a casual self-serve affair, but the opportunity to speak privately had not presented itself.

Till now.

"At last," she said, clasping her hands in front of her as she halted beside him. "I've been waiting for an opportunity to speak with you alone, Mr. Northcott. I'm not intruding, am I?"

Julian breathed in her subtle floral scent. "Not at all, Miss Aitken. Would you care to walk with me, perhaps?"

"A pleasant thought, but I regretfully must refuse." Chewing on her lip, she glanced away briefly and then turned back to him. "Thing is, I am not one for beating around the bush, so I shall simply say that the young lady who has stolen your heart is very fortunate, and I wish both of you much happiness."

Unprepared for such forthrightness, Julian stumbled over a response. "Miss Aitken, I never meant... that is, I hope you don't—"

"You are not obligated to atone, sir," she replied. "After all, there has been no agreement between us. But I have been made aware of a change in the *potential* of our situation. That being the case, I wish to acknowledge it now, so we may place any awkwardness behind us and enjoy this splendid party. I trust this meets with your approval?"

Julian regarded her, his frown dissolving into a resigned smile. "Yes, it does, Miss Aitken, and I appreciate it. Thank you."

She returned the smile, though a touch of regret seemed to linger in her expression. For a moment, Julian had the impression she was about to say something else, but she merely turned and walked away.

Julian filled his lungs and then breathed out, slowly.

"Well, that's that, I presume," said a familiar female voice. "How do you feel?"

"Somewhat winded, but relieved, Your Grace," he replied, turning to see the duchess approaching from behind. "How much did you hear?'

"Just that last part." She moved to his side. "No regrets?"

"None at all."

Head cocked, she regarded him. "You're besotted with this flower girl, aren't you?"

"I am certain of her," he replied, after a moment. "There's a lot to be said for not having any doubts."

The duchess parted with an audible sigh. "Yes, I should imagine there is."

Julian cursed inwardly. "Forgive me, Duchess. That was thoughtless of me."

"Nothing to forgive." She snapped open the parasol she'd been carrying. "No one, male or female, has ever forced me to do anything I didn't want to do. I have calculated, I have considered, and I have made my choices, admittedly not all of them good. Any doubts I've had, however, were set aside in favor of those choices. Now, walk with me, will you? I overindulged a little at luncheon and besides, I believe you owe me a story. I want to hear all about this young lady; where you met, how she came to be arranging flowers at Myddleton, and why she ran off the way she did."

Julian smiled and presented his elbow. "As you wish, Your Grace."

"What a remarkable coincidence," the duchess said, sometime later, as Julian finished his tale. "And so deliciously romantic! I've always been curious about what attracts a man to a woman. And before you say anything, I'm not talking about the frivolous bits, although they do, of course, play a part."

Julian arched a brow. "Frivolous bits, Duchess?"

Eyes twinkling, she peered up at him from beneath her white lace parasol. "The bits that stimulate a man's body rather than his brain."

Julian frowned. "Ah, those bits. There's no denying their appeal, but they're not necessarily an indicator of a woman's authentic beauty."

The duchess gave a soft whistle. "Gracious. I'm beyond impressed, Mr. Northcott."

Julian laughed and paused by one of Myddleton's fountains, its perpetual cascade sparkling like liquid diamonds in the afternoon sun. "I used to play in here as a child," he said. "Invariably got into trouble for it as well. I'm still tempted to jump in, even now."

"I dare you," the duchess replied.

"I will if you will."

"There was a time when I wouldn't have hesitated, but those days are gone, I'm afraid." The duchess settled on a nearby wrought-iron bench and patted the empty seat beside her. "Sit, please."

The sound of laughter, subdued by the fountain's waterfall, drifted down from the terrace and snared Julian's attention. "I think we should consider getting back to the party, Duchess. You'll be missed."

"Nonsense! Just five more minutes." She patted the seat again. "Humor me."

Julian voiced a sudden suspicion. "Is it because I'm his brother?"

She flinched. "What? My wanting to spend time with you? My God, Julian, is that what you think?"

"Just a suspicion. Am I correct?"

"Of course not," she said, scowling. A moment later, the scowl vanished, and she blew out an unladylike breath. "Oh, very well. In the beginning, yes, I'll admit I was drawn to you because of your relationship to Joe. But, as it happens, I genuinely enjoy your company. You don't fawn, which is refreshing. One can grow weary of the sniveling and groveling by those who claim admiration, most of which is insincere."

"Understandable. I dislike pretentiousness myself." He settled beside her. "Does Joe fawn?"

Her mouth quirked as she shook her head. "Your brother neither snivels nor grovels, yet he possesses a remarkable knack of making me feel as if I'm the most important woman under Heaven. And it has nothing to do with my title. But enough about me and your shameless brother. I want to know what it is about this mysterious flower girl who made you choose her over the daughter of a viscount."

"I'm not sure I can give you a precise answer, Duchess." He grimaced. "It's simply that I feel… unburdened, I suppose, when I'm with her. Being in her company is effortless. Natural. There's no pretense, no doubts. I enjoy her intelligence, her forthright-ness, and her naivety. Physically, she is lovely, but she is also beautiful in all the other ways that matter."

"An authentic beauty."

"Yes."

"Miss Aitken never stood a chance," the duchess mused.

"Under the circumstances, no, she didn't."

"And it seems the family is in favor?"

"I have no reason to believe otherwise." His mouth quirked. "Granted, my aunt and uncle were bound to be gracious. They always are. The stumbling block may be my grandmother, who probably won't put in an appearance here till Monday, when things have quieted down. As for my immediate family, I'd venture to say they approve. My mother trusts my judgment, at least."

"Then it had better not be misplaced." The duchess rose to her feet. "So, when will you next see this young lady of yours?"

"Monday," he replied, rising also. "I'm here till Tuesday but I may stay a day or two longer."

"I needn't ask why. How old is the young lady? Will there be a chaperone?"

"I'm not sure of Annabelle's age, but it's certain she'll be chaperoned, probably by her ever-vigilant maid." An idea slid into his head, and he looked back toward the terrace. "Unless…"

The duchess followed his gaze. "Unless?"

"Just considering another possibility. Perhaps I'll invite the twins to join us. Annabelle's maid is a little over-bearing, and the other lady who was here yesterday—Janet is her name, I believe—made it quite clear she disapproved of my being anywhere near Annabelle. Not sure why." He frowned. "I hope she hasn't had a miserable time because of it."

CHAPTER SIXTEEN

T HE PAST TWO days at Ferndale had been disquieting, as if a pall had settled over the house. Mealtimes had been strained, with conversation polite to the point of insipid, any and all references to the Thursday events at Myddleton House avoided.

Janet had remained subdued and distracted much of the time, as if her mind was elsewhere. Hattie's blatant attempts to lighten the prevailing mood, in Annie's opinion, only served to accentuate the gravity of it. Even Ruffy seemed to sense the change, judging by his quizzical expressions, hesitant tail-wags, and the soft little sigh whenever he settled into his basket.

When talking to Hattie, Annie maintained that Janet was growing weary of their presence and that they had outstayed their welcome. Hattie insisted that wasn't the case, but Annie remained adamant about returning to London. Her letter to Archibald Mason now sat in a sealed envelope on the hall table with the other outgoing mail, awaiting delivery to the local postmaster on the morrow.

Without providing a reason, she had advised Mr. Mason of their intent to return to the city and asked that he not renew the lease on the house at the end of September. She'd also asked him to recommend some suitable rental accommodation should she need it before the house was vacated. Writing the letter had been a lesson in regret and disappointment, her smudged signature due to a sneaky tear that had dodged a swipe of her hand and splashed onto the paper.

Yes, indeed. The last couple of days had been unsettling. It didn't help that Annie's emotions ranged from dizzying happiness to regret and confusion. Grief, too, was still very much in residence. Leaving Ferndale would certainly be a wrench on her heart, for she'd come to love the place. But something about Janet's sudden change of mood was troubling. Annie had the distinct impression things had been left unsaid, and she feared the situation might deteriorate further. That being so, she'd endeavored to keep conversation light and polite, avoiding any mention of her Monday arrangement with Julian Northcott. It was akin to walking on eggshells. And she wearied of it.

Now, on this quiet Sunday evening, Annie found herself alone in the kitchen with Hattie and asked a question that had been niggling her for the past three days.

"Do you think Janet will allow Mr. Northcott entry to the house tomorrow? I feel obliged to ask, since it seems clear she does not approve of him."

Hattie looked at Annie as though she'd grown an extra head. "Well, of course she'll allow him entry! Good grief, child, must I keep telling you? Things are not as they seem. Janet is merely… well, let's just say, recent events have stirred up some painful memories, that's all."

"Painful memories you won't share with me."

"Because it is not my place to do so."

"Which leaves me with little choice but to make assumptions."

Hattie heaved a sigh. "Just don't misjudge her, pet. She wants only your happiness, as do I."

"Not the impression she gave me at Myddleton House last Thursday."

"You may have misinterpreted her meaning. Anyway, we've already been over this. Now, since you haven't mentioned it at all, I must ask. Are you looking forward to tomorrow?"

Annie suppressed a sudden shiver of excitement. "I can hardly wait."

"How long will the fellow be staying at Myddleton House?"

Annie felt a touch of pleasurable warmth in her cheeks. "If you mean Julian Northcott, he'll be staying till this Wednesday, I believe."

"Yes, well, don't imagine for a moment the two of you will be galivanting all over Derbyshire without a chaperone," Hattie said, raising a brow. "Who happens to be me, by the way."

Annie frowned. "Once again, Hattie Henshaw, you forget yourself. You're welcome to make suggestions and recommendations for my consideration, but you have no right to give me orders or tell me what to do."

"I am fulfilling a promise I made to your mother, young lady, and that was to ensure your safety and well-being. When it comes to your spending time with a man—*any* man—that promise preempts any and all of your arguments against it."

Annie scoffed. "Are you suggesting Julian Northcott is a threat to my honor?"

"Not unless he argues against my intent to chaperone. Should that be the case, then yes, I would absolutely see him as a threat, for it would imply your honor is of no concern to him."

Annie opened her mouth to respond, but could not, in truth, argue with Hattie's logic. "Oh, very well," she said. "But will you at least try to be polite?'

Hattie's eyes widened. "What on earth do you mean? I'm always polite."

The outer kitchen door opened and Janet, with Ruffy at her heels, stepped inside carrying a basket of freshly dug carrots. "It's a bit chilly out there tonight." She set the basket on the table and looked from Hattie to Annie. "Am I interrupting something?"

"No, not at all." Annie bent to pet the dog and then rose to her feet. "I was just about to go to bed."

"But it's barely eight o'clock," Janet said, mildly. "I thought we might spend some time at the piano. It's been a while since we had a musical evening."

"Now, that's a lovely idea. Don't you think so, Annie?" Hattie gave her a pleading look. "I can make some cocoa for us."

Ready to offer up an excuse, Annie opened her mouth but hesitated and instead summoned up a smile. She doubted she'd be sleeping much that night anyway. "All right, yes," she said, nodding. "It is a lovely idea."

A little more than two hours later, Annie clambered into her bed, turned down the lantern, and snuggled beneath her blankets. The evening *had* been pleasurable, entertaining, and also surprising. This wasn't the first musical evening she'd enjoyed at Ferndale, so she was fully aware Janet played the piano, What she hadn't been aware of, till tonight, was that Janet could also sing, and quite beautifully as well.

In any case, a semblance of harmony, other than the musical kind, seemed to have been restored beneath the house's ancient eaves. And that meant Annie could devote her entire focus to the morrow and what it might bring. How could she possibly hope to sleep? Yawning, she closed her eyes, snuggled deeper into her covers, and hugged herself, imagining it was Julian Northcott who held her.

When next she opened her eyes, it was to the sound of Lancelot's unmelodious racket from outside her window… and a song from the kitchen. Annie, shocked she'd actually slept the night away, rubbed her eyes and stretched out beneath her covers. She frowned slightly, for the song Janet was singing sounded vaguely familiar, though she couldn't quite place it. In the next moment, however, both Lancelot's crowing and Janet's song were totally disregarded. Monday had arrived, which meant Julian Northcott would be calling on her that afternoon.

With a squeak of delight, Annie scrambled out of bed, pulled the curtains aside, and pushed the window open. "Perfect," she whispered, gazing out at a clear dawn sky infused with the rosy glow of sunrise. "Absolutely perfect."

CHAPTER SEVENTEEN

"Y OU LOOK VERY dapper, brother mine." Evie folded her arms and raked another gaze over him. "Very dapper indeed."

"Yes, you do, dear," his mother said.

"Thank you, Mama, Evie," Julian replied.

Clara sidled up to him, leaned in, and sniffed, blatantly. "Hmm, you smell quite nice as well, Jules. Not too overpowering. I'm sure Miss Fairfax will approve."

"And thank you, as well, Clara." Julian frowned. "I think."

The Dowager Lady Hutton, who was observing the proceedings from a nearby settee, made a sound that surely epitomized disapproval. "I despair of our young people today," she said, with a shake of her head. "I truly despair."

"Why, Grandmama?" Julian asked, already knowing the answer.

"Sniffing?" She scowled at Clara. "Good Lord, child, we are not dogs."

Clara cringed. "My pardon, Grandmama. But Julian will be sitting beside Miss Fairfax in the carriage, so I just wanted to make sure he smelled... well, *nice*."

The Dowager's lips thinned. "I should hope they are not so glued to each other that such an assessment can be made."

"Don't worry, Grandmama," Evie said, waggling a brow at Julian. "Clara and I will make sure they behave. Are you ready to go, Jules? It doesn't do to keep a lady waiting."

Julian glanced at the clock. "Yes, perhaps we should," he said. "The carriage will be here any minute."

"And where are you taking this young lady?" his grandmother asked.

"Thought we'd take a ride to the Roman bathhouse ruins, Grandmama, down by the river," he said. "There's a pleasant walk along the riverbank with bench seats here and there."

"Along with clouds of midges," his grandmother responded, shuddering visibly. "You'll be eaten alive."

Julian exchanged a brief amused glance with his mother. "I hope not," he replied. "Right-oh, let's go."

"Enjoy," his mother said. "I shall look forward to hearing all about it later."

"Do you think she'll mind us coming with you?" Clara asked, as they headed out into the hallway.

"Who?" Julian glanced at her. "Miss Fairfax or her maid?"

"Well, both, I suppose."

"I don't think Miss Fairfax will mind at all." Julian barely suppressed a smile. "Her maid might not be too happy, though."

"You do realize, Clara, that we're being exploited by our darling eldest brother," Evie said, slowing to a halt. "Although actually, now I come to think of it, it puts us in an advantageous position."

Julian halted too and turned to face Evie. "Meaning what, exactly?" he asked, hands on hips.

"Meaning compensation, exactly." Evie gave him an impertinent smile. "It seems only fair we be paid for our chaperone services today, wouldn't you agree?"

"Hmm, let me think about that." Julian grimaced and scratched his jaw. "There. Thought about it. It seems I shall have to put up with Miss Fairfax's maid after all. Have a nice afternoon, my dears." With that, he turned on his heel and walked on, smiling to himself.

"No, Julian, wait," Clara cried, scurrying after him. "It was

Evie's idea, not mine. I don't want to be paid. I just want to go with you."

Julian gave a nod. "Thank you, Clara."

"Traitor," Evie said.

"Imp," Julian responded. "Are you coming, or not?'

"Well, of course I am." Evie hurried to catch up. "Wouldn't miss it for the world."

Julian gave the twins a sideways glance. "Just don't make me regret my decision, either of you."

ANNIE HAD SPENT the past hour installed on the window seat in the front parlor, breath misting the glass, eyes fixed on the lane. She wasn't quite sure what to expect. A carriage of some sort, certainly. But she hadn't quite imagined a sleek, blood-red landau, open to the skies and being pulled by two magnificent bays. And not for a moment had she considered Julian Northcott might be bringing someone with him. Any nervousness Annie might have had completely evaporated at the sight of the twins. She pressed her fingers to her lips, stifling a giggle of delight.

"Mr. Northcott is here," she called, and slid off the window seat to smooth her skirts. Ruffy, perhaps hearing the clip-clop of horses' hooves, tore into the room, leapt onto the window-seat, and set about barking a welcome. Hattie wandered in a moment later, untying her apron as she came to peer out of the window.

"Goodness, what a handsome carriage," she said and then frowned. "Has he brought someone with him?"

"It would seem so," Annie replied. "They're his sisters, the Misses Evie and Clara."

"But the carriage only seats four," she said, looking at Annie. "Where will I sit? Not up there with the driver, surely."

"I don't think you need accompany me now, Hattie." Annie shrugged. "I'm going out to greet them. Where's Janet?"

"I'm here," Janet replied, from the doorway. "I'll invite them in. They may like a little refreshment before you go off to wherever it is you're going."

"Yes, they may. Thank you." Annie felt a touch of relief. Though it remained somewhat detached, Janet's gentler mood had continued from the previous night.

"Well, I'm not sure I approve of this arrangement." Hattie, still frowning, followed Annie from the room. "It's not how it's done."

"It's not how you *thought* it would be done," Annie corrected, "and, truthfully, neither did I. It appears to be a family outing to which I'm invited. I met Miss Evie and Miss Clara last week, Hattie. They're fine young ladies."

Janet opened the door and stepped out. Annie, following, shaded her eyes as the driver pulled the horses to a halt. Julian stood and gave Annie a smile that went straight to her heart.

"Good day, Miss Fairfax, ladies," he said, looking at Hattie and Janet before practically leaping down from the carriage. His gaze, and his smile, went to Annie again and rested there for a moment. "As you've no doubt noticed," he continued, "I am not alone. Allow me to introduce my sisters, Miss Evie and Miss Clara. Evie, Clara, this is Miss Caldridge and…" he hesitated as he regarded Hattie. "Forgive me, madam, but I never did learn your name."

"Mrs. Henshaw," Hattie said, with a sniff.

"Well, it's a pleasure to see you again, Mrs. Henshaw," Julian replied, and gave the twins a nod. "Evie, Clara?"

"Pleased to meet you," the twins said, in perfect unison.

"It's nice to see you again, Miss Fairfax," Clara said.

"Likewise, to both of you," Annie replied. "I wasn't expecting this. It's a lovely surprise."

"Welcome to Ferndale Grange, Mr. Northcott." Janet stepped forward. "Would you and your sisters care to come in for some refreshment before you continue with your outing?"

Julian barely hesitated. "Thank you, Miss Caldridge, that

would be most agreeable. A pleasant start to our afternoon." He gave Annie another smile. "How are you today, Miss Fairfax?"

"I'm very well, Mr. Northcott, thank you." An understatement. At that precise moment, Annie was sure she'd never felt quite so happy. "Was the party a success?"

"It was, indeed," he said, helping Evie and Clara exit the carriage. "Though I confess I was looking forward to this outing the entire time."

Clara let out a squeal at the sight of Ruffy. "Oh! What a sweet little dog. Is he friendly?"

"Very friendly," Janet replied, "though a little rambunctious at times."

"Which is a fine description of my sisters, I think," Julian said, winking at Annie. Everyone laughed except Evie, who glared at her brother for a moment before surrendering to a smile.

"Goodness," Hattie muttered. "It's as well they wear different colored dresses. Never tell them apart, otherwise."

What followed was a half-hour of sheer pleasantness. Annie watched in quiet delight as Julian and the twins engaged Janet and Hattie in easy conversation. Even Hattie, who'd been a little aloof at the start, lost the tightness around her mouth. As the visit drew to a close, Annie felt Janet's gaze on her and met it. The grave expression on the woman's face vanished in the blink of an eye, replaced by a smile that surely implied approval. Annie hoped it also indicated an end to the tension of the past few days.

"It's a lovely spot by the river," Janet said, as they wandered down the garden path to where the carriage awaited. "The ruins are fascinating. I think you'll enjoy them."

Annie nodded. "I cannot wait to see them."

"Enjoy yourself, pet," Hattie said.

"I'm already enjoying myself, Hattie," she replied, thinking she could never have imagined such a perfect start to their afternoon jaunt.

"And please be careful," Janet added. "Don't fall in the river!"

"Never fear, ladies," Julian said, taking Annie's hand to help her into the carriage. "I promise I'll have Miss Fairfax back before dark."

✑

"THE VISIT WENT well, I think." Julian closed his fingers against the fading tingle of Annabelle's touch as the carriage set off down the lane. "A pleasant start to our outing."

"The visit went *very* well," Annabelle replied. "I could not have wished for better."

"Told you so." Evie gave her brother an impish smile. "Clara and I can behave ourselves when we want to."

"There should never be a question of wanting to," Julian replied. "And, since the day is not yet over, I'll reserve judgment on your behavior for the time being, but I have to say, so far so good. Keep it up."

"I've decided I'm going to ask Papa if I might have a dog," Clara said, wriggling in her seat. "A little one, like Ruffy."

"I believe there's a lady in the village who has some puppies for sale," Annabelle replied. "Very similar in appearance to Ruffy, I'm told."

Julian barely stifled a grin at Annabelle's implication. "The answer is 'no'," he said, as Clara opened her mouth to speak. "We are not going to look at puppies today."

"Tomorrow, then?" Clara asked.

"We'll see," Julian replied.

Evie nudged her sister. "Which means 'yes'."

As the twins continued to discuss the likelihood of acquiring a puppy, Julian leaned a little closer to Annabelle. "I hope you approve, Miss Fairfax," he said, softly, "of my inviting the twins."

"I most certainly do," she replied. "They are so much fun."

Julian winced. "Well, that's one way of describing them."

She laughed. "No, really, Mr. Northcott, it's perfect. Hattie is a dear, and she means well, but she can be a little…"

"Fierce?"

Annabelle laughed again and cocked her head. "She means no harm. In any case, it seems you won her over today. Miss Caldridge, as well."

Julian's mouth quirked. "Did I?"

"You know you did, sir."

Yes, he knew, though he'd merely been himself, no pretense, no charades. Unlike, he suspected, the two women in question who, in his opinion, were not quite all they seemed to be. The first time he'd met Hattie Henshaw, he'd felt it. A sense of covertness, specifically when she'd denied knowing the location of Annabelle's childhood exodus to the north of England. That same feeling had arisen when he'd met Miss Caldridge, or rather, encountered her in the long gallery.

"They're merely protective of me," Annabelle added. "Especially Hattie."

No, Julian thought, it was more than that. Having just seen the two ladies together, he was more convinced—and intrigued—than ever. He'd surreptitiously watch the looks the women had exchanged during that half-hour. It was a shared language, silent, but well-practiced, the meaning known only to them. Annabelle was either oblivious to it or misread it completely.

He twisted in his seat, facing her. "How long have you known them?"

Annabelle's brows lifted slightly. "Hattie and Jan... er, Miss Caldridge? I've known Hattie all my life. That is, for as long as I can remember. I'd never met Miss Caldridge till we arrived here last month. I didn't even know she existed, actually, although Hattie insists she mentioned her to me in the past. Perhaps she did, but I have no recollection of it."

"So, Miss Caldridge is related to Hattie?'

"Yes. A distant cousin, apparently. Why?"

"Just curious," Julian replied. "They seem very close."

"They are." A frown appeared as Annabelle looked down at her lap. "Actually, Mr. Northcott, I should tell you that I intend to return to London, and sooner rather than later. My letter to Mr. Mason was mailed this morning. In it, I asked he not renew the lease on the house at the end of September and perhaps suggest rooms I might rent should I return to London before then."

"May I ask why? I mean, you seem to be happy here."

"Oh, I am." The frown vanished and a slight flush arose in Annabelle's cheeks. "And more so since last Thursday."

Julian inclined his head. "I do believe we have that in common, Miss Fairfax."

She smiled and then the frown returned. "But I'm beginning to believe my stay at Ferndale Grange has run its course. Miss Caldridge has been rather quick-tempered with me of late."

"From Annie to Annabelle in less than a minute?"

Annabelle chuckled. "Yes, exactly, but it's not just that. Truth is, this was only ever meant to be a temporary situation, and I think it's time I returned to the city."

Julian voiced the one major concern he had. "Is it safe to do so, Miss Fairfax? I know I've asked you this before, but might Leopold De Witte be a threat to you?"

"Well, actually, there has been a development since we last met." Annabelle regarded the twins, who were practically nose-to-nose while discussing something they obviously found amusing. "But I'd prefer to tell you about it when and if we get a moment alone."

A cold hand wrapped itself around Julian's heart. "We last met only three days ago. Are you saying there's been a development since then?"

"Mr. Northcott, please." She glanced at the twins again. "I'd rather wait for a more suitable moment."

"Then tell me this much for now, at least," he said, his voice little more than a whisper. "Are you in danger, Annabelle?"

Her eyes widened at the use of her Christian name. "No sir, I don't believe so."

Julian searched her face for any hint of fear or uncertainty, but found none. Drawing breath, he lifted her hand to his lips and held it there for a moment. That is, until the sound of an exaggerated and unladylike clearing of the throat came from the opposite seat, its intent quite clear. Julian smiled against the back of Annabelle's hand and then released it. "Perhaps we should have invited Hattie after all," he said.

Annabelle laughed. "No. I much prefer this arrangement."

Julian looked over at Evie, who was regarding him with an expression more befitting their grandmother. "Just doing my job, brother dear," she said, wrinkling her nose.

"I appreciate that, Evie," Julian replied, his tone serious.

"Thank you," she said. "I think."

"Actually, Miss Fairfax, our brother would never behave inappropriately." Clara gave her sister a sideways glance. "Evie was just making a point."

"And relished doing so, apparently," Julian added, trying not to laugh. "But thank you, Clara."

"I know he wouldn't," Annabelle replied, glancing at him. "He's an honorable man."

Julian grimaced. "All right, this conversation is becoming decidedly uncomfortable. How about we just acknowledge the fact that I'm a prince, and then change the subject."

"How about we just change the subject?" Evie retorted, prompting laughter all round.

At that moment, the carriage turned onto a narrow stone bridge which spanned the river. Annabelle straightened and sat forward. "Oh! What is that?"

"That," Julian replied, following her line of sight, "is what used to be a Roman bathhouse."

CHAPTER EIGHTEEN

THE ANCIENT STONES, glowing like pale gold in the sunlight, felt warm beneath Annie's touch. Little remained of the Roman ruin, and much of what did had been claimed by the relentless clutches of nature. Still, it wasn't too difficult for Annie to imagine the walls newly erected, and inhabited by those whose empire, at that time, had encompassed most of the known world. She could certainly understand why the occupants had chosen this spot. It was idyllic, romantic, and perhaps, these days, a little bit haunted by spirits of the past. Then again, the original inhabitants had likely placed more value on the proximity to the river.

A horse nickered, drawing Annie's attention to where Julian stood talking to Molesworth, the coachman, who had steered the horses to a shady spot by the bridge. The twins, meanwhile, were standing on the riverbank nearby, heads bent, chatting quietly about heaven knows what. Julian would likely suspect them of plotting some wild escapade, though he'd already told them to behave themselves and more than once. No, he hadn't *told* them, exactly. He'd begged them, albeit with a threatening undertone.

Smiling to herself, Annie shifted her gaze back to the carriage to see Julian approaching. As their eyes met, he gave her his familiar smile, the one that seemed to be reserved solely for her.

"What do you think, Miss Fairfax?" He glanced around. "I've always liked this spot, personally."

"It's beautiful, sir," she replied. "Worthy of being captured on canvas if it hasn't been already. I don't suppose you happen to know any artists, do you?"

Julian appeared to ponder. "Hmm, as it happens, I believe I do. I also have a suspicion he's familiar with this place. In fact, if memory serves, he once fell in the river." He gestured. "Over there, by the steppingstones."

Annie laughed. "Really?"

"Really. Which reminds me, where are…?" Julian looked around again. "Oh, there they are. Plotting, by the looks of it. Lord help us."

Annie chuckled. "If you don't mind me asking, may I know their age? They're so petite, it's hard to guess."

"They'll be eighteen in January, but they were born several weeks earlier than expected and were, consequently, very small and fragile. The attending physician was adamant they wouldn't survive, but they proved him wrong, thank God. My mother was born several weeks early as well, and she also survived against the odds. There's more to that story, actually, but I'll save it for another time. In any case, it seems they inherited Mama's tenacity." He cast a fond glance at the twins. "They would try the patience of a saint, but I'll always maintain the world is a better place with them in it."

"I don't disagree," she replied. "Have they ever fooled you into thinking one was the other?"

"No, and they never will. I always know which twin I'm talking to. That's not to say they're incapable of fooling someone else, mind you, though I don't think they've ever attempted it."

"Well, I think they're wonderful."

"They have their moments." He gave her a wry smile. "I can't decide whether I'm dreading this next Season or looking forward to it. It'll be interesting, of that I have no doubt."

"This will be their first?"

He nodded. "It was supposed to be last year, but other things took priority. Right now, however, my priority is to spend time with you and to not waste a minute of it. So, my dear Miss Fairfax, would a walk along the river be in order? To begin, anyway."

"It would indeed, Mr. Northcott," Annie replied, wondering vaguely what *other things* had taken priority.

Julian glanced back at the twins and presented his arm. "Come on. Let's see how long it takes before they notice."

Annie gave him a sideways glance. "I'm beginning to think you're just as mischievous as they are, sir."

"Worse actually." He grinned. "I like to test them occasionally. Can't help it."

They hadn't even taken a dozen steps before a couple of indignant shouts carried through the air.

"Most inappropriate," Evie said, panting as she and Clara caught up.

"Yelling like that in public? Yes, I agree." Julian scowled. "What must people think?"

"Not what Evie meant," Clara said, her hand pressed to her chest.

"And there's no one here except us," Evie pointed out. "And Molesworth, of course, but he won't care."

"Miss Fairfax and I were never out of your sight," Julian said. "Not for a moment."

Clara huffed. "But you didn't tell us you were leaving. We might not have noticed your absence till after you'd disappeared into the woods."

Julian shook his head. "This chaperone business works both ways, Clara. I wouldn't actually have gone off and left you by yourselves."

"So you say, but we have no way of knowing that now, have we?" She pouted. "We'd have been quite alone."

"Except for Molesworth," Evie pointed out. "Not really fair on him, though."

"God, give me strength," Julian muttered.

"You started it, sir," Annie said, before she could stop herself.

"Aha! There, see?" Clara's face lit up. "Even Miss Fairfax is on our side."

"Serves you right, brother," Evie added, picking up her skirts and brushing past him. "Thank you, Miss Fairfax."

Julian gave Annie an incredulous look. "I can't believe you said that."

Annie feigned a serious expression. "We women must stick together, Mr. Northcott."

"Indeed we must," Clara said, brushing by them as well to catch up with Evie. "*Brava*, Miss Fairfax."

Julian's expression softened and, for a few minutes, they carried on without speaking. Annie glanced at him, puzzled by his sudden silence. Surely he wasn't upset because of what she'd said. But then he paused on the path and turned fully to look at her, the hint of a frown appearing. Annie felt a brief jolt of dismay and tried to read the expression in his eyes. Perhaps he was upset, after all.

His frown vanished. "Please don't take this the wrong way, Miss Fairfax," he said, taking her hand in his, "but bumping into you on the street that day was one of the best things I have ever done."

All traces of dismay vanished, and a pleasant warmth came to Annie's cheeks. "And I, sir, have never been so thankful to have been literally swept off my feet," she replied.

Julian's mouth curved into a smile as they set out once more, his hand still holding hers. Annie glanced down at their joined hands, then at the twins, and then back up at him in silent question.

"They're not looking." He squeezed her hand gently. "If they do, I shall release you. But should the opportunity again present itself, I will reach for your hand once more. Providing, of course, you have no objection."

"None whatsoever, sir." Annie's heart fluttered, leaving her almost breathless.

The path wound its way through the woods, hugging the

riverbank for the most part. It was a pleasant stroll through dappled sunlight, the air cooler beneath the forest canopy, the river's gentle flow calming to the spirit. A few midges made their presence known here and there, but nothing too disagreeable. The twins carried on with their chatter while Annie listened, with fascination, to Julian's tale of his uncle who, having been thought lost at Waterloo, had recently been discovered in a charitable house by Julian's sister. It was a remarkable tale that drew tears to her eyes. That a man, so gravely wounded, had finally come home more than thirty years after riding off to war, was nothing less than a miracle.

"He was the reason the twins' debut into society was delayed. Mama wasn't happy being away from Highfield for long periods, so my parents were back and forth between London and Yorkshire a few times. My cousin Catherine has offered to take the twins under her wing this coming Season, for some of the time at least."

"Do you enjoy it?" Annie asked.

"The Season?" Julian appeared to ponder a moment. "Yes, actually, I do. I'm always happy to return to Highfield, though."

"Here's the footbridge," Clara called over her shoulder, prompting Julian to release Annie's hand. "Are we crossing it?"

Annie eyed the rickety bridge with some consternation, but said nothing.

"No, I don't think so," Julian replied. "I'm not convinced the bridge is safe, and the path on the other side isn't well suited to skirts and petticoats. It's probably best we turn back."

"Good," Evie said, "because I'm starving."

"Where do you walk, Miss Fairfax?" Clara asked, as they set off back. "Are there some pleasant footpaths to be explored in the vicinity of that charming house?"

"Yes, actually, there are," Annie replied. "Freya's Farewell is a favorite of mine. Perhaps you know of it? It's a bit of a climb, but well worth it. The view from the top is incredible. You can see Myddleton House way off in the distance. That was how I first saw the place, actually."

"Freya's Farewell," Evie repeated, as she and Clara glanced at each other and then back at Annie. "No, never heard of it."

"Neither have I," Julian said. "An odd name. I suspect there's a story there."

"With a sad origin, I'm afraid, though Miss Caldridge said it's probably untrue. There's a rocky ledge on top of the hill and a young woman named Freya supposedly threw herself off it when the man she loved abandoned her."

Evie's eyes widened. "Oh, how tragic. We must visit it, Julian."

Clara nodded her agreement. "How about tomorrow?"

"If you wish and weather permitting," Julian said. "Though I cannot help but wonder if you'd be so keen if not for the tragedy attached to the place."

"Of course we would," Evie said, "but the story makes it all the more interesting."

"Besides, Miss Fairfax said it's probably made-up," Clara added. "And we're still going to see the puppies, yes?"

"We'll see," Julian replied, "but I believe I already said that."

"Yes, you did," Evie said, and gave Clara what looked like a knowing smile.

Julian regarded Annie. "Well then, it appears we've sorted out the agenda for tomorrow."

Annie nodded, her stomach doing a flip at the thought of spending another day in Julian's company. "It would seem so."

"Excuse us," Evie said, as she and Clara moved past them again. "But we've decided it's better if we walk ahead of you."

Julian narrowed his eyes. "Dare I ask why?"

Clara parted with an exaggerated sigh. "Because that way, brother dear, we can pretend not to notice if you hold hands with Miss Fairfax."

"Like you did almost all the way to the footbridge," Evie added. "Don't worry, we probably won't tell anyone."

Annie stifled a laugh. "They're incorrigible," she said, as the twins sauntered off down the path.

"Indeed. And since I'm now firmly inked onto their blackmail list, I suppose we needn't be quite so discreet." He took hold of Annie's hand, lifted it briefly to his lips, and then threaded his fingers through hers. "Besides, it's worth being blackmailed for."

On the way back, their conversation wandered into a sharing of childhood likes and dislikes, favorite music, favorite foods, favorite books, and such like. Annie discovered they actually had much in common, especially when it came to art and music. The conversation flowed naturally, as if they shared something that went beyond mere likes and dislikes. It was notable, Annie thought, how at ease she was in Julian's presence. Did he feel the same? It seemed so. She hoped so.

A short while later, they spread blankets on the grass, sat in the shadow of a Roman ruin, and shared more conversation while enjoying a splendid picnic. The hamper, packed in Myddleton's kitchen, contained a veritable feast of roast duck, sliced ham, soft white bread-rolls, crisp lettuce and some local Stilton cheese. Annie barely managed to save some room for one of the treacle tarts, which was washed down by a glass of tangy lemonade.

Now, with the sun settling lower in the sky, Annie knew it would soon be time to return to Ferndale. As if reading her mind, Julian pulled his fob-watch from his pocket and glanced at it.

"Aww, we're not leaving yet, are we?" Clara asked, the merest hint of a whine in her voice.

"In about a half hour," Julian replied, pocketing his watch. "And no arguments."

"Should give us enough time," Evie said, brushing crumbs from her skirts as she got to her feet.

Julian frowned. "Enough time for what?"

"To cross the steppingstones."

"No." Julian shook his head. "Absolutely not."

"Why not?"

"You know why not," he replied. "You'll fall in. And that's

not a guess, it's a guarantee."

Clara, on her feet also, scowled. "No, we won't, Julian. We'll be very careful. I mean, it's not as if we *want* to fall in."

"But you will, whether you want to or not," Julian said, making Annie laugh.

"I'll wager a shilling we won't," Evie said.

"Make it a half-crown,' Julian replied. "Times two."

"You'll lose," they said, in gleeful unison as they wandered off toward the riverbank.

"Just a matter of time, I fear," Julian said, and then assumed a serious expression. "So, tell me, Miss Fairfax, what is this development you mentioned?"

Annie cast a quick glance at the twins, assuring herself they were out of earshot. "I had a visitor," she said, her voice low. "He was actually waiting for me when I got back to Ferndale on Thursday."

"He?" Julian tensed visibly. "De Witte?"

"No." Annie shook her head and gave a brief smile. "Believe me, Hattie would not have allowed him through the door. No, it was an Inspector Taggart from Scotland Yard, and more of a courtesy call than anything."

Julian raised a brow. "A long way to come for a courtesy call."

"I agree, but he's Archibald Mason's brother-in-law."

"Ah, I see. May I know the reason for this courtesy call?'

"Of course." Annie then proceeded to recount all that had been discussed during the meeting. She attempted to keep the account somewhat light, but Julian's expression had darkened a little as she continued. "And that was it, basically," she finished. "He assured me, as he readied to leave, that he did not believe me to be in any danger. Just asked that I remain vigilant."

Julian looked unconvinced. "Nevertheless, Miss Fairfax, I'm not sure returning to London is wise. I should imagine you're safer here."

She regarded him for a moment. "I'm curious about something, sir."

"Which is?"

"Why I'm back to being Miss Fairfax, when I was Annabelle just a little while ago."

Julian looked contrite. "The latter was an unconscious slip. I apologize."

"You don't have to," she replied. "I didn't mind it at all, actually."

A smile appeared. "It's a very pretty name."

"Thank you. Those close to me, however, shorten it to Annie."

"Annie," he repeated, as if savoring the name on his lips. "Even prettier."

"You have my permission to use it, sir, whenever we're alone." She glanced past him again to where the twins were now making their way across the steppingstones. "Unless, of course, you'd prefer to maintain our current accordance."

"Then you shall be 'Annie' from now on," he said, taking her hand in his again. "When we're alone, at least. And hearing my Christian name on your lips, under those same circumstances, would give me great pleasure. I have been called other things, but that comes from having sibl—"

A sudden scream split the air, followed by a squeal of unladylike laughter and another scream.

"No, they didn't!" Julian shot to his feet as did Annie, even as more squeals of laughter rang across the meadow. "Yes, they did. I told you. Did I not tell you? They fell in. They bloody well fell in!"

Annie gasped. "What, *both* of them?"

"Oh, it's never just one of them," Julian said as he set off toward the river. "Never."

Annie laughed, picked up her skirts, and hurried after him. "Looking on the bright side," she said, "at least you won the bet."

CHAPTER NINETEEN

JULIAN GOT TO the river's edge at the same time as Molesworth.

"One went in and then t'other, Mr. Northcott," the coachman said, panting as he rolled down his shirt sleeves and pulled on his jacket. "Gave me a bit of a scare. They look to be all right though, other than being sopping wet."

"Don't worry, we're fine," Clara proclaimed, clutching her sodden skirts on one hand, the other arm outstretched as she waded toward the bank. "The stones were slippery. Evie fell in first, and I went in when I tried to save her."

Julian heaved a sigh and held out a hand. "Any bruises?"

Clara took it and clambered onto dry land. "No, don't think so."

"What about you, Evie?" He held out his hand again. "Do you hurt anywhere?"

"My hair came loose," she replied, as he hoisted her onto the bank. "And my shoes are ruined."

Julian parted with yet another sigh. "Do either of those things cause you pain?"

"No."

"So, are both of you uninjured? I'm not joking. I need to be sure."

"I'm fine, Julian," Clara said, her teeth chattering. "Just a bit cold."

"Same," Evie said.

Julian silently cursed his carelessness. He'd been irresponsible and the burden of blame rested solely with him. *Heaven forbid they fall ill because of this.*

"There's a couple of blankets in the carriage," Molesworth said. "I'll fetch them. Actually, sir, I'll bring the carriage over. I expect you'll be wanting to get the young ladies home as soon as possible."

"Yes, thank you, Molesworth." Julian glanced around. "We'll clear up here and then head straight to Myddleton. Do you have any objections to being a guest for the night, Miss Fairfax? I'll have a message sent to Ferndale Grange explaining the situation. If you'd rather return home, I can arrange that too, of course."

"No, I have no objection at all. But, if I'm to stay the night at Myddleton, might the message include a request for some suitable attire to be sent back with the messenger?"

"Yes, of course. Forgive me, I should have thought of that."

"You have more important things on your mind, sir," she replied. "Priority must be given where it is due."

"Indeed." Julian gave the twins a critical look. "Hot baths for both of you as soon as we get home," he said, and added a touch of levity to hide the depth of his concern and guilt. "And you owe me five shillings."

"Ah, there you are." Julian wandered into Myddleton's ballroom and gave Annie the smile she'd come to love. He looked at ease, unlike earlier when worry had etched lines across his brow. "I've been looking for you. I was beginning to think you'd run away again."

Annie shook her head. "No, just exploring this incredible house. How are the twins?"

"Bathed, dressed, and not in the least contrite." He moved to her side and heaved a sigh of obvious relief. "But they appear to be none the worse for their soaking, thank God. In fact, they're already talking about tomorrow's outing. Oh, and a messenger has been dispatched to Ferndale."

"Thank you." Annie wrinkled her nose. "Hattie will probably think it was all orchestrated to provide me with an excuse to spend the night at Myddleton House."

Julian cleared his throat. "And I fear she may be right."

Annie gasped. "No! Are you saying the twins fell in on purpose? Surely not. They wouldn't do that. Would they?"

"I wouldn't put it past them. Evie alluded to the fact that, thanks to their little escapade, you and I are able to spend more time with each other. In any case, orchestrated or not, I accept full responsibility for what happened. I should have known better." His eyes took on a softness. "But I must also admit, Annie, I'm glad you agreed to stay. I rather like the idea of sleeping under the same roof as you."

Annie pressed her hands to her cheeks as if to halt the sudden blush, which now warmed her fingers. "Mr. Northcott, really. I don't know what to say."

He winced. "Uh oh. I'm back to being Mr. Northcott. Did I offend you?"

"No, you didn't," she replied, dropping her hands. "Quite the opposite. You say the loveliest things. It was just… unexpected, that's all."

Julian glanced at the door and then back at her. "In that case, allow me to give you fair warning that I'm about to kiss you. Unless, of course, you have an objection."

She shook her head. "Not a single one, Julian."

"That's better," he said, and drew her into his arms. Annie laughed and clung to him as she had once before, feeling equally as light-headed as she had on that previous occasion. But this was deliciously different. Intoxicating, exciting, and somehow undeniably *right*. Her gaze flicked to Julian's mouth, and she licked the dryness from her lips, anticipating. Julian touched his thumb to her chin and bent his head.

Annie closed her eyes.

"I've arranged for tea to be served in the west parlor, Julian." Lady Hutton's voice pulled them apart with only a little less force than a physical intervention. "I'm sure you and Miss Fairfax must be ready for some refreshment."

Julian cleared his throat and turned to face his aunt. Cheeks blazing, Annie bit her lip, lowered her gaze, and tussled with an inexplicable urge to laugh.

Julian nodded. "We'll be along in a moment, Aunt Eleanor."

"Good. Be sure not to dally. There are few things more disagreeable than over-steeped tea." Lady Hutton fanned her face with her hand as she turned to leave. "Goodness, it's awfully warm in here."

"Oh dear," Annie said, unable to stifle a giggle once the lady had left. "Am I to be cast out in shame?"

Julian grinned and took her hand. "If you are, I'll be coming with you, but it looks like we're allowed to have some tea first. Besides, you haven't met all the family yet. You should at least do that before being banished."

Annie raised her brows as they set off toward the door. "Who haven't I met?"

A duke, a duchess, a dowager-countess, two uncles, two more aunts, and three cousins later, Annie sank gratefully onto a gold damask settee and placed her teacup on the small adjacent table. A hum of conversation continued around her, but Annie, for now at least, was happy to listen rather than engage.

"Exhausted?" Julian muttered, taking his place beside her.

She nodded. "And overwhelmed."

"You were marvelous," he said, keeping his voice low.

"I was terrified of putting a foot wrong."

"Like I said, you were marvelous. You even managed to make Grandmama Hutton smile. Quite the feat."

"I like her. She's very regal."

"That she is."

"And am I right in thinking that your cousin Catherine outranks her parents?"

"She outranks all of us," Julian replied. "When circumstances allow, I'll tell you her story. It merits telling."

"I shall look forward to that. Anyway, they were all very gracious."

Julian gave her a sideways glance. "With one exception, in my opinion."

Annie barely hesitated. "Your cousin Adam?"

"You noticed."

"I got the impression he didn't approve of me."

"He can be a pompous ass at times, especially when he's had one or two, which is most days."

Annie nodded her understanding and barely fought off a yawn. "Oh, goodness. Excuse me."

"It's all that fresh air," Julian said, getting to his feet and holding out his hand. "Come on, my dear. I'll have someone show you to your room. Dinner isn't till eight. Plenty of time for a nap."

Annie opened her mouth to argue, but the thought of a nap was simply too enticing to ignore. "Are you sure? I mean, is it acceptable?" she asked, rising to her feet.

"Almost mandatory." He winked and squeezed her hand lightly. "Don't worry. I'll make your excuses."

A short while later, having promised to escort her to dinner that evening, Julian handed Annie off to Elsa, a rosy-cheeked maid whose smile never faded as they bustled their way up the stairs and along a corridor.

"Here you are, miss," Elsa said, opening a large, paneled door and standing to the side. "Do you need help undressing?"

"Oh, no, thank you, Elsa. I can manage."

The maid nodded. "Very good, miss. The room has been readied for a guest, but if there's anything else you require, the bellpull is next to the bed."

"Thank you," Annie said again, taking only a couple of steps over the threshold before coming to a halt. Behind her, the door closed with a quiet click, but Annie still didn't move. Frozen in place, she wasn't sure whether to laugh or cry. She ended up doing both, her eyes watering, and the laugh, which sounded more like a hiccup, stifled by her hand.

This couldn't be her room. Elsa must have made a mistake. Then again, it did have a bed in it. An enormous bed, in fact, with an intricately-carved, four-poster canopy, hung with pale gold damask curtains which matched the counterpane. But there was more yet.

The occupant might, instead, choose to sit on the moss-green velvet settee, or perhaps recline on the matching chaise-longue, and admire the tapestries and gilt-framed landscapes decorating the creamy damask walls. And, though dormant at this time of year, the black marble fireplace, centered on the opposite wall, promised warmth on a winter's night. As for the armoire, standing against the wall to Annie's right, it was the grandest she'd ever seen.

But it was the large window, elegantly framed in the same gold fabric, that pulled Annie farther into the room, a single question arising in her mind. What might she see beyond it?

Could it be?

Fingers crossed, Annie hurried to the window and gazed out at the surrounding countryside, which had taken on the soft glow of late afternoon. It took a few moments for her eager gaze to find what she was looking for. The perspective, after all, was completely reversed. But, to her absolute delight, there it was, from this distance little more than a small, grayish-brown anomaly on a sunlit, grassy summit. But there was no mistaking it.

"Freya's Farewell," she whispered.

That she could see it from her room had significance, though she couldn't begin to say why. She could only marvel at the intricate, unpredictable workings of fate. If today was anything to go by, she dared to believe her future was brighter than she could ever have imagined, especially given the sadness of the past few weeks. With that came thoughts of Leo, but she shoved them aside. He didn't know where she was, and even if he did, it wouldn't make any sense for him to come looking for her. Not now.

She turned and regarded the bed, thinking she didn't feel particularly tired anymore. Still, a brief rest wouldn't hurt. She reached around to unfasten her dress, wondering if the messenger had returned from Ferndale. As it was, she had nothing to change into for dinner, though even if she had, it would simply mean swapping one black dress for another. Secretly, she wearied of wearing the same dark garb, day after day.

A short time later, clad in only her petticoats, Annie slid beneath the counterpane and gazed up at the canopy, certain she was far too excited to sleep.

After that, she remembered nothing till a knock came to the door.

"FANCY AN AFTER-DINNER stroll, Annie?" Julian asked, as the dining room emptied that evening. "Or would you rather spend some time with the ladies?"

"A stroll would be lovely," she replied, "but you must join the men if you prefer, and enjoy a cigar. I'm sure I'll be perfectly fine with the ladies."

"I'd much prefer to spend the time with you." Julian presented his elbow. "Truth be told, I've never particularly enjoyed smoking."

Annie tucked a hand into the crook of his arm, her subsequent sigh one of obvious contentment. "Papa didn't like it, either," she replied. "He was of the opinion it couldn't possibly be good for the lungs. Should I excuse myself from the ladies?"

"Consider it done, my dear." Grace fell into step beside them. "Are you heading outside?"

Julian nodded. "It's a fine evening, Mama. I thought a walk

around the gardens and then a seat on the west terrace might be nice. Would you care to join us?"

Grace's mouth twitched. "Perhaps not immediately. I'll see you on the terrace later. Miss Fairfax, here, take my wrap. It gets chilly in the evening."

"Oh, but I can fetch one from my bedroom, Mrs. Northcott."

"No, please, I insist." She held it out. "Take it."

"Thank you." Annie blushed slightly. "You're very kind."

"You're welcome," Grace replied, smiling. "Enjoy your stroll."

"Your mother is so lovely," Annie said, as they stepped outside into the twilight. "You're very fortunate, Julian."

"I know I am, and yes, she is."

Another sigh, then, "Today has been…"

Julian gave her a sideways glance. "Trying? Interesting? Unpredictable?"

She laughed. "Wonderful. It's been wonderful. Well, except for the twins falling in the river, though they don't seem to be any the worse for it, fortunately."

"I think accidentally-on-purpose falling in the river is a more accurate description," Julian replied. "But, if not for that, you wouldn't be here with me now."

She sucked in a breath. "I still can't believe I slept for two hours this afternoon."

"It's the fresh air. Speaking of which." Julian took the wrap from her and settled it about her shoulders. "There. Don't want you catching a cold."

"Why, thank you, sir." Annie gazed up at him, her expression unmistakably one of adoration. "Perhaps you should have brought a coat."

He tutted and shook his head. "We Yorkshiremen are a tough breed."

She chuckled. "Chivalrous, as well."

"Your wish is my command, my lady."

The easy banter continued as they wandered through Myddleton's splendid gardens. Julian quietly calculated they hadn't even spent two full days together, but there was no doubt in his mind. Being with Annie, simply put, felt *right*. It was effortless. Natural. A union of kindred souls, each one different and unique, yet perfectly matched to the other. Julian smiled to himself, amused and somewhat baffled by the fanciful thoughts drifting through his head. A new experience for him.

Later, as the stars twinkled overhead, they joined others on the terrace, where lamplight and candleflame already flickered. The general atmosphere seemed to reflect Julian's mood, contented and just a little bit lazy. As the night chilled and people moved back indoors, Annie leaned over and whispered in his ear. "I've changed my mind, Julian," she said. "Today hasn't been wonderful. It's been perfect."

CHAPTER TWENTY

ANNIE DREW HER shawl around her as the landau, with Molesworth once again at the reins, wound its way along the country lanes. The skies were a little less reassuring than the previous day, the air a little fresher. They'd left Myddleton House after a late breakfast, their destination being Freya's Farewell. For Annie, it was something of a bitter-sweet excursion. After today, she didn't know when she'd be seeing Julian again. Everything he'd said and done implied she had a place in his future, but he'd yet to say anything definitive. Consequently, she couldn't help but wonder about it. And, deeming it inappropriate to do so, she hadn't asked.

"We're going to see the puppies first, right?" Clara asked.

Julian shook his head. "I don't think we have time for that."

"Of course we do," Evie said. "Besides, you said we could."

Clara nodded. "Yes, you did."

Julian scratched his jaw. "As I recall, I believe I said 'we'll see'. Twice."

Evie gave him a cocky smile. "Which isn't a 'no'."

"It isn't a 'yes' either," Julian replied.

"I told Papa that we were going to see them today," Clara said, "and he seemed quite accepting of the idea."

Julian looked skeptical. "Was he reading his newspaper at the time?"

Clara frowned. "Um, actually, yes, he was."

"Then he probably didn't hear a word you said."

"What do you think, Miss Fairfax?" Evie regarded her, eyes wide with obvious hope. "Do we have time to see the puppies?"

Annie feigned a moment of thought. "I'm inclined to say yes, but—"

Evie let out a squeak of obvious delight.

"But," Annie glanced at the skies, "perhaps you might do so on your way back. The weather, at the moment, is fine, and I think we should make the most of it while we can. The climb to Freya's Farewell would not be pleasant, or even possible, in the rain."

"It seems we have a compromise." Julian reached for Annie's hand, linking his fingers through hers. "So we'll visit the puppies on the way back."

Another squeak, this time from both twins and in perfect unison.

Clara clapped her hands. "I cannot wait to see them."

"And in the meantime," Evie said, "we can think of some names."

"Names for what?" Julian asked.

"The puppies, of course."

Julian scoffed while giving Annie's hand a surreptitious squeeze. "We're merely going to *see* some puppies, Evie, not actually acquire one. Names, therefore, are hardly necessary."

Evie snorted. "Then what's the point of going to see them?"

"That's a good question. But there'll be no more talk of puppies for now. As Miss Fairfax has pointed out, it's a fine day for an outing and we should be enjoying the countryside."

The twins' subsequent scowls had Annie suppressing a smile.

"You are wicked," she murmured.

"I am." Julian winced. "And what's worse, I enjoy it."

Annie chuckled. "I've noticed."

A short while later, following Annie's directions, Molesworth halted the landau in a sheltered spot by the woods. From there, Annie led the way to the stile and then the path skirting the woods, where the crows provided their usual welcome. Having been warned away from the stream, the twins went a little way ahead, their chatter audible but unclear. Annie, meanwhile, had come to understand what "walking on air" actually felt like. Simply being close to Julian, her hand tucked into his, was euphoric. As if reading her mind, he spoke.

"Happy, Annie?"

"Exceedingly," she replied. "You?"

"Inordinately." He lifted her hand and kissed it. "I'm already thinking about when I can return to Myddleton to spend more time with you. If you would be amenable to that, of course."

"I believe I would be, sir."

"Good. Then maybe in a fortnight or so. Perhaps a little longer. In the meantime, there are letters."

"In the meantime, there is the rest of this day." Annie gazed at the slope which lay ahead. "And a hill to climb."

"Stay away from the edge," Julian called to the twins, who had already begun to climb.

"We will," they replied in unison and then laughed as they muttered something to each other.

"I mean it," Julian went on. "To disobey will result in depriving a poor puppy of a rather splendid home."

A couple of shrieks followed.

Annie laughed. "You're really going to allow them to have a puppy?"

"Oh, probably, assuming they don't do anything foolish in the meantime." He released her hand as they approached the narrow path. "After you, my lady."

They reached the top to find the twins waiting, both of them standing well back from the ledge. "This view is incredible," Clara said. "We didn't go anywhere near the edge and we're going to name him Mr. Darcy."

"Who?" Julian moved past them. "Good Lord, yes, this is incredible."

"The puppy," Evie replied.

"What if he's a she?" Annie asked.

"Mrs. Darcy?" Julian offered and Annie bit back a laugh.

"Georgie, if it's a girl, short for Georgiana," Clara said, "but we'd rather have a boy."

"Just look at this view! You can see for miles." Julian stepped onto the ledge. "And there's Myddleton House. Magnificent."

"Isn't it splendid?" Annie went to stand beside him. "I was drawn to it immediately. I had no idea you were connected to it, of course. If I'm not mistaken, I think the room I stayed in would be the second window from the right."

"Third window, actually," Julian said. "It has the best view of this place, I'm told."

Annie gasped. "Are you saying you arranged it?"

The hint of a smile came to his lips, though his gaze remained fixed on Myddleton. "I like making you happy, Annie," he said, softly, and then turned to her and took her hand. "Come. Sit with me a while."

He led her to a nearby outcrop of rock, where they sat side-by-side on a flat-topped boulder.

"You told me about Highfield, but what's the history of Myddleton House?" Annie asked, untying her bonnet and lifting her face to the breeze. "Your uncle mentioned that Ferndale was once part of the old medieval estate, but Myddleton isn't medieval, is it?"

"No, it isn't," Julian replied. "It was built in the seventeenth century by the fourth earl, I believe. The ruins of Myddleton Castle are about a mile to the east of the house, though not much is left. It was torn down centuries ago. Castles were originally built for defense, of course, and were big, drafty places. When society became more peaceful, castles were often abandoned and replaced with the homes you see today."

"Fascinating," Annie said. "To have all that history running through your veins is an honor."

"It is," he replied, "and I hope I never take it for granted."

"Um, excuse me, brother dear," Evie said, gesturing to the

distant horizon as she approached, "but have you noticed those clouds over there? They're heading this way, and I don't think we should still be up here when they arrive."

Annie and Julian glanced over at the ominous gray wall that loomed on the horizon.

"They're still some way off, but it's probably wise to start back," Julian said, he and Annie rising. "You two got soaked yesterday. I don't want to risk it again today."

"But we're still going to see the puppies, yes?" Clara asked.

Julian looked dubious. "Whereabouts is this house, Annie?"

"It's not far from the church," Annie replied. "Practically next door."

"All right." Julian turned to the twins, who were already sharing excited grins with each other. "Off you go. Just be careful on the way down and don't get too far ahead."

"Don't get too far behind," Evie countered, still grinning as she picked up her skirts and headed off to the path with Clara.

Annie went to follow, but Julian caught hold of her hand. "Wait, Annie, please."

She gave him a questioning look.

"There's something I..." He frowned, moved closer, and cupped his hand to her cheek, his gaze moving over her face before resting on her mouth. "Something I have been longing to do. That is, if you have no objection."

He didn't need to explain further. Annie's breath caught and a flush of warmth arose in her cheeks. "Yes," she said, and then shook her head. "I mean, no, Julian, I... I have no objection. Not at all."

A smile turned into a slight frown appeared as his thumb stroked her cheek, while his fingers gently buried themselves in her curls. His eyes met hers for a moment, his gaze so intense, it stirred something deep inside. A flutter of desire, and not entirely unfamiliar. Julian's gaze then shifted to her mouth, his frown deepening as he tilted his head, tipped up her chin, and touched his lips to hers. Tentative at first, cautious even, but the sensation sent tingles all the way down to Annie's toes. A soft sound of pleasure came from her throat as she closed her eyes, gripped his coat, and leaned into him.

Immediately, his arms folded around her, the kiss becoming more bold, more demanding, yet still gentle. As Julian's hands slid down to her waist, pulling her close, Annie's hands crept upward, over his shoulders and around his neck, allowing her to move closer still, body to body. Her heartbeat pulsed in her ears as his mouth continued to caress hers. Something else, way down inside, also pulsed to life, demanding she press harder against him, needing, seeking. She became aware of a stirring between them, a telling thickness that strained against her belly. Julian parted with a groan and lifted his head, chest rising and falling against hers. "Annie," he muttered, between breaths, "we have to go."

"Yes, of course." Annie exhaled as her hands slid down his chest. Instinct told her their desire was mutually intense and, given the time and place, in need of taming. She also realized what had stirred between them and what it meant. The intensity of it, the want of it, shocked her. Was it wrong to be so affected?

Julian stole another quick kiss and then took her hand. Neither one spoke till they reached the path. By now, the twins were almost at the bottom of the hill. Evie glanced up at them, halted, and threw her arms wide. *'What is taking you so long?'* was the unspoken message.

"Imp," Julian said.

Annie laughed. "I fear the odds of you being blackmailed have just increased."

"Worth it," he replied. "Unquestionably. Right. Let's go and look at some puppies."

"OH, THEY'RE SO sweet!" Evie said, peering into the stall at the puppies, who were busy wrestling with each other in the straw. "Are there only two of them?"

The owner, a rosy-cheeked gray-haired lady by the name of Mrs. Clayton, nodded and folded her arms over her ample bosom. "There were six at the start, but only two of 'em left now," she said. "Just coming up on ten weeks old. Bitch and a dog. The bitch is the smaller one."

"We wanted a boy," Clara said. "But the little girl is very sweet as well."

"Yes, she is," Evie said, casting a glance at Julian. "Maybe we could take—?"

"One, Evie." Julian gave her a stern look. "Only one. No argument."

"They're grand little dogs," Mrs. Clayton said, nodding. "Good parentage."

"No doubt." Julian exchanged a quick, knowing glance with Annie. "All right, Evie, Clara, make up your minds. Which one is it to be?"

"Um, the boy, I suppose," Evie said, with little enthusiasm, "but then his sister'd be left all alone."

"Or he will, if we take the little girl," Clara said, pouting.

Julian smiled over his gritted teeth. "Either way, I'm sure the remaining pup will be fine. Make a decision."

"Well, having considered, I think we should take little girl," Clara said, throwing a scowl at Julian. "Of the two, she'd likely be more upset if we took away from her big brother and left her all alone."

"You make a good point, Clara." Julian nodded his apparent agreement. "Whereas the big brother will probably be relieved to have some peace and quiet."

Annie made a sound somewhere between a laugh and a cough.

"The bitch, then?" Mrs. Clayton said.

The twins looked at each other for a few moments. Julian arched a brow. "Mrs. Clayton is waiting for an answer."

Evie heaved a sigh. "We'll take the little girl, please."

"Right-oh." The woman stepped into the stall to retrieve the puppy. "Here y'go, then. Lovely little thing." She passed the smaller of the puppies to Clara before closing the stall gate. "Do you have a name for her?"

"Georgie," Evie replied, smiling as she petted the wriggling pup. "Short for Georgiana."

Mrs. Clayton's brows shot up momentarily. "Nice name. A bit unusual for a dog."

"She's lovely," Annie said, as the pup snuggled into Clara's arms. "And she's going to a wonderful home."

Julian dug into his pocket for a coin and pressed a half-crown into the woman's hand. "Thank you, Mrs. Clayton," he said, and then regarded the twins. "Come on, let's go. I'd like to avoid the rain if possible."

"Thank you kindly, sir," the woman replied, her eyes widening at the sight of the coin. "Very generous of you."

They headed outside, where Julian eyed the skies. "Damn it," he muttered, at the ominous wall of clouds looming overhead. He'd hoped to spend more time with Annie, but it seemed the odds were against him. As if reading his mind, she spoke.

"I can walk home from here, Julian. It's not even a mile."

"Absolutely not. I won't hear of it." Julian ushered the twins into the carriage and then helped Annie aboard. "It's too bad about the weather. I was hoping to spend more time with you this afternoon."

"Oh, but it's been a wonderful two days," she said. "Well, three days, actually, if we include last Thursday. I can hardly believe all that has happened."

"I'd like to believe it's just the beginning," he said, taking her hand as the carriage set off. "Like I said, I'll be back here as soon as I can, unless you decide to return to London in the meantime."

"I might reconsider that idea," she said.

A short while later, Julian escorted Annie to the doorstep of Ferndale and found himself facing Hattie Henshaw.

"Are you not staying?" the woman asked, looking past Julian to where the twins sat in the carriage. "How are the young ladies? We heard about their mishap. You're welcome to come in if you'd like some refreshment."

"Thank you, Mrs. Henshaw, but I must regretfully decline." Julian glanced skyward once more. "The young ladies are quite well, but given their mishap yesterday, I'd like to get them back to Myddleton before the skies open."

"I understand, of course." She gave Annie a quick smile. "Janet and I are looking forward to hearing all about your adventures over the past two days, my dear. I'll leave you to say your farewells, though, and bid you a safe journey home, Mr. Northcott."

The door closed.

"Well, it seems safe enough," Julian said, his voice a good deal more cheerful than he felt. "That is, I doubt they're about to lock you in the attic."

"They won't do that." The smile she gave him had an edge of despondency about it. "You'd better go. The weather is about to change."

"I'll write and let you know when I'm able to return," he said, lifting her hand to his lips as he gazed into eyes that shone with a tell-tale glimmer. "In the meantime, Annie Fairfax, do not forget me."

"Never," she replied with conviction, a sweet blush coming to her cheeks. "I cannot wait to see you again."

Turning, he walked away, fists clenching as an unsettling sense of detachment came over him. As if leaving Annie was wrong, somehow. He looked back as he clambered into the carriage, committing the sight of her, still standing by the door, to memory.

"We like Miss Fairfax very much, Julian," Evie said, as the carriage departed. "She's the one, isn't she?"

Julian nodded. "Yes, Evie. I believe she is. And I'm glad you like her."

For a short while they traveled in silence, Julian already immersed in his memories of the past two days. Then Clara, with the puppy sleeping in her arms, squirmed in her seat.

"Um, we have a question, Julian."

Pulled from his contemplation, he regarded her. "What is it?"

"Would you be upset if someone kidnapped us?"

Julian frowned. "What kind of question is that? Are you planning on being kidnapped?"

"No." She wrinkled her nose. "But we can't stop thinking of Mr. Darcy all alone in that stable, wondering where his little sister has gone."

"Ah, yes, of course, I should have realized where this was going. How short-sighted of me." He gave her a thin smile. "And my answer is 'no'."

Evie gasped. "You wouldn't be upset if we were kidnapped?"

"As in 'no', we are not going back to get Mr. Darcy." He held up a hand as Clara opened her mouth. "Don't bother arguing, either of you. You'll be wasting your time."

CHAPTER TWENTY-ONE

THE ATMOSPHERE AT Ferndale Grange had been cautiously calm since Julian Northcott bid Annie farewell. Hattie and Janet had plied her with questions about her stay at Myddleton House, as well as the outings with Julian and the twins. They had not, however, voiced any opinions, a notable lapse which Annie found odd. Certainly uncharacteristic in Hattie's case. They were, she finally decided, simply trying to restore the harmony that had existed prior to Annie's surprise reunion with Julian.

In any case, she was seriously considering changing her mind about returning to London. Perhaps, though, her motivation had less to do with the peaceful atmosphere at Ferndale Grange and more to do with being closer to Yorkshire.

Closer to Julian.

Since he'd left, Annie had been waiting for an opportunity to return to Freya's Farewell, but had been impeded by the weather. She longed to climb the hill again, to gaze at the distant gables of Myddleton House and relive the wonder of her time there. Most of all, though, she wanted to stand in the place where she'd experienced her first kiss. Her first *proper* kiss. She could not think of it, of him, without stirring the familiar sense of longing and desire. It was both exquisite and frustrating at the same time. She missed him. Felt empty without him.

The rain had continued, on and off, till midday on Friday, trapping Annie in the house. Saturday blew in on a south-west wind that drove a thin scattering of clouds across the sky. But no rain.

"I'm going for a walk after these are done," Annie announced, getting ready to dry the dishes after a late breakfast.

Hattie, who had been clearing the table, glanced at the window. "Yes, you should. You've been cooped up for the past few days. Where are you going?"

"Freya's Farewell, I think."

"It'll be very windy up there, so be careful." Janet, standing at the sink, exchanged a brief glance with Hattie. "And wear good shoes. The ground will still be wet."

"I'll see to the dishes," Hattie said. "Go and get yourself ready."

Annie hesitated. "Are you sure?"

"Positive. Off you go."

Barely a half-hour later, Annie, with Ruffy at her heels, stepped out into the wind and headed for the stile. As usual, they followed the path along the edge of the woods. Part way along, Ruffy, who had been zigzagging here and there, came to a sudden halt, pointed his little nose toward the woods, and growled. Annie, who'd been lost in thought, halted as well, a shiver trickling down her spine as she followed the dog's gaze. "What is it, Ruffy?"

The terrier, whose hackles had lifted, answered with a throaty growl, and backed up a couple of steps, his attention still fixed on the woods. Annie held her breath and squinted into the shadowed undergrowth that rippled and danced on the forest floor, but saw nothing out of the ordinary. The only sounds to be heard were the rush of the wind through the trees and the raucous cries of the crows, the latter a little more boisterous than usual.

The hair on Annie's neck lifted. "What is it, Ruffy?" she asked again, still peering into the trees. "What do you see?'

Tongue lolling from the side of his mouth, the dog looked up at her and wagged his tail. Then he scooted off across the meadow once more, following his nose as he usually did.

Whatever had caught his attention had apparently gone. Annie heaved a sigh of relief and continued on her way, her mind once again wandering back over the past few incredible days. As for moving back to London, she'd decided to wait till she heard back from Archibald Mason.

The thought of the city brought her father to mind. "I wish you could have known Julian, Papa," she muttered. "You would have approved. You were right to doubt Leo. Oh!"

Annie grabbed at her bonnet as a sudden gust of wind threatened to snatch it from her head. Drawing near to the hill, her gaze wandered upward. There would be no shelter from the wind up there. Nevertheless, driven by a need to see Myddleton House, to stand in the spot where Julian had kissed her, she continued on. She fancied the wind was challenging her, playing with her skirts, tugging at her bonnet, and mocking any attempt to keep her curls tucked away. At last she reached the top, breathless, but exhilarated, as if she'd met the challenge of nature and beaten it. In a moment of sheer euphoria, she tore the bonnet from her head and lifted her face to the sky, barely staving off a temptation to howl in delight. As if acknowledging her success, the wind howled instead, and then seemed to warn her by wrapping her skirts around her legs as she stepped out onto the ledge. One step only. It was enough that she could see Myddleton House.

"I miss you," she said, thinking of Julian. "I cannot wait to see you again."

Lost in daydreams, she stood there for a few moments, her thoughts drifting from past to future, memories and imaginings sharing space in her head. The wind dropped a little, its howl replaced by a hushed whistle. A mournful sound. Ominous, even.

Unbidden, a prickle crept over her scalp, accompanied by an odd sense of human presence, as if she was no longer alone. She spun around, her panicked gaze raking over the hilltop and the rocks. Empty, all of it. No sign of anyone.

Annoyed at her foolishness, she heaved a sigh and turned

back to regard the landscape. As if to counter her silly fears, she dared to venture a little farther onto the ledge.

It happened again. The sense of someone there, as if a shadow had appeared at her back, stealing the light. A squeal of fear caught in her throat as someone grabbed her from behind and pushed her toward the edge. Her bonnet slid from her fingers to be snatched away by the wind, ribbons trailing.

Terror, like an icy wave, washed over her as the precipice loomed. Only at the last second, mere inches from certain death, did her assailant halt his attack. Annie closed her eyes as his foul breath, heavy and rhythmic, brushed over her right ear.

"You should be more careful, my dear," a male voice muttered. "It is doubtful you would survive such a fall."

Annie's eyes flew open, the world tilting as she whispered his name. "Leo."

A growl rumbled in his throat. "So, you have not forgotten me."

Numb with shock, heart hammering in her ears, she replied with only a whimper. Questions tumbled through her mind, one in particular at the forefront. *How did you know where to find me?*

Lucidity, in a crude form, returned and brought indignation with it. Annie squirmed in his grip and pushed back against him, but he held her fast, arms pinned to her sides. "How dare you, Leo," she said, teeth gritted. "Let me *go!*"

Leo responded with another low growl, his breaths coming hard and fast against her throat. "I suggest you be still, Annie. It is not wise to move against me like that."

Realizing what pressed against the base of her spine, Annie froze. "You're disgusting."

"And I'm disappointed you know what it represents, my dear. I trust it is not through personal experience."

Annie gasped. "How dare you! Release me. You're scaring me."

"As intended." His hold on her tightened a little. "I've been watching you this past while. You have been enjoying yourself, haven't you? With him. That toff." He laughed softly and without humor. "Who is obviously unaware of the truth."

Annie's stomach lurched. "You've been *watching* me? What do you mean? For what purpose?"

"Curiosity."

"You have no right to do so, Leo. None." She tensed against an urge to struggle. "How did you know where to find me?"

"A little bit of detective work. It was not difficult." Leo hissed softly through his teeth. "What has been difficult is watching you with *him*. The hand-in-hand walk by the river. Sharing a kiss by those rocks over there. That, especially, I did not like to see. Not one bit. It angered me, Annie." He inched closer to the edge, his breaths heavy once more. "It infuriated me."

A cry scraped from Annie's throat. "Leo, please, no."

"You spent a night beneath the same roof as him as well, didn't you? Did you sleep alone?"

She gasped. "How dare you! Let me go, please. This... this is madness."

"Madness?" Another soft laugh. "I'm of the opinion it's an opportunity for revenge not to be missed. You, all alone up here. A fierce west wind. She was a foolish girl, they will say, to venture onto the ledge in such weather. An accident was inevitable."

"No, please." Annie's throat tightened as her legs buckled beneath her. "I beg of you."

"As I once begged you, remember?" Leo nuzzled the spot beneath her ear. "And you denied me, Annie. You cast me aside. I told you you'd live to regret it, did I not? It seems that day has come."

"Leo, please. I don't... Oh, God, I don't want to die." Tears blurred Annie's vision as she looked out over the landscape. She blinked them away, strangely furious that they dared to obscure her view. She needed to see Myddleton House. To remember. To regret. She blinked again as her eyes found what she was looking for.

I should have told you, Julian. I should have told you that I love you. And I do. I do love you. I'm sorry. I'm so sorry.

They came back to her, then. The words Leo had spoken:*…who is completely unaware of the truth.*

"What truth, Leo? What truth is Julian unaware of?"

"I was beginning to think you'd never ask," he replied. "The truth about *you*, Annie."

Her teeth chattered. "About me?"

"I thought they'd have told you by now."

"Told me what? Who is 'they'?"

"I can only surmise they've kept it from you because of him."

She parted with a cry of frustration. "Stop speaking in riddles and tell me what you mean."

"Suffice to say, that charming little house is a custodian of secrets."

"Ferndale Grange?" Annie frowned, trying and failing to make any sense of what he was saying. Perhaps he had truly lost his mind. Dread coiled in her gut even as another question arose in her thoughts, one that surely demanded an answer. She dropped her gaze to Leo's hands. Bare hands. Unadorned. "Did you kill Karl Hoffman?"

He scoffed. "I assume that is what Taggart implied when he visited you. I'll admit I was tempted, my dear, but Hoffman was alive the last time I laid eyes on him."

Annie wanted to believe him. Then again, he'd proven himself to be an expert at deceit. Fearful of antagonizing him, she decided against asking about Hoffman's ring, but dared to voice another question. "How do you know about Inspector Taggart's visit?"

"Like I said, I've been watching you."

A suspicion formed. "That's how you found me," Annie said. "You broke into Archibald Mason's office, didn't you?"

Leo remained silent.

"They're looking for you," she continued. "The police."

"Fortunately, in all the wrong places," Leo replied. "If I let you live, however, that will change. And unless Hoffman reappears, I remain the prime suspect in his disappearance."

She shook her head. "I won't tell anyone, I swear."

His hold tightened again as he placed his mouth close to her ear. "Do not insult me with false promises, Annie."

"They are not false, Leo. You have my word. I'm pleading for my life! Believe me, it is not a scenario I would wish to repeat."

Moments passed while Annie prayed in silence, daring to hope Leo was considering her release. But when a sudden and violent gust of wind rocked them, he stepped closer to the edge, causing Annie to squeal.

"Exhilarating, isn't it," he said. "Look down, Annie. I dare you."

She did so, her terrified mind latching on to the story of Freya. But instead of Freya, she saw herself sprawled on the rocks below. "Must I go to my grave not knowing of what you speak?" she asked, tears blurring her view once more. "Do you really hate me that much, Leo?"

She felt, rather than heard, his inhalation of breath and felt his body tense. "Damn you," he murmured, and pulled her back from the precipice. Annie dared to hope. Dared to believe.

"Let me look at you, Leo," she said, surprising herself. "I want to see you."

The response came instantly. "No."

"Why not?"

"We are done here, Annie," he said. "Now, hear me well. When I release you, you will close your eyes and count to fifty before you turn around. Any attempt to follow me will, I swear, not end well for you. Understood?"

"Not the reason behind it, Leo, no. And believe me, I have no desire to follow you, though I admit to being curious as to your direction. Do you still intend to spy on me?"

"Not anymore. Suffice to say, I shall be leaving England to-morrow."

Leaving England? "And what of these secrets?"

"'Seek and ye shall find.' I shall say no more than that. Do not test me further. Close your eyes."

She did as bidden yet Leo remained where he was, his breath still hot and heavy against her neck. Then he pressed his lips to her hair and held them there for a long moment. "Damn you," he muttered again. "I care not who you are, Annabelle Fairfax. When Northcott has deserted you, which he surely will, you might remember that." He released her and stepped back. "Keep your eyes closed and start counting."

Annie struggled to remain upright on her unsteady legs. Despite Leo's demand, she opened her eyes and focused her gaze once more on Myddleton's familiar roofs. Meanwhile, the numbers went by in her head, unspoken.

"Twenty," she whispered at last, and stopped. She'd given Leo enough time to get away. Besides, she'd spoken true when she said she had no desire to follow him. Bracing herself against the wind, she remained in place, consumed by a fading sense of shock, a euphoric sense of relief, and a horde of unanswered questions. If any fear remained, it now rested solely in the mystery of this unknown truth.

When Northcott has deserted you, which he surely will…

Why would Julian desert her?

I care not who you are…

What did that mean? Was her father guilty of something nefarious? Had some crime been committed in the past, perhaps? And how, under God's great sky, might she begin to ask Hattie and Janet about whatever it was? She had no idea how to proceed. To question them would surely result in them questioning her, and she balked at the thought of confessing her encounter with Leo. She wasn't sure why. Perhaps because he was a potential complication, one that might be used as a diversion to the exposure of this mysterious truth. If there even was a mysterious truth hidden somewhere. For now, at least, Leo would remain unseen and unheard. As if to support her rationale, more of his words came back to her.

Seek and ye shall find.

After one last look at Myddleton House, Annie turned and regarded Ferndale Grange, now seeing it through different eyes. Questioning eyes. Before she stepped through its door, she needed to gather herself and show no outward sign of distress. Hattie, after all, could read her like a book. She lifted a shaky hand to her hair as she briefly pondered the whereabouts of her bonnet. Miles away by now, no doubt. Easy to explain its loss, given the weather. In an attempt to calm the tremble in her hands, she clenched and unclenched her fingers several times. To settle her racing heart, she filled her lungs and exhaled slowly; once, twice, thrice. Then, dropping her shoulders and lifting her chin, she set off back, already making plans.

It wasn't till she got to the woods that she remembered Ruffy's earlier reaction. Is that where Leo had been hiding? Had the dog sensed his presence? Annie knew she'd never pass the woods again without thinking about being watched. A shiver ran down her spine as she hurried on her way.

CHAPTER TWENTY-TWO

LANCELOT HAILED DAWN'S arrival in his usual, unmelodious fashion. Annie was already awake. Caught up in the aftermath of the previous day's shocking events, she'd slept little, her dreams bizarre and nonsensical. This new day now lay ahead. A day for finding answers and solving mysteries, if such things even existed.

Annie's return to Ferndale the previous afternoon had raised a few questions. Her disheveled state and the loss of her bonnet had drawn a comment from Hattie but, given the weather, had not required an explanation. As for the frown, Annie hadn't realized it was even there till Hattie mentioned it. She replied that a headache had taken up residence while she was out on her walk. Not a complete lie, as it happened. Hattie had immediately attributed it to the weather as well. The headache had then conveniently lingered on into the evening, giving Annie an excuse for her genuine lack of hunger and a reason to go to bed early. Surprisingly, Ruffy had gone with her, curling up at Annie's feet as she settled down for the night. He'd never done that before. Annie was simply glad he'd come home safely.

Lancelot cackled a second time. Ruffy stirred and jumped down to scratch at the door. Annie let him out and then snuggled back beneath her covers, where she intended to remain for the time being.

Soon, Hattie and Janet would be going to church, leaving

Annie by herself for a couple of hours. On previous Sundays, Annie spent those hours in a variety of ways; her nose buried in a book, embroidering her sampler, or cleaning the brass and copper to name a few.

She would be doing none of those things this morning. This morning, as soon as Hattie and Janet left, Annie would begin searching for something. What that something was, or where it might be found, or if it even existed, was unknown.

A soft tap came to the door and it creaked open. "How are you feeling, pet?" Hattie asked. "Has the headache gone? Did you manage to sleep?"

"Yes, the headache has gone, and no, not much," Annie replied. "I might have a bit of a lie-in this morning, actually."

Hattie approached and touched the back of her hand to Annie's forehead. "Hmm, there's no sign of a fever, but yes, stay in bed if you're not feeling well. You do look a bit peaky. Would you like some tea? Could you eat something? You hardly touched your food last night."

"Some tea would be lovely, thank you. But nothing to eat at the moment. Later, perhaps."

Hattie frowned. "Maybe I should stay home with you this morning."

Annie flinched inwardly. "No, Hattie, there's no need for that. I'm sure I'll be fine." She managed a smile. "Truth is, I actually enjoy my Sunday morning solitude."

Hattie's brows lifted as she folded her arms. "Do you, now?"

"Yes." She winced. "No offense."

"None taken," Hattie said. "And far be it from me to spoil your peace and quiet. I'll be back in a while."

Two welcome cups of tea later, Annie heard Hattie and Janet's voices in the hallway, followed by the sound of the front door closing. Shortly after, she heard the clip-clop of Tulip's hooves on the road, the sound fading into the distance.

Annie sat up, threw the bedcovers back, swung her legs over the side, and took a breath. Apprehension soured her stomach as did a large helping of guilt. She was about to pry, to disrespect the privacy of those she cared about, Janet in particular. Part of her hoped she would find something to justify her actions. Another part of her dreaded doing so. Heart heavy, she rose to wash and dress.

A while later, she entered the small study which contained Janet's writing desk. She'd used the desk herself when writing letters to Archibald Mason, though not for a moment had she considered opening any of the desk drawers or poking around in the cubbyholes.

Even now, it wasn't an easy undertaking. *Seek and ye shall find*, she reminded herself. Chewing on her lip, Annie bent to open the left side drawer, startling when the door to the study creaked open. She straightened and spun around.

"Oh, Ruffy," she said, pressing a hand to her chest. "You scared me."

The dog whined and wagged his tail.

"I know, I know, I should not be doing this. I feel terrible about it. Please don't tell tales." Annie turned back to the desk and pulled the drawer open. As one might have expected, it contained a number of letters and papers, none of which appeared to be suspicious. After closing that drawer, she searched the other, followed by the desk's cubbyholes. She found nothing but a ledger, a number of invoices and receipts, and a list of contacts and suppliers.

The entire, fruitless episode was beyond distasteful. Sick with guilt, Annie stepped back and considered where else she might accumulate more shame. Her gaze drifted to the ceiling, her mind already wandering the upper rooms, including Janet's bedroom and the attic.

The attic seemed to be the logical place to discover hidden secrets. Perhaps too logical. But searching such a space felt less abhorrent than searching Janet's bedroom. Annie had never been up there, though she knew of the small wooden door that led to it.

With Ruffy still on her heels, Annie headed upstairs, pausing before the attic door for a moment before pulling it open. Ahead lay a narrow, half-turn, wooden staircase, dark and dismal. Ruffy parted with a whine. "I agree," Annie said. "We need light."

She went to her bedroom, lit her lantern, and returned, pausing once again at the foot of the stairs to gather her courage. "What say you, Ruffy?" she asked. "Will you be my escort?" The dog wagged his tail and backed up a step.

"Well, thank you for nothing," she said. "That's very reassuring.

Of course, the stairs creaked as she knew they would, and the lantern-light didn't quite reach into the darker corners where Lord-knows-what lurked. The staircase led to another narrow door, apparently the twin of the previous one. Annie's hand hovered momentarily over the door handle. Then, gritting her teeth, she turned it and pushed the door open. It, too, creaked. Annie paused on the threshold and held her lantern up, breath hissing through her teeth at the sight of cobwebs hanging from the rafters. It was apparent no one had been up here for some time.

Lantern still held aloft, Annie moved forward a couple of steps, looking for anything that might merit investigation. The space was not as cluttered as she'd imagined it to be. There were a few items of furniture; several wooden chairs, a moth-eaten footstool, a couple of small tables, a traveling chest, a dilapidated armoire, and one blanket box.

The traveling chest was empty. Annie then went to the blanket box and lifted the lid, which resulted in releasing the smell of camphor and a dust cloud. Waving the dust aside, she peered into the box to see what looked like an old, embroidered quilt.

But nothing else.

It seemed clear there was little of value in this dark space. Coughing, Annie closed the lid, cast another quick glance around, and made her way back downstairs.

"Where to now, Ruffy?" she asked, turning the wick down on

the lantern. There was, in truth, only one other likely place to search. The one Annie had prayed wouldn't be necessary.

Janet's bedroom.

Annie had been in the room before, briefly. It had been a casual thing, random, a sharing of conversation that just happened to occur in that particular space. Once again, Annie paused, her stomach churning as she regarded the bedroom door. She felt like a thief, in this case stealing Janet's privacy and trust. "God forgive me," she muttered, as she opened the door.

It was a pleasant room. Quite large, but with a cozy atmosphere. Worn rugs on polished floors, oak beams, whitewashed walls, floral curtains. And, of course, Janet's bed, neatly made with its embroidered bedspread and topped with a pale green, featherdown quilt.

Furniture in the room consisted of a simple chest of drawers, an oak armoire, a small bedside table, another table beneath the window, a bent-cane chair, and a washstand and mirror. Neat and tidy, nothing out of place.

Gritting her teeth, Annie first went to the armoire and opened the door. Again, she breathed in the faint odor of camphor, this time sweetened with a touch of lavender. All Janet's clothing was in plain view, hanging from the rack or folded neatly on the shelves. Annie then opened the drawer at the bottom of the closet. In it was a lidless, satin-lined box containing a variety of lace gloves and fichus.

The dresser came next, each drawer opened and closed in fairly quick succession. Annie didn't know what she was looking for, but it surely wasn't a variety of woolen stockings or a selection of a lady's undergarments.

She glanced around the room, her gaze coming to rest on the small table beneath the window. Draped to the floor with a fringed, gold velvet cloth, it brought to mind an altar. It had a few items on it; a delicate ceramic dish, a silver hairbrush and matching hand-mirror, and a tiny wooden box.

Annie approached and lifted the lid off the box. It contained a single item. A brooch, edged in black enamel and inlaid with silver. The center of the brooch was clear glass, protecting and displaying what Annie knew to be a woven sample of human hair. It was a piece of mourning jewelry, the hair of a departed loved one.

Seeking an inscription, Annie turned the brooch over, but the silver backing bore only a hallmark. It was a curious object, but not unusual. The mystery lay in to whom the hair belonged. Someone Janet had known, obviously, but it meant nothing to Annie. Heaving a sigh, she put the brooch back in its box and looked around the room once more. The only place she hadn't checked was underneath the bed.

She went to it, dropped to her knees, and lifted the bedspread to peer beneath. There was only one object under there. Annie doubted, however, that Janet's chamber pot would be hiding any secrets. Heaving another sigh, she sat back on her heels, her gaze wandering around the perimeter of the room.

"This is madness," she muttered. "There's nothing here. Nothing at..."

She paused, her attention drawn once more to the covered table by the window. More specifically, the solid, flat base, partially visible through the fringe on the cloth. What kind of table would have a solid, flat base? A prickle wandered across Annie's scalp as she went to investigate. She lifted a corner of the cloth and gasped. It wasn't a table at all, she realized, but a chest. It seemed obvious to Annie that the cloth was intended to disguise it. Her stomach tightened as a sense of foreboding crept over her, as if she was about to discover something that would change her life.

Annie removed the items from the top of the chest and set them on the bed. The cloth came next, folded and placed on the chair. The chest now stood naked, its keyhole empty. Was it locked? Annie tested the lid. No, it wasn't. She glanced over her shoulder at the half-open door, an instinctive reaction. She was, of course, quite alone. There was no sign of Ruffy.

"Get on with it, then," she muttered, and opened the lid fully.

She dropped to her knees, hands gripping the edge of the chest as she peered down at the contents. The first thing that caught her eye was a small, oval portrait of a woman, behind glass, framed in gold, and resting atop a white, satin-edged blanket. Annie picked the portrait up and studied it. The woman looked to be quite young and resembled Janet. But it wasn't Janet. Annie frowned and turned the portrait over, reading the dedication.

Mama, Chesterfield, 1822.

Janet's mother, perhaps? Annie set it aside and reached for the blanket, which fell open as she lifted it from the chest. The original whiteness had succumbed to time, giving it a faint yellowish hue, the small size suggesting it had been made for an infant. Wondering at its significance, she set that aside too, and peered into the chest once more.

The removal of the blanket had revealed a brown card-paper box, stiff with age, color faded, edges worn. Annie lifted the lid, set it aside, and stared down at a small bundle of letters, held together by a yellow silk ribbon. They also showed signs of age, the ribbon faded, the paper discolored. The ink, too, had faded, though she made out the name 'Janet', on the envelope. The ribbon partially hid the rest of what was written. Not that it mattered. Annie wasn't about to read any of the letters. The mere thought of doing so was too repugnant.

Beneath the letters, however, was a leather portfolio. Curious, Annie lifted the letters out to set them aside. As she did so, the ribbon shifted slightly, revealing part of Janet's surname, which leapt out at her.

She moved the ribbon further aside, exposing the surname in its entirety, her benumbed brain unable to make sense of what her eyes were seeing. Using her thumb, she flicked through the bundle, seeing the same name, again and again.

Miss Janet Fairfax

Nor were they addressed to Ferndale Grange, but to an address in Chesterfield. Annie sat in bewildered silence. *Fairfax? Is Janet a relative? If so, why not admit it? What does she have to hide?* Certainly, Annie's father had never mentioned her, or any other relative of his, come to that. The only relative she'd ever been aware of was her deceased aunt. But that was her mother's sister, not her father's. And he'd never spoken of her. He'd *refused* to speak of her.

There had always been gaps in Annie's childhood, but she'd long since learned not to ask about them. Questions remained unanswered, memories discouraged and unshared.

The soft chime of the hall clock drifted up the stairs, reminding Annie her time was rationed. She gave herself a mental shake, set the letters aside, and reached for the portfolio. As she gazed upon its pocked, leather surface, she had the impression she was standing, once again, on a precipice. Blindfolded.

She inhaled deeply, exhaled slowly, and opened the flap.

A WHILE LATER, down in the kitchen, Annie stood back and surveyed her work. Having read the contents of the portfolio, her first task had been to rearrange the kitchen back to the way it was when she'd been here as a four-year-old child. It hadn't taken very long. She'd simply moved the kitchen table and chairs to the center of the room, facing the window.

The table also served as the place to display her exhibit. A sorry exposé of the colossal lies and inconceivable deceit that had, since birth, been a part of Annie's world. The soul-crushing evidence, discovered not a half an hour since, had torn the blindfold from Annie's eyes and thrown her off the precipice, ending her life as she knew it.

"Eggcups," she muttered, clambering onto a chair to remove

them from the cupboard. "Mustn't forget the eggcups, must we?"

Taking one eggcup at a time, she cradled them in the crook of her arm. As she stepped down, one of them slid from her tenuous grasp and shattered on the stone floor. Annie regarded the fragments for a moment, her eyes blurring with a sudden stab of remorse. It faded quickly, shoved aside by resentment, anguish, and the agony of betrayal.

Blinking the threat of tears away, Annie put the remaining three egg cups on the table beside the yellowed blanket and the documents from the portfolio. Then she stepped back and regarded her efforts once more. Satisfied, she pulled out the chair facing the courtyard door and sat down to wait. She wanted to see their reaction when they came through that door, their expressions when they saw the items on the table and realized what it meant.

She heard a noise at her feet and looked down to see Ruffy gazing up at her. As their eyes met, he whined and nuzzled her skirts. "Mind where you step, my friend," she said, the dog's simple display of affection threatening her fragile composure. "I didn't clean up the mess."

Once again, Annie thrust the threat of tears aside. Though her heart and soul begged for it, she refused to cry. She was determined to stay strong. To hold on. To face Hattie and Janet as she might a couple of strangers. For that is what they had become, after all. Strangers.

Whose veins ran with the same blood as her own.

CHAPTER TWENTY-THREE

I T WASN'T LONG before familiar, tell-tale sounds found their way into the kitchen. The clip-clop of hooves and the rattle of wheels on stone. Familiar female voices, their words unclear, the tone light and congenial. Ruffy gave an excited bark and pressed his nose to the door, waiting. Several quiet minutes passed, undoubtedly used to unharness Tulip and put her back in the stable. Then came more conversation and some shared laughter, which had barely faded before the kitchen door opened. Tail wagging, Ruffy barked a brief welcome and then shot outside, as if escaping what was to come.

Annie shifted and straightened her spine.

Hattie entered first. "Ah, you're up. Are you feeling better?" Her smile changed to a puzzled frown even as Janet followed her over the threshold. "Goodness, what on earth have you been doing? Why have you moved the table?" She looked down as her shoe crunched on a fragment of the shattered eggcup. "Did you break something?"

"I put the table back where it used to be," Annie replied, her voice sounding distant to her ears. "And yes, I broke an eggcup. It was an accident."

Janet closed the door and moved past Hattie, her face draining of color as she spied the items on the table. "Oh, Annie, what have you done." She dropped onto the chair adjacent to Annie's, her hand shaking as she reached over and touched the blanket.

"Oh, love, it wasn't supposed to be like this. I didn't want it to be like this."

"What are you…?" Hattie began, then gasped, her hands flying to her face as she noticed the collection on the table. "Oh, dear Lord."

"How did you want it to be, Janet?" Annie replied, her throat tightening with suppressed anguish. "Forgive me if I don't use your names. Since learning the truth of your identities, I'm no longer sure how to address either of you. 'Mama' and 'Aunt Hattie' are, I fear, quite beyond me at the moment." She regarded Janet. "I was led to believe you were my mother's sister. My Aunt Sybil, long dead. And as for you, Hattie, I am in complete awe of your ability to have been someone you are not for the past twenty-one years."

Janet closed her eyes briefly. "Oh, Annie."

Hattie, looking somewhat pallid as well, pulled a handkerchief from her coat pocket in apparent readiness as she also settled onto a chair. "What prompted this, pet?" She gestured toward the items. "Did you remember something from childhood?"

"From when I was here before, you mean?" *Seek and ye shall find.* Annie could almost hear Leo's voice in her ear and feel the heat of his breath on her flesh. "Odd you should ask. Obviously, I remembered the eggcups and where the kitchen table used to be. The song I heard the other morning was familiar as well. Now I know why. But given the extent you've gone to in order to hide the truth of my parentage, I fail to understand why I was brought here all those years ago. It makes no sense. All those years, all those lies. Even your names falsified. I'm no longer sure of what is true and what is not. Did you ever mean to tell me the truth, either of you?"

"Of course we did," Janet replied. "It was just a matter of choosing the right time, the right moment. I swear I did not want you to find out like this."

Annie gasped. "I've been here for several *weeks*. You've had plenty of time."

"But the moment never presented itself." Janet heaved a sigh. "We had other things to consider."

"And I had to lie about my name," Hattie said. "Your father would never have employed me had he known who I really was. It was a blessing we'd never met prior to my brother's death."

"He was *not* my father, though, was he?" Annie cried. "He also lied to me my entire life. I can barely conceive of it. It's as if I never knew him at all. Did he even love me, or was that pretense as well?

Hattie leaned forward, her gaze unblinking and intense. "Hear me well, Annie. Clarence Fairfax was your father in every way that mattered, and you must *never* doubt his love for you. He loved you as his own. I bore witness to it every single day. Please do not judge him too harshly. He was not without fault, but not many men would have done as he did. As for me, I lied my way into a position in his house because it was the only way I could be near you. To watch over you. I'll not apologize for it, either."

"Hattie did it for me as much as for you, Annie," Janet said. "Her presence in that house meant I still had a connection to you and could watch you grow up from afar. There were many times, as well, when I traveled to London to watch you from nearby. From across the street, perhaps, or from a certain spot in Hyde Park." She reached over and squeezed Annie's hand, the touch warm. "And, more recently, from the quiet corner of a church."

An image loomed in Annie's mind, that of a woman, a mysterious silhouette in the shadows of the nave. "My wedding," she said. "That was *you?*"

Janet nodded. "I'm so sorry, love. It was a terrible day."

"For you as well, surely," Annie said. "You watched your brother die."

"Yes, I did." Janet smiled even as tears welled in her eyes. "We hadn't spoken since before you were born."

"So much lost." Annie shook her head. "It's beyond belief."

"The deceit was an unfortunate necessity," Janet said. "I was an unmarried woman carrying a child. I don't need to tell you that society spares neither favor nor pity for such women, or the children they carry. They are judged, scorned, and to hell with the circumstances. Clarence and Muriel were childless. I don't think she was strong enough to bear a child, actually. Maybe that's partly why Clarence offered to take you, to give you an upbringing I could never have provided. Or maybe, deep down in his heart, he found a morsel of compassion. In any case, it was all arranged beforehand. I stayed with Doctor De Witte till you were born."

Annie tensed. "Leo's father?" That little nugget of information likely explained how Leo knew of the hidden truths. But, she wondered, had he always known?

"Yes. It was he who delivered you and who took you to my brother's house," Janet replied. "Clarence had staged Muriel's confinement. Not a difficult thing to do, I suppose, given his profession. He simply made it appear as though she'd given birth, and you were their child. I knew it was for the best, but if you think I gave you up easily, think again. It almost killed me."

"So many secrets," Annie murmured, as much to herself as Janet and Hattie. "I'm unable to recognize myself. My entire life has been a lie. Everyone I ever cared about has deceived me."

"Not maliciously though, pet," Hattie said. "The intentions were well-meant."

"So you say." Annie studied Janet for a moment, seeking similarities in appearance and finding none. "I don't look like you."

Janet shook her head. "No. You look more like your father, with your dark hair and your eyes." Her mouth quivered slightly. "Especially your eyes. They are so like his. It's remarkable."

"Did you love him?"

"Oh, yes," Janet replied, softly. "You were born from love, Annie, I can promise you that. I loved your father very much. I will always love him."

"What was his name? The letter says merely that he died."

"His name was…" Janet's lips trembled, and she pressed a hand to her throat. "His name was David. David Clement Caldridge."

"David," Annie repeated as more questions formed in her mind. "Did he know about me?"

"No." Janet gave her a sad smile. "He died before I knew I was *enceinte*. He died a week before we were to be married."

Annie barely controlled a flinch. "How?"

"Suddenly. His heart, we must assume." Janet glanced at Hattie. "I wasn't here when it happened."

"Here?" Annie gaped at Hattie. "You and my father lived here?"

"No, I lived in Chesterfield, on the same street as your mother. I was merely visiting that day." Hattie glanced around the kitchen. "David had just inherited the farm from our uncle and wanted to show it off. He had all kinds of plans for it, including raising his family here. He went out to the fields that morning and never came back. They found him in the pasture by the stream. You've walked past the spot many times since you've been here."

Annie frowned. "Ferndale Grange belonged to my father?"

Hattie nodded. "Had he not died, this is where you would have grown up."

"It now belongs to Hattie," Janet said. "She gave me a home here when Clarence disowned me. I was, to anyone who asked, a cousin and a Caldridge. To this day, no one around here knows my true identity."

Annie shook her head. "I swear I cannot keep up with it all. And I still cannot fathom why I was brought here as a child. Papa must have known there was a possibility I'd remember some of it. Certainly, it explains why he refused to speak of it."

"Actually, you were brought here at Muriel's insistence," Janet replied. "She knew she was dying and insisted Clarence send you to me till everything was done with and settled. He was against it at first, but in the end he agreed, simply, I believe, to appease Muriel. A dying wish, if you will. She was always sympathetic to my circumstances. Never judgmental, unlike Clarence. I like to believe the time you spent here was her parting gift to me, and may God bless her for it. That said, it broke my heart all over again when I had to give you back."

The familiar image of the lady on the chaise-long appeared in Annie's mind. "I have only a vague memory of her. I think of her whenever I smell roses."

"Her favorite perfume," Hattie said. "Muriel Fairfax was a fine lady. I've no doubt she'd have been a good mother to you, had she lived."

Annie pondered a moment. "A little while ago, you said there were other things to consider. What things? What haven't you told me?"

Janet glanced at Hattie. "I believe we've told you everything from our perspective, Annie."

"Your perspective? What does that mean?"

Hattie cleared her throat and rose to her feet. "Tea. I'm going to make some tea. Then we'll move to the parlor and decide how to proceed further."

Annie shook her head. "Proceed further?"

"We need to discuss what this means for the future, Annie," Janet said, quietly. "*Your* future, specifically."

There it was, subtly delivered, yet like a dagger through the heart. An allusion to the potential, heartbreaking consequence of Annie's true parentage. A fear that had lingered in shadows at the back of her mind from the moment she'd learned the truth of her birth. So far, she hadn't found the courage to face it, yet there was no escape. Even Leo had alluded to it. The fear slid from her mouth, whisper soft. "He'll not want me now, will he?"

"Tea," Hattie said again, shrugging her coat off. "Go and settle yourselves in the parlor. Did you eat today, Annie?"

"No."

"Tea and toast, then."

"I'm not hungry."

"You'll eat something anyway." Hattie set the kettle on the hob. "Go on, off with you both. I won't be long."

Annie followed Janet into the parlor but wandered over to the window, her sight turned inward.

"You know, Annie," Janet said, seating herself on the settee, "this doesn't necessarily mean Julian Northcott will no longer want—"

"Why 'Aunt Sybil'?" Annie, still staring out of the window, folded her arms against the pain of hearing Julian's name. "Was she someone you invented, or was she a real person who once meant something to you?"

Janet replied after a notable stretch of silence. "Though Clarence agreed to let you stay here, he insisted I use an alias for precisely the reason you mentioned earlier; his fear you might remember certain things about the time spent with me. That, and the fact he wouldn't allow my name to be spoken in his presence. I'm certain the last thing he wanted was to hear it from your lips. In any case, I chose 'Sybil' as my alias. Sybil was David's mother's name. Your grandmother's name. And yes, she meant something to me. Might I assume you saw the mourning brooch when you were in my bedroom?"

"You might."

"The hair was hers. She was a sweet lady."

"And the small portrait?"

"My mother, so your grandmother also. She died two years before you were born."

"What was her name?"

"Amelia Elizabeth. I wanted you named for her, but Clarence refused. He settled on the same initials, however."

Annie pondered her father's—her uncle's, she supposed now—lack of forgiveness. He'd been a man accustomed to dealing with all manner of people. People who were suffering and in pain. To have cast his sister aside, especially given the tragic circumstances, seemed to go against his nature and his profession. He had always been a kind man. A kind father. *But not an honest one. Why didn't you tell me the truth? Why?*

"And the dog?" she asked.

"Which dog?"

"I remember a black and white dog."

"Ah, Meg. David's dog. A collie, always at his side. She was with him when they found him. In fact, she wouldn't let anyone…" Janet's voice faltered. "She wouldn't let anyone near him at first. She was always very protective of him. She lived for several years after his death."

Annie heard the unfeigned sorrow in Janet's voice and searched her conscience, seeking a measure of compassion. She found none. It was as if some unknown entity had crawled into the space beneath her ribs, stealing her ability to feel anything beyond her own shock and fear. She turned around and, for the first time, dared to look upon Janet as her mother. And still, she felt nothing.

"Annie?" Janet regarded her through wide eyes. "Was there something else you wanted to ask?"

Annie shook her head. "No. I merely wish to address what you said earlier, about Julian Northcott. You cannot seriously believe he'll want to pursue a relationship with the bastard child of a farmer. And I cannot help but think you might be pleased about that, since I've suspected, from the start, that you disliked him."

Janet flinched and dropped her gaze to her lap. Hattie, who had just entered the room with a tray of tea, paused mid-step, her jaw dropping. Saying nothing, she set the tea tray on the sideboard and then turned to face Annie.

"Given what has occurred here this morning," she said, her expression grim, "emotional exchanges are to be expected, and allowances must be made. I cannot speak for Janet, but I am, at this very moment, making an allowance for what just came out of your mouth. You're upset, Annie, of course, and I'll choose to take that as a reason for your uncharacteristic rudeness. Now, let's have some tea and, hopefully, a civil conversation about how this situation might be handled."

"Upset?" Annie laughed, a sound void of humor. "I am completely lost, Hattie. I cannot even begin to describe how I feel. Betrayed, foolish, and naïve, to begin. I pray Mr. Mason will respond to my letter sooner rather than later, because I think it best I distance myself from all this and return to London."

"And I think it best you wait a while," Hattie said. "Running away will solve nothing."

"Neither will a cup of tea," Annie countered.

Janet parted with a soft sigh, rose to her feet, and went to Annie, halting not even a step away. Annie looked into her mother's eyes, seeking something of herself. Instead, to her bewilderment, she found herself seeing through them, acquiring the perspective of a woman who had lost everything of worth. The emptiness within her dissipated a little.

"I never disliked Julian Northcott, Annie," Janet said. "Quite the contrary. I saw his worth immediately. To my shame, my response to your association with him was, initially at least, purely selfish. You see, I'd planned to tell you everything last weekend, after we'd returned from Myddleton. I was going to tell you who I was, who *you* were, and the circumstances of your birth. I'd waited till then because you'd arrived from London looking utterly defeated. It was obvious you needed time to rest. Time to recover. God knows, you'd already been through so much. But I hadn't considered the possibility of a stumbling block like Julian Northcott. His presence at Myddleton, and your reaction to it, took me completely by surprise. I confess I resented, and feared, your attraction to him, because I knew where it would lead. Where it would leave *me*. So I tried to fight it, tried to turn you away from him. But then I saw the way you looked at him, the way he looked at you, and I knew, before we'd even returned home that afternoon, that my moment had passed. That I'd lost my child all over again." Her mouth trembled as she drew breath. "I had no choice but to submit to fate, to let you live your life unaware of who I really was. I could only hope that, once in a while, I might still have the privilege of being able to watch you, from near or far." Eyes brimming with tears, she smiled and touched Annie's face. "You are my daughter, and I love you. I have always loved you. And I have missed you, Annie. I have missed you so much! All I ever wanted for you—all I *want* for you—is your health and happiness. That being so, nothing of what you've learned today needs to go beyond these walls, if that is what you prefer. We can go on as we were, as you were. I'd already decided the truth would remain hidden and resigned myself to it. Today's events have been, to say the least, totally unexpected."

Annie, absorbing all that had been said, didn't answer. As she continued to look into Janet's eyes, she began to understand, to see beyond her own feelings.

Hattie's voice drifted into her thoughts. "Come and sit down, both of you, and have your tea."

Janet took Annie's hand and held it between hers. "I cannot pretend to know how you're feeling, love. You don't need to make any decisions right now. You've had a tremendous shock, so it's best not to rush anything. Give it a few days, at least. And please, don't worry about how to address me. Do whatever is comfortable for you. Now, come and sit down. Your hands are like ice and you're awfully pale."

For the second time that day, Annie made a decision. The first decision, the most heartbreaking of all, had been made earlier, when she'd read the contents of the portfolio.

Yet she stayed where she was, regarding the woman who'd given her life. Her mother. The only mother she would ever have.

A sense of compassion stirred, tussling with the contradictory sense of betrayal. Annie knew which of the two would be easier to bear. So much had been lost already. Still, she hesitated, not quite able to say the words her conscience now demanded. In the end, she just blurted them out. "I will no longer be your lost child, Mama. Or would you prefer 'Mother', perhaps?"

Janet's hands flew to her face, catching her soft gasp. "Are you sure?"

Annie nodded. "Yes, I am. So, what is it to be? Shall I address you as 'Mama' or 'Mother'?"

"Mama," Janet said, tears falling as she reached into her sleeve for her handkerchief. "I prefer *Mama*. Oh, my dear, you've made me so happy."

"Bless your heart, pet." Hattie also armed herself with a handkerchief, pulling it from her apron pocket. "Bless your heart."

"And I suppose you must be Aunt Hattie from now on," Annie said, with a touch of genuine reluctance.

"Oh, I'm not fussed about that." She shrugged. "I've always been Hattie to you. Actually, I think I'd prefer to keep it that way."

"I'd prefer it as well, if you don't mind. It would feel strange, otherwise," Annie replied. "As for Mr. Northcott…" Her stomach tightened at the mere mention of his name. "I've decided I shall write to him."

"And explain everything." Nodding, Janet sniffed and dabbed her cheeks. "Yes, that's a good decision. I really don't think he'll abandon you."

"No, I'm not going to explain anything." Annie pressed a hand to her chest, wondering if she even had the strength to put her intention into words. "I'm simply going to tell him I cannot… I cannot see him anymore. That I have no desire to continue our association."

"What?" Janet's handkerchief ceased its dabbing. "For heaven's sake, Annie, why?"

"Because that will allow me to end it before he does." Taking a shaky breath, she felt the heavy thud of her heart beneath her ribs. "I cannot bear the thought of being set aside due to the circumstances of my birth, which I would surely be. I have no wish to receive a letter from him telling me, ever so nicely, that our friendship, our liaison, is over. And I cannot even imagine the thought of facing him, of seeing the warmth fade from his eyes when I tell him who—or what—I really am. I would rather end it now and be done with it. It'll be less painful in the long run."

"Annie, please," Hattie said. "Take some time to think about this. I'm not at all sure he'll set you aside. He's quite obviously smitten."

"But it's not just about him, is it?" Annie swallowed against a choking thrust of despair. "Men like Julian Northcott are required to make a suitable marriage. One that has the approval of the family and will not bring shame to the family name or result in scandal or gossip. Before this, my position in society was already less than might be deemed desirable. As it stands now, I am completely unsuitable, no longer worthy of his consideration."

Hattie frowned. "Well, there is another option. Just don't tell him—"

"Do not even *dare* to suggest such a thing," Annie cried. "There'll be no more lies. No more deceit."

Hattie winced. "With respect, love, you'll be deceiving him if you write and tell him you want nothing more to do with him."

"That is true, and I know it's cowardly of me, but the result will at least be the same. I simply cannot face the alternative." She voiced a thought that slid into her mind. "Besides, it's not as if we've known each other for very long. No doubt he'll forget me soon enough."

"Oh, I wouldn't be too sure about that." Janet reached for Annie's hand again. "Julian Northcott is no fool. You're going to have to write a very convincing epistle to keep him away, I think. Now, come and sit down before you fall down."

CHAPTER TWENTY-FOUR

THE REST OF that strange, pivotal day had passed in a dream-like fashion. Annie had functioned as best she could, while secretly longing for the moment when she could retire to her room. Weary of feigning bravery, she craved solitude, that she might finally surrender to the demands of her despair.

At last her solitude had been granted, though she'd found no peace in the confines of her room. For the past few hours, her unshackled emotions had spun her in vicious, unending circles. Time and again she'd wept over the cruel unpredictability of life, and then castigated herself for her weakness and for unfairly blaming others for her predicament. The past was gone. She was grieving, she knew, for the future she'd lost. A future that had promised so much love and happiness.

Weighed down with exhaustion, Annie now sat at her small table surrounded by a halo of lanternlight. Her bed remained unslept in, her letter to Julian Northcott unwritten. Her current mindset was that life went on. That all her grief and self-pity served no purpose. And that she needed to do what had to be done.

The pen in her hand hovered over the paper as she whispered the first words to be written. "Dear Mr. Northcott." Ah, but they were much more than a written salutation, those words. They were a statement. Blinking away persistent tears, Annie dipped the nib and began to write, silently cursing the slight tremble in her hand.

Dear Mr. Northcott,

To begin, please be assured, I take no pleasure in writing this letter. That being so, I shall not fatigue you or myself with extraneous verbiage, but shall simply get straight to the point.

After some consideration, I have decided to end our association. This is in no way a reflection upon your character. You have been most gracious to me, and I shall always think of you with fondness. Beyond that sentiment, however, I am unable to venture and must apologize if I gave you a contradictory impression.

My decision, as it pertains, is absolute and steadfast, the reasons for it personal to me. I must insist, sir, that you set aside all thoughts of responding to this letter and also refrain from seeking me out personally at any time in the future.

I trust you will respect my wishes and thank you in advance for your deference.

Yours most sincerely,
Annabelle Fairfax

"May God forgive me," Annie whispered, shivering as she set the pen aside. "I'm so sorry, Julian."

But the chill edging her words was necessary. There could be no sign of anguish, no hint of agonizing regret, no mistaking her message. She read it again and again before folding and sealing it. Then, in a moment of tearful fancy, she pressed her lips to the seal.

As the downstairs clock struck four, she lowered the lantern wick and, still shivering, climbed into bed. Fatigue swam in her head, yet she was way beyond sleep. She stared into the darkness and prayed that time might pass quickly, for only time would soothe what ailed her. Healing, she mused, would surely take a lifetime.

Later that day, having dragged herself from her bed without a wink of sleep, Annie dispatched her letter to Julian Northcott and took the timely delivery of a response from Archibald Mason.

Two days later, despite pleadings and protests from her mother and aunt, Annie left Ferndale Grange and returned to London.
Alone.

CHAPTER TWENTY-FIVE

JULIAN HEAVED A sigh, sat back in the chair, and read the letter for the third time. Nothing in it, of course, had changed. It read exactly as it had the first and second time. Absorbing each word, he barely heard the creak of the study door as it opened.

"Ah, here you are," his mother said. "Your father's looking for you. And if that letter is for who I think it's for, then you might want to wait before sending it off."

That caught his attention. Setting his letter aside, he looked up. "Why?"

"Because it would appear Miss Fairfax has written to you first." Grace set an envelope on the desk. "So you'll likely wish to amend yours and respond accordingly."

"Ah." His heart beat a little faster as he picked up Annie's letter. "Thank you, Mama. What does Papa want?"

"Your observations and opinion. He and Roberts are heading over to Boarbank Farm. Old Mr. Mulgrew isn't doing very well, apparently, so they're going to see what's required in the way of help. You know how your father likes to take an active interest in the tenants' lives. I think he's hoping you'll continue likewise."

"Yes, of course." Julian ignored a brief twinge of impatience, got to his feet, and tucked both his and Annie's letter into his pocket. "I'll save it for later, then."

"Something to look forward to, dear," his mother said, a smile playing on her lips. "Enjoy the anticipation. I'm sure it'll be worth the wait."

"No doubt," Julian replied, returning the smile. "Where's Papa?"

"He said to meet him in the stables."

The anticipation lasted almost three hours, which included a brief Yorkshire downpour on the way back to Highfield Hall that soaked horse and rider. Fortunately, Annie's letter was saved by being tucked against Julian's heart. Obliged to change out of his damp clothes, he found himself alone, at last, in the privacy of his room. Having stripped off, he put on his robe, settled onto his bed and, acknowledging the pleasure of his anticipation, opened the letter.

The first paragraph alone was enough to halt his breath. By the time he'd reached the end of the short epistle, his mind was in a spin, his heart thudding hard against his ribs. He read the words again and again, his mind hearing Annie's voice as she spoke them, his eyes noting the telltale flutter in her penmanship. Obviously, her hand had trembled as she'd written the words. Harsh words. Unfeeling.

And unquestionably fabricated.

That conclusion was not arrived at through vanity or pride. Though their time together had been comparatively brief, Julian knew Annie as he knew himself. Her anguish showed plainly in her stilted voice and the tremor in her hand. Something had happened. Something had made her turn away from him. He cursed the miles that lay between them, for he was at once desperate to see her, to speak to her face-to-face. To find out what, or who, had forced her hand. A name came to mind. A faceless name. And he could hardly bear to think of what it might mean. It occurred to him she might have returned to London, since she'd hinted at it. He hoped not. In any case, his first priority was to return to Ferndale Grange, and as soon as possible.

"Sorry, my love," he muttered, pulling on some dry clothes. "But no, I will not respect your request, nor will I defer."

———

"But you only just got home," Grace said, a little later, having heard Julian's announcement he'd be leaving for Derbyshire immediately. "What is this about? Is Annie unwell? Has something happened?"

"No, I don't think she's unwell, Mama," Julian replied. "But something is definitely wrong."

"Can you be more specific?"

Julian shook his head. "I cannot, I'm afraid, which is why I must leave. I need to find out what is going on. I need to speak to her."

Aldous cleared his throat. "You know, it occurs to me that this is the second time you've gone looking for this young woman due to ambiguous circumstances. And while it is, of course, your business, I would appreciate an honest answer to one question. Might any of these circumstances cast doubt on the integrity of our family?"

Julian thought but a second before responding. "I don't believe so, Papa. If that were the case, I would tell you, of course."

Aldous gave a nod. "That's all I needed to hear. Then I hope you get whatever it is sorted out. If you need me, let me know, and give my regards to your aunt and uncle."

"Thank you, Papa," Julian replied. "But actually, I've decided not to stay at Myddleton for the reason you just mentioned. Until I find out what is going on, I'd rather keep things within our immediate family."

"Not a bad idea." Aldous frowned. "So where will you stay?"

"The Black Horse, probably. Failing that, The Rose and Crown."

"Right," Aldous said, still frowning. "Well, I hope this young lady is worth whatever this latest issue is."

"I believe she is, Papa," Julian said. "And I have a suspicion as to the actual problem, but it's all speculation at the moment. I'll explain everything when I'm able."

"I'm sure you will," Grace said. "Just be careful, Julian. And give my regards to Annie."

CHAPTER TWENTY-SIX

JULIAN SLID FROM the saddle and tethered his horse at the gatepost. A pellet of rain struck his face as he opened the gate and approached the blue-painted door of Ferndale Grange. By the time he stepped into the porch and rapped on the door, the rain had begun in earnest. If he believed in omens, he might have taken it as a bad sign. He thrust the foolish thought aside and tried to ignore a sudden sense of unease.

The door opened and he found himself greeted by a gasp from Hattie Henshaw. "Mr. Northcott!"

"Good day to you, Mrs. Henshaw," he said, removing his hat. "Forgive the intrusion. I'm hoping I might speak with Miss Fairfax, assuming she's at home?"

To his surprise and dismay, the woman's eyes filled with tears as she opened the door wider. "Annie isn't here, I'm afraid," she said, "but come in, please."

Disappointment soured Julian's stomach as he stepped into the hallway. "She isn't here?"

The woman shook her head. "She went back to London last Tuesday. I must assume you received her letter."

"That's why I'm here," he replied, noting the dark shadows beneath the woman's eyes.

Her expression slackened as she parted with a breath that implied relief. "We've been praying you'd come. You must have questions."

Praying? "I do indeed," he replied. "Might you have answers?"

"I believe we might, yes." She peered past him. "Looks like there's some nasty weather moving in. I'll have Amos see to your horse."

"I would appreciate that."

She gave him a resigned smile and closed the door. "Let me take your coat and hat, and then please settle yourself in the parlor. I'll let Miss Caldridge know you're here. Would you like some tea?"

"No, but thank you." Julian shrugged off his coat. "Mrs. Henshaw, I have one question that cannot wait. Is Miss Fairfax in some kind of danger?"

"No, sir," she replied, hanging his coat and hat on the hall tree. "At least, we don't believe so. She's staying with her solicitor and his wife. For the time being, at least."

"Ah, right." Julian frowned as some of his innermost fear dissipated, while his puzzlement over Annie's departure deepened. "Well, that's a relief."

The woman merely gave him another smile and gestured toward the parlor door. "Please make yourself at home. Are you sure you wouldn't like some refreshment?"

"No, nothing, thank you." Julian entered the parlor as he had once before. On that occasion, sunlight had poured through the windows and the air had hummed with chitchat and laughter. Today, the room seemed dull and empty. Unwelcoming. Heaving a sigh, he sank into a chair, swallowed against his impatience, and drummed his fingers on the chair arm.

Not a minute later, the door opened and Janet Caldridge entered. "Mr. Northcott, we were hoping you'd come. I thought you might, I must confess."

"Miss Caldridge." Julian rose to his feet. "I wish I could say, with honesty, that it is a pleasure to be back here. Truth is, I am unsure of my mindset. To say I'm perplexed is an understatement. To begin, Mrs. Henshaw assures me Annie is not in any danger. I trust you are of the same opinion."

"I am, sir," she replied.

"Good. And can you also explain why she sent me a letter stating she never wishes to see me again?"

"I can, yes, with hope that you'll set her fears aside."

Julian frowned. "Her fears?"

The door opened again, and Hattie entered. "Your horse is being stabled, Mr. Northcott," she said, settling herself on the settee beside Janet.

"Thank you." Still frowning, Julian leaned forward. "So what, exactly, is going on? Why did Annie leave? What prompted her to send that letter?"

Janet cleared her throat. "It is a long and rather tragic story, Mr. Northcott. One that began over twenty years ago. I would ask that you let me tell it without interruption, even when I pause to gather myself, as will surely be necessary. Please reserve your questions till the end as well as your judgment on those involved. I, too, shall reserve judgment, pending your response to what you are about to hear."

Julian drew a steadying breath, nodded his silent assent, and sat back.

Janet opened her mouth as if to speak, but hesitated and glanced at Hattie, who took hold of her hand. "Go on, love," Hattie said. "It'll be all right."

Regarding Julian once more, Janet began to unfurl her tale, her voice soft, her gaze on Julian the entire time. And, as the truth of Annie's birth and parentage revealed itself, the reason for her letter became apparent. Julian also realized that his suspicions, his instincts, had merit. These women had played a game of charades spanning years, hiding a truth he could never have guessed. As requested, he never said a word as the account continued, nor did he show emotion other than the occasional clenching of his jaw when Janet's voice faltered, or when tears shone in her eyes, as they did a few times.

"I don't know exactly what prompted Annie to go looking for the truth about her birth," Janet said, as her tale wound down, "though I knew she possessed a few vague memories of her time with me. I'd fully intended to tell her everything but had bided my time simply to give her a chance to recover from the terrible events at the church. Which brings me to your presence in her life, Mr. Northcott. I was going to tell her the truth the weekend we were at Myddleton House. That is, until I learned of her association with you, which made me reconsider my decision. I owe you an apology for my subsequent rudeness, sir, which was borne from fear and resentment, though I harbor neither one any longer. In any case, now you know why Annie sent you that letter. She feared your rejection once you learned the truth of her birth and simply could not bear the thought of it. We offered to keep the information hidden from you, but she refused outright." Janet heaved a sigh. "And so, there it is. I suppose what happens next is up to you."

A whirlwind of thoughts twisted in Julian's head. He needed to move, needed to think. He rose and went to the window, seeing nothing beyond the rain-spattered glass as he continued to absorb all he'd learned while deciding what had to be done as a result. He voiced the first clear thing that came to mind. "I must return to Highfield as soon as possible."

A soft cry of dismay came from behind him. He turned to see Janet and Hattie on their feet. Janet went to the door, opened it, and stood to the side. "Your response is not what we'd hoped for, sir." She lifted her chin. "Be advised that my daughter will not be told of your visit here today. I'll have Amos bring your horse to the gate. Do you need help with your coat?"

Julian winced and rubbed his jaw. "Actually, I'd rather like that cup of tea you offered earlier. A biscuit as well, if you have one, would be most welcome."

"Would you now." Hattie regarded him with a scowl that made him cringe inwardly. "I thought you had to leave as soon as possible."

"I must return to Highfield, yes, and the sooner the better." Julian cleared his throat. "But I'm sure I can spare the time for some refreshment. This unfortunate business has left me a bit parched."

"*Unfortunate business?*" Janet scoffed and folded her arms. "Your audacity, Mr. Northcott, is astonishing. You judge my daughter, and then expect us to serve you refreshment?"

"I have judged no one, Miss Fairfax," Julian replied. "Least of all your daughter."

"But you surely have, sir," Janet cried, "by your decision to abandon her."

"I have no intention of abandoning her." Julian moved back to his chair but remained standing. "Quite the contrary. I intend to marry her."

"Thank the Lord," Hattie muttered, closing her eyes for a moment.

Janet's hands flew to her face. "*Marry* her? But you said... I mean, I don't understand."

Julian sighed. "I love your daughter, Miss Fairfax, and I want to marry her. But since hearing your story today, things have changed. And yes, it concerns judgments, because whether you like it or not, judgments will be made. Unless..."

Janet shook her head. "Unless?"

"Unless you agree to keep this unfortunate business to yourselves. For that is what it is. An unfortunate business." He held up a hand as Hattie opened her mouth as if to argue. "We would not be having this discussion otherwise. My resolve to marry Annie will remain, no matter what you decide. I simply ask that you consider my position and that of my family. While there are many fine people in the gentry, there are also those who take pleasure in feasting on the misery and misfortune of others. As my wife, should Annie's illegitimacy become known, she will, undoubtedly—"

"Be scorned," Janet finished. "I am fully aware of that, though I'm not sure Annie has fully embraced the likelihood. Has it occurred to you that I would also be similarly scorned should the truth of Annie's birth become known?"

"Of course it has. Your own brother disowned you, did he not? Consequently, you must surely understand my concerns as they pertain to my family. Hence my decision to return to Highfield forthwith. I cannot go to London till I have spoken to my parents, to advise them of the circumstances and my intentions. They have a right to know about this beforehand. Please understand, Miss Fairfax, I'm not saying you must deny your daughter. Not at all. I am merely suggesting we keep the truth of her birth between us."

"A family with secrets," Hattie quipped. "Gracious. Whoever heard of such a thing?"

Julian chuckled. "Quite. Simply put, it means you must continue with your almost flawless performances when among those who are not privy to the truth."

Janet nodded. "Like when we come to your and Annie's wedding?"

Julian laughed. "Precisely."

Hattie's eyes widened. "*Almost* flawless, Mr. Northcott?"

"I had a feeling something secretive was going on between the both of you," he said, with a shrug. "I just wasn't sure what it was. Annie seemed oblivious to it."

"Will this affect how your family sees her?" Janet asked.

"No," Julian replied, without hesitation. "At least, not my immediate family. They trust my judgment. Besides, my mother adores Annie already."

"Then I cannot tell you what this means to me, sir, or what it will mean to Annie." Janet's eyes watered again. "She left here with a broken heart."

Julian's throat tightened. "I shall endeavor to mend it as soon as I can, Miss Fairfax. You have my word. And your apology is accepted, of course."

Hattie heaved a sigh. "Tea and a biscuit you said, right, Mr. Northcott?"

"Yes, thank you." Gratified by the morning's discussion, he decided to throw caution to the wind. "Actually, two biscuits, if you can spare them."

"You may have as many as you like, Mr. Northcott," Hattie said, with conviction. "I was right about you, you know. I liked you from the start."

CHAPTER TWENTY-SEVEN

HAVING PLACED HER simple posy of flowers, Annie stepped back from the grave of the man she had known as her father. Since learning the truth of her birth, however, she felt as though she'd never really known him at all. Though much of the initial shock had dissipated, questions continued to clutter her mind. Sadly, the answers to them lay buried at her feet.

"That you loved me is not in doubt, Papa, but you should have told me the truth," she said, blinking tears away. "To find out the way I did was unfair. You must have known these secrets would emerge after your death, so why didn't you prepare me? And what do I do now? Do I continue with this charade? Is that what you would have wanted?"

There was, of course, no response. Nor would there ever be.

This was her first visit to the cemetery. Though she'd attended her father's funeral service, she had not gone to the graveside afterwards. She'd had no desire to face the small crowd that had gathered as a result of the newspaper report. But aside from that, she knew the practice, for women, was discouraged. Women were considered weak, prone to fits of hysteria and fainting. Heaven forbid they display emotion at such a solemn time.

Since returning to London, it had taken Annie this long to summon up the courage, and the desire, to visit the grave. She had learned to take each day in stride, lowering her expectations while making allowances for her moments of weakness. As for the nights, well, they were another matter entirely.

Despite everything, however, Annie had cause to be thankful. Archibald Mason and his wife had been more than gracious, providing room and board while refusing any kind of remuneration. Curious to know if he was already aware, Annie had told Mr. Mason the truth about her birth. Apart from a fleeting, and telling, expression of shock, the man had retained his usual, serious demeanor. He had then commiserated, assured Annie of his discretion, and said what had already been said, that her adoptive father had accepted her as his own, evidenced by leaving his entire estate to her, and in good order. Annie couldn't help but think that marriage to Leo would have meant surrendering her inheritance to him. She wondered, briefly, where her former fiancé might be, and then set the thought aside. As it was, she didn't have to worry about starving or keeping a roof over her head.

Finding a new roof had become a priority. Though there had been no indication of it, Annie already felt as though she'd outstayed her welcome at the Mason household. Returning to Ferndale Grange anytime soon was not something she could consider. Too many painful memories. The same applied to her home on Chester Street. She'd either have to lease the house permanently or sell it. Archibald Mason would undoubtedly advise her on the merits and pitfalls of each option. Maybe she should find some rooms to rent in the meantime.

Nearby voices drew her attention, as did the sudden brush of gentle raindrops on her cheeks. Opening her umbrella, Annie turned from the grave and, with a nod to a passing couple, set off for Chester Street. There was still work to be done. The proverbial road ahead needed to be cleared, so that she might dare to move forward.

ARMS FOLDED, JOSIAH leaned against the door jamb. "Good luck, brother," he said, as Julian pulled on his coat. "I'll see you at one o'clock, hopefully with Annie hanging off your arm."

"From your lips to God's ear." Julian studied his reflection in the hall mirror and straightened his collar. "I suspect getting past Archibald Mason's defenses will be nigh on impossible."

Josiah shrugged. "Set the formal claptrap aside and tell him what lies in your heart."

Julian threw him a doubtful look. "He's a solicitor, Joe, not a priest."

"Trust me."

"I'll think about it." Julian opened the door. "But if I have to wait a few more hours to see her, so be it." His heart skipped at the mere thought. "In any case, I'll see you at one o'clock."

He stepped out into the morning rain and hailed a cab. Not a half hour later, he stood before Archibald Mason's desk.

"Mr. Northcott." The solicitor stood and extended his hand. "It's good to see you again, sir."

"Likewise, Mr. Mason." Julian shook the man's hand. "Thank you for taking the time."

"You're most welcome," Mason replied, retaking his seat. "Sit, please, and tell me how I might help you."

Julian wondered if the man knew the truth of Annie's birth. In any case, his approach merited discretion. "Basically, sir, I'm here for the same reason as before," he replied, as he sat. "I'm hoping to have an opportunity to speak with Miss Fairfax who, I'm told, is staying with your good self and your lady wife."

"I see," the man replied. "Then if you'd care to leave a message, I'll be sure to deliver it to Miss Fairfax this evening."

"This evening?" Julian cleared his throat. "Actually, I'd hoped to speak with the young lady sooner than that, if possible."

The solicitor's brows rose. "Is there a matter of urgency I should be made aware of?"

"No. That is, nothing alarming, I assure you. It's simply a matter of..." he hesitated. There was nothing *simple* about the matter at all, and a verbal dance around the issue would serve no purpose.

"*...tell him what lies in your heart.*"

Julian drew breath and leaned forward slightly. "To hell with propriety, sir. The situation is this. I'm in love with the lady and I'm damn well certain she is in love with me. However, a situation has recently arisen which has led Miss Fairfax to believe she is no longer worthy of me. And I swear to you, Mr. Mason, nothing could be…" He swallowed over the sudden dryness in his throat. "*Nothing* could be further from the truth. I came to London to find her, to set things straight, and I will not leave the city till I have done so. Obviously, the sooner this issue is resolved, the better. For her, and, God knows, for me." He swallowed again. "Please."

Archibald Mason sat completely still for a moment, his expression remarkably unchanged. Then he shifted in his seat and frowned. "While I appreciate your predicament and your eagerness to resolve it, sir, the most I'm able to do is to let Miss Fairfax know you are here in London and looking for her, but that will not be until later today. Are you residing at the same address as before?"

"I am, yes." Julian pinched the bridge of his nose. "Is there any way at all I might call on her this morning?"

"At my private residence?" The man shook his head. "That is not an option, sir."

Julian heaved a sigh. "I will not insult you by offering a bribe, Mr. Mason. Must I beg, then?"

"Neither one would make any difference, Mr. Northcott." Archibald Mason rose to his feet, and extended his hand. "I regret if this is not quite the answer you hoped for. It has, however, been a pleasure to see you again."

Julian regarded the man's outstretched hand, and was tempted, momentarily, to do something he had never done, which was to use the family name in an attempt to force that hand. But the mere thought of doing so left a sour taste in his mouth. Instead, he stifled another sigh and then rose, slowly, to his feet. "I understand, sir, of course," he said, as he shook the man's hand once more. "I shall wait for Miss Fairfax's response, then. Thank you. I appreciate your time and consideration."

As he turned to leave, Mr. Mason spoke again. "I believe you're familiar with the lady's London address, are you not?"

Julian paused. "Yes, I am. Chester Street."

A brief smile appeared. "As I thought." He cleared his throat. "Miss Fairfax has been spending quite a lot of time at the house of late, sorting things out. Not an easy task for her, I'm sure you understand."

Julian's heart quickened at the inference. "Might she be there this morning?"

"I couldn't say," he replied. "I cannot, however, prevent you from going there to check." He smiled again and gave a nod. "I appreciate your discretion, Mr. Northcott, and bid you a very good day."

ANNIE PAUSED IN the dining room doorway and regarded her morning's work. The past few days had been spent sorting through the boxes that had been locked in the attic. She'd lost count of how many times she had ascended and descended the stairs, burdened or not. There had been moments when she'd regretted her refusals of help, due mostly to her physical exhaustion. Otherwise, she had no desire to share this deeply personal experience with anyone. She didn't want to be stoic. She wanted to be the weak woman at the graveside, prone to hysteria, succumbing to whatever her emotions demanded. Doing so, she hoped, might finally grant her a measure of peace.

So far, it continued to elude her.

The sad pile of clothes on the chair by the window, including her wedding dress, was destined for charity. The items on the dining table would be kept. It was notable, she thought, eyeing those items, that the things she cherished most had little to no monetary value. Daisy was nothing more than a raggedy cloth doll from childhood, well-worn and somewhat frayed around the edges. The stack of her favorite books had been read and re-read and would absolutely be read again. The carved wooden trinket box was a treasure in its own right and contained yet more childhood treasures within. A marble she'd found in the park. A cockleshell collected from the beach at Eastbourne. A French coin she'd also found in the park. And a fragment of pottery, with a little blue sailing ship on it, that the gardener had dug up in their small rear garden one day.

How innocent and happy she had been back then, confident of her place in the world, blissfully unaware of her true circumstances. She'd never seen herself as anyone but Annabelle Edwina Fairfax, daughter of a respected physician. Now, whenever she looked in the mirror, she saw someone else. A stranger with familiar features.

Annie's gaze shifted to his chair, and the usual knot of grief tightened beneath her ribs. A memory drifted into her head, one that had established itself at Myddleton House when she'd questioned the duplicity of men.

Papa, at least, was an honest and honorable man.

Not quite.

She looked down at the sleeping-cap grasped in her hand, the one she'd purchased for her father the day she'd bumped into Julian Northcott. For some reason, she hadn't been able to put it with the other items slated for charitable donation. She still needed to inventory the actual contents of the house and decide which to sell and which to keep.

On the positive side, with the exception of her father's trunk, she had all but emptied the attic. The trunk could wait. For now, exhausted by the endless turmoil of heart and mind, Annie wandered into the room, sat at the table, and put the sleeping-cap next to her cloth doll. Bad enough that echoes of the past rang mercilessly through the house. Worse that the echoes no longer rang with quite the same resonance. And, of course, that was not all that weighed on her. The most devastating thing of all was the loss of a potentially wonderful future and the love it had promised.

Almost a fortnight had passed since she'd sent the letter to Julian Northcott. As far as she knew, there had been no response. At least, she'd not had any word forwarded to her from Derbyshire. Of course, she had no cause to expect a response. She'd made it quite clear she didn't want to see him again and her mind was made up.

More lies. More shame. Hers, this time.

But her lack of expectation did not prevent her from daring to hope. Hope had filled the blank spaces between each and every heartbreaking word she'd written. Hope that Julian would see beyond the lies she'd spewed, and question them, challenge them. In her dreams, she dared to imagine he would not hesitate to seek her out, demand to know the real reasons for the letter, and then swear he didn't give a damn about any of them. That he loved her, despite everything.

So much for dreams.

The hall clock began to strike, the chimes accentuating the silence as it announced the hour. Eleven. The morning was almost over. Annie's stomach growled, reminding her she hadn't eaten that day. She didn't actually feel hungry, just weary in heart and mind. Maybe a walk would be beneficial. She glanced at the window. At least the rain had stopped.

A short while later, suitably attired, she stepped out and locked the door behind her. Then, giving the cloudy skies a dubious glance, she descended the steps and paused to look right and left. And then right again.

As always, she recalled that first day when Julian Northcott had turned and walked away from her. Which was why she silently cursed her sudden and ridiculous reaction to the man who was currently walking toward her, a bouquet of flowers clasped in his hand.

Damn her lying eyes, it wasn't him. It couldn't be him. Such things only happened in dreams and romance novels. But, God help her, it looked so much like him. Maybe her weary mind was playing tricks. Maybe it *was* a dream. As she had on one other inconceivable occasion, she dug her nails into her palm.

Doing so changed nothing.

The man drew closer, his identity now undeniable, yet still unthinkable. Annie's vision misted, blurring his image. She blinked once, twice, releasing her tears, and his image returned, clear and sharp. Her hand fumbled as it sought to grasp the iron railing that fronted her house. A necessary crutch.

Julian Northcott halted an arm's length away, jaw clenching as his gaze searched her face, but he remained silent. He was wearing the pearl pin, the one he'd worn the first time they met.

Annie drew a shaky breath. "Good day to you, Mr. North-cott."

A slight frown came and went. "Good day to you, Annie."

The sound of her name on his lips almost robbed her of breath. "Wh…what are you doing here?"

"Looking for you, of course."

"But, how did you know where I was?" She shook her head. "Did you not get my letter?"

"The one where you said I mustn't come looking for you?"

She hiccupped on a sob. "Yes, that one."

"Yes, I got it." He pulled a folded handkerchief from his coat pocket, and moved closer to dab the tears from her cheeks. "Please don't cry. Look, I brought you some flowers. I don't suppose you happen to have a vase in the house, do you?" A smile appeared as he eyed the bouquet. "Red roses. I thought we might arrange them together. They represent love, I'm told."

"You obviously don't understand, sir." Annie's grip on the railing tightened. "There are things you need to know. Things about me. Things I didn't mention in my letter."

He put the handkerchief back in his pocket as his gaze flicked to the railing. "If you're feeling a little unsteady, Annie, take my hand." He held it out. "I'll not let you fall."

"Julian, pl… please," she said, her voice breaking. "I'm not… I'm not who you think I am."

A softness came to his eyes. "I know exactly who you are, Annie Fairfax. Your mother and your aunt explained everything to me."

Annie gaped at him as the meaning behind his words sank into her brain. "You went to Ferndale Grange?"

He groaned. "Well, of course I did! Did you seriously think I wouldn't? That's how I found out where you were. I didn't believe a word of that damn letter. To do so would have meant that everything I'd felt in your presence had been a fallacy, the love in your eyes an illusion. I might not be the most insightful man in the world, Annie, but I've always been certain of you. Always! What I *didn't* know was what, or who, had caused you to lie to that extent. I feared De Witte had got to you. Threatened you, somehow. Truth is, I was relieved when I discovered the real reason for your letter. That said, we do need to discuss it."

He obviously had no idea how relevant his fears had been. Annie drew a shaky breath, wondering if she should mention her encounter with Leo. "I was afraid," she replied. "Afraid that if I told you the truth about the circumstances of my birth, I'd see disapproval in your eyes or hear it in your voice, and I couldn't bear the thought of it."

Frowning, he thumbed an errant tear from her cheek. "Then it appears I must make something abundantly clear. And that is, you can be certain of me as well, Annie. Always."

"Oh, Julian." Annie let go of the railing and reached for his hand, the warmth of his flesh blissful against the chill of hers. "I'm so sorry for doubting you."

"Hmm." He looked down at their joined hands and then glanced about. "You know, it occurred to me, as I turned onto your street just now, that this is the third time I've approached your door. The first time, I was obliged to bid you farewell and never thought to see you again. The second time, I actually knocked on your door, even though I knew you weren't at home. And, once again, I thought you were lost to me. Today, to quote Shakespeare, *is the third time, and I hope good luck lies in odd numbers.* In any case, I have no intention of losing you again." He parted with a soft sigh. "That being so, before anything else is said, I want you to promise me something."

"Anything," she replied. "What is it?"

"That you will never again run away from me. It's becoming very tiresome."

Smiling, she drew a cross over her heart. "I promise."

"Thank you. Given your past record, however, I'm of a mind to hold you to that promise legally." He lifted her hand and kissed it. "Marry me, Annie. Be my wife. Honor me by being forever at my side. Please say you will. I swear to you, there is nothing I want more."

Annie gasped, hardly daring to believe what she'd heard, thinking no daydream she might have conjured up could ever be this perfect. Choked by a sudden rush of emotion, she merely nodded, while grappling with a fresh swell of tears that mocked her attempt to prevent them. "I will," she managed at last. "Of course I will. There is nothing I want more, either."

"Then it's official," he said with conviction, as he pulled his handkerchief out and mopped her cheeks again. "I have just become the happiest man on Earth."

Annie laughed and decided that before this incredible day was through, she would tell him the truth about Leopold and what had taken place at Freya's Farewell. There would be no more secrets, no more deceit. For now, however, there was something else she needed to say. "It nearly killed me writing that letter, Julian," she said, gazing into his eyes. "I swear it was the most difficult thing I have ever done. Please forgive me."

"Nothing to forgive, my love." He regarded the bouquet as if he'd just remembered it was there. "We need a vase for these. I don't suppose you happen to have some tea in the house as well, do you? I'm parched."

IN TRUTH, JULIAN couldn't have given a damn about a vase for the flowers, or a cup of tea. What bothered him to the depths of his soul was the pallor of Annie's face, the uncertainty in her beautiful eyes, and the dark shadows lingering beneath them. She'd lost weight, and her hand, clasped in his, had felt like ice. She had suffered and it showed. Thankfully, she looked a little better now, seated beside him at the messy dining table, her cheeks faintly pink, hands cradling a cup of tea. His proposal of marriage had chased the uncertainty from her eyes, though the shadows beneath still lingered.

He hadn't intended to propose on the street. He'd envisaged somewhere a little more romantic. Beneath the spreading branches of a handsome oak, perhaps, or beside a sparkling fountain in a park. But the way Annie had looked at him, hopeful and fearful at the same time, had clawed at his heart. Asking her to marry him, at that precise moment, was almost instinctive. She needed to be assured of his commitment, of where his heart lay. What could be better than a promise of forever?

But he hadn't quite finished yet. The promise needed to be sealed, and he wasn't about to do that on the street. He reached into his pocket and pulled out the small, green leather box he'd tucked in there that morning. "Annie, my love, I hope this is to your liking. If not, please say so." He opened the box, removed a ring from its velvet cushion, and reached for her left hand. "May I?'

"Yes, of course!" Annie's eyes widened as he slid the ring, with its cluster of diamonds, onto her finger. "Oh, Julian, it's beautiful."

"I'm glad you like it," he said. "It belonged to my maternal great-grandmother. Her name was Margaret, and that center diamond was originally in a brooch owned by Queen Elizabeth. At least, that's the story that's been passed down, though no one seems to know exactly how the stone came to be in our posses-sion. Does it fit?"

Annie held up her hand, a look of wonder on her face. "It fits perfectly. I hardly know what to say. I can't believe all this is happening. You here, like this. It's more than I hoped for. More than I prayed for."

"Your happiness is all I want, Annie." Julian took her hand again, gratified by its warmth. "Now, as I mentioned earlier, there are things that need to be discussed. Will you hear me?"

She regarded him for a moment and then looked away, but not before Julian saw something else reflecting in her eyes. *Fear? No, surely not.*

"May I begin, please, Julian?" She regarded him once more. "There is something I must tell you before we go any further."

A prickle of apprehension wandered across Julian's scalp. "Of course."

She gave a quick smile. "Did Jan… that is, did my mother and my aunt tell you how I came to learn of my illegitimacy?"

Julian nodded. "They said you'd remembered things from your childhood and found the documents and letters while they were at church. Why? Was that not how it happened?"

There followed a short stretch of silence, then, "Sort of, but there's a bit more to it than that."

"Oh?" Julian raised a brow. "What didn't they tell me?"

"It's not what they didn't tell *you*," she replied, looking down at her teacup. "It's what I didn't tell *them*."

A sense of unease had him shifting in his seat. "Go on."

She released a slow breath and met his gaze once more. "On the Saturday after you left, I set out on a walk to Freya's Farewell. I thought to revisit our Thursday outing. To relive it in my mind." Another smile came and went, followed by a touch of deeper color in her cheeks. "It was a fine day, but terribly windy. Ruffy was with me, as usual, sniffing here and there. As we were walking along the edge of the stream, he halted suddenly, pointed his nose into the woods, and began to bark. His hackles lifted as well. I'd never seen him do that before, so it was unsettling, especially since I couldn't see any reason for it. There was no sign of anyone or anything in the woods. Anyway, after a few moments, he stopped barking and his hackles went down. I told myself he must have spotted a fox or some other creature. In any case, he went off across the fields and I continued on my own, though I confess my uneasiness never quite left me."

As she'd been speaking, a seed of suspicion as to where this was going had sprouted in Julian's brain. Something he hardly dared to contemplate. The mere thought of it chilled his blood.

"When I got to the top, I hesitated to venture onto the ledge because of the wind," she continued. "It was so strong and so loud, which is why I didn't see him, why I didn't hear him." Her lip quivered. "I was looking at the view, Julian. I was looking at Myddleton and thinking about you. Not for one moment did I suspect someone was there, that I wasn't alone. Not until someone grabbed me from behind. A man, obvious from his size and strength. He pushed me onto the ledge, and I thought... I thought I was about to die." She closed her eyes briefly and pressed her hand to her mouth as the sweet blush in her cheeks faded.

"Christ." Julian pushed his chair back and went to lift her into his arms. "Leopold?"

Trembling, she all but fell into his embrace. "Yes, but I didn't know that at first." She gazed up at him. "It was only when he spoke that I realized who it was."

Molten rage coursed through Julian's veins. It took an effort to keep his voice steady. "Did he hurt you?"

"He frightened me. I mean, he implied he was going to push me off the ledge. I feel sick just thinking about it." She shook her head. "I never once saw his face. I asked what he was doing there, and he said he'd been watching me for some time. Watching *us*. You and me and the twins."

"How did he know where to find you?"

"I can't be certain. Inspector Taggart said Mr. Mason's office was broken into, but didn't think it had anything to do with Leopold. Yet he knew about our day at the river, my night at Myddleton, and our outing to Freya's Farewell. He even mentioned our kiss. Then he laughed in my ear and told me I'd been wasting my time, because once the truth came out about who I really was, you'd abandon me. He said my entire life had been a lie, that I was not who I thought I was, and that Hattie and Janet knew the truth of it. I asked him what he meant, but he just laughed again and said I had to ask them. I had no idea what he was talking about. I thought he'd lost his mind."

Julian's arms tightened around her. "Promise me you'll never go out alone again. At least till this cad is caught."

"I don't think he will be caught."

"Why do you say that?"

"Because I remembered the ring that Hattie mentioned, and I looked at his hands to see if he was wearing it, but he wasn't. He wasn't wearing any rings at all. So I asked him if he killed Karl Hoffman. He denied it immediately, but said he had to leave England because the police were looking for him and he didn't want to hang or be transported. Then he released me, but demanded I close my eyes and count out loud to fifty without stopping or I'd regret it. I got as far as twenty, by which time I knew he'd gone. I stayed up there for quite a while afterwards, trying to make sense of all he'd said. I was so confused by it all and knew I needed to gather my wits before returning to Ferndale, because I'd already decided I wasn't going to tell Hattie or Janet about any of it."

Julian frowned. "Why? Surely you don't harbor some kind of sympathy for the fellow."

"No, it had nothing to do with sympathy. What he told me about my life being a lie made no sense, but there was a measure of conviction in his voice that made me hesitate to reject it out of hand. I mean, why would he concoct such a tale? It was vague, yet also specific, somehow. And I just had this… this *feeling*. What I couldn't get straight in my head was how I could approach

Hattie and Janet about it. If they were harboring secrets, how could I be sure they'd admit to them? And if they denied everything, how could I be sure they were being honest? So, I decided I needed some kind of proof. Something tangible that left no room for doubt. If secrets did exist, perhaps their origins lay within the walls of Ferndale Grange. I went home eventually, of course, told them I had a headache, and took myself off to bed. The next morning, I waited till they'd left for church and then set about searching the house for something—anything—that might explain what Leo meant. And I found it, Julian. Some yellowed papers, hidden away in a chest in my mother's bedroom." She winced. "I cannot begin to describe how I felt as I read those letters. In a matter of minutes, everything I'd held true crumbled into dust. It was as if my life, the life I'd always known, had been lived by someone else. The real me, the secret bastard child, possessed nothing more than a handful of vague memories; a childhood visit to a house in the countryside, fields and stone walls, a black-and-white dog, an eggcup. And a song." She laughed softly. "The funny thing is…"

Julian groaned. "I fail to see anything remotely funny in this, Annie."

"I know. It's just that in those first few seconds at Freya's Farewell, when I thought I was about to die, all I could think of was that I'd never see you again, and I regretted, with all my heart, not telling you that I loved you when I'd had the chance. As it happened, learning the truth about the circumstances of my birth had the same result. I made a decision that, as far as I knew, meant I would never see you again. Which is why, now that I am blessed with this chance, I must say it before anything else is said." Her sweet gaze wandered over his face, before settling back on his eyes. "I love you, Julian Northcott. So very much."

"And I love you, Annie Fairfax, with all my heart." He stroked her hair. "You should have had more faith in me."

"Yes, I should have, of course," she replied, "but I wasn't only thinking of you. I was thinking of your family as well. Do they know the truth about me?"

Julian nodded. "That's why it took me a while to get here. Since I knew I wanted to marry you, I had to return to Highfield to discuss everything with the family. Then I came here to find you."

"Dare I ask what they thought of it all?"

"That's what we need to talk about." Julian cast a quick glance at the clock. *Time yet.* "After some discussion, it was agreed that, on the face of it at least, it would be best to leave things as they are. Or were. That is, if asked, to say that you are a physician's daughter from London."

Annie blinked. "But why would...? I mean, that's not really who I am, though, is it? Are you saying they disapprove of my circumstances? Of the truth?"

"That is not what I'm saying at all," he replied. "What I *am* saying is that your family and mine knows the truth, as they should, but when it comes to anyone else, the truth is none of their business."

She wrinkled her nose. "Even so, I'm not sure I'm comfortable with more deceit. There has been enough of it already."

"I see your point, but you have to consider the world to which you have recently been introduced and will soon be a part of. Its occupants might be described as gentlefolk, but they are not all gentle. If meddlesome Lady Marzipan, who means absolutely nothing to you and me, corners you at some society event and asks about your background, what would you rather tell her? The truth you've embraced for most of your life, or the somewhat complicated truth you've only known about for the past fortnight? And which of those responses, do you think, is more likely to elicit a malicious hailstorm of gossip followed by a blatant snub?"

Annie appeared to ponder for a moment, then, "Lady Marzipan, Julian?"

Julian chuckled. "She's not real, of course."

"I actually find that disappointing." A slight frown appeared.

"But even if she was, I wouldn't actually be obliged to tell her anything, would I?"

"No, but dodging the question, no matter how graciously, would be guaranteed to set her nose twitching and to send her off in search of whatever it is you're not willing to share. And, mark my words, she will not stop till she finds it. And when she does, she will take immense pleasure in sharing it with anyone who'll listen." He pressed a kiss to her forehead. "I just want you to think about it."

"Given what you've just described, I don't believe I need to think about it."

"Don't misunderstand me," Julian said. "There's no shortage of wonderful people either."

"I know, I've met some of them already." She fiddled with a ringlet. "Um, may I ask how Jan—um, that is, my mother and aunt were when you visited? Are they well?"

He'd been wondering when she'd ask, hoping she would. "Yes, they're both well. They were concerned about you, of course, though that went away once I told them I intended to marry you. They understand that all this has been a tremendous shock, and that you need time to sort things out. They love you very much, Annie."

"I know they do." Annie heaved a sigh. "Did my mother tell you she was in the church that day? That she saw everything?"

"Yes, she did. We had quite the chitchat over tea and some rather excellent biscuits."

"Oh, I'm so glad." Annie glanced away for a moment. "Would it be acceptable, do you think, to invite her to our wedding? I mean, given what we've just discussed, would it even be wise? And my aunt too, of course."

"They'll be there, of course," he replied. "Bear in mind, they've been playing a game of charades for years, They're experts at it! Nothing needs to change, and not just to protect you, but also to protect your mother."

Annie gasped. "Oh, my goodness. Yes, of course. How selfish

of me not to think of her."

"I'm sure they don't see it that way. As far as they're concerned, the most important thing is that you know the truth. That's all they ever wanted. Well, that and your happiness. So the answer is *yes*, of course they'll be invited to our wedding. I've no doubt they'd have found a way to be there anyway. Which begs the question, where would you like the ceremony to take place? Here, in London? Or would you prefer we go to Highfield and have the banns read in the local church?"

"Highfield, definitely." Her face brightened. "I cannot wait to see it."

"I cannot wait for you to see it."

"Oh, and I forgot to ask. How is Georgie? Is she a well-behaved pup?"

"Georgie is doing very well." Julian cleared his throat. "And so is Mr. Darcy."

Annie gasped. "You didn't!"

Julian winced. "I did."

She laughed. "Well, I cannot wait to see them. And the twins, of course."

"I'm looking forward to introducing you to Louisa. I have a feeling you'll become the best of friends." Julian glanced at the clock as it struck the half-hour. "For now, though, we should perhaps think about leaving. I'd like to take you out to celebrate our engagement. We still have a couple of minutes, however, and I was wondering if I might spend it kissing my future bride."

Annie's answer was to lift her chin in readiness. Julian smiled and lowered his mouth to hers. Eyes closed, she leaned into him, her mouth parting slightly as he gently caressed her lips with his. Sliding his hands down her back, he drew her closer, breathing in her sweet scent, molding her body to his as much as her petticoats would allow. Lord, how he wanted her, *craved* her. A new limit to his self-control, thus far untested, loomed ever closer.

Too close, in fact.

He lifted his head. "Annie," he said, huskily, "we should leave."

Biting her bottom lip, rosy from his kiss, she peered up at him. "Do we have to? This isn't Freya's Farewell. We could just stay here."

Julian parted with a groan. "Believe me, my sweet, the idea is extremely tempting, but—"

A loud growl from Annie's stomach interrupted him. She grimaced. "Excuse me. I missed breakfast this morning."

Julian frowned. "How come?"

"I wasn't hungry."

"So, when did you last eat? And I mean, a proper meal."

"*Um*, it was…"

"You actually have to think about it?" Julian sighed. "Right, let's go. I'm going to feed you, and by hand if necessary. No arguments."

ANNIE FELT THE scrutiny of curious eyes as she and Julian were ushered through the restaurant to their table. Male eyes, for the most part. This was, after all, a masculine world. The few women present were noticeable solely by their scarcity, Annie included.

It was a grand establishment, with white linen cloths, gleaming cutlery, and sparkling glassware. Judging by their direction, Annie guessed their table to be the solitary one situated by the window and next to a rather splendid palm, which promised some privacy. There was, however, someone already seated at it.

The man, who appeared to be of a similar age to Julian, rose to his feet as they approached and stepped forward to meet them. With his tousled mass of tawny curls, brilliant blue eyes, and a solid physique that matched Julian's, he was utterly striking in appearance. Though immaculately-dressed, his smile gave the impression of easygoing charm, void of arrogance. A suspicion of his identity brushed across Annie's mind.

"Annie," Julian said, as they halted, "I'd like to introduce you to my brother, Mr. Josiah Northcott. Joe, this is Miss Annabelle Fairfax." He gave her a fond glance. "My *fiancée*."

Annie felt a flush of pleasure from the top of her head to her toes. But she couldn't let the moment distract her from the expected niceties. "It's a pleasure to meet you, Mr. Northcott," she said, her suspicion confirmed. "Your brother speaks very highly of you."

Josiah, whose eyes had widened briefly at *fiancée*, studied her for a moment, then, "She's perfect, Julian," he said softly. "Absolutely perfect."

"Indeed," Julian replied, as a blush warmed Annie's cheeks, "and she is awaiting your reply."

"Yes, of course." Josiah gave her a friendly grin. "Forgive me, Miss Fairfax. It's simply that I've heard much about you as well. It's truly an honor to meet you at last. And since you've apparently agreed to become part of the Northcott family, you needn't bother with the formalities. Josiah is perfectly acceptable, or Joe if you prefer."

"Then you must call me Annie," she replied, returning the smile.

"Annie," he repeated, and gestured to the table. "Well, Annie, I think we should sit down and order champagne, since it appears we have something to celebrate."

The next hour of Annie's life was yet another to be added to her list of most pleasurable. If she had any nervousness at all, it disappeared minutes after taking her seat. The close bond between Julian and Josiah became evident immediately, their brotherly exchanges ranging from friendly arguments about nothing of consequence, to hilarious accounts of their foolish childhood escapades. Yet, not for a moment, had Annie felt left out or ignored. To the contrary, she found herself being entertained, and with obvious consideration for her fragile emotions. Some subjects had been notably avoided, and she was thankful for it. Besides, to be in the company of two very handsome and charming men, one of whom she loved beyond words, could never be anything but wonderful.

As for the food, Julian had not been joking when he'd said he was going to feed her. He'd fussed over her from the soup to the dessert. Annie now sat back in her chair, her stomach no longer growling, her head perhaps a little fuzzy from her two glasses of champagne.

"Is any of your art on display at Highfield Hall, Josiah?" she asked. "I would love to see some of your work."

"There is only one of mine at Highfield," he replied. "Most of my paintings are commissioned and displayed in private homes."

"Family portraits?"

"A few," he replied, cradling his brandy snifter. "Individual portraits tend to be more in demand at the moment. You know, the usual thing. Stony-faced lord, hand on hip, polished boots you can see your face in, and his favorite hound beside him."

"But how wonderful to have such a talent." Annie's thoughts drifted back to Myddleton House and its majestic foyer. "Do you also paint ceiling murals?"

Josiah, who had just taken a mouthful of liquor, sputtered and spat most of it onto the pristine white tablecloth.

Julian raised a brow. "Brandy not to your liking, Joe?"

"I do beg your pardon." Eyes visibly watering, Josiah blinked and cleared his throat. "The brandy is excellent. It just went down the wrong way." He cleared his throat again and pulled a watch from his waistcoat pocket. "Lord above, where has the time gone? This past hour has been truly splendid, but I have an appointment this afternoon and really should be going. Besides, I'm sure you'd prefer some time to yourselves. Two's company and all that. Do you have plans?"

Julian reached over and covered Annie's hand with his. "Apart from spending the rest of our lives together? Not really, no."

Annie's heart somersaulted, stealing her breath.

Josiah gave a soft whistle. "I'm impressed, brother," he said. "That was beautiful."

Julian smiled. "Actually, Annie and I do have to make arrangements." He squeezed her hand. "Because I am not going back to Highfield without her."

CHAPTER TWENTY-EIGHT

"THERE'S A LETTER here addressed to Hattie," Annie said, handing the sealed envelope to Julian. "How odd."

"This is your father's writing?"

"Yes." Annie, kneeling beside her father's oak storage chest, sat back on her heels. "I wonder why he didn't give it to her?"

"Maybe he meant to and never got the chance."

"Do you think it might have something to do with my adoption?"

"It might." Julian knew that's what she hoped to find. Something in writing from her father that might compensate, in some way, for the shame of her birth. So far, her hopes had been dashed. "We can take a detour to Ferndale Grange on the way to Highfield if you like. Maybe stop off for a day or two, give Hattie the letter, and learn what it's all about. Assuming she decides to tell us."

Annie's eyes widened and a touch of pink came to her cheeks. "Would that be possible?"

"Of course." Though she'd never asked, Julian had a feeling she wanted to visit her mother and aunt even before she found the letter. The past three days, spent in his company, had seen Annie daring to embrace a future that held no fear. A future where she knew she would be protected and loved. And in embracing her future, she had become more accepting of her past. The shadows beneath her eyes had all but disappeared and her appetite, while still that of a bird, had more or less returned.

All this despite the fact they'd been clearing out what remained in the house on Chester Street, a difficult exercise for Annie, but cleansing, nevertheless. Everything had been inventoried, whether to be kept, stored appropriately, or given away.

Annie had put off clearing out her father's trunk till this final day.

"That would be lovely, Julian, thank you." Eyes bright, she leaned over the edge of the trunk once more. "Let's see what else is in here."

Her disappointment continued. The contents of the trunk were mostly an inventory of Doctor Clarence Fairfax's professional life. Lists of patients going back decades, medical records and ledgers. It also contained a few personal letters to Muriel before they married, which Annie set to one side. But, with the exception of the letter addressed to Hattie, there was little else that fostered intrigue.

"I assume it's to be shipped as well?" Julian asked, getting to his feet as Annie closed the lid on the chest.

"Yes, I think so." Annie heaved a sigh. "I'd like to keep it for the time being, at least."

A short while later, they stood together on the step, Annie clutching the house key. Her hand shook as she inserted the key into the lock. She held it there for a moment as if readying herself, drew breath, and then turned it.

The lock clicked.

"There." She removed the key and gazed up at the house's façade. "It is finished."

Julian stroked his knuckles down her cheek. "Are you tired, sweetheart? Shall I hail a cab?"

Smiling up at him, she shook her head and looped her arm through his. "Thank you, but I'd rather walk if you don't mind. Besides, we're not expected till seven, though I don't suppose they'll mind if we're a little bit early."

"I'm looking forward to it," Julian said.

"So am I," Annie replied. "I'll miss them. They've been so kind to me, Julian."

It seemed Julian had gained Archibald Mason's full approval, having been invited to dine with them that evening. It was to be Annie's final night at the Mason's house. Indeed, it was their final night in London. Tomorrow, they would begin the journey to Yorkshire, which, as of a half-hour ago, now included a detour into Derbyshire.

As it turned out, dinner for four at the Mason's house became dinner for five, due to the unexpected arrival of Inspector Taggart. He had not come intending to eat, however. He had come to relay some news to Annie, which he did after being introduced to Julian.

"Karl Hoffman has been found," he announced, taking a glass of vermouth from the servant's tray. "However, I consider the harsh facts of his case to be unsuitable for a lady's ear. Suffice to say, he was discovered some weeks ago somewhere down near the docks, barely conscious and in a sorry state, his identity unknown, his speech incoherent. He was taken to St. Thomas' hospital, though he was not, initially at least, expected to live. God, evidently, decided otherwise. Though still weak, Mr. Hoffman is now alert and talking. A letter has already been dispatched to his family in Germany."

Julian, aware of what Annie was about to ask and what the likely answer would be, moved to her side.

"Was Leopold responsible for Mr. Hoffman's injuries, Inspector?"

The man inclined his head. "I fear he was, Miss Fairfax, and although Mr. Hoffman's memory of that night is not fully intact, he claims he did not go down without a fight. Suffice to say, Leopold De Witte likely carries a scar on his left cheek. And your lady companion was also correct about the stolen ring. At least, Mr. Hoffman no longer has it, and assumes it was taken from his finger by De Witte, though he has no proof."

"How dreadful." Annie heaved a soft sigh. "That poor man. Thank God he survived."

"Indeed. In any case, we're still looking for De Witte. I assume you've had no correspondence or dealings with him since we last spoke?"

Julian held his breath and waited.

"Um…" She glanced at Julian. "Actually, yes, Inspector, I have had dealings with him."

Taggart looked momentarily taken aback. "In person?"

"Yes, sir."

"Where and when was this?"

"The Saturday after your visit to Ferndale Grange."

"Good Lord." A flush of red crept over the man's face. "He came to the house?"

"No, sir. I was out on one of my walks when he approached me."

Frowning, Taggart put his hands on his hips. "Why have I not been informed of this? I assume you contacted the police."

Annie shook her head. "I did not, sir."

Taggart gaped at her. "Why the hell not?"

"Easy, Taggart," Julian said, stepping partially between them. "Miss Fairfax has been through a lot lately."

"Yes, of course. I beg your pardon, Miss Fairfax." The man scrubbed a hand over his face. "But we should have been informed, nevertheless. How did he know where to find you? Did he threaten you?"

"I don't know for certain how he knew where I was," Annie replied. "I did wonder if he'd been the one who broke into Mr. Mason's office, but you said my file was untouched. He didn't actually hurt me, Inspector, but he frightened me with his presence. Then he told me he had no intention of being jailed or transported and was leaving England the next day. That being so, I did not see the point of telling the police about the incident. Leopold De Witte is long gone by now."

"Is he, indeed." Taggart narrowed his eyes. "Can you be

certain of that, Miss Fairfax?"

Archibald Mason cleared his throat. "If it is necessary to continue with this discussion, might I ask that you do so after dinner?"

～

"THE YOUNG LADY should have informed us, Northcott." Taggart tucked his pipe between his teeth and struck a match, cupping his hands around the pipe bowl, cheeks hollowing as he drew on the flame. "We might have caught the bastard before he left the country," he continued, speaking through his teeth. "If he has, in fact, left the country, which I seriously doubt."

At Julian's request, following the somewhat tense dinner party, he and Taggart had removed to the small terrace in the Mason's rear garden. It was obvious the inspector still harbored frustrations following Annie's admission. However, Julian wasn't there to placate the fellow. "Miss Fairfax had her reasons, Inspector."

"The devil you say." Taggart gave a sardonic laugh. "May I know what they were?"

Julian shook his head. "I would be breaking a confidence, sir. I do, however, share your misgivings about the fellow leaving the country, which gives me concerns about Miss Fairfax's future safety. De Witte seems to be adept at keeping track of her whereabouts."

"Which might not be the case had the young lady kept us informed."

Julian clenched his jaw against a twinge of impatience. "I don't disagree, which brings me to the reason I wished to speak to you in private. I'd like to be prepared should the fellow decide to show up at Highfield Hall. More specifically, invite himself to our wedding, which is to be held there."

The man huffed. "I get the impression he's arrogant enough

to do so. Is it police protection you're after?"

"An unofficial police presence, perhaps," Julian replied. "How would you feel about being invited as a guest? Better yet, bring a colleague."

"Have you set a date for this wedding?"

"Not precisely. I estimate four or five weeks from now, all being well. It's to be a private affair in the family chapel. I secured a license for it just this morning."

"Not wasting any time, are you?"

"I don't see the point of doing so."

"Hmm." The man appeared to mull as he drew on his pipe, releasing several puffs of smoke before he gave Julian a sideways glance. "We'd be housed and fed, I assume?"

"In comfort and in copious amounts, Inspector."

A definite gleam came to Taggart's eyes. "Very well, North-cott, get the details to me as soon as you can, and I'll see if I can arrange it. If this scoundrel happens to show up, we'll nab him."

CHAPTER TWENTY-NINE

"HERE WE ARE," Julian said, as the carriage drew to a halt outside Ferndale Grange. There followed the distant sound of a dog barking in the house, followed by the sight of a familiar, furry face at the parlor window. "And it would appear we've just been officially announced."

Annie laughed. "Aww, Ruffy. I have missed him." Excited and apprehensive at the same time, she regarded the house, which now held new meaning for her. "Are you sure you won't stay, Julian?"

"No, my love, not on this occasion." Julian stepped down from the carriage and turned to assist her. "This visit is meant only for the three of you. I'll be back for you in the morning, of course."

Annie's feet had barely touched the ground before Ferndale's front door flew open and Hattie appeared, nudged aside a moment later by Janet. There could be no doubting the delight on their faces. Fighting a sudden rise of emotion, Annie hesitated, swallowing against a threat of tears.

"Come on," Julian said, opening the garden gate for her. "They're waiting for you. Do you have the letter?"

"I do." Annie patted the cloth bag in her grasp and looked up at him. "I wonder if you truly know how much I love you, Mr. Northcott. You have saved me in so many ways."

Julian's eyes softened. "I love you too." He kissed her cheek.

"Promise me you'll not go wandering off alone."

"I already did."

"I want to hear it again."

"I promise," she said, drawing a cross over her heart. Then she picked up her skirts, and all but ran along the path to the front door. Stifling a sob, she flung herself into a dual embrace, breathing in Janet and Hattie's sweet, familiar scents.

"I have missed you," she said, kissing Janet's cheek and then Hattie's. "I have missed you both so much."

"We've missed you too, love," Hattie said, dabbing her eyes with her apron. "Oh, but you look well. How long can you stay? Is Mr. Northcott not joining us?"

"I'd like to stay the night if I may, and no, Mr. Northcott is not joining us. Good day to you as well, Ruffy." Annie bent to pet the little dog who'd been pawing at her skirts. "But he'll be back here in the morn—"

"Oooh!" Janet's squeal startled Annie and Ruffy. "He proposed, Hattie. Look at that ring. Oh, Annie, it's beautiful."

"What? Let me see." Hattie grabbed Annie's left hand, her eyes widening. "Lord above, the size of that diamond. It's a wonder you can lift your hand. Oh, but it's magnificent, pet. I'm so happy for you. Only one night?"

The sound of the carriage leaving drew Annie's attention. She turned and raised a farewell hand to Julian. "Yes, only one, I'm afraid," she replied. "We're leaving for Highfield tomorrow. We have a wedding to arrange. And you're invited, of course."

THE ATMOSPHERE AT Ferndale Grange had changed. Or perhaps it was simply that Annie finally recognized what had always been there. Whatever the case, gone were the feelings of uncertainty and resentment, in their place an impression of comfort and love. A sense of coming home. Annie hoped the ambience was not about to be disturbed by the mysterious contents of a letter.

Frowning, Hattie regarded the envelope Annie had just given her. "You say you found it in a storage chest?"

Annie nodded. "The one where he kept all his paperwork. It was tucked into a bundle of receipts. I have to assume he didn't want you to read it till after his death."

"Why would your father write a letter to me?" she muttered, still staring at the envelope.

"That is for you to find out, Hattie." Annie, seated at the kitchen table, took a sip of her tea, and tried to hide her eagerness to discover the answer.

"Are you going to open it?" Janet asked. "If you'd rather do so in private, we can leave."

"Goodness, no, you don't have to do that. Let's see what it says." Hattie went to a drawer, pulled out a letter opener, and sliced the envelope open. "Whatever it is, I cannot imagine it would be anything bad."

"I hope not," Annie replied, crossing her fingers beneath the table.

Drawing breath, Hattie removed the letter and began to read, her expression going from one of puzzlement to shock, her eyes filling with tears as she sank onto a chair. "Well, I'll be," she murmured. "All that time and he never said a word. Not a word."

Annie shared a questioning look with Janet.

"Is it bad?" Janet asked.

Hattie sniffed and shook her head. "He knew all along," she said, her face crumpling as she gave the letter to Annie. "All along."

Annie drew breath and pored over the paper.

My dear Mrs. Henshaw,

Well, it would seem I have gone to pastures new, otherwise you would not be reading this epistle of mine. That being so, it is possible my beloved Annie is now aware of her unfortunate beginnings and how she came to be my daughter in name only.

If she is as yet unaware, I trust you will reveal the truth to her gently, for it will surely be a shock. I confess I never found the courage to tell her myself. The words, I fear, would have tasted too bitter on my tongue. It is of little consequence now, of course. Though I trust she knows it in her heart, please impress upon her that Muriel and I loved her as our own. She must never doubt it.

At this point, Mrs. Henshaw, I wonder if you have asked yourself why I am soliciting you to reveal the circumstances surrounding Annie's birth. After all, you should not be cognizant of them, should you? That is, not unless you happen to be related to the child in some way. Which, of course, you are.

Yes, Harriet Caldridge, I am quite aware of your impertinent charade and always have been. Your attempt at falsifying your references left much to be desired. The motivation behind it, however, intrigued me, though I had my suspicions. So, I decided to do a little digging. Much to my indignation, my suspicions turned out to be correct, and I fully intended to challenge your deception and send you on your way.

Muriel, however, changed my mind. Or perhaps I should say I acquiesced to the pleadings of the woman I loved. When I told her of your chicanery and the reason behind it, she begged me to make a concession, the only concession my conscience would allow. So, despite a multitude of misgivings, I employed you. I did not, however, do so for your sake. I did it for Muriel, whose sympathetic heart insisted my sister be allowed to maintain a connection with her illegitimate child, albeit a clandestine one. Which was, of course, the original objective of your attempt to deceive.

My dear lady, I am compelled to concede, false references and misgivings aside, that your employment proved to be more than a reluctant concession on my part. Your service to my household has been totally without blemish. I am indebted to you for your kindness to Muriel during her final years, and I am thankful for the love and guidance you have shown Annie as she has grown into womanhood. I depart this world comforted by the knowledge of your continued presence in her life.

As for Janet, though she disappointed me, I never stopped loving her. That love, in the end, was the cornerstone that determined my concession and my acceptance of you into my household.

More than this, I confess, would have taken a better man than I was able to be, may God forgive me.

I leave you with my sincere gratitude,
Clarence Fairfax

Scrubbing tears from her eyes, Annie read the words again, secretly admitting they were not quite what she'd hoped for. But then, what she'd hoped for was of her own creation. The letter in her hand actually epitomized the man she had known and loved as her father. They were honest words, written from his heart, a testimony to his compassion and the steadfastness of his doctrine.

"He's right, Hattie," she said, passing the letter to Janet. "You have been an invaluable part of my life. Of all our lives, Mama's included."

"A privilege and an honor," she replied, as Annie passed the letter to Janet.

Janet eyed the paper with obvious reluctance. "Given that you're both in tears, I'm not sure I want to read it."

"You must, Mama," Annie said. "I suspect it might give you solace."

Hattie, still sniffling, nodded. "Yes, indeed. Oh, my goodness, I did not expect that."

Janet read quietly, her expression unchanging. Even when it seemed apparent she'd reached the end of the letter, she remained silent and continued to stare at the paper.

"Are you all right, Mama?" Annie asked.

Janet flinched as if waking from a dream. "Yes, dear, I am. I was just thinking that my brother was under no obligation to do what he did. He could quite easily have cast us both aside. I cannot deny I'd have struggled without him. All things considered, I've been fortunate, as have you, Annie." She laughed softly as she glanced about. "I find myself thanking him for this day, with my child seated beside me, a royal diamond on her finger, readying herself to marry the nephew of a local earl."

"I had a happy childhood, Mama," Annie replied. "I truly did. I wanted for nothing."

"I know," she replied. "And that is all that matters."

"I agree." Hattie scrubbed her handkerchief over her nose and pushed her chair back. "Right, well, I'm going to put the kettle on, then I want to hear all about your wedding plans and how we fit into them."

"They're not quite finalized yet," Annie replied. "The ceremony is to be a little different to what you're imagining, I suspect."

Janet wrinkled her nose. "So, not Westminster Abbey then."

She chuckled. "Not quite. Actually, it's to be a quiet ceremony in the family's private chapel. Julian has already obtained the necessary license. His grandparents were the last to be married there, apparently."

"Oh, I see." Janet smiled and glanced away briefly. "Well, I'm sure it'll be lovely."

"I can guess what you're thinking, Mama, but you're wrong," Annie said. "You and Hattie will be there, I promise. The decision to have a private ceremony has nothing to do with my birth."

"Well, that's good to know." Janet pressed a hand to her chest. "Admittedly, I did wonder."

"I'm sure it'll be lovely, pet," Hattie said, busy at the stove. "I have to say, without mentioning another name, you've had a narrow escape."

"Odd you should say that," Annie replied. "You see, I have a confession to make and you're not going to like it, though it will certainly explain our decision to have a private ceremony. It's about the weekend when I found out the truth of who I was. I didn't go looking for proof because I'd suddenly remembered something. I went looking for proof because I had an encounter with someone atop Freya's Farewell."

Janet exchanged a glance with Hattie. "What kind of encounter?"

"A rather unpleasant one," Annie replied. "You're right, Hattie. I've had a narrow escape."

"Uh oh." Hattie's hand paused over the tea caddy. "I have a feeling I don't want to hear this."

"Probably not, but you have to," Annie replied, and proceeded to recount her meeting with Leopold, softening the more unpleasant details of it substantially. Even so, their response was, as expected, a combination of remorse, horror, and indignation.

"Well, there'll be no more walking out alone, young lady," Hattie said, scowling as she set the teapot on the table. "At least not until this scoundrel is captured or, better yet, pronounced dead. Till then, he remains a threat."

"Which is why Julian will not risk a church ceremony," Annie said. "He fears an interruption, hence the need for privacy."

"It makes sense, of course." Janet cocked her head. "Are you disappointed, love?"

Annie tutted and shook her head. "Mama, I'm to be married in a private chapel located in an historic house which sits on the edge of the Yorkshire moors. In my opinion, that exceeds the Westminster Abbey option by miles. Truth is, I'd marry Julian Northcott in a barn if that had to be the case. As for walking out alone, he made me promise I wouldn't. Twice, actually." She smiled at the memory. "Anyway, as you can see, I am perfectly fine, so do you think we might set all this unpleasantness aside for now and enjoy the rest of our day together?"

"Yes, of course." Janet folded her arms atop the table and leaned forward. "So, what would you like to do? Piano? Card games? A jigsaw puzzle?"

"Actually, I wondered if I might spend some time learning more about my parents' families," Annie said, taking her mother's hand. "If that's all right with you."

A slight flush crept into Janet's cheeks. "Why, Annie, that's a lovely idea."

"Well, I'm going to do some baking," Hattie announced. "Specifically, a batch of biscuits for my future nephew-in-law. He told me they were the best he'd ever had."

ANNIE WENT TO bed that night with a sense of fulfillment, as if all the loose pieces of her life had been gathered up and put into order, a puzzle complete. Well, almost. One piece of the puzzle was missing. Without it, she could not sit back and take joy in what lay before her. A touch of resentment had her frowning into the dark. Even now, wherever he was, Leopold De Witte was influencing her life. Influencing Julian's decisions about *their* lives.

Would it ever cease? The answer surely lay in Hattie's words, which drifted back to her. *At least not until this scoundrel is captured or, better yet, pronounced dead. Till then, he remains a threat.*

Annie gave herself a mental shake and shifted her focus back to the pleasures of the day and her future journey to Highfield Hall. Allowing her thoughts to wander, she closed her eyes. When next she opened them, it was to Lancelot's piteous clamor. And, to her mild surprise, she realized how much she'd missed it.

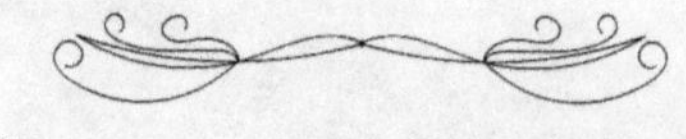

CHAPTER THIRTY

HIGHFIELD HALL WAS not nearly as palatial as Myddleton House. As Julian had described, it was an intriguing hodge-podge of renovations representing several eras. But, from its beautiful, coffered ceilings to its creaking wood floors, Highfield possessed a wealth of character that Annie had not felt at Myddleton. The deep sense of history and the lingering impression of past lives was as tangible as the air in her lungs. Having arrived with Julian, not even two hours ago, she could hardly believe this incredible place was to be her future home. It was a fairytale reality, yet to be fully grasped.

The welcome Annie received allayed any residual nervousness. Captain and Mrs. Northcott had been gracious, the twins enthusiastic. And then, of course, there were Georgie and Mr. Darcy, who looked uncannily like replicas of Ruffy, and followed the twins everywhere. "It is a match made somewhere other than Heaven," Julian quipped. "I cannot believe I agreed to it."

Arthur, meanwhile, had gone off to boarding school the week before, but would be returning, briefly, to attend the wedding.

The most poignant introduction of the day had been to Grace's brother, the uncle Julian had told her about the day they'd visited the Roman ruins. Annie had been warned that to look upon the man's face was not for the faint of heart.

"I grew up in a physician's household," she said. "I'm not without some knowledge of sickness and injury."

It was, indeed, a shocking disfigurement, much worse than Annie had envisaged. Yet she felt neither fear nor revulsion. Rather, she found herself seeing a courageous man whose fight had continued long after the war was over. His one functioning eye was a brilliant blue, a family trait obviously passed on to Josiah. While he showed no awareness whatsoever of Annie's presence, his face lit up at the sight of Grace. Annie thought it said much about the Northcott family that, despite the man's disabilities, they'd chosen to keep him near, rather than placing him in a dreadful mental institution somewhere.

Finally, Julian had brought Annie here, to Highfield's private chapel, where they were to be married. It was a serene space, perfect for contemplation, prayer, or the exchange of holy vows between two people entering into marriage.

Two small lancet windows, one on each side of the altar, gave entry to daylight. Bare sandstone walls of a soft golden hue supported a vaulted stone ceiling. A stark white altar-cloth, edged with several inches of fine lace, draped gracefully over the top of the intricately carved, wooden altar. A marble cross, as white as the cloth upon which it sat, and edged in gold, served as the simple but exquisite centerpiece.

"What do you think, Annie?" Julian asked, folding his arms. "It's somewhat bare at the moment, but will no doubt be decorated for the wedding. I don't suppose you happen to know anything about flower arranging, do you?"

Annie, who had been absorbed in the serenity of her surroundings, stifled a bubble of laughter. "I think it's beautiful," she replied, mouth twitching. "And you, sir, are incorrigible."

Grace, who had accompanied them, chuckled. "Personally, I'm delighted the chapel is to host a wedding. It's almost fifty years to the day since the last one, being that of my parents. There were almost a hundred guests at my wedding, so using the chapel wasn't an option. Not that I'm complaining. Our day was perfect, as I'm sure yours will be."

"How many guests are we expecting, Mama?" Julian asked.

"Twenty-two, I believe. I'll go over the list again this evening and the invitations will be sent out tomorrow." She glanced about. "Plenty of room. The chapel seats thirty comfortably."

Julian nodded in apparent agreement. "Have we included Messrs. Taggart and Lloyd?"

"We have indeed," his mother replied. "Though I trust their services will not be required."

"Hopefully not." Julian glanced at one of the lancet windows as if gauging the weather. "Well, Annie, the grand tour of Highfield Hall is all but complete. We could take a stroll around the gardens, or perhaps you'd like to rest before dinner."

Annie nodded. "A stroll around the gardens sounds most agreeable, but might I ask something of you first, Mrs. Northcott?"

"Of course, dear. What is it?"

"Well, I have a gown for the wedding, but it's rather plain and would benefit from embellishments. Can you recommend a seamstress?"

"I can, indeed," Grace replied. "She goes by the name of Francesca Corvinelli, and she owns a wonderful little dress shop in Knaresborough. I'm sure Julian would be happy to escort you. Knaresborough is a charming place. It would be a nice day out for you both, and should probably take place sooner rather than later, I think."

"Then let's aim for Thursday, weather permitting," Julian said.

"If it's not too much trouble," Annie replied.

Julian shook his head. "No trouble at all."

"Then I shall leave you to your stroll." Grace smiled at Annie. "Once again, welcome to Highfield Hall, my dear."

JULIAN TUCKED ANNIE'S arm into his as they followed the gravel path that wound its way around the lawns and flowerbeds. "All right, Miss Fairfax, out with it," he said, aware of her subdued mood. "Tell me what's bothering you and I'll tell you why it shouldn't."

Annie laughed softly. "You are very perceptive, Mr. Northcott. For a man, that is."

"I'm not sure that's actually a compliment but go on."

"It's just that I fear your mother might be a little disappointed."

Julian had an idea where Annie was going with her concerns but played ignorant. "Disappointed with what?"

Annie heaved a sigh. "Well, I can't help but wonder if she's actually nurtured a different vision for her son's marriage. A grand affair, something more conducive to your status and without the awful necessity of a police presence."

"Conducive to my status?" Julian halted and regarded her. "Well, first of all, my status does not dictate whom I love. Yes, I have a social standing to consider, and abide accordingly, but I will always be governed by my own personal principles and my judgment of character. I cannot claim to have acquired these things without influence, however. They've been impressed upon me by parents whose own morals and principles, while conducive to their status, are to be admired. If my mother has nurtured a vision for me, Annie, I guarantee it is this one. Me, preparing to marry a woman I love, certain I have made the right choice. My mother—my *parents*—are happy for us, believe me." Julian shrugged. "As for a grand affair, our wedding vows are just as pertinent, just as sacred, whether declared before a couple of witnesses or in a church full of people. You heard what my mother said. She's delighted the chapel is being used again, as am I." He smiled and ran a fingertip along the edge of her jaw. "I'd marry you in a barn, Annie Fairfax, if that had to be the case. As for the police presence, I very much doubt it will be necessary, but I'll do whatever is required to protect the woman I love. Always. There. Does that settle your mind?"

"Yes, it does." Annie brought his hand to her mouth and kissed it. "It's also odd that you should mention marrying in a barn."

Julian winced. "Well I wasn't joking, but I think I prefer the chapel."

She chuckled. "Oh, most definitely. It's just that I said exactly the same thing to my mother. I'd marry you in a barn if need be."

"Something else we have in common, then." Julian gave her hand a gentle squeeze. "Barn or chapel, Annie, I cannot wait to marry you. It's going to be a long three weeks."

As it happened, the subsequent days passed at a pleasant pace. The arranged visit to Knaresborough took place as planned and was declared a success. Annie had been thoroughly indulged, though not without some protest.

It pleased Julian that his prediction of a friendship between Annie and Louisa had come true. The women were of a similar age, after all, and shared several things in common, including a mutual love of the written word.

"Annie's perfect for you, Jules," Louisa had confided, as the wedding day drew near. "She puts up with you admirably."

Julian blinked. "Do I thank you for that remark? I'm not certain."

"You don't have to. In any case, it's obvious you adore each other, which is as it should be." Louisa rested a hand on the swell of her belly. "And Annie is wonderful company for me. I adore her."

"How much longer, Lou?" Julian asked.

"Another three months, or thereabouts," she replied, smiling as her gaze flicked to where her hand rested. "An early Christmas present."

"I'm looking forward to meeting him or her." Julian laughed softly and shook his head. "This past while has been an endless calendar of events. Your marriage to Maxwell. The miraculous return of our long-lost uncle. My soon-to-be-marriage to Annie. A first grandchild on the way for Papa and Mama. What's next, I wonder?"

"The twins' debut," Louisa replied, without hesitation.

"Ah, yes." Julian frowned and cleared his throat, which had gone dry at the thought of those two imps released upon an unsuspecting Society. "I can hardly wait."

"And, perhaps later that year, a child of your own," Louisa added, touching his arm. "You'll make a wonderful father, Julian."

Julian allowed himself to visit the real possibility of fatherhood. He'd considered it, of course. He wanted an heir. He wanted a family.

The deep love he shared with Annie had yet to evolve. She had no idea how easily she aroused him. At times, it took nothing more than an adoring glance, or the touch of her hand, or the way she bit her lip. Kissing her was both pleasurable and torturous. He longed to show her the intimate side of love, to take their relationship to a higher level. He smiled to himself as he thought about the honeymoon. Specifically, the location, which he had not yet revealed. And so far, Annie had yet to ask about it.

It had been an early wedding gift. A surprise from an unlikely source. Or perhaps, in hindsight, not so unlikely. In any case, Julian had resolved to keep it a secret until after the wedding.

"What are you smiling about?" Louisa asked.

"Oh, nothing." He tugged gently on one of her ringlets. "At least, nothing I can tell you about."

Louisa cocked her head. "It's rather nice, isn't it?"

"What is?"

"Being in love."

"Yes," he replied, "it is."

CHAPTER THIRTY-ONE

FOR THE SECOND time that year, Annie turned to a mirror and regarded her reflection as a bride-to-be. The face was the same, but the person it belonged to had changed. No longer an uninformed, somewhat naïve girl, but a young woman richer in the knowledge of love and trust, less likely to judge carelessly, and blessed with the protection and devotion of family. Her wedding gown, with its skirts of cream silk and embellishments of cream lace, was an exquisite accessory to the fairytale. She also quietly acknowledged the relief of being allowed to discard her mourning clothes.

Almost four weeks had passed since she'd first laid eyes on Highfield Hall. On this bright summer morning, she would officially become part of the family that lived here. The Northcotts. A family who shared a closeness unlike anything Annie had ever known. Not that they didn't argue, but she had yet to witness anything that resembled a genuine disagreement. That is, unless Captain Northcott, heaving a sigh and rolling his eyes as he snapped open his newspaper, might be classed as a genuine disagreement.

As for ghosts, there'd been neither sight nor sound of one, leaving her equally relieved and disappointed. She slept undisturbed and awoke each morning with a sense of joy. If anything was lacking, it was Lancelot's unique fanfare.

"You look beautiful, my darling." Janet's voice, quivering

slightly, meandered into Annie's deliberations. "I have to say, being with you on your wedding day, seeing you like this, is a dream come true."

Annie smiled at her through the mirror. "I'm so glad you're here, Mama. You look beautiful as well. That gown is very becoming. You too, Hattie. You look splendid."

"Splendid, eh?" Hattie leaned in to fiddle with the garland of flowers on Annie's head. "A suitable epithet for a ship, perhaps."

Annie laughed. "Elegant, then."

"Better." Frowning, the woman stepped back, her gaze critical. "I must admit, the modiste has done a remarkable job on your gown, pet. It's exquisite."

"Francesca Corvinelli is her name," Annie replied. "She's making several more outfits for me. Julian and I spent the better part of an afternoon in her shop."

"Oh, you poor thing." Hattie leaned in to fiddle with the garland once more. "I'm sure it must be difficult being treated like a princess."

Annie chuckled. "Yes, it was rather trying."

Once again, Hattie stepped back. "There," she said, her tone indicative of satisfaction. "Perfect."

A knock came to the door and a maid peeked in. "They're ready for you, Miss Fairfax."

Annie nodded a response and suppressed a shiver of excitement. "Thank you. I'll be there shortly."

A HUSH FELL over the chapel indicating the bride's arrival. Julian straightened a little and turned to face the door. As tradition demanded, he had not seen Annie that day. Now he saw nothing but her. The vision she presented, the sensual mystery of her veiled face and the graceful, unfaltering step as she approached, stole his breath. She was the epitome of innocence, yet at once incredibly alluring. Julian swallowed over the knot in his throat and blinked away the telltale burn in his eyes.

Annie passed her bouquet to Louisa and stepped to Julian's side, gazing up at him. Julian regarded her for a moment, anticipating. Then he lifted her veil and found himself gazing into the eyes that had captivated him from the first moment they'd met. "You are exquisite, Miss Fairfax," he murmured, breathing in her soft, floral scent. "Absolutely exquisite." Annie inhaled, bit her lip, and closed her eyes briefly, as if savoring the happiness so evident in her smile.

"Dearly beloved," the vicar announced, and the ceremony began. Naturally, memories of that dreadful day in May threatened to overshadow Annie's happiness, but she pushed them aside. Though tragic, the events of that day had set her on a different path. A wonderful path, full of promise. This was where she was meant to be, beside the man she truly loved. Vows were exchanged without interruption, the ring given and received, and the union officially pronounced. Their subsequent kiss was the final, sweet attestation.

"My wife," Julian murmured, as their lips parted.

"My husband," Annie replied, her face alight with joy.

Julian, who couldn't stop smiling, escorted Annie to the dining hall where a spectacular Wedding Breakfast had been laid out. There followed a verbal shower of compliments and acknowledgments as guests wandered in.

"Congratulations you two," Josiah said, squeezing Julian's shoulder as he wandered past. "Lovely service. Excellent spread as well. Please excuse me, I'm starving."

Julian laughed. "Only here for the food, Joe?"

"You know it," he replied and winked at Annie.

"Welcome to the family, Annie." Louisa leaned in and kissed Annie's cheek. "You look beautiful. Your dress is magnificent."

And so it continued. A while later, with Annie chatting to the twins and everyone mingling nicely, Julian sought out his father.

"So far so good, Papa," he said. "No sign of trouble."

Aldous gave him a sideways glance. "You've only been married for five minutes, Julian. If you want my advice, it's best to agree with everything she says. That's always been my philosophy."

Laughing, Julian shook his head. "That is not what I meant."

"I know what you meant." Aldous took a sip of what looked like port. "And may it continue, but the day isn't over yet."

An echo from a familiar voice found its way into Julian's ear.

"So far so good," Taggart said, repeating Julian's words as he approached. "Which disappoints me, if I'm to be honest. Worth coming for the food, though."

"I agree." Lloyd patted his stomach. "Ain't never seen a spread like it."

Aldous' mouth twitched as he took another sip.

"Yes, I'm relieved, Inspector." Julian's nonchalant gaze wandered over the room. "Though I also share your disappointment. Nothing I'd like more than to see the fellow caught and dealt with."

"The day's not over yet, gentlemen," Aldous said. "Don't let your guard down."

"Quite right." Julian's gaze halted, his attention drawn to Annie and the footman who'd approached her. The man, silver salver balanced on his hand, said something to her, and she immediately looked about, searching, Julian knew, for him.

A prickle of unease crept across Julian's nape. "If you'll excuse me, gentlemen, Papa, it appears we might have a problem. Wait here, please."

Annie, who had been chatting to Hattie and Janet, locked eyes with his as he approached. Panicked eyes, and unspoken words which were written plainly on her face. *He's here.*

"What is this?" Julian asked of the footman.

"Um, a message for the lady, sir," the footman replied, looking somewhat confused.

"Who delivered it?"

"I don't know, sir. Mr. Barnes bid me deliver it."

Frowning, Julian picked up the folded paper. Of cheap quality, it was addressed simply to "Annie".

"Ask Mr. Barnes to join me, please."

"Certainly sir." The man nodded and sped off.

"It's his writing," Annie said, fear in her voice.

Julian frowned as his fingers touched something solid enclosed within the folds. "You're sure?"

"Positive. We exchanged many letters over the years."

"That damn scoundrel," Hattie muttered.

"Will you open it, Julian?" Annie asked. "I dare not."

"Of course. And I must ask that we all stay calm." Julian smiled at Annie as he opened the paper, catching the enclosed object in his palm as it slid free.

It was a wedding band. A small, gold wedding band. Annie gasped softly.

Julian kept his expression quiet as he opened the paper fully and read what was written. Five words only. Yet they chilled his blood and lit a flame of fury in his gut.

It should have been me.

Barnes approached. "You wanted to see me, Mr. Northcott?"

Julian tore his gaze from the paper and managed a smile. "Yes, Barnes. This note. Who delivered it?"

"He didn't give his name, sir. Just asked that the letter be given to Miss… er, that is, your lady wife." Barnes gave Annie a quick smile. "Is there a problem?"

Julian feigned nonchalance. "No, no, I don't think so. We're just curious to know who delivered it. Can you describe the fellow?"

"I can, sir." The man frowned. "Tall, blond hair. Well spoken. Of reasonable appearance, I suppose. Perhaps a little rough. A scar on his left cheek, which looked to be recent."

Janet cleared her throat and dropped her gaze to the floor.

"That's very helpful, Barnes, thank you. That'll be all." Julian pocketed the ring and turned to Annie. "Listen to me, Annie, I swear there's nothing to fear. De Witte is toying with you.

Toying with *us*. Do not let him ruin this day."

"I won't," she said, shaking her head. "I'm more angry than fearful, Julian. I'm tired of his interference. I *hate* what he's done. What he's trying to do." She looked to where Aldous stood with the two police officers. "If they're going to catch him, they'd better get going."

Julian chuckled and bent to kiss her mouth. "I love you, Mrs. Northcott."

He hurried over to where his father stood with Taggart and Lloyd. "De Witte is here," he said quietly. "Come with me, both of you. I want to keep things quiet if possible. Unobtrusive."

"Wait, what?" Taggart cast a glance around the room. "What do you mean, he's here? How do you—?"

"Keep your bloody voice down, man." Julian gritted his teeth. "Just follow me and look as though you're enjoying yourselves."

He led them and his father into the hallway where he explained the situation.

"The arrogance of the fellow," Aldous said, shaking his head. "It beggars belief."

"We'll catch him, Captain, I guarantee it," Taggart said, patting his hat onto his head as he opened the front door. "He's on foot and not long gone. We'll be on horseback."

"Well, if you catch him quickly enough, I'd be obliged if you'd bring him back here for a visit." Julian shrugged. "I've never met the fellow and I'd like an opportunity to introduce myself before I leave on my honeymoon."

Taggart grinned. "Understood, sir. Where would we hold him?"

"There's an unused room in the gatehouse," Julian replied. "It has no window and a door that bolts from the outside. Put him in there."

The man gave a nod and opened the door. "Right Lloyd, let's go catch a rat."

As the door closed, Aldous gave Julian a slow smile. "Gloves off, son?"

Julian tutted. "I'm a gentleman, Papa."

"Yes, of course. I've no doubt you'll assert yourself accordingly." Aldous continued to smile and patted Julian's shoulder. "Let's get back to the party before we're missed."

When they returned, they found Annie in the company of his grandmother, the dowager countess. "Grandmama." Julian dropped a kiss on her cheek. "Did you enjoy the ceremony?"

"I did indeed," she replied. "As I was just telling Annabelle, there's a lot to be said for simplicity."

Aldous turned his head and cleared his throat. Julian suppressed a smile. "It was what we wanted, Grandmama."

"Oh, don't misunderstand," the dowager replied. "Truth be told, I've always found those grand affairs to be rather tiring. This smaller celebration is far more pleasurable. I hope it becomes a trend."

"I'm glad you're enjoying yourself, Mother," Aldous said.

"I am. You know I've always loved this house." She tapped her fan on the lapel of his jacket. "I must also assume, since those two police officers have left, that the reason for their presence no longer exists. And please, do not attempt to gainsay me."

Annie gasped softly and Julian exchanged an amused glance with his father. "How did you know they were police officers, Grandmama?"

"I overheard them mention 'the Yard' while they were ploughing their way through the buffet." She frowned. "It was also obvious they were not the sort who'd normally be included on the invitee list, though I don't really care about that. I'm just wondering *why* they were invited. Were you expecting trouble? Is everything all right?"

"Everything is fine, Mother," Aldous replied. "The expectation, such as it was, no longer exists, and it was never a grave concern to begin with. There's nothing to worry about at all."

"Glad to hear it." She regarded Julian. "And it must be about time for you to leave."

Julian barely managed to keep a straight face. "We'll be leaving in about an hour, Grandmama."

"An hour?" She turned to Annie. "Then you'd better think about getting ready, my dear. It doesn't do to dawdle."

JULIAN HAD ALMOST given up hope of confronting Leopold De Witte. Indeed, he was just about to excuse himself and prepare for his and Annie's departure when Barnes approached him. "Been asked to give you this, sir," he said, handing Julian a folded paper. Julian opened it and read the one-word message.

Gatehouse.

Which is where he now found himself, gazing upon the scarred face of Taggart's handcuffed prisoner. The musty air carried the faint odor of sweat and unwashed skin, though the man's general appearance was less slovenly than Julian had expected.

"I'll leave you to it," Taggart said, "but I'll be right outside the door."

Julian waited till the door creaked shut before speaking. "Leopold De Witte, I assume," he said, raking a gaze over the fellow, his focus resting on the scarred cheek for a moment. "Due to your recent surveillance efforts, I must assume you know who I am. It's a displeasure to make your acquaintance. I was hoping you'd left the country."

De Witte responded with a cavalier tilt to his chin and a smirk on his face. "I confess to being wrong about you, Northcott," he said. "I felt sure you'd abandon the chit when you found out she was born on the wrong side of the blanket."

"Happy to disappoint you." Julian grimaced. "You know, there's something repugnant about a man who's responsible for fathering an illegitimate child yet vilifies illegitimacy. You're an arrogant fool, De Witte. I fail to understand why you persist with these absurd little games. You should have left England while you had the chance."

"My absurd little games amuse me. They ensure I'll not be forgotten that easily. As for leaving England," he shrugged. "I considered it but changed my mind. Why should I leave? Which laws have I broken? I know nothing of Hoffman's fate, nor do I accept responsibility for his sister's bastard."

Julian narrowed his eyes. "Where did you get that scar?"

"None of your business. Suffice to say, I was the victim." He assumed a sullen expression. "You misjudge me, Northcott. I am not a violent man."

"I read the newspaper report, De Witte."

"Which was misleading." De Witte sniffed. "Hoffman was the aggressor, not I."

Julian scoffed. "My wife tells a different story. Which reminds me, allow me to return your paltry offering." He pulled the little gold ring from his pocket and flicked it at De Witte. It bounced off the man's chest and fell to the floor. The man's smug expression faltered slightly, then the smirk returned. "I'm curious, Northcott," he said. "Did Annie tell you about our little meeting atop that hill?"

Annie's name on De Witte's tongue had Julian clenching his fists. "That's *Mrs. Northcott* to you, and yes, she did."

De Witte tilted his chin again and smiled a cold smile. "Well, there's your proof. I could easily have ravished her that day or thrown her off that ledge and got away with murder, but I merely kissed her instead and let her go."

Julian's fragile restraint snapped like a dry twig. With a hiss of fury, he closed the gap between them and landed a bone-crunching uppercut to De Witte's jaw. The man's head snapped back, and he crumpled to the floor.

Julian hovered over him. "I hope you hang, De Witte," he snarled, through gritted teeth. "In fact, I'll volunteer to pull the lever and watch you drop, you worthless piece of shit."

From somewhere beyond the rush of blood in Julian's ears came the sound of the door opening, followed by a familiar voice. "All right, Northcott, you've had your fun. Step away."

"Thought you were a gentleman, Northcott." Blooded spittle bubbled in the corners of De Witte's mouth as he tried, and failed, to sit up. "Bad form to hit a shackled man."

"Yet I feel not the slightest remorse." Julian stepped back, clenching and unclenching his sore fist. "I want to be the one to tell him, Taggart."

"Go on, then," Taggart replied. "I'll allow that."

De Witte winced as he waggled his jaw and then managed a smile. "Tell me what?"

"That Karl Hoffman is alive," Julian said, gratified to see the smile fade from the man's face. "Alive and talking. We know how you got that scar."

"Alive, eh?" Wincing again, De Witte propped himself up on an elbow. "Told you I didn't kill him."

"Attempted murder is still a hanging offense," Julian replied.

De Witte huffed. "Not guilty."

"It'll be your word against his, you fool. And if asked, I'll be happy to provide a statement. How you spied on us, threatened my wife more than once, and intruded upon our privacy today. By the time I'm finished, they'll be throwing you into the hold of a transport ship."

"Take a breath, Northcott," Taggart muttered.

"Oh, I'm done here," Julian replied, straightening. "He's all yours. I'd appreciate it, however, if you'd keep me posted."

"Will do." Taggart cocked an eyebrow. "Feel better?"

"Much. Thank you, Inspector."

"You're welcome. Best get back to the party, or they'll be thinking the groom's done a runner." Taggart touched the brim of his hat. "Give my regards to your lady wife."

De Witte coughed and spat out some bloody phlegm. "And be sure to give her my love."

Julian tilted his chin and gave the man a cold smile. "Go to Hell, De Witte.

ANNIE LOOKED BACK as the carriage pulled away from Highfield Hall. Everyone, including the staff, had come outside to bid them farewell. Among them were those she had always loved and those she had recently come to love. And all of them standing in front of the remarkable old house that was now her home. She'd come to love that as well. It was an image she wanted to commit to memory, for in her mind it symbolized the end of a chapter. The first chapter of her life.

Today marked the beginning of the second one, and she could hardly wait to see where it led. As the carriage passed beneath the gatehouse, Annie turned and looked forward. As to their destination, she knew only that it was somewhere in England. A flutter arose in her stomach as she thought about their first night together. Of course, she was aware of what would take place. She wasn't afraid, though admittedly a little nervous.

She fidgeted. A warm hand covered hers. No words spoken. Just a gentle squeeze, calming. Reassuring. Annie heaved a soft sigh and rested her head against Julian's shoulder, assured of her place at his side. There was a lot to be said, she thought, for not having any doubts.

EPILOGUE

F IRTH HOUSE HAD sat atop the Cumberland cliffs since Tudor times, its Gothic façade scrubbed and wind-worn by storms rolling in from the Irish Sea. Though not exactly a storm, it had rained solidly for the past three days; relentless, window-pelting drops that obscured the sea views and effectively trapped Julian and Annie indoors. Not that Julian was about to complain. Annie didn't appear to be too bothered about it either. They'd kept themselves deliciously busy. Besides, the house, fully staffed and catered, was theirs for an entire month, so they had plenty of time yet for exploring beyond the Firth's rather splendid grounds.

Though the letter offering them the private use of Firth House had been signed by His Grace, the Duke of Rothbury, Julian was sure Her Grace had been the influence behind it. He couldn't help but wonder if Josiah had a hand in it, too.

No matter. It was a generous gift.

On this, their fourth night, a cozy fire cast shadows around the rather splendid bedchamber. Julian, wearing only his underpants, was reclining atop the bed, propped up against the pillows, watching Annie, who was seated at the dressing table, brushing her hair by candlelight.

"You do realize I'm about to mess it up again," Julian said. "The minute you climb into this bed, in fact."

Annie laughed, set the brush down, blew out the candle, and wandered over to him, her silk nightgown molding to her curves.

Julian, partly erect, shifted slightly, drawing her into his arms as she settled at his side. She heaved a soft sigh and trailed an idle fingertip down his breastbone.

"You're not tired of me yet, then," she said, her fingertip halting at his belly button.

"Not in the least." He settled his hand over hers and pushed it lower, over the waist of his underpants. "There are some buttons awaiting your attention."

Biting her lip, Annie reached down and stroked his erection through the fabric. Julian hissed softly through his teeth and hardened further. Then her fingers found the buttons, which fell open at her touch, and she reached inside. "I just cannot believe how silky it feels," she said, running her hand up and down his length, "or how rigid it is. It's like steel."

Julian groaned "Give me strength, woman," he muttered, lifting his hips. To his utter delight, Annie had embraced the intimacies of the marriage bed with enthusiasm. Being held to ransom by bad weather had been no hardship at all. Other than the staff, who were more than discreet, Firth House was all theirs. Day and night. "You drive me to madness."

Annie smiled, sat up, and straddled him, pulling her nightgown off before guiding him into her. He groaned again as she sank onto him, her hips moving slowly at first. Lips parted, eyes half-closed, she gyrated in a lazy fashion. Julian, riding a growing wave of ecstasy, pushed up against her, a sensual resistance that brought a soft cry from her lips. She met his upward thrusts with an ever-increasing rhythm, riding him with unabashed passion.

"Annie," he muttered and reached up to caress her breast, pinching and tugging at her nipple. "You're incredible."

"My God, Julian," she said, on a gasp, her head tilting back. "I…"

He inserted his fingers into the tight gap where their bodies were joined, heightening the stimulation of her most sensitive part. She whimpered and he felt the beginning of her orgasm, the increased tightness, the rhythmic ripples of pleasure. Annie let out a cry as her body went rigid, a response that pushed Julian off the edge, his own body tightening with the intensity of his climax.

Replete, they tumbled together on the bed, breathing hard. For a while they lay in the contented aftermath of their satisfaction, no words necessary. Julian allowed his thoughts to drift. "I think, this time next year, we'll take a trip to Europe."

"Europe?" Eyes wide, Annie turned to look at him. "Really?"

"Mmm. Belgium, Switzerland, Italy. What do you think?"

"It doesn't appeal to me at all, Julian," she replied, snuggling against him.

Julian feigned a dejected sigh. "Right, well, we'll forget that then."

"But I might change my mind," she said, making him chuckle. "In the meantime, I confess I'm looking forward to the Season, though I'm not really sure what to expect."

"Afternoon teas," Julian replied, and pressed a kiss to her hair. "Parties, lots of them. Theater. Ballet. Rides in the park, weather permitting. Socializing all over town."

"Goodness," Annie replied. "It sounds dreadful."

"Well, it might be challenging," Julian said. "We have to bear witness to the twins trying, and failing, to behave appropriately."

"Aww, you should have more faith in them. When it comes to finding a suitor, I suspect Evie will be quite selective. I hope she finds someone worthy of her. Someone who deserves her."

"And Clara?"

Annie tutted. "Clara might enjoy the socializing, but I doubt very much she'll be looking for a suitor. Louisa happens to be of the same opinion."

Julian frowned. "And how, pray, did you both arrive at that conclusion?"

"We share a mutual suspicion that Clara is already enamored of someone."

Julian shifted onto an elbow and regarded her. "Who?"

Annie waggled a brow and gave him a knowing smile. "I can't believe you haven't noticed."

"Come on, Annie, who is it? As far as I know, Clara hasn't been anywhere to meet anyone."

"She was at our wedding."

"Well, yes, of course." Julian pondered a moment. "But everyone there, other than Taggart and Lloyd, was family."

"Not everyone."

"Who else…?" As realization sank in, his eyes widened. "Finlay? Maxwell's brother? Is that who you mean? No. You're mistaken, surely."

"We don't think so. First of all, how many times has she and Evie visited Northcott Manor in the past few weeks?"

"Numerous times, but that's easily explained. Louisa's condition means keeping travel to a minimum, so it makes sense the twins would go to see her rather than her traveling to Highfield."

"True, but according to Louisa, Clara looks at Finlay the way I look at you. I watched her for a while on our wedding day, and it's true. She appears to be besotted. She hardly took her eyes off him."

Julian frowned. "Is it reciprocated?"

"It doesn't seem to be," Annie replied. "We don't think Finlay is even aware of it."

"Does Evie know?" Julian huffed. "Never mind, don't answer that. Of course she knows."

"Does it bother you?"

Julian pondered a moment. "No," he said at last. "It doesn't bother me at all. *The heart has its reasons which reason knows not.*"

Annie parted with a soft gasp. "Julian! What a lovely thing to say."

"Can't take the credit," he replied. "A French fellow by the name of Pascal wrote it, apparently."

"Well, I'm very impressed."

"Actually, it was Josiah who said it to me the day I met you," he said. "I told him all about you, Annie. How I felt about you. How it shouldn't be possible to feel what I felt when I'd only known you for half an hour. It didn't make sense. And yet, somehow, it did."

Annie touched his face. "I felt the same, Julian," she said. "When you walked away from me that day, I felt as though I'd made a terrible mistake, but there was no way to fix it. And yet, despite everything, here we are."

"Yes, here we are," Julian replied, drawing her closer. "As it should be."

End of Book Two

Other books in this series, present and future:

Book 1 – Doubts and Desires
Book 3 – Passion and Principles
Book 4 – Pride and Propriety
Book 5 – Obsession and Obligation
Book 6 – Vices and Virtues

Novellas connected to this series:

A Solitary Candle
(written under my other author name, Avril Borthiry.)

If The Fates Allow
Loving Lysander
Of Christmas Past

To keep up to date with my book releases, please follow me on:

Facebook:
facebook.com/Wrenbooks
facebook.com/borthiry

Amazon:
amazon.com/Charlotte-Wren/e/B08FFBR14W
amazon.com/Avril-Borthiry/e/B006RNN04W

About the Author

Charlotte Wren writes heartfelt historical romances set in the Regency and Victorian eras.

You can find Charlotte at the following social media sites:
Facebook – facebook.com/Wrenbooks
Amazon – amazon.com/Charlotte-Wren/e/B08FFBR14W